MW00479982

THE SEEING

Achill Island, Ireland 1913

By

Steve Peek

"Everything exists, everything is true, and the earth is only a little dust under our feet."
W.B. Yeats

1913 September, Dublin, Ireland, Trinity University

Branna recognized the man at once. He sat where he should be, in the library's current events alcove filled with daily, weekly and monthly publications. From a distance, Albert Lewis was his name, struck Branna as a human evolved from the Order Rodentia: furtive, ready to skitter into a dark recess off the highly polished stone floor. But he didn't. He sat reading his notebook, looking up every few seconds to glance around. He was trying to recognize Branna but had no idea of her appearance.

Branna recognized him by the description provided by her superior, Chancellor Ian Fannin, head of Trinity University's School of Irish History and Antiquities. Fannin had, on occasion, conducted business with Albert Lewis, acquiring odd pieces for the museum. Even the Chancellor's tenure and reputation at the University would offer little protection if anyone ever proved the purchases of ancient relics were contracted knowing their origins were legally questionable.

Standing a few feet from the jittery man with the thin face and slightly bucked teeth peeking from beneath his bushy, unkempt mustache, Branna noticed the library lights. Normally almost too bright, they dimmed and flickered as thunderous clouds darkened the day and speared Dublin with lightning.

It was foreboding, Branna thought, looking out the room's tall windows to glimpse a portion of roiling cloud and a nearby streak of lightning.

Branna stopped at the opposite side of the table occupied by Lewis.

"I am waiting for Professor Butler." Albert Lewis said, placing his notebook on the table in front of him. His voice was of a man unnerved by his mission to the university.

Branna turned toward the window as if she did not hear Lewis' remark. Branna suffered this assumptive insult when meeting people for the first time at the university. She had grown accustomed to it. She was only the second female to obtain a professorship at Trinity in its long history of exclusively educating boys.

Branna turned from the window and gazed at Albert Rodent who remained seated, looking at her with dark, glistening eyes. Lewis was extremely thin, enough to suspect ill health. He was also very hairy. Branna saw the curling black hairs on his hands as well as a few errant curls emerging from his buttoned collar. Lewis had shaved, but his skin was hardly clean. Dark shadows covered an otherwise pale face. He also had small tufts of hair growing from his ears.

"Yes, I am Professor Butler," was all she said.

Lewis' eyes grew large, and in a moment an expression of grave error crossed his face. He stood immediately, shooting his hand out too quickly.

Branna was not inclined to shake the extended paw-like hand.

Of course, Branna, a meticulous lady of civilized traditions, shook hands and asked, "How may I help you?"

"I hope you don't take offense, Ms. Butler, but I was hoping to meet with the chancellor himself. We share a long relationship and, I dare say, have almost become friends. It's a bit disappointing I don't get to see him," Lewis said, his squinty black eyes peering into Branna's own.

"It is Professor Butler, Mr. Lewis, but you may call me Branna. Everyone does." Much as she already disliked having to deal with Mr. Lewis, she certainly did not want this nefarious-looking fellow contacting the chancellor. That is precisely reason the chancellor had sent her, to screen Mr. Lewis as on this occasion the layman seeking audience had nothing to sell, nothing physical anyway.

A better look at Mr. Lewis gave Branna the impression he was of the black Irish. Their heritage included dark eyes, black hair and olive complexions, generally rare in Ireland. There were those in the anthropology department who argued the black Irish lineage originated in eastern Europe as opposed to the more common belief they descended from an expeditionary group of Moors who shipwrecked and began homesteading. Either way, they were not generally well received among the general public who regarded them as untrustworthy, seedy and without common morals. Labeling them gypsies encompassed the feelings harbored by those who used the label. Albert Lewis fit the description to a T.

"I'm sorry, Mr. Lewis, the chancellor is quite busy. He sent his apologies and asked you tell me what it is you've discovered that might be of interest to the university."

Branna indicated Mr. Lewis should reseat himself before taking the chair next to the one occupied by Lewis.

For a moment, Lewis did not look at Branna. He stared

at the folder on the table. Suddenly his body language signaled he reached a decision. Opening the folder, he extracted two black and white photographs and offered them to Branna.

Branna studied each.

After a reasonable amount of time, she held the grainy images out for Lewis to reclaim. "I'm sorry, Mr. Lewis, I really can't make anything out. Can you explain what it is I am supposed to see?"

"Yes, yes, I know, they are of poor quality. I am not even an amateur photographer, but please look at this one more closely." Lewis held one of the photographs in a way they could both see it.

"What you are looking at, Professor Branna is the bottom terrace in a peat farm. It is a very deep as peat digging goes. Now look more closely at the shape in the center of the image. Use the shadows in the photograph."

Branna looked closely and still recognized nothing more than a hollow space in the exposed peat tier. Other than thinking it was the deepest peat terrace she'd ever seen, she saw an empty cavern that had been exposed using a peat, or humble spade for cutting bricks of peat. The digging rendered the once solid hillock of peat to foot-high tiers allowing workers to dig deeper. She refocused her eyes to see the whole image then saw, as Lewis had suggested, the shadows formed the shape of a buried human. Branna looked at Lewis as she thought through the possibilities of a human form found deep in the acid-loving, low-oxygen, decomposing plants of the wetlands, or bogs, of Ireland. More important than who or how, the intriguing question was when did it get there?

"How deep is this level?" Branna asked, interest growing.

"At least a dozen feet," Lewis answered.

"It may just be nothing more than an oddly shaped large gas pocket, trapped in the bog. It has happened before," Branna asserted.

"That's what I thought at first," Lewis returned, blinking his eyes as the lights returned to their normal brightness. Then added, "But there was something in it, more solid than condensed gas."

Branna waited for the furtive man to continue. When Lewis failed to offer an explanation she asked impatiently, "Well then, what was it, and why would Chancellor Fannin be interested?"

Lewis opened his notebook, extracted the third photograph and handed it to Branna.

She looked at it, looked at Lewis, then back to the paper. "You can't be serious," she said.

Branna Butler sat on a too-thin and too-used red velvet cushion in a shared passenger car on the train to Achill Island. Two days before, Branna departed the eastern port of Dublin, bound for the most western piece of Ireland, a place of boulders, rolling hills, low bogs, crashing waves and people who, while good Catholics, never stopped believing in myths and creatures from Irish lore.

The first part of the journey went well. Branna had a well-appointed private compartment on the Midland Great Western Railway from Dublin to Claremorris. There, she changed trains and shared a compartment to Westport. Her sole companion was a chatty nun returning to the Mission Colony, where she served as head nurse in the clinic that tended after the small population of old fishermen, shepherds, peat diggers and their wives or widows, living their last days in the self-contained community of fifty, two-room cottages.

She introduced herself as Sister Francis O'Toole. When Branna offered her name, Sister Francis quickly asked, "Are you descended from the Butlers of Ormonde?"

"I don't believe so," Branna lied, avoiding the topic as

she always did with strangers.

She was, in fact, directly related to the fabulously wealthy and important Butler family.

Theobald Walter commanded the Cavaliers in the 12th-century invasion of Ireland. King Henry II promoted his rank in the court to Butler of England and Butler of Ireland. Walter originated Branna's branch of the Butler family. The butler's official duty was tracking all shipments of spirits, wines, and ales. Failure to obtain the Butler's stamp on a product allowed confiscation. The price of the Butler's stamp was a small percentage of the value of the beverage based on what it might be worth.

The Butlers gained royal titles and lands along with great wealth. By the time Branna became a leaf bud on the family tree, the family had achieved the distinction of a dynasty having secured its future in banking, industry, and commodities throughout Europe.

Branna knew obtaining her position at Trinity University was because of her family and their donations. She knew this because both her mother and father reminded her of it every time they questioned her as to the reason she was so willing to throw away her future by not marrying while still young and scooting more baby Butlers into their world of indulgence and influence. Why couldn't she write books or something that allowed her to stay at home, instead of pursuing studies of the dirty and broken bits of bones and tools?

In addition to avoiding acknowledging her connection to such enormous wealth, her second reason for anonymity was the Butlers were not original Irish. Though they lived there for more than eight hundred years, many people still considered them invaders, plundering the spoils of the Emerald Isle.

☐

September 23, Keel, Achill Island, Ireland

She spent the night at the Amethyst Hotel at Keel on the south coast of the island. She dined alone. She enjoyed a lobster taken from the sea three hours before arriving on her table and several glasses of port. Two other hotel guests, young men, kept glancing at her as they ate but she kept her head down and retired for the night without incident.

The next morning, she waited inside the hotel's small lobby. Mr. Lewis was to take her by carriage to meet the person who supposedly possessed the thing taken from the peat bank.

When he did not show up at nine, the scheduled time, Branna ordered another pot of tea and read a journal from the Royal Academy. At ten, she paced near the door, glancing up and down the dirt and gravel road, angry that Lewis could be so inconsiderate.

Hearing something like an enormous bumblebee and seeing a few people on the road turned toward the sound, Branna tried, but couldn't see what caused the racket.

In a few seconds, a bicycle with a petrol engine stopped on the street exactly in front of the door. The rider, a broad-shouldered man wearing goggles that looked intended for swimming, a helmet-like leather cap, and gloves, dismounted, lowered the bicycle stand and came toward the hotel entrance.

He removed his gloves, goggles, and cap. His fingertips smoothed his mussed auburn hair. Instead of tipping a hat, he offered a polite smile as he passed Branna.

The goggles, though removed, had been worn tightly and the reddish imprints on his pale complexion prevented Branna from getting a fair look at his face. Branna turned back toward the door and continued to watch for Lewis.

"Missus Butler," a young man said behind her.

"Yes," she turned to see a bellboy facing her.

"Excuse me ma'am, but this man," he indicated the bicycle rider who entered a moment before, "would like to speak with you if that is agreeable."

The teenage bellman seemed a little nervous. The boy stuttered slightly while saying, "He's the county sub-inspector from the Royal Irish Constabulary in Westport."

Branna glanced at his face then back at the boy, who seemed awed by the presence of a county sub-inspector.

But in that glance, like many women, she saw a man, probably in his early thirties. His clean-shaven face was handsome, with a straight nose, ocean blue, almost violet eyes that held something appealing. Maybe his eyes showed honesty, Branna thought.

"Hello, Inspector, or should I call you sub." Branna extended her hand. "I am Branna Butler, which I suspect you already know. It is a pleasure to meet you, but I cannot imagine what reason you have to seek me. I've just arrived yesterday and am fairly certain I've not had the time to break any laws." Her eyes smiled at him as she spoke.

Gently taking her hand, he offered, "I am Michael Doyle. You may call me Inspector the 'sub' is a formality. I was here two days ago on a case, a quite serious case."

"What sort of case? Surely, you are aware I arrived by train yesterday? What could this have to do with me?" Branna, more curious than concerned, spoke quickly.

Michael Doyle, trained to observe, noted the woman did not lose her composure or jump to any conclusions. He answered her, "Someone you might know, an Albert Lewis, is involved. Do you know him?"

"Yes, Inspector, I came here to meet him. We just met a little over a week ago, so I don't know him well. What has he done?" she asked.

Doyle listened closely to her choice of words and inflection. He reasoned she would not wilt. He decided both he and Miss Butler would conclude this business more quickly if he just told her about Lewis and asked his questions. But then, he'd been on the bike for nearly twenty miles. He could use a break, so why not spend as much time as possible with this beautiful woman?

"I would prefer you to be seated," the inspector said softly.

"Please, just tell me if Lewis will be here or not," she queried.

"I'm not so worried about you, Miss Butler, I'm just wondering if you might sit with me at a table in the restaurant and have an early lunch."

"Why, Inspector," she said, hiding her delight, "Are you allowed this sort of flirtatious behavior while on duty?"

His face reddened, and his expression waxed serious again. He wondered what made him act so out of character. "I'm sorry, Miss Butler, it was forward of me. Please forgive me."

"Quite all right, Inspector," Branna said.

Michael Doyle straightened to attention and said just loud enough for Branna to hear, "I am sorry to inform you, Albert Lewis is dead." He waited for her response.

Branna was shocked. She had not expected that to be

10

the news. She thought perhaps he'd been caught with stolen antiquities. "Perhaps, I'd better sit down," Branna said, slowly moving toward the restaurant.

Michael offered his arm as if to steady her.

She did not need it, but she took it.

As they ate sandwiches, Branna, watercress, and cucumber, Inspector Doyle, a plowman's special, they spoke little, mostly uncomfortable chitchat as the news of Lewis' death settled with Branna.

"How did he die?" Branna asked. "I am assuming his death did not occur from natural causes or you would not have come all this way."

Michael thought before answering. Branna certainly seemed to be taking the death well, but then again, she hadn't known him long. Michael looked into her face then said, "I'm afraid Mr. Lewis was murdered.

"I came all this way hoping you might shed some light on the reason Mr. Lewis decided to come here at this time," Michael said. "We found Mr. Lewis' journal at the scene. It contained an entry with your name, today's date and this location where he was to meet you at nine AM. Lewis arranged to hire a coach for your journey. He retained the coach and driver, but Mr. Lewis had the bad luck to die before you arrived."

Branna thought before she answered. She certainly did not want to implicate herself, the chancellor or the university in anything so sordid, but she knew better than to lie.

"I am a professor at Trinity University in Dublin. My specialty is Irish history and antiquities. Mr. Lewis previously worked with my department's head. On this occasion, the chancellor asked me to meet and explore whatever it is Mr. Lewis discovered. Mr. Lewis insisted the discovery's importance was self-evident," Branna stated carefully.

"And what had Lewis discovered?" Michael asked.

11

"I don't know," Branna replied honestly.

"Well, why come all this way if you have no idea what he wanted to show you?" Michael asked.

"I said I didn't know. I did not say I had no idea," Branna said, correcting his inquiry. "He brought us poor photographs, and he may have found a mummified bogman."

"Ah, yes. A corpse found in the peat. I understand bogmen are rare, but what about this specific relic would interest someone as expert and familiar with this sort of thing as yourself, Miss Butler?"

Branna reassessed the inspector's intellect. His questions indicated a quick mind. She responded, "The photograph was of a peat tier displaying a hollow cavity shaped like a reclined, possibly buried, human figure. There was no bogman, as you call it, in the photo. A second photograph might have been a close-up of the back of the bogman's head in a state of advanced decomposition. What is fascinating, and the reason I came, is the carved-out area of the human form was approximately twelve feet beneath the surface of the peat, and the close-up photograph appeared to show a portion of a metal band worn on the head."

"Thank you, Branna. We found the photographs at the scene with Lewis' other documents," Michael stated.

Branna could see the wheels turning in the inspector's mind.

"Being a lay person in your field, would it be wrong of me to assume the depth of the," he paused looking for the proper word, "of the discovery indicates it is quite old, most likely ancient?"

"And now, you know why I am here," Branna answered. "If the content were what we suspected, it would pre-date the pyramids of Egypt. It would pre-date our earliest estimation of human habitation of Ireland by at least a thousand years, probably more."

Branna watched Michael's face for a reaction. She continued, "The metal headband adds to the mystery because it indicates a level of civilization never before believed to exist that far back in our past."

Michael sat back, looked up at the ceiling in thought, then decided to reveal a piece of information, "Normally I would never say this, but since you could not possibly have been involved in the murders, I would like to further discuss the case with you."

"Murders, you said, not murder," Branna replied, "How many victims are there?"

"A man named Paddy Healy," Michael responded. "Interestingly enough, he is, or was, a turf farmer on the north side of Achill Island. The murders took place in one of his peat shelters."

"Secondly, Sub-inspector," Branna said in a teasing manner, "How do you know I could not possibly be involved in the murders? I might have played a part in a murder for hire scheme and arrived in my innocent appearance to claim the mysterious and valuable bogman."

Michael grinned. "This sub-inspector thought of that early on in our discussions. He discounted it for two reasons. First, smuggling the corpse of a bogman back to Dublin is dirty, strenuous work. You would need to hire someone with a wagon, and that would alleviate the need for you to travel to the end of Ireland, to be here talking to me, a sub-inspector investigating the crime you committed. Second, Lewis, one of the victims, was scheduled to pick you up here today. So, in this sub-inspector's logic, you are eliminated as a suspect. That is of course unless you would like to become one, or, even better, confess." Michael grinned.

"Bravo, Inspector," Branna said, "I think you might be a successful author of penny dreadful books."

"Thank you," he replied, "I wish I could say the same for you."

They laughed.

"Oh my," Branna said, "You must think me awful to laugh at such a serious subject."

"Normally, these circumstances would not allow a display of humor, even if some existed, but, if I may be so forward, something about you brings out the devil in me, Miss Butler," Michael said, "I hope you take no offense."

"Likewise, Inspector Michael Doyle." Branna smiled. "Now, how else do you think I can help you?"

"I will be back in touch with you later in the day," Michael said before leaving.

Once the RIC Station in Westport replied to his telegram confirming the victims' bodies were removed from Paddy Healy's peat farm, Michael returned to the hotel and sent a note, via a bellman, asking Branna to speak with him in the lobby.

While waiting, he obtained a room at the Amethyst Hotel then brought in the saddlebag from the Triumph motorized bicycle parked outside. He scribbled notes in his case journal.

"Inspector," Branna spoke as she approached the man writing in his notebook, "delighted to see you again."

Michael stood to face her, wearing a smile that refused to professional suppression. "The delight is all mine, Ms. Butler."

A slight pause ensued, and they spoke in unison, "Would you have tea…"

"Of course, I welcome the chance to learn more about this case. I am particularly interested in knowing the whereabouts of the item found buried in the peat," Branna said, looking expectantly at Michael.

"I am afraid we don't know its whereabouts," Michael replied. "It may have been stolen and the motive for the murders. If that is the case, then we assume it is of great value to someone, and that person, or his agent, took possession of the bogman with the headband. Our problem, you see, is we must confirm what we are trying to find before we can effectively look for it."

"I see," Branna said as if the handsome detective had just said something profound.

"I am hoping you can help us determine if what Healy removed from the peat before Mr. Lewis contacted you is, in fact, an ancient relic and not some hoax," Michael said.

"I am certainly game to try," Branna replied, "Though I don't want to get your hopes too high. It remains a possibility nothing ever filled the space in the peat bank, and it is part of an elaborate scheme to gain money from the university."

"Yes, it is possible I suppose, but if nothing ever occupied the cavity, then what was the motive for the brutal murders of our victims?" Michael offered.

"Ah," Branna said. "Now they are brutal murders. I must admit the dripping of information is an effective way to keep my attention."

"Ma'am, I simply wish to avoid offending your sensibilities," Michael replied.

"You sound like my father," Branna quipped. "Why do you suppose my sensibilities are different than yours?"

"Miss Butler, you are a lady of station and breeding. I cannot imagine you have been exposed to the more gruesome aspects of crime, especially murder," Michael Doyle offered, watching her face. "If I am wrong, I apologize and hope you will forgive me for wishing only to avoid exposing you to new types of ugliness."

"Oh, now you sound like my mother," Branna said, offering a smile and patting Michael's hand. "I have no interest in viewing 'new types of ugliness,' as you so delicately named it, but I will assure you, many dead animals have felt my steady knife dissecting their carcasses. So, please tell me, how can I help you?"

"If you are agreeable to a day's journey to the island's

north side, I will hire a carriage to take us to Dugort, the location of Paddy's farm in the heart of the largest bog on the island.

"A day's journey going means a day's journey returning and probably a half-day investigating Paddy's shed and the bog. The victims' bodies have been removed from the scene and taken to the medical clinic and embalmer.

"The Slievemore Hotel was the first hotel on the island; I will make arrangements for the RIC to pay for your room and meals." Michael paused, then asked, "So will you come? I think your knowledge will be enormously helpful in determining what, if anything, is missing from the hollow in the peat."

"I will participate in your investigation on one condition," Branna said.

"And that is?" Michael asked.

"The sub-inspector from the Westport region of the Royal Irish Constabulary join me for dinner this evening. They have lovely lobsters here," Branna stated as if an official point of negotiation.

"Ms. Butler, I am sure the sub-inspector has no other plans for this evening and will be happy to enjoy your company. What time should he expect you?"

"I'll be down at eight. Make sure he is prompt," Branna said rising to leave.

Michael stood as well, "Until then. And thank you for agreeing to help."

Michael watched her walk toward the stairs thinking what a remarkable woman she is. Making her way in the man's world of academicians, quick-minded, clever and, most obvious, possessed of soft, radiant beauty. She would age well blossoming in the different stages of beauty.

Then the cloud of Victorian class-based society hovered above him. Branna was a daughter to one of Ireland's wealthiest families. Beyond rich, titled in Ireland, Wales, and England, the mention of the Butler name was

16

often enough to end disagreements. Branna had so far exhibited none of the superiority or sense of entitlement ever-present among the upper classes.

Though she seemed nearly unaffected by her station in society, it was impossible for her to be raised by so prominent a family and not feel the differences between herself and the lower classes.

Michael knew about the lower classes. He was from one. While Branna walked one step behind a princess, Michael walked forth behind a simple fisherman. The family's two currachs, lightly framed boats covered with stretched canvas, were designed for fishing within sight of shorelines in the North Atlantic.

Though light, when fishing for the giant basking sharks that migrated past Achill Island in the spring and summer, they were used like whaling boats. Armed with harpoons and coils of rope, the craft, pulled by the forty-foot whale sharks, sped through the water until the exhausted fish came to the surface and succumbed to a volley of harpoons.

Towed back to the pier, the huge fish rendered edible flesh, animal meal, and tough fabric, but the main commercial use was the oil in their liver.

An average fish weighed roughly twenty-five thousand pounds of which their liver weighed three thousand. Once processed, the shark's liver produced a ton of oil purchased for many uses including a lubricant for textile mills and factories, and widespread use as fuel for street lamps.

Michael Doyle's father and brothers fished for these great fish. Michael did not.

The maximum number of useful crew in a currach was four. The father and three older brothers formed the crew. Michael, the youngest in the family, stayed ashore with his mother and sisters. He hated exclusion from the male Doyles, and his brothers went out of their way to tease

oing women's work while they fought with
nsters to provide for the family.

s after Michael's twelfth birthday, like so many
ilies' youngest sons, Michael was sent to live in
a Catholic secondary school. The end goal was to be
selected to attend a seminary and become a priest.

Michael succeeded in attending a Catholic university,
St. Patrick's. He fell far short of the priesthood.

The young sub-inspector decided, much as he wanted
to get to know Branna personally, nothing good could
come of it.

□
September 24, Coach on Bog Road

"I would have brought a pillow to sit on if you warned me the road was this rough," Branna said, looking at Michael seated next to her.

The 'coach' Michael hired to take them to Dugort had seen better days — much better. Dugort was located on the island's north shore and at Slievemore's southern slope, the second highest mountain on Achill Island.

They shared the coach's single seat, a hard plank covered with faded, cracked black leather. Branna's bags and Michael's motorized bicycle were strapped to its boot.

Two huge dray horses pulled the vehicle, powerful animals bred to move heavy loads all day. The horses seemed to be the only ones not struggling with the uneven, rocky incline that was Bog Road. Dugort Village was less than five miles north of the Amethyst Hotel, but the narrow road made it slow going.

"You are quiet today," Branna said when Michael made no reply to her pillow comment.

"Oh, sorry," Michael said, keeping his gaze on the road ahead, "just thinking about the case."

"Anything in particular?" Branna wanted to know.

"The motive. If an ancient bogman was discovered, then who would be interested in buying it? After all, according to the British Antiquities Act, it is the property of England but may be allowed to remain in Ireland. So, whoever bought it would be receiving stolen property and committing a crime against the Crown." Michael paused.

"True," Branna agreed. "But in candor, universities purchase things like this for their museums and studies. They pay well, but not enough to cause a murder."

"Does Trinity buy stolen antiquities?" Michael asked.

"Oh dear," Branna exclaimed, "Not since I've been there," then added, "As far as I am aware, anyway."

Up ahead, the road to Dugort curved to the right following the base of Mount Slievemore. A smaller trail continued straight. Branna saw the ruins of a village at the smaller trail's end. "What is that?" She pointed toward the ruined cottages.

Without looking, Michael answered in a flat tone, "That is a famine village."

"Can we go there?" Branna asked. "I know of them, of course, but have never actually been in one."

Michael spoke to the driver. "Driver, please stop at the fork. The lady and I want to walk to the abandoned village for a few moments."

The driver stopped, turned in his seat and kept a keen eye on the two outsiders making their way toward the abandoned village.

Along the overgrown trail to the village, they passed a narrow brook, gurgling its way down the slope like a miniature river with waterfalls every few yards.

Branna thought she caught movement at a flat stone across the flow, creating a five-inch drop for the tiny waterfall. She stopped and watched for a moment. When nothing untoward appeared, she quickened her pace to catch up with Michael.

They reached the fallen stones and ruined walls that made up the abandoned village.

Branna slowly walked into what had been its center.

She studied the fallen stones and rotted lintels spanning doorways in small cottages with vanished roofs. She stopped at a stone cistern, three feet across. Its once watertight walls no longer reached the three-foot height on the down-flow side where a stone would have been absent from the top edge to allow water flowing into the cistern from uphill, to flow out the low side when the cistern filled.

The water flowing in these hills picked up their rusty-blood color from the peat over and through which it flowed. Supposedly healthy to drink, Branna questioned the wisdom of drinking from the small trickle passing where she stood. Its color was a darker red than the other springs she'd seen on their trip from the Amethyst Hotel.

She squatted and put her finger in the shallow dark water trapped in the cistern, thinking she might taste a drop.

Suddenly, feelings of grief and sadness overwhelmed Branna. Tears ran from her eyes. Sobs, painful and deep, wracked her body and a long terrible wail came up her throat and sounded against the wind.

She felt herself standing, no she wasn't standing. Someone, Michael, helped her stand, then held her up as she walked away from the ruins. She began to feel better but did not speak. She wanted to sort out her experience at the cistern.

The driver, hearing the scream, dismounted and hurried toward them.

"Can I help, sir?" he offered, looking not at Michael but studying Branna's eyes.

Branna straightened and took her weight from Michael. "Thank you, no. I'm fine now."

The driver turned back toward the coach.

Branna and Michael passed the five-inch fall at the flat stone. A small rainbow formed in the mist caused by the water splashing on rocks below.

Back in the carriage, a concerned Michael poured water into a tin cup, helped her drink, then poured more on his handkerchief to cool her brow.

The driver shifted in his seat to examine Branna. Michael told the driver to stand steady. When she appeared recovered, he asked the driver to continue. The driver gave Branna once last curious look, turned around and slacked the reins, signaling the horses to move.

As the carriage rolled again, Branna, somewhat embarrassedly, said, "Well, that's never happened before. I have never even felt faint. Thank you for helping me."

"You are welcome," Michael said, a concerned expression still discernable on his face. He was silent for a moment thinking about asking Branna about the experience. Before he could ask, she started talking.

"Just before I," she paused, "fainted if that is what happened, a terrible sadness overcame me. Feelings of sorrow, great loss, never-ending grief. It was quite extraordinary."

Michael thought before he spoke then asked politely, "How do you feel now? Normal? In charge of your faculties and thoughts?"

"Oh heavens, yes," she answered, brushing the incident off as trivial. "Why would you ask me that?"

"You are not the first person to be deeply affected in a famine village. The hunger in those places during the time of the Great Famine caused unbelievable suffering. Men went to the cities taking any kind of work. Children old enough immigrated: America, Australia, and Canada were the most popular," Michael said, then put his hand to his mouth as if to cough.

Branna saw him wipe a tear away and thought, "What a sensitive man."

Michael continued, "The women and the small children had no place to go. Charity, what there was of it, offered soup made with water and little else. People starved slowly, day after day, the woman and children in those villages grew weaker. The infants died first. They lacked reserved fat. Then the children, from youngest to oldest, slowly became skeletons as the mothers watched. Achill was one of the hardest hit in all of Ireland."

"So, many, religious or not, believe the pain and suffering never left the villages. It resides in ruins, of the stones themselves, waiting to be released when a kind soul walks among them." Michael turned his head away from Branna and wiped tears from both eyes. Michael looked up the road, turned to her and said, "If you truly feel well, would you be willing to conduct an experiment?"

"How delightful," Branna exclaimed. "I enjoy experiments so long as things don't explode or smell bad," she joked.

"All right," Michael said, "Here we go. Relax as best you can and close your eyes. You may think about anything but must not speak and keep your eyes closed until I tell you to open them."

She complied with his request.

She heard the horses clopping. She noticed one of the wheels offered up a slight squeak once per revolution. Their seat squeaked as movement rocked it. She heard Michael breathing next to her.

"How much longer?" she asked, breaking the no talking rule.

"Just a little bit longer," Michael replied.

Since she could think about anything, she considered the recently met man seated next to her. She thought Michael a lovely man. He displayed compassion and sincerity, both grand qualities for someone in law enforcement. She began to think of his physical aspects and soon entered a daydream. Her imagination showed her introducing him to her family and, most surprisingly, they were all happy to meet him and treated him as one of their own. Then she envisaged their home, a small manor house, with children and dogs playing outside. She and Michael held hands as they faced each other in conversation. She sighed happily. She knew contentment for the first time in her life.

Then, in her fantasy, a darkening cloud rushed into view. She started to warn Michael, but before she could say anything, the cloud swirled and formed a spiraling vortex-like mouth, then the rough contours of a demonic face with remorseless eyes. The mouth pulled Michael from the ground. She stood paralyzed as Michael floated into the air, rising faster and faster until he entered its mouth and vanished.

Next, the cloud's eyes grew more detailed: a single, yellowish sclera and a fiery pupil. The eye found her. Just as she suffered the sense of intense loss and grief before in the village, she now knew true terror for the first time in her life. Branna experienced fear before, but nothing of this magnitude. Her heart hammered, her stomach knotted, her legs gave out from under her, and she vomited and wet herself at the same time . The cloud's eye winked at her and lifted at the corner in proud jest. Then it squinted into something beyond evil, and the real fear gripped her.

She found her voice and screamed.

Her eyes flew open.

The driver swung to look.

The horses stopped on their own.

Michael put an arm around her.

The driver watched her with interest, then touched the horses ever so lightly with a long reed, and they moved up the road.

"I am so sorry. Everything will be fine," Michael repeated several times, holding her close to him in the carriage seat.

After a few minutes, Branna said, "I've no idea what has gotten into me." She wiped her eyes with the damp handkerchief from earlier, then said, trying to lighten the atmosphere, "Do you think the lobster was spoiled?"

It took a second for Michael to realize she meant her dinner the night before. Following her lead, he continued attempting to lighten the moment.

"I hope not. I was hoping to have another when I get back down," Michael kidded. He moved a little away from Branna and asked, "Have you had experiences similar to the one at the ruins and the one just now in the coach?"

"Most certainly not," she answered quickly. "I'm not sure my mind could endure many of those spells." She thought about revealing details of the fantasy in which she was his wife but thought better of it.

"What do you think brought on the second one?" she wanted to know.

"We passed an ancient burial site. A full-court portal tomb. We were within feet of it," Michael replied.

"May we go see it?" Branna said excitedly.

"I think your experience just now precludes a closer examination for a time," Michael said, amazed by how quickly she recovered.

The driver made faster work of the road, and the carriage pulled to a stop in front of the Slievemore Hotel. Facing the sea, the building, small for a hotel, displayed a fresh coat of whitewash over the plaster façade.

Michael dismounted, then helped Branna out of the coach.

The portly hotel manager and his equally portly wife bustled from the front door, introduced themselves and welcomed Professor Branna Butler and Inspector Michael Doyle to the hotel.

What had once been the best hotel on Achill, now a shadow of better years, lacked many of the modern amenities at the newer Amethyst Hotel. The furnishings were clean and functional but worn beyond their life in a prosperous lodging. The small restaurant offered a narrow dining room with only ten tables placed in a single file. The tables all provided a view of the grass between the hotel and the sea. Unseen from the hotel's first floor, the coarse sand beach lay below a four-foot escarpment and was reached by cut stone stairs at the end of a flagstone path.

An electrical update finished two years ago, and the cords running between switches and lights were still visible despite the management's best efforts to hide them with paint.

While the hotel manager stretched the tour longer than necessary, Branna seemed tired and wanted to go rest in her room. The manager showed Branna to her room, then Inspector Doyle to his.

About an hour before sundown, Michael knocked on the door to the professor's room.

"Feeling better?" Michael asked, looking at her for signs of fatigue or stress.

"Rejuvenated! It must be the breeze and salt air. I feel positively excited to visit our crime scene," Branna said with genuine enthusiasm.

Michael smiled and marveled at Branna's appearance. Her long black hair in a tight bun, she wore a camel-colored sweater and canvas overalls that ended with drawstrings below the knees. The perfect outfit for working in a site digging for ancient pottery, or whatever remained. At the same time, Michael thought she looked stunning.

"Well, then, we best hurry, as there's just enough daylight left to view it," Michael said, questioning his decision to go with so little light left.

The manager, a Mr. Thomas Corrigan, darted from behind the registration counter, motioning them to a cabinet in the mudroom portion of the hotel's entrance.

"As you requested, Inspector," Corrigan said proudly, opening the cabinet door revealing two sealskin coats and two pairs of rubber boots. "And," Corrigan said, pulling a paper-wrapped package from the top shelf, "These are the shirts and trousers you wanted from the local shop. I hope everything fits."

Corrigan handed one jacket to each of them. Branna's was slightly too large and Doyle's too small.

"I'm sorry we couldn't provide better sized coats. These are borrowed from two local fishermen," Corrigan apologized.

"They will do nicely," Michael Doyle said.

"I hate to deprive the men of their coats," Branna spoke hesitantly, taking in the slight odor wafting from the inside of the jacket around her. "I can tell the owner of this one must work very hard at whatever he does."

"Not to worry, Professor Butler," Corrigan replied, "They vanished two summers ago while fishing for the great sharks." He crossed himself then added, "They were both good boys, and they are in a better place. Their mother was glad to let you borrow them."

"Oh, dear," Branna whispered, thinking about being wrapped in a dead man's jacket.

"And here are your boots for your walk in the bog." Corrigan picked up the smaller pair of black rubber boots known throughout the UK as Wellies, named after Marshall Wellington from the battle of Waterloo. Corrigan carried them to a bench and encouraged Branna to sit while changing into the boots.

The coats were very warm, and soon Branna and Michael had them unbuttoned as they made their way along the path to Paddy's peat farm.

When a person purchased a property on Achill, it almost always came with a plot of bog, a private source of fuel for the owner's fireplaces. Men like Paddy bought or leased other pieces of bog to make a business out of it.

The path was like walking up a slight incline on a moist sponge, and many areas were overgrown with gorse.

They arrived at the official site of Paddy's farm: two

sheds, each with three walls and opened to the south, two long wheelbarrows, and an assortment of picks and specialty shovels in various degrees of wear.

Handwritten signs nailed to wooden stakes had been posted by the local constabulary around the buildings, warning people not to enter the area under investigation.

August is the warmest month on Achill, but by mid-September, the chill and a quickly shortening of daylight announces winter approaching at a gallop.

Enough sunlight remained for Branna and Michael to see clearly, but the shadows lengthened quickly.

Michael pointed to several small pieces of thin wooden stakes placed in the soil flooring. "These are very odd. What do you make of them?" he asked Branna.

"Is that blood?" Branna asked, a shaky finger pointing to dark stains in evidence on most of the tools, counters, walls, and structures in the shed.

Michael watched to see if she might faint again. "Yes, Branna, it is. Should we return to the hotel?"

"Heavens no," Branna said, "I'm just surprised by the quantity. Are you sure only two people were killed here?"

"Excellent question," Michael replied. "There were only two bodies present, but that does not preclude one or more other victims being carried off." Michael pulled his notebook and made a note.

"You called me Branna, a moment ago," she said as she bent down to examine the small stakes Michael indicated before.

"I must apologize," Michael stuttered, "It just slipped out. I did not mean anything..."

"Oh, stop it," Branna said without looking up at him. "Truth is, I liked it. There are few men with whom I am comfortable enough to allow them to use my first name. It turns out, you are, apparently, one of them." She looked at him as she said, "And stop apologizing every time you think you have offended me. I am capable of letting you know when you have crossed a boundary."

Michael liked this side of Branna. Her independence and lack of false demure represented exactly what the fledgling women's movement in England and America represented.

Michael squatted next to her. "Those two are men's prints wearing different sized Wellies," Michael said, indicating the two closest footprints pressed into the soft ground.

Looking beyond the scattering of rubber boot prints, Branna pointed and asked, "Those are odd tracks. What are they?"

Michael rose and walked around the small stakes sticking in the ground. Branna followed.

They stopped and examined a different print. Whoever made it wore no shoes and walked on the balls of their feet. There were no heel prints. The tracks clearly showed the ball of these particular feet had only four toes.

"If that is not odd enough," Michael pointed out, placing the toe of his boot next to a track, "This footprint is nine to ten inches wide."

The ability to compare the track's size to Michael's boot caused Branna to widen her eyes. Then she said, "No wonder it's not wearing shoes. Have you compared the depths of the tracks?" Branna wanted to know. She removed a notebook of her own and began making a pencil sketch.

"Yes," Michael answered. "We know Paddy Healy weighed close to two hundred pounds. His boot prints range between a sixteenth and a one-eighth inch deep. The ball of the footprint's depth measures as deep as one-half inch. Our math puts the print's owner at between four and five hundred pounds."

Branna's eyes opened wider. She continued to sketch, making an excellent likeness of the odd print.

"Since people weighing more than five hundred

pounds are scarce, we think it is possible the murderer, or murderers, may have carved or sculpted these odd tracks at the end of short stilts and managed to sink them deeper than a normal footprint," Michael posited.

"Why would they do that?" Branna said, studying the detail of the print more closely.

"I am not sure," Michael responded. "Perhaps to throw the investigation off by adding another layer of mystery?"

Branna looked up at Michael. She wore a puzzled expression as she spoke, "If in fact, your theory is correct, the sculptor of these fake feet knows a great deal about anatomy. Look closely, and you can see the barest traces of calluses, lines, and at least one scar."

Michael moved closer and squatted next to Branna. His shoulders touched hers as he did so. She did not move away.

"I do not see anything," he said, studying the bottom of the print.

"Look here," Branna said, pointing to a slightly deeper circular area just behind the two toes on the left. "And here," she pointed to a similar area behind the toes on the right side.

"Those are callus pads, normal for bipedal animals," she said. "Now look at this slight long indenture between the callus pads. I suspect that is a scar."

"You have extremely sharp eyesight, Branna," Michael said, trying to more clearly make out the details Branna described. The marks were there, but he would never have noticed them if he even knew to look.

"Thank you very much, Michael," she responded.

Michael stood and stepped from beneath the shed's roof. Twilight deepened rapidly. "It will be dark soon. We should start back. We can come again tomorrow and spend more time examining the blood stains."

"Agreed," Branna said, rising and putting her notebook in a pocket.

The north breeze was enough for them to button their coats.

The sun descended faster than anticipated. A low, thick fog arose slowly above the peat. Another larger fog bank moved inland from the sea. They were still on the bog trail when they saw the silhouette of someone approaching.

☐

September, Achill Island, Lynott's Pub

Lynott's Pub in Cashel was small, even by Achill standards. The front offered very old stones divided in the center by a single door in the center and a window on either side. Door and trim were painted kelly green. The bar could seat six and the two small tables combined could squeeze in eight. It was exactly the kind of place generations of islanders congregated to complain about conditions, whisper conspiracy, gossip, and laugh. A long-standing tradition prevented sons from entering if their fathers were in residence, so the pub was usually crowded with older men.

"I am telling you, she is one," Ryan O'Neal said for the third time, "I saw her with me own two eyes. At the village ruins and again at the cairn. I seen one before, so I know it's true."

"O'Neal, nobody's ever going to believe you so long as you keep that jug of poteen under the seat in your carriage. There ain't been one here in three hundred years, so you never seen one neither, at least not in this life!" Manus Moran shouted across the small room.

"Aye, she's worse than a witch, I hear she's a Butler, and you all know what them did to us on the island," Thomas Quinn added to the verbal scrap.

Manus stood and loudly stated so no one would miss

his comment, "Butler, witch, what's the difference? It's known around the world, Butlers are feckers. I'm knocked on my arse she's got the gall to come here!"

"Now that's the truth of it," someone at the bar chided.

"Me father told me the story, but I was too young to remember. What was it those bastard Butlers did to us?"

The bar hushed.

The man who spoke was young, by pub standards. His father died of cancer the year before and the young man, Sean O'Malley, was earning his stool at the pub.

Manus asked, "How can you call yourself a man from Achill and not know?" Before Sean could answer, Manus said, "I'll tell you the story, but it will cost you a pint."

Sean said, "For a pint, it better not be worthless lies like most of the tales in here."

"Oh, it's the truth all right, every word of it, burned into the memories of those who lived through it and passed down father to son, mother to daughter, ever since."

Manus stood at the bar near Sean and waited for the bartender to finish pouring his pint of dark beer.

He took a long draw, then said, "That's to keep my voice from giving out."

"A man came to the island in 1831, before the Great Hunger. He was the right reverend bastard, Edward Nangle. He had plenty of money and said he had come to convert us to Protestantism as if there was any chance in hell. Anyway, as I just said, he had plenty of money, bought some land, put some of the islanders to work building things. No one complained so long as he was hiring our men." Manus looked around the room, he loved it when everyone listened to him tell stories.

"But then the trouble starts. Nangle brings protestant families to live in the buildings we built for him. Pretty soon, he is buying more land until he owns half the island. They built their churches, schools, orphanages, farms, a whole damned town. In a couple of years there were more of them than there were islanders."

"The Protestant mission prospered, and the people of the island suffered. Then the Great Hunger arose and cursed the land and ate the spirits of the people, but not those who lived in the mission. Money and food kept coming to them. Butler money. Soon, Nangle and his Protestant devils set up a kitchen in Keel and right here in Cashel. They offered free meals for all." Manus stopped and looked at Sean.

"So, what's wrong with that, you asked? I'll tell you what's wrong. The food wasn't free. Oh, they didn't ask for money. They made you come inside and sit in their makeshift churches and participate in Protestant services. After a while, if you wanted to keep your family fed, you had to convert. That's right, abandon the Catholic Church. The food cost no money, only your immortal soul.

"And the Butlers, supposedly a good Catholic family, were part of a group of rich feckers who paid to make us abandon our faith.

"Now it's true, when the famine ended, those who survived converted back to being Catholics, but the damage was done. Once Nangle died, a mysterious death some say, the colony ran a streak of bad luck: crops failed, sheep died, boats sprung leaks. It was not much time at all they packed up and left.

"Now it's true, Achill was changed forever; backed by the Butlers, they tried to kill the Catholic Church and our old ways. But they failed. But I for one will hate them to my dying day."

Manus took another long swig of beer then sat down as conversation resumed.

"That's a fine and well-told bit of history, Manus, but it don't change the fact, I seen the way she acted. You yourself just said they failed to kill the old ways, so maybe all of you better start thinking them old ways are returning.

Because, on my poor mother's grave, I swear to you and to God, that girl's not a witch, she's a changeling and, mark my words, nothing good will come from her being among us." Ryan O'Neal banged his empty glass on the marred table top to punctuate his prediction.

"Aye, Ryan, if what you say is true, then what are we prepared to do about it?" Manus challenged.

A new voice was heard. A man standing beside the small fireplace, holding a half-empty glass of Guinness and smoking a pipe spoke. His free hand adjusted a patch over his left eye and drew attention to the scar that ran past his bad eye from brow to cheek, "We may have more mischief to worry over than a well-formed rich girl. We may have real trouble."

"Quinn," Manus said, "We know all about the murders up to Dugort. That inspector from Westport is up there now, solving the crime. He and the Butler girl will be gone in a day or so."

"My youngest son was up there, in Dugort Bog, where the killings took place," Quinn said as if he had not heard Manus. "He saw something that scared him. He stood just outside the shed where the killings took place. He said it looked like they were slaughtered more than just killed a little; blood and lots of it, splashed on everything. He didn't go in because the constabulary marked footprints with small wooden posts and he did not want to leave his boot print inside."

"True enough," Sean said, "Jack Ford, they hired him to move the bodies to St. Thomas' Cemetery, said it looked like humans butchered. Cut into pieces, legs and arms ripped from their sockets. He turned white as a ghost when he told me about it."

"My son saw something else: strange tracks sunk deep in the bog. Something with four toes, something big. He said it walked on the balls of its foot, never a heel mark, which means maybe it has no heels," Quinn said, looking at the faces staring back at him.

"There's your answer, boys, to why the changeling is here now. Something's afoot, and they've called her back," Collin Gallagher, the oldest man on the island, said. "Quiet now, boys. This is the story my great-grandfather, Seamus Gallagher, told me from his bed on his dying day. I was still a young lad, and the tale scared me. My mother told me it was not true, just old lore, but I never forgot a word of it."

Collin began his great grandfather's story, and the room grew deathly quiet. "The first thing to know is don't look at them. They want you to look. Seeing is believing."

☐

September, Achill Island, Trail to Dugort Bog

The silhouetted man blocking the trail stood motionless in the dying light.

"Branna," Michael instructed in a quiet official tone, "I'm going to approach the man, then stop a few feet away and speak with him. Please stay three paces behind me. In case there is trouble, I will engage him, and you run to the hotel for help."

"Do you not have a pistol?" Branna asked.

"Not on my person," Michael answered.

"Perhaps we should make a tactical withdrawal and arm ourselves with shovels and picks from the shed," Branna said, only half joking.

"It is probably just a local coming out to collect some peat," Michael offered, seeing the man did not push a wheelbarrow and knowing it was too dark for normal peat collection. "Follow me, and stay on guard," Michael said as he stepped forward at a normal pace.

The man on the trail ahead remained a statue.

As Michael drew nearer, he saw the man was large and dressed in all black.

"His apparel is not comforting," Michael heard Branna whisper from behind.

The man on the trail came slowly toward Michael. They

37

were yards apart when Michael thought he caught a flash of white beneath the man's chin.

Michael increased his pace as he said, "You frightened us near to death! Why didn't you call out?"

"I was not sure it was you," the big man laughed as he embraced Michael in a bear-like hug. "I heard you were here and came looking to thrash your impudent pagan soul for not visiting me right off."

Branna caught up and stood just off to the side.

The big man stepped back from Michael and looked at Branna. "Professor Butler, I presume," he inquired.

Able to make out details of the man's appearance, Branna said, "You presume correctly. Now tell me why a priest is in the bog in this growing dark."

"I must sadly inform you, Professor Butler, most priests I have come to know are never out in the dark. It is a hazard of the business," the priest quipped, then added, "I am Father Bob." The priest extended his hand.

Branna accepted it, asking, "Does everyone call you Father Bob?"

"Everyone except the college of cardinals and the Pope. They call me Father McGuire," the big man responded.

"I think Father Bob rather suits you," she said. "Not usually one to cut short joyful reunions…" Branna began, then paused.

"Not at all. We need to get out of the damp. My knee tells me a storm will be upon us in two to three hours. Allow me to walk you back to the Slievemore for warm tea, or strong whiskey," Father Bob said.

They followed him back toward Dugort.

Branna felt the north wind grow stronger and she sensed the storm over the horizon.

Thomas and Mary Corrigan arranged chairs and footstools so the three of them could sit comfortably in a semicircle, its center the fireplace. The manager and his wife brought them a tray of tea and biscuits then went about their tasks but often glancing to see if the trio required anything else.

"How did you two become friends?" Branna inquired. It only took a few moments of observation before she realized how close the two men were with each other. She envied never having known that depth of friendship. Her father, or her mother, or their wealth and power always interfered and eventually ruined Branna's personal relationships.

Father Bob responded quickly, "We met at Saint Patrick's University in Dublin. Long ago, when we both dreamed of saving souls the Catholic way."

"And what way is that?" Branna smiled as she asked.

"Oh, you know, the usual way; make them feel guilty then charge them for forgiveness," Father Bob answered.

When Branna grinned and nodded, Michael continued answering the first question. "Bob and I had the same classes and studied together. After two years we each knew the other better than we knew ourselves," Michael added.

"That's about the time I informed Michael he would be a lousy priest," Father Bob said, smiling at Michael.

"How did you reach that conclusion?" Branna wanted to know.

"Michael is a natural cynic. He never believes anything just because someone says so. Even if he thinks it might be true, even wants it to be true, he questions everything. At first, the questions are in his mind only but once formulated, tested, and refined, he can't keep them in. I told him the Catholic Church despises being questioned, at any of its many levels of hierarchy. At best, Michael would have been limited to running a parish in a small, out of the way county with very little funding." Father Bob looked at Michael.

Michael's face reddened.

"So," the priest continued, "I told him the best place

39

for that type of thinking was the law, either catch criminals or prosecute them."

"Bob was right," Michael said smiling. "He saved me a life of misery, for which I am forever grateful."

Branna placed her cup and saucer on the side table, smiled at the priest and asked gently, "It sounds as if you were perfect for the church's hierarchy and have climbed the Papal ladder to the top and are now running a small, out of the way parish with very little funding."

Father Bob looked at Branna with new appreciation. "Touché, Professor. I knew I would receive my just rewards."

"So, tell me, Father, how did you wind up here?" Branna was curious.

"A long and sordid tale, perhaps another time. I believe, if I walk briskly, I will reach my ark before the deluge strikes." Father Bob stood, offered his pleasantries, said good night and exited into a strong wind coming off the sea and a near constant rumble of distant clouds.

"Your friend must be terribly disappointed to manage Achill Island for the church. He seems fit for grander things," Branna said to Michael as they walked up the stairs to their rooms for the night.

"He doesn't manage anything. He is a Cistercian Monk who works and prays at St. Thomas Church here in Dugort. It's a long story, more interesting and complicated than you might think. It is his to tell."

Michael walked with Branna to her door. Branna spoke of making some kind of casting of the track she sketched earlier. She opened her door.

Michael said, "Good night."

Branna surprised him. She raised on her toes and leaned in just enough to provide him a brief, gentle hug. "That's for being my knight in sealskin armor in the bog when we thought Father Bob someone more sinister."

Michael, blushing again, said, "It was my pleasure. I will

meet you for breakfast at eight?"

"I look forward to learning more about you and your friend, the reluctant priest," she said and closed the door, watching his eyes until the door latched.

He had such marvelous eyes, she thought, innocent and honest. They held no deceit. Michael, she began to believe, was a man of honor, a very rare thing around all the 'honorable' politicians and magnates of industry in her personal world. His broad shoulders were another of his visual assets.

The nearly continuous thunder moved closer. Lightning flashes managed to illuminate slices of the room even through closed drapes.

Branna reclined and pulled the covers up to her neck as the rain began to fall against the windows. Rain always caused her to drop right off to sleep. She dreamed all night, dreams that caused her to toss and turn, to kick off the covers, to talk in her sleep.

Mostly unremembered, the common threads in the dreams were the odd tracks in the shed on Paddy's peat farm and Michael's recurring death. She woke before dawn. Not wishing to go back to sleep, feeling somehow disconnected from herself, she readied to meet Michael in the lobby. Brushing her hair back, Branna looked closely at herself in the mirror. She possessed a natural attractiveness: clear complexion, straight nose, full lips and light blue eyes, framed by raven hair that often caused people to take a second look at her. As the brush gently moved through the hair on top of her head, she saw something. Leaning in, using the brush to separate the hairs growing from her hairline. She discovered her first gray hair. How it became as long as the others without being noticed was beyond her. She thought about plucking it then decided that was silly vanity.

On her way down to breakfast, she remembered she had yet to see the reason she visited this remote island.

By morning everything outside was drenched. The storm came and went, dumping what seemed rivers of water on the island. Worry disturbed Michael's rest. His concern was Branna had yet to see the human-shaped cavity in the peat. Though the local constabulary covered the hole with a weighted down tarp, another rain like last night's might have filled the hole and destroyed its usefulness in the investigation. It was, after all, the main reason he wanted Branna's help. Of course, it was the main reason before he began to know her.

Before descending the stairs for breakfast, Michael decided to forgo his concerns regarding the difference in social strata between Branna and himself. He reasoned if nothing serious could come of the relationship, and he was fully aware of this fact, then no reason existed not to enjoy his time with Branna.

The morning air was bracing, decidedly colder than yesterday. The wind continued coming off the sea from the north, and brooding clouds promised coming storms.

Suited in sealskin and boots, they walked back toward the bog.

Passing St. Thomas Chapel, Father Bob exited the back door, waved and moved toward them. His long strides made his progress deceptively quicker than first thought.

The three of them exchanged greetings, and Father Bob fell in step on their way to the peat farm.

The rain had not affected the bog's surface as much as Michael feared. The sponge-like peat held more water than the day before but walking on it was the same.

They first stopped at the shed so Father Bob could see the tracks.

He grew pale as he knelt to better see the marks on the earth.

"That print there," he pointed, "that's Paddy's shoe. I

know because he accidentally cut a notch in the outside of the sole. You can see it on the left side."

"What about this one?" Branna directed his attention to the four-toed track.

He waddled a foot toward it. His eyes grew large as he studied it. "I'll wager that's a never-seen-before clue for you, Inspector."

"What do you make of it?" Michael asked.

"It's a mystery," he responded. When he stood, he continued, "I buried them, you know. I'll never forget the carnage, the horror of trying to place pieces in the right coffin."

Michael did not want Branna dwelling on that thought.

"Over here, beneath that rise, is the peat layer with the cavity, if the rain didn't fill it."

The flat bottom tier marked the last piece of bog Paddy Healy worked. The local constabulary along with some volunteers placed a canvas sail over the hole and drove stakes through the grommets in the material to keep it close to the ground. Not satisfied, they used fresh-cut bricks of peat to further secure the edges. Along the high side, where water's natural course would drain it into the cavity, the volunteers created a wall of cut peat.

Their efforts preserved the evidence.

All three worked to remove the stakes and the cut peat bricks on the low and perpendicular sides. Michael and Father Bob pulled the sail back, revealing the cavity.

Branna was on her hands and knees peering in before the canvas was completely pulled back.

Two inches of reddish water covered the cavity's bottom. It had not come directly from the rain, but the cavity's walls allowed the liquid to seep in from the surrounding soil, which absorbed the rain.

"Would one of you go and bring back the two buckets from the shelf along the shed's back wall?" Branna did not pause her investigation. "I need to get as much water out as possible.

Father Bob answered by heading toward the shed.

"What do you think?" Michael asked.

"Can't tell much of anything with all this bloody water," Branna responded. "But I have one question." Not waiting for a reply, "Why is the hole so long? Was the thing in here long enough to warrant it?"

Michael didn't answer.

"Well, have you no idea?" she asked.

"'There were giants in the earth in those days; and also, after that, when the sons of God came in unto the daughters of men, and they bear children to them, the same became mighty men which were of old, men of renown,'" Michael quoted from the Bible.

Branna looked up, "Of course you would know that, you studied to be a priest. Do you really think whatever was buried here was celestial?"

"How deep did you say this layer is from the original surface?" Branna asked, looking at the step-like tiers cut into the side of the hill.

"Twelve feet, but looking again, and allowing for the slope of the original hillside, I'm going to say fourteen," Michael said, revising his estimate. "How old would that make this thing?"

"Too old," Branna answered.

"What do you mean?" Michael asked.

"I've worked in peat bogs before. One of the things we know about them is an accumulation of depth is slow, so items found at depth in peat are older than items found at the same depth in the soil. Another thing, important in our case of the elongated bog man, is peat's water content makes it heavy. As peat deepens, the layers above compress the layers below, like a sponge pressed upon. This means that if a bog accumulates one inch of depth per decade, then a one-inch layer compressed by the weight above might have required a century to accumulate.

"The numbers vary from bog to bog, but that's a general idea," Branna concluded. "To answer your question, I said it was too old because my estimate at the moment is this layer of bog is ten thousand years old, and that is too old in which to find human remains. It is a time when the Ice Age glaciers were still retreating." Branna said, looking toward the shed as Father Bob came with two buckets and a gallon tin can.

The three of them worked carefully, making sure the buckets' lips did not touch the bottom surface of the cavity.

Ninety minutes later, when the water's depth was less than a half an inch, Michael said, "It seems to me we have reached the point of diminishing returns."

"What?" Father Bob said, carefully letting the water run into a bucket.

"The walls around the hole are currently seeping as much water in as we are taking out and we can't work any faster without damaging whatever imprint is left," Michael pointed out.

Branna stopped bailing and made a close, inch-by-inch study of the imprint under the water.

Michael and Bob stood by if she needed assistance. They talked quietly.

With the sun descending, Michael spoke, "Branna, sorry to disturb, but there are about two hours of good light remaining. It is likely to storm again tonight so we will have to recover the pit. If there is something critical you need Bob or me to help with, let us know."

"Plaster," Branna answered. "Unless you can fetch a barrel of plaster, there's not much else you can do here."

"There's not that much plaster on this side of Achill. We would have to get it in Cashel, and there's not enough time to do that today," Father Bob stated.

"What have you discovered?" Michael asked, seeing Branna standing up and stretching her lower back.

Branna rolled her head around her shoulders, working out kinks. "The wet peat does not keep impressions well as it spongy quality swells and ruins details. I will need to study my notes and drawings, but I think, speaking in broad generalities, the subject was human, or something similar. It was buried face down, which may indicate primitive superstitions. It is almost nine feet tall when standing. It has four toes on each foot. Its fingers are relatively long and appear to be taloned. It is a female," Branna ticked off. "Like I said, I'll know more after reviewing my notes and thinking through the information."

"Would you like me to make arrangements to bring in plaster?" Father Bob offered.

Branna thought a moment before answering. "Michael, do you have photos of the impression other than the ones you obtained from Lewis' journal?"

"No," Michael said, "the department does not as yet possess a camera. I will use this case to further argue the value of one."

"The water will continue to seep in, storm or not. By tomorrow, the swelling of the peat will destroy what details remain. Unless you have something else in mind, I don't see any reason to recover it," Branna said, looking at the rusty coloring under her fingernails.

"Well then, let's take a walk around the area to see if we missed anything and then head back to the hotel to get cleaned up. Branna, you will be happy to know we will leave tomorrow, and you can hurry back to proper civilization," Michael said with a sad smile.

As they strolled the bog, gazing about for things unusual, Father Bob said to Michael, "I cannot join you for dinner, but I insist you come for brandy later. There is something I want to discuss with you, and I may need my books about."

"And I still want to know the story of how you came to

be on Achill Island," Branna said, accepting his offer for Michael and herself.

"We will take an early dinner. You can expect us around eight if that is acceptable to Branna," Michael said, looking to Branna, who nodded approval.

The hotel bathtubs were not ensuite. Michael made an excuse so Branna could bathe and prepare herself for dinner.

At dinner, the management team of Thomas and Mary Corrigan fussed over the couple as if they were royalty. Their behavior, while well intended, embarrassed Michael and annoyed Branna as they left hardly any time to chat.

After dinner, the two of them donned their sealskins and boots before stepping outside to go visit Father Bob at the rectory, a small but classic coastal home with a slate tiled roof and heavy shutters for the windows.

The sky was clear. Stars winked above them. It was a cool, beautiful night, for the moment. The horizon presented lightning, frequent bolts flaring to expose a high bank of black clouds. Too far away to hear the thunder, Michael said, "We should make sure to leave the rectory in time to return to the hotel. In the morning, I will arrange for a carriage to take you back."

"Just me? Why are you staying?" Branna sounded almost hurt.

"I have a much to do in my investigation. Boring things, like interviewing people who knew the victims," explained Michael.

"What if I am not ready to return home?" Branna pouted. "What if I want to spend more time studying the bog itself and ask locals about things that have been found buried before?"

"I suppose," Michael said, "I would be delighted to enjoy your company after my interviews and your discoveries."

Father Bob opened the door almost as soon as they

knocked. He showed them through the parlor and into a tidy office. On the farthest wall, a painting hung over the fireplace. The other three walls were floor to ceiling shelves filled with books. A small fireplace hosted two comfy chairs for reading. The center of the room contained a polished oak parson's table. Their host offered them two chairs at the table facing the fireplace. He took the single chair opposite it.

By his chair, a small side cart had been placed. Topped with an ancient-looking bottle of brandy and three rounded glasses, it stood ready for guests.

Father Bob chatted distractedly as he poured and served the drink made by monks several decades earlier and only available to members of the church — high-ranking members.

The parson table's surface contained a large rolled up piece of heavy paper and a stack of three books to either side of Father Bob.

After everyone enjoyed their first taste of the rare beverage, Father Bob began, "So, Branna, you want to hear how I came to be here."

"I do," Branna replied.

"I will make it the short version," Father Bob started. "Michael and I met at St. Patrick's University. When we graduated, Michael chose his current profession, I stayed with the church. I excelled while at St. Patrick's, I received the rite of ordination but was not sent to save the souls of fellow Irishmen. Instead, the church sent me to study further at Trinity, a place with which you are familiar. While not a Catholic institution, per se, it offered religious, philosophical and history courses nowhere else available in Ireland.

"But then again, you know all this. I spent four years there focused on the history of Ireland, England, and the Celts. Once armed with my doctoral degree, I waited for the church to assign me to teach at a Catholic college. I was totally surprised when my assignment arrived. I was to continue my education in Italy, at the Vatican."

Branna's eyes widened, and she said, "That is an honor afforded very few men, especially few Irishmen."

"Yes, I was proud and honored to be asked to learn there," Father Bob said. "The first order of business was to become a Cistercian Monk. I can tell you about the order later if you are interested, but for now, it is enough to know they are among the strictest members of the Catholic clergy which requires their members' beliefs to be stronger than any other order."

"I'm sure a few Jesuits might draw their swords to argue that point," Branna said.

"They do a bit of killing for Jesus and think their life is hard. They mostly drink and pray their enemies are slower than themselves." Bob took another sip of brandy and continued, "This is the part of the story where most people suddenly remember polite excuses and ask to see the door."

Branna waited expectantly.

"Jesuits, as you probably know, are warriors of the church. They have carried shields and swords and physically fought for the holy church.

"What you may not know is Cistercians are the institution's spiritual warriors. We are trained to oppose evil when and where we see it." Father Bob paused, watching Branna. Father Bob knew Michael was intimately familiar with his story and focused on the woman's reaction.

"I am aware of some aspects of your order. Do you mean, oppose evil where you find it as opposed to seeing it?" Branna wanted to know.

Father Bob replied, "Both find and see." He hoped she required no additional explanation.

"I see. Tell me, please, with whom do these spiritual warriors battle?"

Father Bob looked at Michael for affirmation to continue.

Michael nodded almost imperceptibly.

Father Bob took another drink, made a deep sigh, leaned forward, looked in Branna's eyes and said, "Demons."

Branna instinctively leaned back from the man across the table. Being a Catholic herself, at least in name if not in spirit, knew some of the things Father Bob told her. But to hear a man who appeared sane and rational say he fought demons shook her faith in her judgment of the character of others to the core. She considered Michael and the priest were having fun with her, playing an outlandish prank. After a quick glance at Michael, she knew this was no joke.

"Do you mean to say you fight demons metaphorically?" she asked.

"Sometimes," the priest responded watching her eyes. "Mostly I fight demons."

"Just to be clear, you fight actual demons," Branna said, wondering if maybe it was time for her to make excuses and head for the door.

"Branna, I see the recognition of my insanity dawning in your eyes," the priest said softly. "It is a most natural reaction, and I've seen it often enough to know you are a little frightened at the moment. I assure you, I am not mad, you are in no danger and I will explain more after you take another sip of brandy and your heartbeat slows."

"Perhaps we should return to the hotel before the rain begins." Michael offered Branna an easy retreat.

"Michael," Branna began, "Father Bob's story is fascinating, and I have no intention of leaving just when it's reaching the climax." Branna took a larger than usual sip of brandy. "Please, Father, continue. I am most interested to know where and how you find your enemies. I already know your choice of weapons: a cross and holy water."

"We use other weapons sometimes, lesser known. Finding demons is the easy part," the priest said. "Those chosen by the church to fight demons are trained to see and hear them. The ability to do that is mostly belief in their existence. Belief is so important to the shaping of human history."

Michael sat, slowly sipping his drink and studying Branna for any sign of distress.

"I am fine, Michael," Branna stated, "I find your protective nature charming, though a bit silly and wish you would allow me to enjoy Bob's tale, whether I believe all of it or not. Please continue, Father."

"Do you believe in sea monsters?" he asked.

"I'm sure there are monstrous creatures in the depths, but do I believe some seven-headed, tentacled beast is going to surface off the beach and eat us all?" She paused. "Certainly not."

"Well, we have that in common," Bob said. "What about dragons and goblins? Do they exist?"

"Not as most people think, but they may be latent memories from a more primitive time when people confused something else and labeled them as such. Over the years, their descriptions and proportions have become exaggerated by time." Branna said, "I don't believe in ghosts either so I can save you that question." Branna smiled, showing her nerves were settled.

"Then I am sure you don't believe in faeries, or leprechauns, or any other of the Irish pantheon of the ridiculous," Father Bob stated before confirming, "Do you?"

"Not any more than dragons," she replied.

"Well, the people on this island believe in all of them, at least most of them," the priest said. "This place is the last bastion of true belief in Irish lore. The people here are a representation of what all of Ireland was like long before the invasions began.

"I am sure, Branna, you are familiar with the string of invasions Ireland suffered in the distant past." Father Bob waited for acknowledgement.

"Anyone who has studied our history knows of the four invasions. If you are talking about the mythological invasions and not the real ones of the Norse, Viking, Britons, Moors and finally the Catholic Church, I am familiar with those as well.

"Let me see if I get them in order. From first to final the invaders were the Cessair, Partholon, Nemed, Fir Bolg, and the Tuatha De Danann," Branna said, "Did I get them right?"

"You did, and even having only just met you, I expected nothing less." The priest beamed. "For now, let's assume the old adage to be correct, there is some truth in every myth. Many historians have taken these mythological people and placed them in different parts of Europe at different times, and their names change from those you listed to Spanish, Greek, Turks. But there are two other early people of myth you did not mention," the priest said, pouring himself another glass of brandy.

"Who?" Branna asked, always annoyed at missing an answer.

"The Fomoir, or Formor," the priest responded then sipped his brandy.

The thunder and lightning had slowly advanced during the conversation. As if on cue, the storm was upon them. Wind howled. Thunder rattled the windows. Lightning brightened the room in bright bluish rays. Rain hammered the slate roof and poured from the eaves.

Branna took the last of her drink, looked at the priest, indicated the storm outside, and said, "Quite a show your boss arranged for us."

They all laughed.

Branna hinted for more brandy as did Michael. Father

Bob poured.

"Unless you plan on transforming into seals, you will be here for a while," Father Bob stated the obvious.

"I for one am delighted to be trapped in your lair of frightening stories. The effects of the storm make it all the better. Please, Father, continue," Branna mused.

Feeling useless, Michael rose, went to the bucket by the fire and carefully placed two broken pieces of peat. The peat took his mind off the myths and onto reality. Two men were murdered in the most horrible way possible. It was his responsibility to bring the killer to justice, but at the moment he had no idea who might have committed the murders.

Father Bob exclaimed, "Excellent. We might even be forced to finish what we started." He pointed at the bottle. "Now, where were we?" the priest posed. "Oh yes, the Fomoir."

Branna remembered more Irish lore and said, "I left them from the list because they were not one of the five invaders. When the Fir Bolg arrived, Ireland was supposed to be without people, but the Fomoir were here."

"True enough, Branna," Father Bob replied, "So where did they come from?"

Branna could not find the answer, perhaps the brandy dulled her mind. "I'm not sure," she said, "But if you give me time to clear my head of brandy, I am sure I will remember."

They laughed again.

"There are many theories for their presence. The one I find most interesting is the etymology of their name. While the experts disagree on the minutiae, they generally agree Fomoir is a translation meaning either demons from the sea or, even less pleasant, demons of nightmares. Take your pick." The priest reached and picked up the roll of paper.

"Another interesting aspect is Irish mythology is the

only culture on earth that does not have a creation story. It assumes Ireland has always existed as part of, and separate from, the rest of the world. It assumes it was populated with all the creatures of faerie lore long before humans arrived." Father Bob sighed, as he came to what he considered the saddest part of the story.

He unrolled the paper revealing a map of Ireland inked with notes.

"To understand why the church, in all its divine wisdom, stationed me in Dugort, you need to follow the eradication of original Ireland." He paused.

An enormous lightning bolt struck somewhere nearby. The blinding flash was followed instantly with a peel of thunder that shook the entire building.

"Since you are stuck here for a while, I will assume your silence at this point is not from drowsiness." Father Bob emptied the bottle, pouring equal shares in their glasses.

"I follow your theory," Branna said, emphasizing the last word. "I am curious as to where your trail ends; not, I hope, down a rabbit hole."

"Maybe a hole," the priest responded, "but certainly not a rabbit hole."

"I'll be the judge of that," Branna smiled.

Michael stood. "I need to stretch my legs. I am not accustomed to spending so much time in a chair," he said, stepping to the window. In the glass, he watched the reflection of his old friend and the lady professor from Trinity.

He and his friend were fast and true. Always speaking the truth to each other, never sugar coating. He would ask Father Bob his opinion of Branna and what chance Michael might have with establishing a personal relationship with her.

He looked at his own face reflected in the window, distorted by streams of rain running down the outside of the glass. His expression was sad, anticipating Father Bob's answer regarding Branna and dreading parting with her knowing they would never meet again.

He heard Father Bob take up the discussion he and Michael shared numerous times over the years. Branna did not seem bored, but her demeanor was not as talkative as Michael thought.

Michael cupped his hands on the window and tried to see out into the night, trying to stop thinking about Branna.

Pointing at various places on the map, Father Bob said, "These arrows indicated the areas where invaders, mythical and historical, entered Ireland. Notice they all come from the north, east or south. They conquered lands, dominating many of the people in the area. But many moved away from the invaders."

The priest placed one of his books and covered the northeast of the map. A second book covered the southeast section.

"These two books represent the advances over centuries of all of Ireland's invaders." Father Bob began to move the books slowly toward one another. The books' spines met and passed over Dublin.

"The black 'X's' you see are the sites of battles. The Irish won some, but in the end, unrelenting expansion pushed them farther and farther west." He moved the books westward. As the ninety-degree angle where the books touched reached an area on the map near County Mayo, he took his hands off the books.

"This is where the great and final battle for control of Ireland was fought." He placed a finger inside a circle someone had drawn and written 'Moytura (the plain of battalions).'

Branna leaned forward, studying the map. "Yes, the final battle between the Fir Bolg and the Tuatha De Dananns supposedly lasted four days. Both sides erected cairns, monuments, and tombs to honor their dead.

"Legend has it the Fomoirs allied with the Fir Bolg in this war and used their magical powers against the Tuatha De Dananns, but in the end, when the Fir Bolgs lost most of their army and their king, they retreated northwest and acknowledged defeat," Branna described, her finger now touching the map near the circle.

"Move your finger northwest to where the Fir Bolgs ended their retreat," the priest asked.

"I do not have to," Branna answered, "it leads right here, to Achill Island." She said, thinking about the implications. After a moment she spoke again, "It seems your theory establishes evidence indicating Achill Island, as you put it, became the last stronghold of the old Irish."

"Yes. It is my belief the remaining beings of myth and legend could survive only in a population where belief in their existence remained strong," the priest said, removing the books and rerolling the map.

"This brings us to 'the seeing.'" Father Bob began a new direction in the conversation.

The thunder and lightning moved past, but heavy rain beat a primordial tattoo against the window.

Michael turned from the window. "Bob, I think someone is outside."

☐

"In ancient days, we feared the things we knew, the things in woods, and caves and the night. We made them gods that they might spare us. Now, we think them merely figments of ignorant ancestors. They have only retreated. They are the woods, the caves and the night, waiting."

Collin Gallagher

Achill Island's oldest resident

Achill Island, Lynott's Pub

Sean O'Malley nearly slid off the barstool twice while Collin Gallagher told his great grandfather's frightening tale of days when humans first encountered the otherworldly beings of Ireland. Sean could not remember ever being so drunk, maybe never. The volume of dark beer he downed dulled his consideration of what the older patrons thought of him.

Collin said, "In the beginning, the humans and the not-so-humans could barely see each other. They appeared and vanished like shapes of flickering mist in the air where there was nothing a second before then gone a second later.

Sean remembered the first portion of Collin's story, but at some point, he went to the toilet to piss. When he finished the long bladder draining, he felt the urge to evacuate his bowels, and he splattered the toilet bowl with an explosive blast. Then, while bent over washing his hands, he vomited bitter beer into the sink. He washed his face and hands, returned to the bar, ordered a shot of Jameson's, pulled out a chair and slumped into it.

Old man Gallagher seemed to like the attention as the men in the bar paid reverent attention to his story. Who knows, maybe his great-grandfather really did tell it to him all those years ago. Even less likely it held any truth, but it was a damned good story. Everyone acted as if they enjoyed and hung on every word. Everyone except Sean.

Sean went back to the bar for another shot of Irish whiskey. He bumped into a table and nearly toppled over. Every head in the room pivoted as one.

Sean knew he should apologize but fuck these old men. Most of them were older than his father was before he died. They thought they were such hot shite because of their goddamn club in the pub.

Sean stood at the bar and slammed down the whiskey.

He turned and, in a loud drunken slur, interrupted Collin Gallagher again. "So, you ol' sod, you are saying that the faeries, leprechauns, Sidhe and all the other stupid superstitious fuckall rubbish was true but didn't exist until humans began to see them and they, us. What a load of shite, old man. I think your head's gone soft."

"Quiet, Sean." Manus Moran's voice was serious, but not yet threatening. "You're drunk and being disrespectful."

"Of what? An old man who needs help getting up the steps to the pub's door and makes up lies to grab a bit of attention? It's not disrespect, Squire," Sean said, emphasizing the last word, a title the Moran family lost decades ago. "What it is," continued Sean, "is something there's damned little of in this shoddy little room of yours that smells of stale beer, cheap tobacco and the sweat and piss of old men who can't get their peckers out in time. It's the truth, and there's no one here but me with the guts to say it."

Ryan O'Neal rose from his barstool, his enormous, callous and scarred hands clenched at his sides. "Your father, a good man, is spinning in his grave, you saying such things to his dearest friends."

Sean took a step toward the door, eyes never leaving Ryan.

Ryan was old, but large and tough nevertheless.

"If this lot is the best he could do for friends, then he's better off dead," Sean said, in a lower, hateful voice.

"Shame on you, Sean O'Malley! Shame on you. Even knee crawling drunk, you've no right to say such things," Manus, who was not standing, said, voice quivering with anger.

"Shame on you," echoed from the others in the room.

"Goodnight, Sean O'Malley," came loud and clear from the bartender and pub's owner. "You know I stay out of my guests' way, but I'm making an exception tonight before the pub fills with broken chairs. Now, please leave."

Sean's bleary eyes half-saw the fuzzy-looking angry men. "I'll go. I'll go, and you'll never see another quid come out of my pocket."

Drunk as he was, Sean felt the anger smoldering and wanted to exit before the flames erupted.

He staggered toward the door, grabbed its handle for balance and paused to regain balance before opening it. He stepped outside, let the door close behind him and stood for a moment in the waning rain.

The passing storm soaked everything. Puddles in the road sometimes caught and reflected the light coming from occasional homes' windows.

It was a miserable night, and he dreaded the long walk home to Attawalla on the island's southeast side near Achill Sound. He thought about the walk. Three and three-quarters miles if he stuck to the road, two and a half if he cut across the country through Sraheens Bog.

59

Sraheens Bog yielded up a bogman when he was a young boy. Its skin, stretched tight across its bones, frightened Sean when his father took him and his brothers to see it before the people burned it on a funeral pyre. Boys of his age at the time whispered horrible things they or someone else saw while crossing the bog after sunset.

Sean didn't believe in any of it, except for the bogman, he'd seen that. It was scary, but it was just a body from a few hundred or so years ago. It wore a warrior's rotted leather armor and weapons, which the discoverer stripped before telling anyone about his find. It was no demon or mythical thingee.

Sean decided, though more distant, he would make better time on the road and, in the end, get home sooner.

Three hours later, soaked and muddy from the journey, he saw his mother's home set off from the road near the sound. Sobered by the walk, he trudged toward it, a headache forming.

He stepped behind the house to urinate before going to bed. He heard something in the direction of the water. He finished his peeing, put his penis away and stood quietly listening. Not hearing or seeing anything in the dark, wet night, he turned to go inside.

Then the sound again. Like someone dragging something over the rocky, weedy sand. Sean turned back toward the beach and waited. He heard it again, closer.

Sean froze; had he not just urinated, he would have wet himself. All the talk at the pub about demons, monsters and other things that go bump in the night had him on edge.

He decided to go inside the house. He was deciding whether to turn and run and not see if anything chased him, or keep his back toward the house, keeping his eyes strained for whatever moved in the night.

He heard the sound, much closer. The decision made, his now nearly sober legs moved as fast as they ever had until he reached the door and let himself inside. He moved to the window by the door and looked out. At first, it was the empty night. Then he thought he saw someone, or something, moving north along the Sound's coast. Thing or man, he guessed it might be eight feet tall.

But he wasn't sure he'd seen anything. Collin's stories affected him more than he admitted and he may have imagined it all.

He undressed, climbed into bed and fell asleep immediately.

He did not see the large, very human, face, peering through the gap in the window's curtains. His intoxicated coma was so deep he did not hear the wood and glass of window above his small bed shatter, nor did he feel the powerful hand at the end of the long arm reach down, grip a foot and lift him out of bed as if he weighed a pound. Sean O'Malley finally roused when his foot and leg were pulled through the window opening from the outside. Nowhere close to understanding his predicament, he cursed loudly and used his hands and arms to press against the inside wall to stop his outward progress.

For a moment, the pulling ceased, his ankle burned from the tightness of whatever gripped it.

Sean appraised the situation as best his drunken stupor allowed and took comfort when he realized the window's frame was not large enough to allow his torso to be pulled through.

The pulling began again, a slow, irresistible force that relentlessly brought him to the too small window a fraction of an inch at a time. Obtaining a better position for his hands and arms, Sean redoubled his resistance.

The pulling stopped again. A second later, Sean felt the tension on his leg slacken. Then, as soon as the pressure stopped, his leg was jerked.

The first jerk crushed his scrotum against the window and dislocated the leg at the hip and knee.

Sean screamed a prayer to God for mercy.

God's answer was another jerk that pulled his torso and the other leg, its foot next to his face, most of the way through the opening in the wall. Many ribs broke, his chest so compressed his lungs stopped working. He wanted to scream again, but with no air in his lungs, a pitiful gasp was all that emerged.

There was a merciful pause.

Something breathed hot breath on his distended leg.

The final jerk shattered his collarbones, and what remained of Sean O'Malley popped from inside the house to outside the house, body and head slamming to the ground.

Barely alive, no part of his body working, he moved his eyes to see what monster did this. When he looked down toward his foot, the one that was now by his face, he saw a huge, bald man, grinning at him.

Sean realized his hearing functioned when he heard the blast of the shotgun.

The giant stood and moved toward Sean's mother at incredible speed.

She fired the other barrel then screamed as the man swept his arm out, grabbed her by the neck, then snapped it like a breaking branch.

He came back to check on Sean. Seeing he remained alive, though by the thinnest of margins, he walked back toward the woman, ripped her nightshirt off with one movement then began to eat her breast.

Helpless, Sean saw the man denigrating his mother's corpse.

The giant took another bite. Mouth full, he turned to look at Sean. Chewing, raw meat and blood dripping from the corners of his mouth, he smiled. A horizontal line across his forehead flicked open. A putrid yellow eye stared back from the giant's forehead.

Sean prayed for God to take him. He wasn't sure if it

The SEEING

was God, but something took him.

☐

Achill Island, St. Thomas Rectory

"I do not see anything," Father Bob said, looking into the darkness. Nothing was visible at all unless seen in the flash of now distant lightning. "I hope my stories aren't making you nervous again."

"Certainly not," Michael Doyle, fearless sub-inspector from the Westport Barracks of the Royal Irish Constabulary, said, turning from the window.

"Branna, I suggest we return to the hotel while the weather has let up," Michael said, looking at the beautiful black-haired lady, wishing the European social class system could be made to disappear. Michael knew what he felt for her happened too quickly and that, even if the class difference was not in play, her feelings for him were not at a mutual level of affection.

"Michael, I admit to a little drowsiness, and agree we should return to the hotel," she said, pausing.

Michael was delighted she had finally agreed to one of his suggestions.

"I think, if Father Bob is up for it, we stay for 'the seeing' part of his lecture series," she said, glancing at the priest.

"I never liked leaving unfinished business," the priest said. "Besides, this is close to the part where I tell you why the Vatican-trained Cistercian is in Dugort, Ireland."

"By all means, Father, please continue," Branna said smiling.

Michael returned to the chair he occupied earlier and shook his head wearily at Father Bob.

"Brevity shall be my goal," Father Bob replied to Michael's signal. "The Buddhists and the Hindi share many philosophies. One is the creation of manmade reality. This is a grossly simplified explanation," Father Bob said, watching his guests to make sure they were not too tired to absorb the importance of what he was about to say.

Judging them alert and listening, the priest continued, "If you think something, you speak it. When you speak it often, you begin believing in it. If you believe it long and fervently enough, it becomes part of your unconscious. When it takes root in your mind, and your belief is strong enough, you eventually see it. When you see it enough, it becomes real to you. You have created it, and it becomes part of your reality.

"If a person believes a lie long enough, it becomes their truth," the priest said, watching his audience for signs of acceptance or rejection.

Michael knew this story by heart and seemed close to nodding off.

Branna probably knew some other version of the theory but seemed alert and receptive.

Father Bob went on. "At first a single person sees an improbable thing. A second, then a third, then six, then a dozen, then the whole village grows to believe in and see the thing. Imagine whole peoples seeing the same thing, incorporating whatever they see, into their reality, shaped by their collective 'seeing."

The priest paused.

"I've heard this theory before, but not near as well presented. Bravo, Father Bob," Branna said then asked, "Michael, this is brilliant. I'm not sure how much truth it offers, but your friend presents it in a wonderfully understandable manner."

"Father Bob honed this theory on me fifteen years ago. I've heard it enough that I can offer the lecture but never, in my occupation, converse with anyone interested enough in social anthropology," Michael replied. "Father Bob, try to get us out of here before sunrise, if possible," Michael said, relinquishing the floor to the priest.

"This theory is not new. The Catholic Church not only understood it but used it in their quest to make their faith a truly universal one," Bob said. "One method the church used in its rapid expansion in Europe was the hijacking of pagan deities and holidays and sacred places.

"They spread throughout Europe not by true conversion, but by enlisting pagan populations to join a religion the pagans thought little different than their own."

Branna took advantage of a pause to ask, "I know of this as well. The Catholic Church studied a pagan population's beliefs then explained to them the sacred place where they worshipped one of their gods on a specific day was actually the same place the church held services for the same gods on the same days."

"Exactly," the priest agreed. "Brigid is the perfect example. The Irish Celts believed Brigid, a triple goddess, was the original god, mother of all things. Their belief in her so strong, they would have nothing to do with any other religion that did not accept her. The Catholics not only made her a major saint, but they also allowed her to maintain all the powers her followers believed in. This switch from pagan god to Catholic saint occurred over and over throughout Europe.

"In conjunction with turning deities into saints, the Church took the pagans' sacred places away from them. To the pagans, a sacred spot was a place of repeated spiritual experiences of the seen and unseen so out of the ordinary as to fill the soul with fear and awe. When multiple people shared the experiences or saw the same strange phenomena in the same place, that place became sacred. As worshippers attended services at these sacred spots on specific days when the spiritual experiences occurred, more and more people accepted and believed the reality. As more people believe, more see or experience at other places. Eventually, as people 'see' the same event or deity at places other than the first sacred spot, the new places become sacred until the entire area is sacred land for the things seen and unseen by the people.

"When invasion comes, as it always does, the new population, not engrained with the local beliefs, refuse to accept the primitive experience and will not participate in the 'seeing,' so the sacred lands begin shrinking until what was once commonly experienced reality is extinguished."

Father Bob went on, "Not to bite the hand that feeds me, the Church knew all of this, learned over a thousand years of folding religions into their Universal Church. As time passed, and Europe fell to the Church's efforts, the leaders became content with their progress.

"So, by the time they reached Ireland, the elimination of pagan beliefs was much more difficult than they encountered in centuries. They conceded to incorporating Celtic gods, and it worked in most of the country. But here, and other places, the pagan and magical beliefs were so strong, the people pretended to accept and convert to the new faith, but they never let go of their old gods.

"The church decided a genuine conversion was not worth the effort or expense, so they allowed things on Achill and other areas to remain as they were, knowing future generations would become true Catholics."

Father Bob stopped and looked at Branna. She started to say something, but the priest interrupted, "Almost finished. If you have questions, you may ask them later.

"Branna, your grandfather, Henry Butler, was an exceptional man, more than most people know. He was a good Catholic, contributing vast sums of money to

Catholic charities and schools. But he was also a most learned man. He knew the things I just told you. He feared the people of Achill would one day return to 'the seeing' of their old gods and demons if they were not converted to Christianity in more than name only. He funded most of the Nangle Mission, in this very town in the mid-eighteen-hundreds."

Branna stood. "But the Mission here was not a Catholic work. Why would Granddad Henry support it?"

"Because Henry Butler knew the Church's position of continuing to do nothing for more generations until the final pagan holdouts died out. What are three or four centuries to the Catholic Church? Henry feared what might happen if enough people on Achill began experiencing 'the seeing' again."

Branna, still somewhat perplexed said, "I am more tired than I thought. My grandfather's involvement in this is unexpected. Please, before Michael and I leave, finally tell me why you are here?"

"For all its faults, the Church monitors everything. It may be slow to react, but it eventually takes action. The per capita number of demonic possessions in the Achill Island area is three times anywhere else in Ireland and increasing. I was sent here to perform exorcisms and watch for demons out of the ordinary or anything that might be interpreted by the people here as a returning pagan god. Such a presence would fuel their latent beliefs and feed power to the returned pagan deities."

"You are saying," Branna said, "you essentially are a well-trained watchman."

"I suppose that provides an adequate description of my function here." Father Bob chuckled.

"Well, let us hope the Church is wasting your time," Branna said, rising to leave.

Whether the brandy, the lateness of the night or Father Bob's mythic sermon or a combination of the three,

Branna's sleep was fitful and filled with strange dreams. She dreamed she was fevered and her mother, more caring and concerned with Branna than she ever demonstrated in the waking world, nursed her. The fever was severe. The doctor came, placed a folded wet cloth around her head. The doctor looked like Father Bob. Her mother's image flickered between the mother Branna knew and another woman. Branna did not know the other woman, yet Branna accepted the person as her mother.

Twice she woke, once needing water and again feeling nauseous. Branna stood before the washbasin to catch whatever might come up. Nothing did, her stomach settled, and she went back to bed.

After the first interruption of her sleep, she quickly fell back into the same dream, only this time only the mother she did not know tended her illness. Branna watched her as she sat in a chair by the bed, reading an ancient book in a language unknown to Branna. The woman was very tall and stately. Her pale skin and flowing silver hair seemed to place a radiance around her. Branna looked away from her toward a sound in the dark; when Branna looked back, the woman appeared dressed as a queen. She told Branna not to fear, that the illness was reversing and soon her health would be restored.

No sooner spoken then Branna curled up with stomach cramps and moaned toward the sound coming from the room's impossibly dark corner. She woke, stood over the washbasin then returned to bed.

This time she dreamed of Father Bob and Michael and their conversation. In the dream, Father Bob vanished from the rectory to perform some emergency priestly task. She and Michael sat together on a plush Chesterfield sofa covered in soft fabric. They were both tired and were drifting off to sleep when Branna felt something touch the hand next to Michael's. She was surprised to see she had placed her hand on top of his. He seemed asleep and did not react. Her hand, as if under its own command, stroked his hand. She looked at his face, asleep; without the worries and responsibilities of his duties as an inspector, Michael looked like an innocent, beautiful young man at peace with himself and the world around him.

Branna's view of Michael shifted. She found her arm across his back and her head on his shoulder. She listened to him breathe. Branna found her lips touching his neck with the gentlest of kisses. Her eyes were closed as she inhaled his aroma.

Branna opened her eyes, and Michael was awake. Their faces very close, looking into each other's eyes, she leaned forward and kissed Michael on the mouth.

His lips were warm and moist.

Michael returned her kiss, demanding nothing more than the pleasure derived from that moment.

Branna wanted more. She wondered what was wrong with her. This was new behavior, but the kiss was so perfect, she pressed further against his mouth and put her arms around his neck.

"Oh, Michael," she said. "I want to stay like this forever." The kiss deepened. "Oh Michael, my Michael," she nearly moaned.

"Branna." It was Michael's voice but muffled and not the man in her arms. "Branna, I am sorry to wake you," Michael said, rapping on the door to her room.

Branna shot up in bed. For a brief second, she thought about the dream Michael was interrupting. She wondered where it might have gone had she not been disturbed.

"Oh, Michael." Branna sounded disappointed. "Just a moment." Robed and slippers donned, she opened the door. Still half asleep, she asked, "Am I late for breakfast?"

"Not at all, Branna. I'm sorry to disturb you, but something critical arose, and I need to leave for part of the day. I'm wondering if you can see fit to delay your return to Dublin until I come back so I can give you a proper farewell." Michael spoke quickly, and his eyes would not leave Branna's.

"What something critical?" Branna asked, finally waking more fully.

"A case on the island. I'm here already, so it's fallen to me to investigate," Michael replied.

"A case? Another murder?" Branna said, more statement than a question.

"I am not sure," Michael half-lied. He knew two more bodies were involved; though he suspected murder, he was not positive.

"Give me a moment, let me dress and accompany you," Branna said, finding spending time with the broad-shouldered, good-hearted man important to her.

"Much as I enjoy your company, if I am to get there, investigate and return this afternoon, I have to ride my motorbike. I really want to see you before you leave," Michael explained.

"If you must. I'll be here. We'll have dinner together. I want to discuss parts of Father Bob's sermon last night," Branna said.

"I thought you were leaving today," Michael replied.

"I said no such thing, Sub-Inspector Doyle. You are the one who said I should leave," Branna said, smiling up at his blue eyes that seemed to gleam with excitement at her comment. "I will consider your request as my schedule permits."

"Well, I know better than to spend time arguing with you," Michael chuckled.

"I should hope so. Now run along on your contraption. I'll see you at dinner," Branna said, then, out of the blue, she took a half step, rose on her toes and lightly kissed his cheek. She stepped back, both surprised and confused at herself. "Good day, Michael. Be careful," she said as she closed the door.

She sat at the dresser and picked up her hairbrush. The

mirror showed a pale-skinned woman with hair tousled and matted from a rough night's sleep. "Oh my," Branna said, then grinned, thinking Michael's face provided no indication that her appearance was anything other than perfect. She located a second gray hair.

After breakfast, she went looking for Father Bob. Discovering he was away for most of the day on church business, she returned to the hotel. She marched into the restaurant's kitchen and called to an ancient-looking woman who sat in a chair polishing silverware.

"Hello, I'm Branna," she didn't want to include Butler in her name, "I'm staying at the hotel. You are Gladys, right? I am working with the RIC inspector on the case of Paddy Healey's murder."

The old woman looked up, her arthritic hands holding a soup spoon. "I've chased a few drunken louts out of me house, but I never killed a man, at least, so far." She smiled, exposing two missing teeth.

Branna laughed. "I'll bet you make your men toe the line."

"No other way to have them. They are all stupid boys, no matter how old." The woman looked back at the spoon and continued polishing.

"I am a student of the old ways," Branna said, sounding as humble as she could, "I'd like to speak to some people who know the lore of Achill. Can you help me?" Branna asked.

The woman's cataract-dulled eyes looked back at her for a long moment, appraising something. "Normally, I keep my own business. I wouldn't send a stranger to talk to anyone I know. But, and I'll tell you true, I've a feeling I should send you to talk to Collin Gallagher. He's the oldest person on the Island and knows more than he should about the carrying ons of the Good Neighbors."

"The Good Neighbors?" Branna asked.

"Oh, child, it's something we sometimes call the Other

Ones," the woman replied. "It's bad luck to speak their names."

"Oh, I understand." Branna suppressed a smile. "So, where do I find Collin Gallagher, and will he speak with me?" Branna asked.

"In the daytime, you can find him smoking a pipe and reading books in his house on the road to Cashel. At night, he'll be a Lynott's Pub, holding court over the younger men," Gladys said. "Whether he'll speak with you or not, I don't know. My guess is, he'll look you up and down then ask you to sit or send you on your way."

"How do I find his house?" Branna queried.

"When you reach a signpost along the road that says, 'Cashel, one mile,' look to your left. You will see a path leading to a stone cottage a bit off the road. That's Paddy's place," Gladys offered, adding, "And be warned, a high-bred girl such as yourself will find the house in need of a good dusting and scrubbing." The old woman bent back to work and spoke in parting, "Good luck, Branna Butler. One more thing, Miss Butler," Gladys said, standing and retrieving a coarse sack from a cubbyhole. She reached in then held out a quart fruit jar filled with clear liquid. "If you'll offer me a pound, I'll send you on your way with Collin's favorite drink. He's more likely to ask you to stay if he knows you might offer him some poteen."

Branna asked Mary Corrigan, who busied herself tidying up the hotel lobby, about hiring transportation. Mary suggested a carriage. Branna wanted a horse to speed things along. Mary sent a bellboy out. Thirty minutes later he returned with a sturdy-looking animal fitted with worn tack. Branna decided it was worth the time to change into her overalls before heading out on the three-mile ride that took her through Dugort East Bog, where the horrid murders occurred.

Attawalla, O'Malley Home

Michael Doyle came out of the general store in Cashel with a newly purchased empty jug. He approached the manual fuel pump and turned the handle on the iron wheel. The smelly liquid flowed through the hose and into his bike's fuel tank. Then he filled the new jug, sealed it and affixed it to the bike's frame.

Reaching Attawalla, he asked two boys walking back from Achill Sound, each carrying a string of fish, where to find the home of Sean O'Malley.

Michael saw a small crowd had gathered at the front door when he arrived. A man in his early forties broke from the group and walked toward him. Michael dismounted, leaned the bike on its stand and started toward the oncoming man.

"Hello," the man said and stuck out his hand as they stopped. "You must be Inspector Doyle. I heard about your motorbike. I've never seen one before," the man said, hinting to get a better look at it.

"Then you must be Liam Williams," Michael said, ending the handshaking and motioning toward the house.

Williams was an acting RIC constable, he received a small stipend to compensate him for the limited services rendered on the island. His primary purpose, other than availability to report local crimes to Westport, was to listen for conspiracy against the crown. While most of Ireland's pubs rang with rebel songs and low talk of Ireland's independence, Achill Island residents seemed indifferent. There were more pressing things to tend to, like putting food on the table.

The small crowd of people watched Michael approach them. Their expressions and color ranged from about-to-be-sick to flushed anger.

A woman, unkempt brown hair streaked with a white strip on either side, looked into Michael's eyes. "Now we have four murders on our island. We haven't seen four murders in the last twenty years, and now there's four of them, each worse than the one before it." She paused. Then, looking at other faces for support, she said, "We need protection. Whether you know who or what is doing the killings, we need protection."

The others mumbled agreement.

Michael answered the woman directly in a soft voice. "I agree completely. After I finish examining the crime here, I'll contact Westport and have them send some armed constables to watch over the island." Then he looked at the other members of the group, "Also, we'll bring some firearms and train local men to augment the force and cover more ground."

Michael looked at their faces again. The woman who first spoke was calmer but not happy. The men, having heard the part about islanders being asked to work as guards, refused to look Michael in the eye.

"If you don't mind," Michael addressed them, "I will begin my examination of the scene."

Sub-inspector Michael Doyle entered the cottage's front door.

Moving slowly through the hall and rooms, he saw nothing awry until he came to Sean O'Malley's bedroom. There was blood everywhere.

Michael noticed Williams had chosen to remain outside the room.

The window frame was completely torn out. Blood coated the wall below it like red paint. Bloody handprints on the plaster wall demonstrated how the victim struggled to remain inside. The fragments of glass and window frames remaining in the window sill were bloodied, and some had pieces of flesh attached.

Michael left the room.

"Where are the bodies?" he asked Williams.

"Around back," the volunteer constable answered, adding, "I'll go question the people to make sure I didn't miss anything the first time."

Michael suspected Williams was avoiding returning to the carnage.

When he saw the bodies, or what remained of them, he understood Williams' reluctance.

The first body belonged to Margaret O'Malley, a widow by storm at sea and the mother of Sean O'Malley and two other children who immigrated to England. Her nightshirt, torn from her body, lay on the ground, soaked in coagulating blood. Her head tilted left at an impossible angle and vertebrae in her neck bulged unnaturally. Michael hoped the broken neck killed her before the other injuries.

Her breasts had been removed. Closer examination revealed teeth marks and Michael realized the breast were bitten away by someone with an extremely large mouth. The bite marks looked human, but the size of them seemed impossible. Yet here he stood, seeing them with his own eyes.

The rain of the last two nights left the ground wet. Unlike the bog, the ground here was composed of a mixture of rocky soil and sand. Firmer than peat bog, the rain most likely ruined any footprints.

Margaret's right hand was missing, and it looked as if it

had been bitten off at the wrist. The bite mark indicated the mouth enclosed the hand as the teeth separated it from the arm. Margaret's right eye was removed from the socket and placed on her forehead then smashed like a plum.

Michael squatted next to Margaret's body for fifteen minutes, taking fresh looks at her remains and jotting notes.

He stood and moved to Sean's body. Standing four feet away, Michael stopped, initially unable to understand how the misshapen human form came to be. When his mind flashed back to the bloody handprints on the wall by the window, he understood. Sean had been pulled through the window, and not all at once in a clean, quick motion, but in stages.

After a few minutes of scanning the wrecked human body, he formed a mental image of Sean's body contorting, and breaking in stages as he lost the fight to remain in the house. Again, a hand, bitten off like his mother's, lay on the ground near the body. Sean's eye also rested on his forehead like a smashed piece of fruit.

Michael struggled to finish his notes. His stomach lurched, and bile rose in this throat. Much more of this and he would be vomiting in a most un-inspector way.

"There's something here," a voice called from behind him.

Michael turned and saw Williams forty yards away from the house, standing in the noonday sun, looking down at the ground.

Michael knew it was a waste of time to expect Williams to explain anything, so he walked across the rocky soil. As he neared, Williams used a walking stick to point to an impression in an area that was more sand than rock.

Michael studied what might have been a human footprint. All the right parts, five toes, and a heel. If this was a print, it meant someone other than what killed Paddy Healy may have done this destruction.

Michael had Williams place his walking stick along the length of the potential track, then across it at the ball of the foot. Using the cane, he determined the barefoot print was at a minimum double the size of his foot, including the boots he wore.

"What do you think, Inspector?" Williams asked. Before Michael answered, he said with a shocked and honest voice, "In all me days, I never seen nothing like this. Mother Mary, I never even heard of nothing close."

Michael looked at Williams and spoke softly, "Me either."

Michael signaled for Williams to follow him around to the front of the house.

"You tell these people I'm off to bring help to solve the mystery as well as bring guards to Achill," Michael said. "Don't let anyone go behind the house. I'll be back in a few hours."

Michael peeled off to his motorbike and heard a flurry of questions fired from the members of the crowd. He did not turn to look.

It felt good to have the cool wind in his face, blowing away the vision and smell of slaughter.

☐

Collin Gallagher's Home

Branna found the house exactly where Gladys said it would be. She rode the horse to the ruins of a wooden fence in front of the cottage door. She tied the horse then knocked on Collin Gallagher's bright green wooden door. It might be the only part of the house to feel fresh paint in twenty years.

At first, there was no answer, so she knocked again, more firmly.

Still no answer.

She tried looking in the windows but they were thickly coated with years of dust, and the house was too dark inside.

She walked around to the back of the house.

There sat Collin Gallagher, slumped into a wooden chaise chair with feet propped on a wooden vegetable crate. He snored with great volume and rhythm.

Branna didn't want to disturb him, but at the same time, she didn't want to have to return later. She went to the side of the house and, head peeking around the corner, called out loudly, "Collin Gallagher, are you home?"

He stirred but not enough to wake, only break the

rhythm of his snoring.

She tried again.

It occurred to Branna the old man's hearing might not work well. She was thinking up her next move when a large matted mongrel appeared near some trees then streaked toward the house, barking non-stop.

Branna went to the front and remounted. She rode the horse back toward the road and waited.

First, a lanky, shaggy dog rounded the corner. As it drew close, it stopped barking and eyed Branna suspiciously.

Next Collin made his way around the house using a long walking stick to speed his progress.

"Steady, Cromwell," he said to the dog, which took one more look at Branna then ran off. Branna noticed how quickly it covered ground.

"Collin, Collin Gallagher?" Branna called, trying to make her voice sound sweet.

"Who wants to know?" Collin answered, "I hope it is not an uninvited guest astride a horse in me yard."

"I am afraid it is, Mr. Gallagher. My name is Branna Butler, and I would…" she said as Gallagher interrupted.

"I've been wondering how long it would take you to find me," Gallagher said, neither friendly nor unfriendly. "Get down off the horse and come inside." Gallagher didn't wait for her to reply. He turned and went inside his front door.

When Branna entered the already opened door, he lit a second lantern, slumped into a worn fabric club chair and put his feet up on a wobbly footstool. He motioned for her to sit next to him in a chair covered with a sheet.

"Who told you how to find me?" Collin asked.

Branna felt if she were anything but honest, Collin might send her away. "Gladys, at the Slievemore Hotel," she said.

"Oh, she did, did she? That Gladys is a wise old

crone," Collin responded. "If I know that Gladys wanted you to find me, she also wanted me to talk with you, which means she sent a bribe along with you." Collin sat silent, waiting expectantly.

Branna handed him a drawstring bag.

He reached in, extracted the jar and held it up so the sunlight filtering through the smeared windows could shine through it.

Collin smiled and said, "A smart old bird, that Gladys is. Would you go to the cabinet and bring two glasses?"

Branna returned quickly and handed Collin two short whiskey glasses. He poured an inch of the liquid into each glass then handed one to Branna.

Gallagher lifted his glass to her and waited for Branna to do likewise. Then he moved his glass to his lips and again waited, watching his guest. When Branna followed his movements, the old man took a sip, smacked his lips and said, "That's the best thing the devil ever invented."

When Branna finished her sip, he watched for a reaction. Seeing none, he smiled and said, "Well then, I imagine we best be about our business."

"Since you appear to know I was coming, tell me what you think our business is?" Branna said.

Gallagher looked hard at her. His old eyes looked directly into hers. He leaned toward her, straining to catch a glimpse of something.

He leaned back and said, "You don't know, do you?"

"Know what?" Branna's curiosity was roused by this mysterious old codger.

"I'm not sure it is my place to tell you," Gallagher said, "I thought you were coming to see me because you knew."

"Knew what?" Branna fought to control her annoyance.

Gallagher looked at her again then said, "Alright, then, you can't say I didn't warn you. This is your last chance. Once you know, you can't unknow."

"Please, Mr. Gallagher, I am a grown woman, I can handle what it is you have to say," Branna said, a feeling growing inside suggesting she might not be able to handle the information at all.

"Branna Butler, you are a changeling," Gallagher said softly, watching her.

Branna made herself appear calm. She knew the people on this island were more superstitious than any other part of Ireland. After a moment, even though she thought she knew the answer, Branna asked, "What exactly is a changeling, Mr. Gallagher?"

Gallagher took his turn at waiting to reply. "I think you think you know, Branna, but you don't know everything. If you'd like to learn, I'm here to help you along your journey." Gallagher paused, then said, "And call me Collin. Saying Gallagher takes longer and I don't have all that much time left."

"Please, Collin, I would like to hear what you have to say," Branna said, knowing there were no such things as changelings.

Collin began, "The fact you don't know you are a changeling means you don't believe they exist. That's only natural. How and why you don't know what you are is not my concern. Branna, you think a changeling is a story from lore, where the Gentry or other Good Neighbors replaced a human baby with one of their own. If the human parents aren't wise to the Sidhe's ways, they may never know their child is not human. There are many signs, but mothers and fathers tend to look the other way when one of their own children is a bit odd."

Gallagher finished the poteen in his glass and poured another inch before continuing, "Now the story most people believe about changelings is that the Good Neighbors need human breeding stock to make their race stronger. That's true sometimes, sometimes it's not. There are other reasons. Often a member of Gentry royalty changes babies to keep their child safe from assassins, plague or war."

Branna's face offered neither belief nor disbelief.

Gallagher took another sip then said, "Branna Butler, you are the child of a queen in the other world. I don't know exactly why she gave you to humans, but now she is calling you home."

"What is my Sidhe mother's name?" Branna said, knowing it was a ridiculous conversation but at the same time wanting to know.

"Her name is Oonaugh. She's known by many other names, but that's her true name." Collin said the name as if it were sacred, then added, "It's not safe to say their names. It calls attention to you."

Branna remembered her strange dream and had to shake an odd feeling of truth about what Collin said.

"You're Catholic?" Collin asked.

"Yes," Branna responded.

"Then you believe in guardian angels. This is no different than that." Collin leaned toward her and continued, "Did you ever wonder how the Butlers became so powerful and wealthy in Ireland? Did you ever question how Butlers always showed up at the right place at the right time to grow their fortune?"

Not waiting for her answer, he continued, "The Sidhe pick families they favor through the decades. They make the family's path easier. They do this because they are manipulating things to come. The Butlers are such a family. The Sidhe have given a bounty over the years, and now it is time to repay."

"How do you know this about me? What makes you so sure it is true?" Branna could not stop the growing feeling this old man's words stirred in her soul.

"First, there's Ryan O'Neal, your coach driver on the road to Slievemore. He watched you at the famine village and again at the portal tomb. Then, I've known for a long time you, or someone like you was coming because strange and dangerous signs have been building here on Achill Island. And last, but not least, I've finally met you, and now there is no doubt you are the one called back to set things right in the otherworld. The longer you remain here, the more you will see it yourself." Gallagher seemed tired, but he wanted to finish.

"The Sidhe live in an otherworld connected to our own. It is connected to a dozen more worlds. Every world is filled with beings and creatures. Just like here on Earth, the worlds have those who crave power and war for dominance of this place or that." Gallagher's eyes drew heavy. "I can't tell you any more than that, other than pay attention to your dreams. Your mother may use them to help you."

Branna sat silent for a few minutes. She didn't know exactly how she felt about her decision to come here. She intended to find out about what kind of creature might possibly have left those tracks in Paddy Healy's shed. Now she was going away with this strange, impossible, superstitious tale, yet something in her would not let it go.

She heard Gallagher snoring.

Branna quietly left the cottage, mounted the horse and headed back to Slievemore.

☐

Royal Irish Constabulary Barracks, Westport, County Mayo

Michael felt no choice but to return to the RIC offices in Westport and present the situation to County Commissioner Oliver Milling, a long-time lawman who had worked his way up the ranks. He was near retirement, and holding the County Commissioner title since 1889, he knew the territory. More importantly, he knew the people. Had anyone else tried to contain the troubles incited by the United Irishmen's League, the bloodshed of the semi-rebellion might have been ten times what it was.

Hugh Lowndes, normally Michael's superior officer, was away on duty. Westport was unaccustomed to the current volume of troubles that plagued most of the rest of Ireland, but lately, County Mayo bubbled continuously with crimes, riots, and incitements. With Lowndes absent, Oliver Milling agreed to see Michael, but he made him wait for nearly two hours.

Michael fidgeted, walked between Milling's office and his own desk, anxious to return to Achill Island. One reason returning to Achill quickly disturbed his usual unflappable outward appearance was his promise made to the people at the O'Malley house in Attawalla; the other, more urgent, though it should not have been, was to speak with Branna before she returned to Dublin.

When admitted to Milling's office, the sun nearly touched the western horizon.

The County Inspector, jacket hanging on a wall-mounted coat hook along with his hat, sat with feet up on his desk, smoking a clay pipe. Three large, thick envelopes remained in his in-box, a fourth, its contents of papers containing columns of numbers, was spread across the center of his desk.

"Sorry to keep you waiting, Michael," Milling apologized. "Monthly reports are due in Dublin, and it is all I can do to keep the bloody paperwork flowing. I'll tell you this, young man, never aspire for my job. It wasn't always like this, but now I have time for little else other than balancing columns of numbers with receipts and pay stubs and submitting reports of hours each officer worked and on what cases."

"Yes, sir," Michael said, wanting to conduct his business and head back to Achill.

"I'm told Achill Island is the location of some unusual and frightening events. As briefly as you can, provide the details of the murders," Oliver said, removing his feet from the desk and relighting his pipe.

Michael told him everything. Using his notebook, Michael covered the details in as few words as possible. Milling liked efficiency in conversation.

Milling did not interrupt. He sat quietly, listening, focused entirely on what Michael said.

When Michael finished and looked to Milling for reaction, Milling spoke. "Horrible, horrible, no wonder the population is nervous."

He looked into Michael's eyes, his own hooded with age that appeared as a constant squint. "Doyle, I know your record. I've followed your career. You are considered someone who will see several promotions. Therefore, I know you are normally very levelheaded. Your record indicates you never before entered into fanciful speculation, but there are parts of your report I had heard before and, quite frankly hoped were not true. The hoof-like prints at the murder scene at the bog, the human footprint of a giant at the O'Malley residence."

Milling scraped the pipe's bowl, tamped down more tobacco and paused before striking a match to relight it.

"Yet here you sit, an otherwise up-and-coming sub-inspector with a record for solving crimes quickly, with no drama or unwarranted theories. I have no choice but to respect your beliefs that these deaths were perpetrated by something inhuman, based on these two pieces of evidence combined with the morbid methods of murder. I know you believe that. Most men would." Milling stopped and lit his pipe.

Michael's confidence sank to a lifetime low. Milling did not believe him. He probably thought Michael a fool.

"Don't feel too badly, Doyle," Oliver Milling offered, seeing the younger man's expression, "There are things at play of which you are blissfully unaware." Oliver stood, peered down at his desk. "Fecking paperwork," he said, "What I would not give to ride back to Achill with you and unravel these wicked deeds and expose the cowards executing innocent folks.

"You see, Doyle, only a fortnight ago, a mile south of Castlebar, some members of the UIL attempted to scare a landlord into selling properties to tenants at unreasonably low prices. They obtained the amputated hooves of cattle, strapped them to their feet, and, costumed as banshees, set the landlord's house afire. In the morning, the only clues were tracks of cows, all around the ruins." He paused, then asked, "So, Doyle, in your thinking, is it possible that the crimes on Achill Island might possibly be something similar to the incident in Castlebar?"

Michael absorbed the information, considered it then replied, "Colonel Milling, as you stated, I was not privy to the knowledge of the UIL's attack at Castlebar." Michael paused, considering the importance of what he said next. "Yes, I suppose something like that might be possible in the Achill killings. There is evidence the 'hoof-like' print at the bog was not made by a human; even so, it is possible."

"Good to hear you understand, Doyle," Milling replied, smiling at his ability to calm Doyle down.

"At the same time, sir, if the evidence is manufactured, there is something else, sir," Michael continued. "Fanciful, hoax or not, the people on the island are frightened, and, in my mind, with good reason. Hoax or not, four people suffered terrible deaths."

Milling's eyes looked to the ceiling in thought. He took a deep breath, held it for two heartbeats, then exhaled. "You make an excellent point, Doyle. I am going to issue an order allowing you to pick up two acting constables in any towns you pass on your way back to Achill.

"Now if there is nothing else, Sub-inspector, I must work late into the night confirming the whereabouts of each constable in County Mayo for the past thirty days."

Michael sat astride his Triumph motorbike, strapping his riding cap tight and adjusting his goggles. Darkness came quickly, preventing him from racing back to Achill Island and arriving at the Slievemore Hotel at an hour early enough to knock on Branna's door. Then, knowing several stops were required to locate and notify acting constables of their new assignment, his heart sank. He would not arrive at the Slievemore Hotel on the north side of Achill before morning.

He started the bike's engine and drove north toward Newport. He hoped to find one constable there and another at Mallaranny. Michael had Liam Williams, acting constable, already on Achill Island. Three acting constables and himself.

He shook his head, accelerated, and moved along the dark road at speed too dangerous for the visibility. The fog grew denser with every mile.

☐

Slievemore Hotel, Gladys

Branna took her time riding back to Dugort. She thought about Collin Gallagher's tales.

Her mind discarded his advice as a combination of folklore and an old man's attempt to maintain some kind of respect in the only community he had ever known. Granted, much of what he said was accurate. Well, as accurate as Irish myth can be. But revealing Branna as a changeling — well, preposterous was too inadequate a word to attach to the claim. She put it down to old Collin's brain being marinated in alcohol for too many decades.

Her heart kept tugging, asking nagging questions. Why had this place energized her shortly after arriving? Why the dreams of the two mothers occurring in her sleep now? Why did she feel so drawn to Michael? While she expressed more forwardness toward Michael than any other man she'd known, she knew she struggled to hold her feelings in check. She realized she wanted Michael. Something about him, or this place, or a combination of the two, stirred up feelings she never had before for a man. In a way, it was great fun, to look forward to seeing him each time they met, to feel the electricity in their bodies when their hands or shoulders brushed. But there was the dark side of her desire. She hardly knew the man. He would not fit in with her family well, if at all. Her father might accept him, set him up in some respectable business, but her mother would forever be quietly and indirectly insulting him, tearing Michael down. Branna was not the kind of girl to give herself physically to a man for a fling. She experienced sexual relationships twice in her life with a boy, a distant cousin that stayed with her family one summer when she was fifteen. The experience failed to make her understand why so many people discarded established relationships for hidden rendezvous to obtain a physical release of bodily tensions.

So, a short-term relationship with Michael, or anyone else for that matter, was not an option for Branna. She admitted to herself how powerfully she was drawn to him. She found no suitable reason as to why the attraction was so intense, but she could not enter into a fling. The darker side of the coin was that long-term it simply would not work.

They were too different. Not just in the invisible, but very real, social classes, but in their taste for things. Michael seemed content living and working in the thinly populated rural west of Ireland among peat farmers, fishermen, and shepherds. She did not dislike them individually, in fact, she found herself drawn to their folksy charm and sincerity.

Branna, lost in thought, realized her horse, receiving no instructions from its rider, had slowed and eventually stopped. She was on a rocky dirt road along the east side of Dugort Bog. High enough to see the ocean to the north, she saw fog banks forming out to sea as the sun hung just above the horizon.

Just off the road to her right, she saw another small spring bringing water to the surface. Following the trickle-like stream of peat-stained water down the slope, she saw shrubs, weeds, gorse, and the now familiar stones creating miniature waterfalls that babbled with their own language.

She turned her attention back to the track and readied

to make the final mile back to Dugort when she caught something in the corner of her eye near the small brook. Whatever it might have been, a butterfly, a small bird, it was gone before she could focus her eyes.

As the horse took the first steps forward, the breeze from the north stopped, and for an instant, the babbling sounds of the brook added flute and string music to their rhythms. She paused the horse and looked toward the sounds but then the north wind returned and drowned out whatever sound she thought she heard.

She reached the Slievemore Hotel a few minutes before the sun sank beyond the horizon. It was beautiful, but at the same time, she found it sad.

There had been no word from Michael, and the management team of Corrigan and Corrigan informed Branna someone told them Michael went to Westport but would be back in Dugort tonight or tomorrow.

Eating dinner alone, consumed with alternating thoughts of Michael and Gallagher's story, she saw Gladys in the kitchen. Branna kept an eye on her, and when she caught Gladys glancing into the dining room, she motioned for Gladys to join her.

Gladys shook her head indicating she would not come out and returned to scrubbing a pot.

Branna did not insist but asked Thomas Corrigan as he brought her a glass of port to end her meal why Gladys was reluctant.

"Oh, Miss Butler, it wouldn't be proper for the kitchen help to be with guests in the dining room," Corrigan replied. "That's the reason there's a rule against it." He paused then added quickly, "Has she done something to trouble you?"

"Not at all," Branna answered. "We spoke this morning. She told me where to find Collin Gallagher. I just wanted to thank her for the help."

"Well, that's no bother at all, Miss Butler," Corrigan

offered, "I'll tell her for you."

"That will not be necessary, Mr. Corrigan. I'll tell her myself when the opportunity occurs." Branna sipped her port and looked out the window toward the ocean where a huge storm raged just inside the horizon.

Corrigan excused himself. A few minutes later Branna saw him enter the kitchen then exit a minute later.

Shortly after, a young boy came to clear a table near Branna's. He seemed nervous, having to speak to an important guest. "Gladys can see you now if you're of a mind to go into the kitchen."

"Thank you." Branna pushed her chair back, lifted the remaining port, downed it and moved toward the kitchen.

Gladys stood waiting in the small cloakroom by an outer door.

"Mr. Corrigan said you wanted to speak with me," the old woman said, no longer eager to talk to the stranger.

"I just wanted to thank you for helping me meet Mr. Gallagher," Branna offered.

"I'm happy to have been of service," Gladys said quickly.

"Gladys," Branna asked, "Is there some reason you do not wish to speak with me? Have I offended you?"

"Oh, no ma'am, not at all," she said, sitting on a stool and indicating Branna could sit on the one next to her.

"Then why do you seem so nervous?" Branna questioned.

"Well, missus," Gladys spoke softly, "you're an important personage from Dublin, for one reason. You are also a stranger, helping that inspector with the murders. There's people about who'd rather you not be here, the inspector neither."

"I am sorry to make you uncomfortable, Gladys," Branna consoled. "If it causes you trouble, I will not intrude again."

"Thank you, ma'am." Gladys' face showed relief. Then

it clouded.

Branna saw a question coming.

"Missus Butler, would you tell me what Collin Gallagher told you?" Gladys asked.

Branna thought about her conversation with the old man, considering which part of the story Gladys wanted to know. Since Gladys probably knew as much about the old ways as Collin, she would want to know something else.

Branna looked at her and said, "Gladys, I believe you know what he told me. I believe you have known the whole time and wanted Gallagher to confirm your belief."

Gladys looked down at her hands clasped in her lap and whispered, "So, it's true."

"I didn't say it was true, Gladys. I said it is what he told me. But just to make sure you already knew, you tell me what he told me," Branna requested.

"You're a changeling, Missus Butler," Gladys whispered, her voice a little frightened. "He told you what I thought, and it's the God's truth. God help us."

"Why would you say, God help us, Gladys?"

"It's started, Missus Butler." Gladys' voice trembled, "It started, and you've been called back. I don't know if you are here to help or hurt us, but they've called you back to your home."

"Gladys," Branna placed a hand tenderly on Gladys's clasped hands, "Please, let me assure you. I have never gone anywhere with the intention of hurting people. Random circumstances related to Paddy Healy's murder brought me here."

Gladys looked up from her hands; she seemed calmer. "That's the way it works, missus, it's always circumstances that move people where they want them. But make no mistake, Miss Butler, it's started, and now, for better or for worse, you are in it, like it or not."

"What has started?" Branna asked.

"The Seeing, Miss Butler, The Seeing. You are a part of

it. If you don't believe me, look at your hair. You're changing before our very eyes."

Gladys stood up, put on her wool coat. "I have to go now, ma'am. Once you understand, if we have the chance, I'll try to help. But for now, that's all I know." She opened the door to the outside; a cold wind pushed her back then she leaned forward, moved through it and struggled to close the door.

Branna went to her room, wondering what the woman saw changing before her eyes.

Inside, remembering this morning, she went to the mirror. A narrow streak of white hairs brushed back from the center of her forehead's hairline.

Branna sat in the chair and stared into the mirror. There had to be a logical explanation. There had to be.

☐

Achill Island Guard Posts

Inspector Michael Doyle recruited two acting constables, one from Mallaranny and another from Newport. They would follow on the Safety Bicycles issued them by the RIC and meet Michael at Lynott's Pub in Cashel. If Michael knew the islanders, the men would gather at Lynott's, sip beer, and talk about the murders and what needed to be done to prevent others. Michael hoped to enlist four more temporary-acting constables for the island's east side. He would eventually make his way to Keel and swear in more men for the west side of the island.

But first, before the men from Westport and Mallaranny could arrive pedaling their bikes, he would make a fast dash to Dugort to see Branna.

He purchased more fuel in Cashel. Just as he suspected, even before the pub opened, four men clustered outside, talking among themselves. Michael found a lad in the store and offered him a Victoria crown coin if he would find Liam Williams and ask Williams to meet that afternoon at Lynott's.

About a mile north of Cashel, Michael stopped in front of a weathered cottage to watch two men helping a grizzled old man onto the back of a wagon. Michael felt it his duty to provide help if he could.

He waved. The men returned his visual salutation and gave no indication of things amiss. Michael restarted his Triumph and hurried toward Dugort and Branna.

Though early afternoon and the sky overhead showed only sun and blue, the northern horizon already brooded with the next storm aimed for Achill. Michael leaned forward to reduce air resistance and gain extra speed.

He parked his bike just outside the Slievemore Hotel's front door. Upon entering, he saw Branna eating a late lunch, reading a newspaper.

"May I join you?" Michael asked with a large, genuine smile.

Branna, knowing his voice, smiled before she looked up at him, "Sit down, Michael Doyle, I've missed you." The last part slipped out.

"I was afraid you might have returned to Dublin," Michael said, happy to see her across the table. "I sent word to you at the hotel. I went to Westport to brief the County Inspector. I suppose you already know of the murders in Attawalla. Very gruesome." Michael could not give cause for his absence quickly enough.

"Calm down, Sub-inspector," Branna said. She folded and placed the newspaper on the table. "First, I never said I was returning to Dublin yesterday, or any day, for that matter. You told me to go." Branna emphasized the word told. "I will, as I am sure you know by now, Michael, always consider a reasonable request. I will not, however, be told what to do or when or where to do it, especially by a County Mayo RIC sub-inspector. You will need to hold that desire for control over me until you are, at the very least, an inspector in Dublin."

Her face projected a false seriousness. Michael's eyes grew large, wondering how he might extract himself from Branna's displeasure.

"Next," Branna held up the folded newspaper and continued, "I am busy reading about the killings of the O'Malley mother and son. Gruesome is an understatement based on the reporter's description of the bodies." Branna, in a softer voice, said, "I am glad you discouraged me from going. Seeing the scene with the victims' corpses in place may have been too much for me. It is, I imagine, very different, more brutal, than seeing the place where Paddy Healy and Albert Lewis perished. So, thank you for that."

"It was very nearly too much for me," Michael agreed.

"It says here," Branna opened and read the newspaper, "Constable Liam Williams was in charge of the investigation and offered a most disturbing clue: a giant's footprint pressed the earth near Sean O'Malley's mangled body." Branna put the paper back on the table, locked eyes with Michael and inquired, "Is it true? The part about a giant leaving a footprint?"

Michael looked down then back to her. He noticed, for the first time, the silver streak in her otherwise raven black hair. He thought better of saying anything at the moment so as not to appear as an attempt to change the subject.

"Yes," Michael replied. "Though not perfectly preserved, a large human footprint was near the body."

"How large?" Branna wanted to know.

"At a minimum, double the size of my boot." Michael extended his leg, so his boot became visible to Branna.

"Oh, my," Branna spoke excitedly, "I've never noticed. You have enormous feet."

"What?" Michael's boot vanished beneath the table.

"Oh, Michael, I am teasing. I am quite sure your foot is proportionate to the rest of you," Branna said, giggling.

"Did the giant's print have four toes and no heel?"

"No," Michael answered, recovering from the remark about his foot, "It was very human, five toes and a heel. I'll have to return to Cashel soon. I'm deputizing some additional constables to organize a night watch for the island." Michael sounded concerned.

"I'll come with you," Branna said, not wanting to be apart again.

"There's no time for a carriage. I have to take my bike now, or I will miss my own meeting," Michael said, wishing she could come.

"If I stay here much longer, I will have to telegraph my father and have him provide an automobile," Branna laughed.

Michael saw a woman in the kitchen staring at Branna through an open door.

"Someone is watching you," Michael said, looking at the woman over Branna's shoulder.

"Probably Gladys," Branna said. "She is the one who sent me to visit a man named Collin Gallagher near Cashel yesterday."

"I've heard of him," Michael said. "He is supposedly the Island's greatest authority on superstition and lore. What did he tell you? Anything about the footprint at the peat farm?"

"Gladys also warned me about something called, 'the seeing.'" Branna watched Michael's face for reaction.

"Sounds like another evening with Father Bob," Michael said. "At the moment, I have to return to Cashel. I will return as quickly as possible. In the meantime, perhaps someone," he paused, knowing Branna caught he did not name her, "should set up a meeting with Father Bob."

Michael stood to leave.

Branna caught his hand. Looking into his eyes, she said, "Hurry home, dear, and stay away from any footprints larger than your own."

Michael smiled, started to leave, then turned about and said, "Branna, may I ask you a personal question?"

"I don't believe there is anything I would like better or hate worse, depending upon the question." She beamed her smile.

Michael considered her answer, then forged ahead, "Have you somehow altered your hair?"

"Someone has. I'll tell you about it this evening." She smiled and waved him off.

Michael stood on the top step of Lynott's Pub's front door and spoke to the fourteen men gathered. "Thank you again for volunteering." Eleven were volunteers, the other three were Liam Williams and the two acting constables recruited from the nearby towns. They were not happy to have to work after pedaling their bicycles all the way to Cashel.

A few volunteers brought their bird hunting shotguns. The others brought axes, pitchforks, knives and old-fashioned shillelaghs.

"Tonight, you will be deployed in pairs," Michael continued his address. "Liam will tell you to which lookout post you are assigned and which wagon to board to take you there. The wagons have a filled lantern for each of you, a tin with extra fuel, candles, matches and, maybe most importantly, four phosphorus flares. Liam will instruct you as to how to activate them, but I want to warn you, they are very bright, and once fully burning, will cause eye damage if you look at them. The flares are incredibly hot and will burn through anything you place it on other than stone. I cannot express the dangers any more clearly, pay attention to Liam's instructions and, for your own sake, be careful." Michael tried to make eye contact with each man as he said, "Do not fool about with the flares. Lighting one out of curiosity will cost you the night's wages and unnecessarily call your comrades to your location, wasting everyone's time.

"If you have any questions, ask me after Liam's assigned you to location and wagon," Michael said and added, "Again, please be cautious and stay alert."

The men lined up by Liam. He paired them up so at least one member of each team carried a firearm. After receiving their assignment, the men one by one went and sat on a bench strapped to the wagon bed.

When the wagons were out of sight, Michael left Liam in Cashel and rode back toward the Slievemore Hotel. In a matter of minutes, Michael passed one of the wagons taking newly appointed acting constables to their assigned locations on Slievemore.

The incoming storm rained itself out before making landfall. There might be another storm later, but for now, the moon and a few scattered stars were visible in a hazy sky.

Mary Corrigan bustled from behind the registration counter and handed Michael an envelope before he reached the staircase. He recognized Branna's handwriting from things she showed him in her notebook.

Michael read the note then exited the hotel as Mary Corrigan chased after him asking if he wanted dinner.

The note was cryptic. It read, "Meet at Father Bob's. Rather interesting developments."

Michael saw flashes of lightning over the horizon as he rode to the rectory.

Three people were seated in the library. The priest, Branna and an old, weathered man, marked by a long history of strong drink and hard work.

"Michael," Father Bob greeted the new arrival. "Please take a seat and let us catch you up."

Michael touched Branna's shoulder as he passed her chair, "Good to see you, Branna," he said more formally than if they were alone. "It has been a long day."

Michael looked at the old man. His chair, brought from

99

another room and placed near the fire, was upholstered with hunter green fabric and pillows were present to allow the man reasonable comfort. He slumped in the chair. He looked very tired.

"You must be Collin Gallagher," Michael said, stepping to the green chair and extending his hand. "I'm Inspector Michael Doyle with the RIC."

"Sub-inspector," Branna chuckled from her seat at the table.

The old man's cataract-glazed eyes looked into Michael's eyes. Collin took the offered hand and held it in an unexpectedly strong grip and for a second or two longer than most.

Michael saw something in Gallagher's eyes. Something he'd seen before. Criminals readying to confess sometimes offered similar looks: unsure of coming clean, knowing what they knew must be said.

The priest poured Michael a small glass of port and brought over a tray of bread, butter, and cheeses. "You must be hungry, eat while we talk." There was a long pause broken by Father Bob, "Before Branna begins her portion of the tale, Michael, you should prepare to hear some very strange things. As a priest, I must deny most of what will be said, as a man I cannot deny them. As a human being, I pray they are false."

Michael placed a buttered slice of bread near his mouth and looked at Branna. The silver streak in her hair had widened since breakfast that morning.

Michael asked for water and then said, "Please, Branna, tell me what you discovered."

Branna moved about the room, another signal Michael recognized as someone who did not want to tell the truth. Like a small girl hoping to avoid a reckoning.

"You know, Michael, I visited with Mr. Gallagher yesterday. He told me a great deal about the ancient beliefs of the otherworlds and their populaces. He is certain I am the daughter of Oonaugh, a queen among the Sidhe. Mr. Gallagher explained Queen Oonaugh is calling me and that is the reason I am here at this time." Branna paused, appraising Michael's reception of the information.

"He also said, this afternoon, the same thing Gladys told me last night after you left, my hair is part of the visible change. The longer I remain on Achill, the faster I will change. At some point I will be able to physically enter the tomb and pass through to the otherworld," Branna said, watching Michael closely.

Michael smiled and responded, "I am not sure who is responsible for the deaths of four people on Achill. I almost half believed the murders involved supernatural creatures, giants if you will. The county inspector briefed me on activities of the United Irishmen's League in other parts of the county. Activities that included attacks and fires committed by men dressed as banshees and wearing the amputated cattle's hooves. It makes more sense to me that we are dealing with the UIL more than resurrected gods from Celtic lore."

"Your inspector is a daft shite," Gallagher piped in a gravelly voice. "The UIL has no reason to poke around on Achill. There's only two pieces of land owned by absentees, the rest is owned by the people who work it. So, you see, Sub-inspector, your man Milling needs to come see for hisself."

"What about my hair, Michael? I have done nothing to it, yet the amount of white hairs increases every day." Branna held her finger next to the center of her hairline, pointing to the one-inch swath pulled back into a bun.

Michael looked closely at Branna. The amount of white hair had increased since morning. He noticed her eyes seemed a darker green. Expanding his focus, he realized her complexion had lightened. He decided not to mention this in front of the other men in the room.

"We have all heard about a giant man murdering the

O'Malley's," Father Bob said. "Three of us saw the actual footprint at Paddy Healy's peat shed, Gallagher saw Branna's drawing of the four-toed print. What Gladys told Branna about 'the seeing' is new. Collin, would you mind telling us what you know about it?" Father Bob looked to Gallagher, so scrunched down in the soft chair his legs were straight out, and his chin nearly touched his chest.

"It's a sad day when we have to talk about these things," Collin said, assuming the wise old man persona he loved so much when holding court in Lynott's Pub. "But before I start, do you have anything with more bite than port?"

Father Bob left the room. Collin watched the peat burning in the fireplace.

The priest returned with four glasses and a bottle of brandy.

Distant thunder tolled across the sea.

Gallagher pulled himself to a more or less seated position in the chair, graciously accepted the glass of brandy from Father Bob, cleared his throat, and sipped the amber liquid.

"Ah, Father, that's the brandy the monks make. You are a most gracious host," Gallagher said then turned to face Branna and Michael.

"These creatures were put away long ago. I think the good father here has told you about some of it already, how they were defeated by waves of invaders and wound up fighting their last battles along the west coast." Gallagher paused for another taste of brandy.

"So as the Sidhe and all the others were driven from other parts of Ireland, the people slowly gave up believing in them. They didn't try to give up the belief, it was just other things took their places. The Father's church tolerated some of their pagan ways, but sermon by sermon separated the Irish from their old beliefs.

"The first thing the people noticed is they no longer

saw their old gods and demons and other things that bumped in the night as often or as clearly as they once did." Gallagher paused before taking up the story. "Like the old Irish saying, 'seeing is believing.' When they could not see them, the power of their belief drained until they no longer heard them and what once was a stable full of heroes, beasties and magicians shrank until there was nothing left but mouse turds." Gallagher's eyes glinted in the firelight.

"As the people stopped believing, the strength of these beings withered. They lost more power, more battles, until they were driven back and returned to their own worlds where they came from in the first place."

"The old Irish believed if they ever returned, the people would experience 'the seeing.' As more and more people saw them and believed in them, they gain power again, and soon they are, amongst this very small part of our nation, real enough to us again. They become strong enough to move outward, gaining more and more followers."

Branna interrupted, "Collin." Her voice was soft, not questioning the validity of the old man's story. "Why do they come here? What do they gain from this place?"

Gallagher held out his empty glass to Father Bob. Once the priest began to pour, he answered her question, "I don't know, lass. Maybe there's wars or famine. Maybe there's just too many of them or the oceans are all fished out. The only thing I know is they were once here, were driven out, and now they are returning."

Father Bob pulled a book from a shelf, thumbed to some pages and said, "No one knows why, but in folklore, Ireland was always considered the best place to cross from one world to the next. All nations' myths tell of people and things crossing back and forth between worlds, but Ireland offers doorways to more of the otherworlds than any other place on earth."

With no fanfare, the rain pounded down in huge drops.

As the wind increased, the falling water angled across the windowpanes. Enormous lightning bolts flashed in rapid succession, lighting the room with bright, flickering light for a few seconds.

"Michael, Branna, we spoke before about the power of belief. If you allow me, the Bible, approved by my church, provides examples of this truth." Father Bob did not read as his fingers looked at a verse then flipped pages to the next quote.

"Here, in the book of Matthew, miracles occur for the Centurion with the dying friend, the woman who touches Christ's robe's hem and is cured, and the woman from Canaan with the possessed, dying child. In each case, Jesus takes no credit for the miracles but instead says, 'your faith' brought about your wish.

"Then we go to another part where Jesus goes to the town in which he grew up, and we are told the people knew him as the carpenter's son and the brother of other sons and daughters. They did not see him as a prophet. The Bible tells us when Jesus left the town that he did not perform miracles because the people there lacked faith."

"So, if we accept the power of belief, for sake of conversation, then the aspect of belief in Collin's story might also be true. While the story illustrates a theory regarding the disappearance of mythical creatures, it provides no evidence." Father Bob looked at Michael and Branna.

"Keep your eye on that lady," Gallagher said, pointing at Branna. "You'll have all the evidence you need soon enough."

The rain passed overhead, leaving soggy ground and a slight mist.

Michael stood by Branna's chair. "Father Bob, I am unconvinced any of this is true, I cannot disprove the possibility, but until there is stronger evidence, I have to act as if yours is one of several theories. We have fourteen acting constables posted on prominent points around the island watching for anything out of the ordinary. I need to check on each of these posts. When I return, I will share everything I learn with you. In the meantime, you should all try and sleep." Michael turned to face Gallagher. "Do you have a room at the hotel?"

Father Bob answered, "There's a small guest room here with a warm bed. Mr. Gallagher may stay if he likes."

Gallagher had returned to his deep slouching position. "I choose to stay with the brandy," was all he said.

Michael turned to Branna, "Can I walk you back to the hotel?"

Branna looked up at Michael's face. She found it charming and annoying he found it necessary to protect her. "I suppose if everyone else is going to bed, I should as well."

Walking to the hotel, Michael asked, "You don't really believe Gallagher, about you being a changeling, do you?"

"On the surface, it is the most preposterous thing I've ever heard, but," Branna replied, "something is occurring. There is the question of my hair as well as I bear no real resemblance to anyone in my family. While I remain staunchly in the 'I am not a changeling' camp, I also am discovering more and more feelings swinging me toward the other camp."

Branna paused at the bottom of the hotel stairs. She turned to face Michael, took one of his hands in each of hers, looked up, and spoke softly, "Michael, please be careful. Something on this island is killing people, and I want to make sure you come home safe and sound." She rose on her toes and kissed his neck.

Michael stood frozen for a second.

"The sooner you leave, the sooner you return," Branna said. "Now off with you on your dangerous mission, and please, take care of yourself."

"Thank you Branna," Michael said.

"For what?" Branna responded.

"For," Michael paused, then said, "for caring."

He turned and went out the door. Before starting his bike, he checked his fuel and removed the .455 caliber Webley revolver from his saddle bag, a powerful pistol with a top-break loading cylinder that self-extracted the spent cartridges for faster reloading times. All five rounds were in the cylinder.

If he found himself dealing with a man, he has no doubt the service revolver will provide a solution to any encounter. If, on the other hand, he faces something other than a man, he doubted any firearm would suffice.

He lit the lantern affixed to the bike's handlebars, checked his water canteen and the items remaining in the saddle bag, then drove south toward Keel on the wet and rutted Bog Road. Within minutes the road curved right along the base of Slievemore.

The ruts in the road made it difficult to maintain balance and impossible to travel at speed.

Two minutes further rounding the curve, he saw two flares glowing a hundred feet up the side of the mountain.

He stopped his engine, looked at his list of watch stations and men assigned to them. He called out, "Ryan O'Neal! Are you up there?"

Other than the bright glow of two flares silhouetting some large rocks between himself and the bright light, Michael didn't see or hear anything.

He called again, "Manus Moran!" He paused to hear a reply.

None came back.

"Moran, O'Neal, I'm coming up. For God sakes, do not shoot me. I'm bringing my lantern so do not fire your weapon." Michael began moving up the slope.

With the lantern held forward and low, he worked his way toward the flares. When the lantern's light illuminated the rocks, before seen in silhouette, Michael realized he stood slightly below the portal tomb where Branna fell ill.

Moving upward, trying to see further than the lantern's light allowed, he pulled his pistol from his jacket pocket and stopped to listen.

Hearing nothing but wind, he moved forward, but much more stealthily.

Passing the portal tomb's stones, holding his arm high to block the bright flares, he reached a more or less flat area on the mountain's side.

His worst nightmare was not unveiled. There were no bodies. There was nothing but the two flares.

Michael called to the men again with no results.

He looked southwesterly, toward Croaghaun, the highest place on the island, rising above the Atlantic Ocean.

He saw a bright pinpoint of light halfway up its eastern slope in the distance.

His heart sank, it was a single flare. Probably the reason O'Neal and Moran ignited their two flares. He hoped he would find them on the way to Croaghaun, but somehow knew he would not.

He called the men's names one more time then started down to his bike.

His dim lantern light caused a glint near the burial cairn.

Michael stepped toward it, peered hard trying to see something other than shadows.

The glint appeared again.

Michael walked to where it had shown itself.

A silver belt buckle.

A belt buckle attached to a brown leather belt threaded through the loops on a pair of badly soiled work pants.

Using his boot, Michael toed through the wet pile and quickly realized it contained two sets of men's shirts, pants, and boots.

Michael smelled the stench coming from the pile.

This was not a promising beginning for the night watch. His first stop revealed both men missing, apparently without clothes, and one had shite himself.

He wanted to return to the hotel, but his first duty was to check on the men posted on Croaghaun, on Achill's western shore.

☐

Branna's Room

As Branna snuggled into the bed and tucked the linen duvet next to her neck, she wondered if she might dream again of her mother of the other world. Her day caught up with her and sleep, unnaturally deep, descended.

She dreamed she stood in a dark stone cave, looking out the oval-shaped entrance at a beautiful sky of powder blue. Every so often, a small random white cloud glided into view, and the sunlight made the shadowed side of the cloud sparkle with flecks of silver, reflecting the sunlight that filtered through the cloud.

The cave was dark. Its only illumination came through the cave's mouth and cast a weak puddle of light below the entrance.

The cave was dank. Sour smelling water seeped through various places on the stone walls and trickled down to form rivulets that flowed across the floor forming a small stream that carried its sulfur smelling liquid into the depths of the cave.

The cave was alive with death. The absence of any living thing, plant, animal or fungi, warned visitors not to tarry.

Yet sounds came from the depths of the cave. An

occasional muted thud, like a heavy step, or probably the wind moving through, sounded like something quite large breathing.

Branna listened to the cave in her dream.

The breathing wind called her name. Just once, in a deep whisper only a strong wind can make, but she heard it clearly. She heard it in her head as much as her ears.

Branna moved toward the mouth of the cave and surrounded herself with the light.

The cave's entrance was just out of her reach. As she sought ways to climb up, then pull herself out, she saw the surface outside the cave nearly glowed a wonderful green and here and there, gorse offered up the brightest yellow flowers she had ever seen.

Branna heard the great breathing. Closer. She looked toward the cave's maw. Only dark. Only shadow. And then, enough light glinted off an eye larger than a dinner plate. A single eye that seemed to hover just below the cave's roof.

"Branna," the wind whispered, and she felt warm, fetid air stir past her.

The dream scared her.

As a child, Branna's father taught her his techniques for defeating bad dreams. One was to turn and face the imaginary creature stalking you. Something told Branna there was nothing imaginary about the sickly-eyed monster. The other technique was to will yourself awake.

Branna woke herself up terminating unpleasant dreams hundreds of times. It was easy, once you knew about it.

She willed herself awake.

Branna sat up in her bed, relieved.

There was no light in the room. She retrieved a match from the bedside table and lit a candle.

Branna was safe in her bed.

The problem was: it was quite literally her childhood bed in the bedroom in which she grew up.

She heard a floorboard squeak outside her bedroom door.

"Mother," she inquired in a normal adult voice, "Is that you?"

No answer. No more squeaks.

"Mum, this is not funny." Branna's tone was flavored with a little petulance.

The door handle turned, and the door unlatched.

"Mummy!" Branna cried out. "Wake up," she told herself over and over.

The door slowly opened inward.

Branna could not see what hand held the handle and pressed the door in on her, but she heard its husky whisper clearly. "Branna, I mean to have you. If not tonight, then tomorrow. We've waited so long."

Branna was afraid before the door opened. Now she knew terror. A blinding, paralyzing knowledge that all hope was lost. All her life, she kept herself brave and showed no fear. That façade fell away.

Branna's mouth was bone dry. She stood at the foot of the bed in her hotel room. Her feet were wet. Branna had wet herself. She lit a lamp and saw she had not wet the bed. Instead, she soaked her nightgown and made a puddle standing at the foot of her bed. A hint of sulfur wafted into the room. Her mind would not allow her to revisit the cause of so great a fear.

She cleaned herself up. There was no going back to sleep, not on this night. As she picked up her hairbrush, she saw herself in the mirror. The streak in her hair was nearly a two-inch wide swath of silver hair. Not white, not gray, but silver as polished metal.

Branna dressed, then waited for the sun to rise. Pieces of her dream niggled her memory, making her recall more and more of the night terror.

She sat in an upholstered chair and tried to read a recently published book authored by a cousin, William

Butler Yeats. She brought it along only because it was a relative's book, but as she turned the pages, a sense of doom darkened the room. The book, The Celtic Twilight, provided background for this current madness.

☐

The Flares

Michael worried what he would find at the outpost on Croaghaun. He tried to stay the deductive realist as inspector investigating multiple murders, but something in him rebelled, knew something powerful unfolded. All the logic in creation could not explain the things he had seen on Achill.

Colonel Milling shut down his theory of supernatural activity. Colonel Milling had not seen the bodies, the tracks. This was not the work of the United Irishmen's League. Gallagher demonstrated they had no reason to protest on Achill. Michael knew danger grew every hour. The atmosphere of the island itself was fearful and becoming more so. If something wasn't done and done quickly, the next murder might cause an insurrection of the Islanders.

Before Michael reached the base of Croaghaun, the flare burned out. It would make it more difficult to locate the site of the outpost. As he dismounted his bike, a new flare spewed white light and smoke.

Good news, Michael thought, at least someone was

there.

He called the names of the men assigned to this outpost. "Thomas O'Toole! Peter Riley! Are you there?"

No answer.

"This is Inspector Doyle. I am coming up. Do not shoot." Michael held his lamp high to make sure the men could see it.

When he reached the top, O'Toole and Riley were on their knees, facing north. Each worked a rosary and repeated the Hail Mary. They spoke softly but quickly, trying to complete some magic number of Hail Mary's. Their voices were hoarse.

Obviously, something had happened to flame their religious fervor. Michael walked around and stood at their fronts, watching them.

Their commitment to prayer held them trance-like, and they made no acknowledgment Michael stood before them.

Michael had to bring them back to reality. "O'Toole, Riley, what happened?"

No response.

Stepping forward and touching O'Toole's hat, he said, "Men, your families are at risk."

The men continued, "Hail Mary, full of grace, the Lord is with thee."

Michael did the first thing that came to mind. Standing in front of them, he lifted his hand to his head and made the sign of the cross as he said, "The Lord be with you, and with your spirit. May almighty God bless you and keep you. In the name of the Father, the Son, and the Holy Spirit. The mass is ended, go in peace."

The words weren't perfect. Truth be known, Michael's presence at mass was somewhat rare. His words worked. The men crossed themselves, stop praying and looked up at him.

As if waking from a long sleep, they looked at each

other then quickly away. O'Toole stood first. "Is it time to go?" he asked.

Riley was on his feet but still in a sort of stupor.

"Why did you light the first flare?" Michael asked cutting to the quick.

"What flare?" O'Toole replied, eyes squinting from the burning white fire.

"Jesus," Michael said exasperated, "One of you lit a flare, like the one burning now. Then after it went out, you lit another. Why did you light the first flare?"

Riley, still coming around to full awareness, answered, "Oh. We lit it to make the thing go away."

"Yes, that's right. To make it go away," O'Toole echoed.

"What thing?" Michael asked, hoping for something that made sense.

"It was the banshee. The great, huge banshee from hell," Riley blurted as if saying it out loud would make it go away. "A giant in black tattered lace. It called my name, it did. I swear, it knew me and everything I ever did. It was like Jesus with the woman at the well. It told me I had," he paused, collecting himself, looking for a way to continue without finishing the original thought, "I had sinned. It knew specific sins, and it said God would send me straight to hell for them."

"He's telling the truth, Inspector," O'Toole injected, "It did the same to me. It made me stare into its eyes. Oh, those eyes! Hell was in those eyes."

The men paused as they remembered everything.

"Did the thing you saw, whatever it was, leave when you struck the flare?" Michael wanted to know.

"No, your honor," O'Toole said, recovering composure. "It told us to tell everyone we seen it or it would come back and get us and our families. It made us swear to tell everyone. Then it left."

Michael, now completely unsure of anything, reasoned

there was no point discussing the apparition any further with Riley and O'Toole. They were far too shaken. He decided to interview them tomorrow.

From where Michael stood, he could see enough of the island to spot any other flares. Thankfully, there were none.

He turned to the two men. "Go home," Michael said softly. "Get some rest, and we will speak again tomorrow."

"Aye, your honor, we'll speak, but after morning mass and before evening's bells," Riley said, letting the inspector know where he intended to be.

Michael drove back toward the hotel in Dugort, but the trip seemed as if time itself stretched and slowed. His mind went over the missing men at the portal tomb and what O'Toole and Riley claimed to have seen. None of it made sense.

As he neared the town of Keel, he saw people in the street outside the Amethyst Hotel. They were vocal, animated and not a little anxious.

Michael parked and entered the conversation.

"I tell ya, I seen it with me own eyes. Running on goat legs as long as a horse's. It left those tracks over there," a rotund woman in a robe spoke frantically.

Michael moved in the direction the woman indicated tracks were.

He could hear two more people in the small group arguing. They saw something, but nothing like the woman described.

The tracks were fresh and deep in the rain-soaked soil by the street. The light from the rising sun revealed four toes, the ball of a foot but no heel.

Michael sighed deeply. He could no longer doubt the supernatural aspect of the case.

Rather than engage in a non-productive argument about who had seen what, Michael mounted and rode north, back up Bog Road.

Halfway along the road to Dugort, the road appeared as if a herd of cattle crossed it. Michael stopped and walked among the tracks. There was the familiar four-toed print, a few feet away the large human print, between and around the two were dozens of tracks of different animals, animals that did not exist. Michael observed they all led to the portal tomb.

Were the creatures of this strange menagerie among the rocks of the cairn? Or, as Gallagher said, had they passed over to another world?

Sub-inspector Michael Doyle stood for a long time staring toward the ancient tomb on the slope. Something was changing, right in front of him; the world shifted away from light, toward a bone shivering darkness. He was afraid. With no other explanation, he had to believe his friend Father Bob, and old Collin Gallagher: the ancient gods were back to reclaim what was theirs. Michael did something he had not done in a long time. He prayed.

☐

Gladys

Branna stared out the dining room window to the sea. Most of her uneaten breakfast and half-empty cup of tea forgotten.

Mary Corrigan pretended to clean a table between where Branna sat and the door to the kitchen where Gladys watched from the corner of her eye. Both women wanted to know about the silver streak of hair. Mary was too embarrassed to ask someone from so powerful a family, and Gladys waited until Corrigan was gone so she could signal Branna.

Branna lost herself thinking about the dream cave. As terrifying as the dream was, she felt drawn to the horrid place. More than that, she could not shake the feeling it was real, not too far away.

"Ma'am," Gladys spoke and gently touched her shoulder. "I couldn't get your attention, so I had to touch you. Come to the kitchen when you can," she said scurrying away and looking to make sure Corrigan didn't see her.

The touch broke Branna's focus. She looked up at

Gladys' wrinkled face. Fear flamed in the old woman's eyes. She drank her cold tea and waited until Gladys reached the safety of the kitchen.

Mary Corrigan busied herself at the reception counter, occasionally glancing toward Branna. When Mary finally went into the closet behind the counter, Branna moved to the kitchen.

"Are you ready, child?" Gladys whispered.

"For what," Branna replied.

"To visit your mum," Gladys answered, taking her coat from a peg on the mudroom wall.

Branna didn't answer. She couldn't bring herself to speak anything that might solidify the reality of this experience.

"It's alright to be afraid," Gladys soothed, "but your mother is calling you, and you know it now. You will go sooner or later."

When Branna didn't answer, Gladys finished buttoning her coat and opened the door to leave. "Well then, I've tried my best. Them that would stop you are growing stronger. If you don't go to her now, they will have you, and that will be your end."

"Wait," Branna implored. Something connected in Branna's mind when the old woman said, 'they will have you.'

After a moment, Gladys said, "Well, child, are you coming, or aren't you?"

Branna slowly put the sealskin coat over her canvas overalls and followed Gladys out the door.

She followed Gladys toward the beach, neither spoke as they descended the stone steps leading to the beach. Gladys turned right and stayed close to the escarpment's face.

"What am I doing?" Branna screamed in her mind. "This is madness."

"Just a little farther, child," Gladys cast back toward

119

Branna.

"Please stop calling me child," Branna said, rousing from her fugue.

Gladys walked on like her legs were twenty years old.

A man further up the beach waved his arms in their direction. Gladys returned the gesture.

Branna thought the man looked familiar and something about that comforted her. He somehow represented sanctuary for her. She didn't understand it. She didn't need to. Any form of comfort was welcome at the moment.

She made out he was a big man, dressed in a long black coat. Another man, shorter, stout, with bowed legs, hobbled to the big man.

A moment later, she recognized Father Bob and Collin Gallagher. It surprised and relieved her.

"Branna," Father Bob said, "we've come to help you along the journey. Collin and Gladys say you are ready, and the last night's rampage proves we must proceed. Your hair tells me you're ready. I know you do not feel up to this, but there really is no choice."

Branna's mind cleared. She still felt fear and anxiety but suddenly was able to manage it. "What about Michael? Is he in on this?" she asked.

"Not exactly," Father Bob replied. We haven't seen him today, but I am sure he would understand the necessity."

Father Bob indicated for them to continue walking. A short distance later, Branna recognized one of the canvas-covered whaling boats. The women and Collin seated, the priest pushed the boat knee deep into the small waves and climbed in. Together he and Collin rowed about a half mile to sea, then turned westward, toward the north face of Slievemore.

Collin stayed in the boat holding it in place with oars and a stone anchor while the others made their way up the steep embankment. Near the top, under an outcropping of rock, were three small caverns locally known as seal caves. A narrow terrace allowed the party to stand.

Branna saw three caves, one of which sent a shiver down her spine and made her knees weak. It was the cave in her dream, at least the opening was shaped like it, but it was much smaller. Still, the dark entrance appeared as a human eye, emptied socket, filled with blackness.

Stones were arranged on the terrace's western end, as if placed to enclose a small garden with a larger stone at the far end.

"This is the hard part, Branna," the priest said, unrolling a blanket worn across his shoulder. "You will have to be here alone for a bit."

Branna inhaled deeply. Alone, by the caves, not just any caves, the nightmare cave. She sickened with nausea.

"We will be in the boat below. If you need anything, just call down, and I'll be at your side in a few seconds," the priest promised.

He placed the blanket in the area enclosed by the stones and indicated for her to sit.

"If you can find it in yourself to sit here for a while, you will discover your mother and her world," Father Bob said soothingly.

"How long?" Branna asked. "How long must I sit here?"

"Not long," Gladys answered. "I envy you. Whole new worlds wait to welcome you."

Though the terror remained, she resolved to try.

She watched the two of them depart the terrace and climb down the escarpment. She felt terribly alone.

Branna studied the cave, half afraid something might emerge from it. A breeze picked up and looking to the sea, dark clouds walled the northern horizon threatening another night of storms.

Branna smelled lavender. She didn't see any. Of course not, lavender would not grow here.

Yet she smelled it on the breeze.

She felt tired, in need of a rest. She lay on the blanket. Branna rolled to her side facing the sea, her hands paired beneath her cheek like a little girl. The breeze felt wonderful.

Her eyes closed, only for a second.

When she opened them, she stood inside the nightmare cave.

☐

Branna is Missing

"Why did you let her do that?" Michael asked Mary Corrigan. "Do you have any idea what is happening on this island?"

"I'm sorry, Inspector. I didn't feel it was my place to tell Missus Butler what she could or could not do," Mary spoke in a nervous whisper. "I'm sorry. I'll get Thomas to help look for her."

Michael studied her. He wasn't being fair. The Corrigans were not responsible for Branna, but her missing scared him. "I'll go along the beach. You say they went east?"

"The tide's coming in, but you can still see their tracks in the sand," Mary answered.

Michael left with not another word.

Down the stairs, on the beach, he picked up the two women's tracks and followed them briskly.

What that crazy old kitchen woman told Branna was anyone's guess, but Michael was surprised Branna had gone with her without leaving a message.

The women's shoe tracks converged with the tracks of two men. The four of them looked to have stood talking then, together, continued eastward.

One of the men's tracks indicated his feet were separated from right to left by an abnormal distance.

The tracks turned toward the sea and vanished in the rising tide.

A boat, Michael deducted. The four of them boarded a boat.

His heart sank. He could not continue to search for Branna. Even with a boat, there was no way of telling in which direction they headed.

Michael had spent the entire night checking the outposts. He was on his way back to the hotel when his conscious succumbed to guilt and the weight of responsibility.

Checking the outposts and relieving the men on duty took longer than he expected. Everywhere he went, people were huddled in their houses staring out windows, or walking in small silent groups to their church or to the ferry to the mainland. Everyone had seen something or knew someone who witnessed a horror of one kind or another. Most of the people, gripped by fear and terror, wanted help and assailed him with questions.

Michael had no answers.

He sent his temporary acting constables in pairs to churches to help people any way they could.

Lewis and the other two recruited constables were provided horses and told to position themselves in Keel. Lastly, he sent a telegram to the barracks at Westport informing Colonel Milling of his manpower on Achill and of a night full of mischief. United Irishmen's League or not, trouble was brewing, and he needed help.

All in all it was not much of a plan, but it was all he had.

Guilt assuaged, Michael drove as fast as he could to the hotel in Dugort to check on Branna. He arrived at half past ten. He was exhausted and confused by the night's events. He really wanted only to confirm Branna's safety then sleep for a couple of hours before regrouping with Father Bob.

When Mary Corrigan told him Branna left hours earlier with Gladys, his soul moaned. There would be no rest. His concern for Branna Butler wrenched the last bit of strength from him, and he sat out to find her.

Now, standing on the beach, having failed, Michael tried to focus on what next to do. His thoughts refused to remain orderly. The things his men and others saw last night were of superstitious primitives from thousands of years past, not things admitted to by people of the twentieth century.

His tired mind would not stay still. One second it terrified him with images of Branna's body floating on the ocean, the next second he imagined the four-toed beast walking goat-like on two legs, rising from the sea and attacking him. His thoughts weren't rational. He had to calm himself.

Looking westward along the beach, back the way he came, he saw Father Bob's rectory and church. Bob could help him.

As he walked back, he again noticed the wide gait of one of the men. But his usually reliable mind refused to provide a hint.

He knocked on Father Bob's door. No answer. He knocked again and turned toward the church while he waited. Small groups of people entered and left Saint Thomas Chapel across the road from his position.

A woman wrapped in a thick gray shawl hurried from the church toward him.

"He's not in, Inspector," she said, nervously glancing around.

"Do you know where he might be?" Michael asked.

"No. I came to clean like I do every day, but Father Bob told me to go home. That my family needed me more than the spiders in the rectory. We are gathered at the church, praying for protection from them demons," she said with absolutely no embarrassment.

"The door's open. Let yourself in. Father Bob would welcome you," she said before turning to leave.

Michael entered, hung his coat on a hook in the small mudroom then went to the library. A half bottle of brandy sat corked on the table. He picked up one of the two empty glasses on the table, wiped it clean with his handkerchief and filled it within a half inch from the brim.

He sat in the cushioned chair Collin Gallagher found so comfortable. Michael stoked the dying fire, brought it back to life, threw on two pieces of peat, then settled back to sip the calming beverage.

After twenty minutes, he became bored. He stood and paced for a while. Fatigue overtook him, and he sat back down, propped his feet on a stool, finished his drink and watched the fire.

As his head bobbed and sleep covered him, Michael realized the odd tracks on the beach might have been made by Gallagher's bowed legs. As he settled into exhausted sleep, he knew he should be looking for Branna. He should not be wasting precious time sleeping. Then his mind switched off.

Three hours later, neck stiff, Michael woke to the sounds of someone entering the house.

Michael roused himself, stood and called, "Father Bob? Is that you?"

The priest appeared in the library's doorway. "You look as if you have had quite a night," he said, wearing a nervous smile.

Ignoring his comment, Michael inquired, "Have you seen Branna? She's missing. Left the hotel with a woman named Gladys."

Gladys chose that exact instant to appear behind the priest.

126

"Where is Branna?" Michael asked, some of the worry draining from his expression.

The old woman started to speak. The priest turned his head and shushed her.

Collin Gallagher's voice sounded from inside the house but unseen. "I'm going to bed. Wake me when it is time."

Michael looked into Father Bob's eyes. "Where is Branna?" His tone was deadly serious.

"I am going to tell you, Michael, but let me finish speaking before reacting," Father Bob said, studying his childhood friend's composure. "First, she is safe. That's the most important thing for you to understand."

"Where... is... she?" Michael asked, eyes narrowed.

"We took her to the seal caves on Slievemore's north face," Father Bob responded softly.

Michael's hands balled into fists. "Have you lost your mind? What were you thinking?" Michael's eyes flamed. "We must find her at once. Where's the boat?"

"Before you storm out of here and race to her rescue, I'm telling you as your best friend, she does not need rescuing. She is safe and exactly where she needs to be." Then the priest added, "For herself and the rest of us."

Suddenly what Father Bob alluded to dawned on Michael. "In the name of God, Bob, do not tell me you have taken her to cross over to the faerie world." Michael's voice rose in volume and filled with incredulity. "You've all gone insane."

Michael looked at his friend and the old woman who had not moved. Father Bob, though larger than Michael, knew the strength Michael mustered when angered. "Please, Michael. Can we discuss this?"

"The only thing to discuss is how soon we can recover her from the elements," Michael responded, anger building in his eyes.

"Very well," the priest said softly, "we can return to the caves, but she is no longer there. She's with her mother."

127

Michael's emotional state would not allow discussion or reason. He wanted Branna, safe and in his arms. That was all that mattered. Michael took a step toward the door, "I am going, with or without you. If she's not there, I am holding you responsible, Bob."

"She is not there. I just told you, she has crossed over. We stayed, checking on her every few minutes until I poked my head up over the rocks and she was no longer there," Father Bob said, standing resolutely in the doorway.

"You and your ever-present demons are insane," Michael snapped. "How dare you expose that girl to any of this?" Michael said, moving toward the door, where he announced, "If you are not going to help me, then step aside. I am going to find someone to take me to the caves."

"You are making a mistake, Michael," Father Bob said, stepping out of the doorway. "That place will be crawling with demons by the time you arrive. You will end up like Paddy Healy or the O'Malleys, or worse. We can't afford to lose you. Last night was a skirmish. A battle, unlike anything ever experienced, is coming. It is a battle we can only win with the help of God's angels."

Stepping through the door, Michael turned to face the priest. "You may be right. I am not sure of anything anymore other than I am not going to allow Branna to suffer any more than she has. I'm going to bring her home," Michael said, taking another step toward the front door.

Bob, eyes wide, watched Michael's face. It was filled with anger and determination. The priest looked away.

A sharp crack filled the room as the knobbed end of Collin Gallagher's blackthorn tree shillelagh ended its swift swing against Michael's skull.

Michael's face registered surprise, then a grimace, as he fell forward and Father Bob tried to catch him.

"Do you think I'll go to prison?" Gallagher asked. "You know, for striking a constable."

"I think prison might be a safer place right now than where we are. Help me get him to my bed," the priest said.

The days grew shorter and night cloaked the rectory like a sprung trap.

In the Belly of the Beast

Branna stood inside the cave, the eye-shaped entrance far out of her reach. Outside, the sun shined brightly, and she could hear small waves breaking on a beach. The sky was flawless blue, gulls sailed effortlessly in the ocean breeze.

She did not want to turn around. She knew the idyllic scene outside the cave would be replaced by darkness and stinking water. She felt putrid air blow against her back.

"Branna, I mean to have you," the coarse whisper from deep inside the cave touched her with its foulness.

Branna's eyes grew accustomed to the darkness, and she could see more. The mouth of the cave, where she stood below the eye-shaped entrance was exactly like a real mouth. It was a large dark place, juicy with sulfur-like saliva, dripping from its walls, excited by the morsel ready to be swallowed.

The back of the cave formed the esophagus, a smaller tube leading back and down out of the mouth. Branna imagined the horrible odors and sounds came up from the thing's stomach.

Two gulls, flying outside the cave, squabbled over a

piece of food. During their aerial maneuvers, one flew into the cave.

Branna turned at the sound, saw the fowl soar swiftly into the cave. It landed on the stone floor then fell over dead.

Branna saw herself outside the cave's entrance. It was her mother who looked about the same age as herself.

Branna called, "Help me, please. Get me out."

The mother shook her head. She pointed toward the back of the cave, toward the esophagus.

In her mind, as clear as any sound, she heard, "Through the belly of the beast."

And Branna knew the only way out of the cave was through the hellish darkness behind her.

Her mother gestured and pointed more firmly. "Go now, while it is day," the woman said.

All her life, Branna was brave or at least acted brave. She watched her father and knew that sometimes when he was afraid, that was when he acted his most brave. She tried to emulate him now as in the past.

Walking slowly toward the narrowing tunnel, she allowed her eyes to adjust even more to the blackness.

The darkness became a living thing, moistening her with its unseen tongue. Her hand pressed against a damp stone wall as she went deeper.

It occurred to her this was what it was like to be completely blind. To live your day seeing nothing, feeling your way along the streets.

At that moment, the cave's stomach belched a huge bubble of noxious fumes that rose, encompassed her and moved through the tunnel.

Branna surrendered to her fear. She could not do this. She was blind and helpless in this foul place. She had to go back. Turning, putting her left hand on the tunnel wall, she took a step the way she had come.

She shook with fear. Her every breath offered a moan

of terror.

She wished Michael were here. Something about his broad shoulders and easy smile offered safety, protection from all things. He would get her through this. But he was not here. Then his voice asked in her mind, "If you think I can do it, why do you think you cannot?"

She stopped in her tracks. It was all about belief, just as Father Bob said. If she believed Michael could get her through this, then she could save herself.

She took ten slow, deep breaths, turned and continued through the tube.

She found moving easier if she closed her eyes.

Her feet felt the tube's downward grade steepen.

Her hand felt the wall's dampness change to running water.

Her foot stepped on something slimy.

It moved.

She fell.

She fell for what seemed a long time.

She knew she would die in this darkness.

The sun felt pleasantly warm on her face.

She heard birds sing and a brook burble.

Lavender, honeysuckle, lilac and other flowers created an aromatic symphony.

Her hands and bare feet felt the grass, which held her in repose.

"This is heaven," she thought, afraid if she opened her eyes it would dissolve.

A lyrical voice spoke in her mind, "Oh, poor child, would that it was, but it is not even a fleeting shadow of that perfection."

Branna decided to allow her eyes to remain closed another moment.

She lay on her back with her head turned to the left. The turf beneath was soft and thick. When her eyes opened, she saw the honeysuckle thickly woven onto a low stone wall. Bees went about their chore, collecting nectar and pollen.

Branna barely felt a hand softly stroke her hair. She realized her head rested in someone's warm lap.

She looked up and saw the slightly older version of herself gazing lovingly down into her eyes.

"Mother?" Branna asked.

"Yes, my child. At last, we are reunited," the gossamer-skinned woman answered.

Branna studied the woman, taking in her features. Her long, silver-streaked hair was black as raven's wing, her eyes green as emeralds, and her lips full and red. Branna wondered how she could be so vain to think she looked anything at all like the perfect countenance looking back at her.

"You are beautiful," Branna whispered, sighing and feeling perfectly content for the first time in her life.

The woman replied, "I am as I appear." She continued to gaze into Branna's eyes. She wore an expression of wonder and pride, a mother's pride.

"Where am I?" Branna asked.

"With me, in our world," her mother replied soothingly.

When Branna tried sitting, a rush of dizziness flushed through her, and she quickly reclined again.

"The journey, twixt here and there, takes a toll. Especially the first time it is taken. Rest a little longer so you can recover," the woman said.

Branna allowed her head to roll to the side and her eyes to close. Sleep came immediately.

When she woke again, nothing in the surroundings changed. She felt rested, restored, strangely energized.

"How long did I sleep?" she asked.

"A good amount of time," the woman replied. "I think we can go now."

Branna stood with her mother, and they walked across a meadow of lush grass, flowers and fruit trees.

At moments, when the sun hit a certain angle, Branna thought she could almost see through her mother's form.

"Where did I get these sandals?" Branna wanted to know, stopping to look down at the white leather straps with silver buckles.

"Did you need them, daughter?" the woman asked.

"Yes," Branna replied, "I suppose I do need them."

"Well, then, you thought them on your feet." The woman moved next to Branna but appeared more to float than walk across the meadow.

Branna thought before replying, "That is a delightful new talent."

Her mother chuckled softly.

"Should I call you Mother?" Branna asked.

"You may call me mother if you like, though you may not think I have been much of one to you. Here, my name is Oonaugh. Either is fine. I am just happy you are finally here to call me," the woman said.

"Ah, so you know Collin Gallagher?" Branna asked.

"We know of each other though never have we met," Oonaugh said.

"He said you are a queen, the queen of the Sidhe," Branna stated in search of an answer.

"A queen? Gallagher said that, did he?" Oonaugh looked ahead to a hill in the distance. "Here, daughter, a queen is a job no one wants," Oonaugh chuckled. "The queen does all the work and makes all the decisions."

Branna looked at the hill ahead of her. It had somehow become more solid, more defined. It was no ordinary hill, it was manmade, a huge tor. She glanced toward her mother and saw her eyes focused on the hill.

When Branna again saw the hill, what looked like a cloud of sparkling dust particles roiled in the sunlight. Slowly the cloud took the form of a castle.

"We must hurry," her mother said. "Others will arrive soon, and I need time to prepare a feast and dance."

When Branna crossed the drawbridge that spanned a moat filled with crystal clear water and schools of colorful fish, she realized the castle walls were made of pure quartz, which, from a distance, reflected the colors between the walls and the observer. It was only when close enough could she see light dancing through the translucent blocks in the castle walls.

Branna found it odd the castle was empty of people other than the two of them. They walked past a covered market area, devoid of goods or customers. There were spotlessly clean shops tucked into areas along the route to the palace, but again, no sign of life.

"Where is everyone?" Branna asked, discovering her mother's pace required more effort than Branna usually exerted.

"Do you need someone else?" Oonaugh asked.

Branna thought before answering spoke, "It just seems odd, that's all."

"Daughter, you surprise me. Not that long ago you died in the cave, then woke up in a garden unlike any you have seen on Earth. You watched this castle form from a dust cloud, and you ask nothing. Now you think it odd no one else is here." Oonaugh flashed a look of pure joy at Branna.

"I suppose, when viewed from that perspective, you might conclude my desire for people is much more prevalent than it actually is," Branna said.

"Soon enough," Oonaugh said, "you will not want for visitors. Now you must rest, then freshen yourself for the feast tonight.

Branna found herself stopped in front of a sixteen-foot-tall door made from white birch and polished to a glass-like finish.

Branna did not realize they had even entered the

135

palace. The last she noticed, they were outside passing more empty shops and homes.

The door opened on its own, swinging into the room, a room of soft colors and canopies and cushions. Branna allowed herself to fill with the awe of its beauty.

"You will find all you need in your suite," Oonaugh said. "I must be off doing queen's busy work."

"I have so many questions, Mother," Branna said. "Can we talk first, before your guests arrive?"

"No, daughter," Oonaugh responded. "There is much to prepare for this gathering."

"Would you mind calling me by my name, Branna," Branna said.

"Your given name is Branaugh," the Sidhe said, "but I am happy to use the name you like."

"Branaugh, Branaugh," Branna pronounced the name, "I like it. It demonstrates a connection between the two of us."

Branna, newly dubbed Branaugh, was concerned how quickly she came to trust this Sidhe woman who before, a few hours or minutes ago, she wasn't sure, had existed in dreams only. Perhaps this was all a dream. A very pleasant dream. If it were, she was dying in the belly of the beast in the dark cave.

"Mother, am I dead?" Branna asked.

"Most certainly not . Do you feel dead?" Oonaugh replied.

"Come to think of it, I have never felt better," Branna said smiling. "When are we going to discuss why you called me here?" Branna asked, remembering this, as wonderful as it seemed, was not her world.

"Branaugh, you are in such a hurry. That is the half-human side of you. Humans' lives are too short, and they are conditioned to believe they have no time to waste. I hope you come to understand, no time is wasted," the Sidhe said, shaking her head. "Now, you are under the queen's orders to bathe, relax then dress for the feast," Oonaugh finished then turned for the door.

"I do not understand why you will not answer my questions," Branna said, growing petulant.

"Not another word, young princess!" Oonaugh smiled. "Or I'll send you back through that horrid cave."

"Yes, Mum," Branna said and watched the stately female Sidhe close the door as she left.

Branna did not remember ever seeing anything made by human hands that compared to the beauty of the castle's great hall. The outside castle wall's quartz stones offered a soft glow providing natural light for half the room. The other side of the room's wall held sconces containing egg-size, teardrop-shaped crystals which illuminated the rest of the hall.

Huge round tables were placed in columns and rows. Each table's surface formed a circle with a top that was four feet across. The circle was not closed. Part of the table was left open so guests could enter to sit inside the circle facing outward. Each table sat sixteen guests on the outside and eleven on the inside.

Suspended from a fifty-foot high ceiling, a twenty-foot long banner hung over the center of each table. The banners were of different colored material, all fringed at the bottoms with silver cording. Each banner contained a large silver symbol embroidered in its middle. Branna didn't know what each symbol conveyed, but she did recognize many of the markings as those left on Neolithic stones.

"These are the forty-two clans of our race," Oonaugh said, standing to Branna's right and slightly behind her.

Branna jumped slightly. "I didn't see you approach."

"It is time for your introduction," Oonaugh said stepping so Branna stood to the right and a half step behind her.

Two trumpets sounded. Their notes were deep, harmonious and short. Branna looked but saw no trumpeters.

Kettle drums announced the queen's speech. Again, Branna saw no drums or drummers.

The great hall filled with unearthly silence. Every eye looked to Oonaugh.

"Welcome, people of the Sidhe, Watchers of old, Warriors of the Way and Teachers of creation."

She paused, looking out across the room, glancing at each of the forty-two tables. "Tonight, we welcome the return of one of our children. I present to you, Branaugh, my own daughter, come to fulfill a prophecy."

The queen motioned Branna to step forward and whispered, "Bow your head."

As Branna moved, every person in the room rose as one. Their applause was thunderous. It interrupted Branna's thoughts. They all wore garments of woven silver, somewhat like her overalls but much finer. It was essentially the same style of clothing left in her room for her to wear.

Branna saw silver hair on nearly every head. They gazed at her as the applause's volume increased. Branna noticed their eyes seemed a little oversized and none of them moved their hands, which made her wonder where the applause came from.

Oonaugh raised her hands, so they were level with her eyes. The applause slowly died.

"Tonight, we feast, dance and sing. Tomorrow we convene the Gathering of Governors," she said.

Branna followed her to a small table for two in the center of the room.

The most enchanting music Branna ever heard played as the guests returned to eating the scrumptious looking food provided in unending quantities. The rest of the night was nonstop entertainment as the guests danced, sang and drank a most marvelous elixir.

Near the end of the feast, the unseen musicians began a strange symphony. Branna found herself drawn to it and listened intently. For some reason, the melody reminded her of childhood memories, pleasant, joyful. Branna's mind watched herself grow up as the music quickened. Before Branna realized it, the music placed her in the middle of the worst storm ever. Unending rain poured to earth as sheets of water, flooded rivers devoured everything within miles; the oceans slowly rose until a single mountain provided refuge for the remaining animals and people. The rain ceased. The few survivors' only views were water to the horizon in every direction.

The music slowed to a soft tune of spring, flower blossoms, the smell of fresh grass; the earth felt moist and soft with no stones beneath.

Branna's mind held her captive. She saw herself and the other guests at their tables, all entranced by the soothing sounds of unknown instruments. As she watched, the Sidhe began to fade. Their solid appearance became made of mist. As they vanished completely, each spirit shone as a soft, glowing white light. She looked back to her own table, and her mother and the light that was her slowly rose from their seats and drifted toward the ceiling.

Branna's vantage point changed to that of her own ascending light.

Soon, the other lights, which Branna realized were souls, formed a single light. Though Branna knew she remained herself, she became part of the greater light.

There was only the light: endless, protective, unfettered love and goodness. The light streaked heavenward. Suddenly, in a state of bliss, Branna realized she was in the light, and the light was in her. She knew all things, but none of it was important. She never had before known power, but it felt tiny and unworthy compared to the light hurtling toward God. She felt His presence.

The sounding trumpets and drums woke Branna from a dead sleep. She did not remember going to bed but remembered the vivid dream of the souls unified into a single euphoric light. It must have been the elixir, she thought.

Branna found the silver overalls laid out for her. As she cleaned up and brushed her hair, she heard her mother speaking in her mind, "Branaugh, The Gathering of Governors convenes in the Great Hall. The meeting is about you."

Oonaugh's voice triggered Branna to finish dressing and make her way to the cavernous room.

Last night the room was festive, and the forty-two tables filled the great space. This morning the room, completely transformed, was arranged with narrow-topped, curved tables placed to form a ninety-foot diameter circle around the center of the room. One opening in the table's circumference allowed movement through the table. The forty-two clan leaders sat around the table facing the room's center.

In the center of the circle formed by the larger table was a smaller circular version of the outer table. Inside this table's circumference sat three Sidhe, each facing the outer, larger table.

Centered inside the smaller table, a round, three-tiered dais containing two thrones rose three feet above the polished quartz floor.

Above the configuration of seated Sidhe, last night's pennants floated over sections of the table occupied by the forty-two clan leaders. A separate, larger banner hung suspended above the thrones. The silver embroidery formed an opened eye.

Oonaugh waited for her daughter at the foot of the stairs. She hugged Branna, whispered not to be nervous, and together they took their first steps toward the dais.

Branna did not hear applause, but she felt a flood of

appreciation and welcoming flowing into her. The trumpets played a fanfare, and the unseen drums beat a rhythm of purpose. The two, mother and daughter, so similar in appearance, walked down the aisle and stepped up the dais. Oonaugh indicated for Branna to sit.

Branna heard her mother's voice filled the room, or perhaps it filled her head, it was impossible to tell.

The Sidhe queen looked out from her seat. "Branaugh answered our call. She is our proxy, and we are her weapons in the coming war."

More feelings of deep appreciation filled Branna.

Branna understood instinctively, even before exiting the cave, she was to play a part in the battle against the creatures rampaging on Achill Island. It might be her destiny, but she still wanted to know who or what she was fighting. Instantly, when that thought ended, a new voice entered her head.

"Branaugh, God sent two hundred angels to watch over, protect and guide humans. The Watcher angels succumbed to the temptation of power and flesh. They took human women and produced children, the Nephilim: half-angel and half-human. The Watchers taught their children to create weapons and war against other humans with the goal of ruling the Earth.

"Some of the Watchers repented and begged God's forgiveness; the rest sought the enslavement of humans.

"The repentant Watchers were given a place between Heaven and Earth and eventually allowed to cross between their world and Earth to help men move toward God. We, the Sidhe, are the children, the Nephilim, of the repentant angels. We live forever, until the judgment day, but will never be allowed in heaven. Before seeing the error of our ways, we became jealous of humans whom God loves more than any angel, who may all pass through the gates of Heaven. This jealousy weakened our spirits and manifesting ourselves on Earth became difficult."

Branna looked around, studying the faces of the Sidhe around the tables, trying to identify the speaker.

The voice stopped.

"Mother," Branna said, "Someone was telling me about the Sidhe. He said they are the children of fallen angels."

"I am Sidhe," Oonaugh said, "half-human, half-angel, a Nephilim from before the great flood. You are my daughter, part Nephilim, part human, who was created to help the Sidhe keep humans safe. As our jealousy and dislike for humans grew, we lost power. As humans stopped believing in our existence, we lost more power. Finally, humans' belief in God waned and further diminished our ability. We set about creating changelings to help restore the balance of power between us and demons."

"The creatures attacking Achill Island, are they demons?" Branna wanted to know.

"They are Nephilim of the unrepentant Watchers who escaped the great flood by finding their own world between Heaven and Earth. We have fought them for thousands of years. But the things that weakened us give them strength. Some of them are already strong enough to show themselves and their power on Earth. The fear of them will grow the belief in them, adding to their power. Their goal never changed: enslave and slaughter mankind," Oonaugh finished.

Branna looked into her mother's large eyes. She knew her mother would never send her to pointless slaughter. "But what can I do? I possess no powers or skills to combat demons," Branna said, discouraged.

"You have no idea of the strength inside you," Oonaugh said, her voice encouraging. "We will train and give you the things you need to defeat the evil that rises again. We will funnel energy to you from our world. You will be ready and able to defend humans."

Branna thought hard. She was afraid, but fear no longer

controlled her thinking. "Then we should waste no more time. When do we begin my training?"

"It started in the cave, but now you begin the next phase," Oonaugh said. "Come with me to the training field where you will learn and develop skills against faux demons we conjure for this purpose."

She trained sunup to sundown every day. Her mother never left her side. They taught her ways to gather power. How to summon energy from the Sidhes to her location on Earth. She learned to create weapons, shields and spells with her mind using the energy she called forth. After nearly three months, Branna, now a Sidhe Changeling Warrior, sat in a ghostly boat in fog, listening to surf break against the shore and looking at the lights in the Slievemore Hotel's windows.

She was ready.

Branna Returns from the Sidhe

Michael Doyle's consciousness slowly rose through stages of awareness. At one point his head hurt. An undetermined amount of time later, his eyes opened and saw vague shapes in fog. He squinted his eyes closed and rubbed them with his hands. This time when he looked out the fog was gone, but he thought he was in severe need of glasses. Everything was blurry. He could make out someone in a chair next to him but only because of movement.

He raised his head. A sharp pain stabbed the back of his head, but his vision began to clear.

Michael recognized Father Bob in the chair next to the bed. In that instant of recognition, his mind cleared completely. He remembered everything.

"Have you lost your mind?" Michael challenged the priest. "Don't you know you may have killed Branna?" He rose and sat on the edge of the bed. "If she is dead, friend or not, I will arrest you for negligent homicide at the very least."

"If she is dead, it won't matter," Father Bob said softly. "I think she is our only chance."

"It damned well matters to me," Michael shot back.

144

"I am sure you hate me intensely at the moment," Father Bob spoke, "but I did what had to be done."

"How long have I been unconscious?" Michael said, reaching for his boots.

Father Bob looked at his pocket watch. "Fourteen hours, give or take a quarter hour."

Michael stood.

"Before you go," the priest said watching his friend, "I need to tell you of last night's events."

"I think I would rather learn about them from someone I trust," Michael said, giving the priest a withering look.

"Please, Michael," the priest intoned, "do not be so quick to judge me until you know the whole story."

"The story," Michael snarled, "is you and the old drunk pagan Gallagher are so sure the old gods have returned to destroy everyone on Achill that you risked the life of someone I care for. That's the story, case closed."

Father Bob rose to face Michael.

At that moment it no longer mattered the priest was physically the larger man, his shame at waylaying Michael made him feel small.

"There's a boy at the door," Gallagher called from the parlor. "He says the Butler girl is back at the hotel."

Michael's face filled with relief as did Father Bob's but not to the same extent.

"I would say you have been very lucky," Michael said. "But this still is not over."

Michael moved quickly to let himself out of the rectory.

"She's at the hotel, sir," the boy said before running to the chapel. The boy's terror of being outside was clear.

Inspector Doyle ran toward the hotel.

Opening the Slievemore Hotel's front door, Michael saw the Corrigans hurrying toward him and heard them speaking simultaneously, "She arrived a few moments ago. We sent the boy straight-away."

145

"Where is she?" Michael asked as Father Bob and Gallagher entered the hotel.

Like Punch and Judy hand puppets, Thomas and Mary Corrigan both pointed toward the dining room.

Michael, heart hammering, walked toward the table she occupied.

She turned her head.

"Hello, Michael," Branna said, wearing an expression of genuine happiness to see him.

Stopping by her chair, Michael asked, "Are you alright? Injured in any way?"

Branna looked at Michael's worried face. She had much to tell him but felt it best not to throw it at him all at once. "Never felt better," she said, then added, "in my entire life."

Michael's trained eyes inspected her. She wore a pure white dress of linen and lace. Her hair was brushed back, held by an inscribed ivory headband, and flowed to below the middle of her back. Its silver streak, now three inches wide, looked like polished metal. Michael never saw her wear rings before, but now she wore three on her left hand and two on her right. She also wore a jeweled cuff bracelet clamped to each wrist and a clear crystal sphere pendant on a silver chain. Her eyes were alive with vitality. Her smile, warm and inviting, made him want to press his lips against hers. Michael realized he could no longer deny that he was smitten by Branna. Social class division aside, an invasion of murderous creatures or not, he loved her and was terrified she did not feel the same way toward him.

Michael admitted to himself there was something different about her. An aura, confidence, he could not put his finger on it, but, whatever it was, it suited her.

Thinking she must have called out to a fisherman, Michael asked, "How did you get back from the seal caves?"

Branna looked into Michael's eyes for a full three

seconds, saw what she needed and replied, "Michael, I know you care for me and want to protect me, and I appreciate it. I care for you as well. But I will not allow your obsessive inspector's mind to chase me away from what we are building between us. Do you understand?"

Michael knew Father Bob and Collin Gallagher stood only a few feet behind and could hear the conversation. He looked down at his feet feeling a little ashamed for pressing Branna as if he were interrogating a criminal. "I'm sorry," Michael said. "You are right about my obsessive nature. I will try and control it, and I am sure you will let me know when I fail." Michael gave a boyish grin.

"Good," said Branna, "It will be my pleasure to make you aware when you stray." She smiled as well. "Now, to answer your question as best as possible for the time and place: I was brought to shore in a boat," Branna said, picking up her teacup. She saw Father Bob and Collin Gallagher observing her with larger than normal eyes. "I know you are eager to learn what happened after you left. I suggest we continue our discussion in the seclusion of the Rectory. That seems to work so far."

"Excellent," replied the priest, "I am assuming you intend for us to convene now."

"And we have a thing or two to tell you about last night," Collin's whiskey-coarsened voice spoke up.

"I have to do something first, before nightfall. I will meet you in Father Bob's library in two hours," Branna said, finishing the last drop of tea.

Michael started to demand he stay by her side but took to heart her earlier message. "Branna, would you mind if I accompany you on this mission? There is a dangerous presence on Achill, and I would feel much better keeping you in sight."

Branna recognized Michael's compromise, thought about telling him her mission might prove too dangerous for him but said instead, "I will be delighted to have you with me on one condition."

Michael expected to argue with her to allow his presence. "Anything, what is it?"

"You may stay with me, and I will always be within your sight, but if I tell you not to come any closer, then I take you on your word as a Constable you will follow my instructions," Branna said, standing. "Now, I must change into something more relevant to the task. Excuse me, gentlemen, I will be down as quickly as possible." She turned and headed toward the staircase. "Oh," she said, looking back, "We will need two horses. Will you arrange that, Michael?"

Something about her behavior made Michael want to answer, "Yes, ma'am," but instead he nodded to her and said, "I'll be here when you come down."

All three men hurried out the door, Michael heading to the town stable and Father Bob and Gallagher to the market to purchase vittles for a hearty meal to get them through the night if necessary.

Riding side-by-side, so close sometimes that one's knee touched the other's leg, Michael struggled not to grill Branna about what happened during the time she was missing. He held his tongue.

Branna, completely aware of Michael's struggle, said, "I know you are holding your questions in check, and I appreciate it. I will tell you everything, but I believe my story will be better received in the presence of Father Bob and Collin Gallagher. But thank you, for not pressing me."

"Branna," Michael began. He felt like telling her at his moment he would do whatever necessary to stay with her. He wanted to tell her she owned his heart, but instead he said only, "I want only to be at your side."

Branna stopped her horse and dismounted.

Michael followed her lead.

He recognized the spot. It was where he left his

motorbike the night he found the men's clothes by the portal tomb. It was also the area where unidentified tracks from at least a dozen creatures indicated they were going toward the portal.

"Michael, please stay here. I'm going up to the tomb, you can see me every step of the way," Branna said, checking her recently acquired jewelry.

Michael did not like it, not one bit, but he had given his word. "I'll stay, but you should know, the night I left Father Bob's house to check the guards, two of them were missing and their clothes, all their clothes, were in wet piles at the entrance to the tomb."

"I'll be careful," Branna said as she moved to the tomb's opening.

"Call the minute you even feel anything is wrong," Michael said, removing his pistol and making sure it was fully loaded.

She stood in front of the tomb's opening. She stooped down behind the mantle rock, and Michael could see only her head.

Her head dipped out of sight. Michael heard hissing coming from Branna's direction. The hissing was quickly followed by spewing, rust-colored smoke and the odor of sulfur.

"Branna," Michael called.

"No worries, Michael, just a little warning note left on the gate latch," she called back.

She held her breath, bent low to the ground and peered into the opening.

She saw the tomb contained a tunnel. It more than likely connected to the seal cave. As she watched, eyes began to appear in the smoke-spewing clouds. Yellow eyes, green eyes, red eyes, large and small, dozens of pairs of eyes, held in check until darkness came.

Branna withdrew, stood, and hurried down the slope to Michael.

"Did you find anything?" Michael asked.

"Yes. When we reach Father Bob's, I will explain everything and answer your questions," Branna said as she mounted and turned the horse to head back the way they came.

Branna rode back to Dugort not daring to glance at Michael. She knew Michael saw the fear in her eyes.

In less than an hour, when the sun sank behind the horizon, Satan would unleash his hounds of hell.

☐

The Night of the Morrigan

As the sun's last rays retreated from the coming night, a large crow lands atop the gray stone cliff on Croaghaun's seaward side. The female crow stands on the edge of the two-thousand-foot drop to the ocean below. She opens her wings, and the stiff breeze lifts her into the air where she hovers comfortably for a few seconds then drops to the clifftop and caws several times.

Croaghaun is composed of quartzite, a stone formed when sandstone and quartz are metamorphosed by extreme heat and pressure. Its superconductivity allows non-directional energy to flow freely until something brings it to focus. It is a source of energy for the denizens of the otherworlds. The Sidhe mastered the ability to focus and direct the energy with great efficiency and accuracy. The Nephilim, children of the fallen, use the energy as well, but only in gross, unhoned ways.

A second crow screams before landing near the original bird on the cliffs. It caws as if speaking as it walks toward the first crow. After a moment the first crow extends its neck, and the newly arrived begins preening the other's neck feathers.

A third crow arrives. The preening stops. The crows move to form the points of an equilateral triangle, three feet per side. They take turns speaking crow language for a few minutes.

A full moon rose before the sun disappeared. Now its brightness casts soft shadows of the rocks and crows, which stop talking and stare at the moon, waiting.

A storm forms in the north.

As the moon approaches its zenith, it slowly disappears in the Earth's shadow and the sky darkens.

The crows' feet glow a soft red. The red changes to purple and emits dancing veins of electricity. The purple changes gradually to light blue and begins moving up the crows, surrounding each in a cyan vortex. When the color becomes white, little lightning bolts in the swirling blue vortex fly outward. When they connect with those emitted by the other crows, a white light blossoms into a dome around the birds. The dome's brightness is such that the color inside the dome becomes washed-out. The black crows appear light gray. The birds begin to grow and change .

The intensely bright dome faded until gone and the full moon, emerged from the eclipse, shone brightly in the southern half of the sky. The storm, writhing with lightning and bruised roiling clouds, grew closer, gathering strength over the ocean.

In place of the three crows stood three tall women, dressed in royal battle gear with bronze shields. Their names were Badb Catha, the Raven of Battle; Macha, the keeper of the realm; and, Nemain, the maker of madness, frenzy, terror and fearful sound.

Together, the unholy trinity is the Great Queen, the Morrigan. She derives her power not from energy trapped in mutated stone, but from war, death, destruction, fear, and loss. Each of the three sisters wields the powers of hell, but when they are together, and become the Morrigan, they are at their most mighty.

Badb Catha had flesh the color of the recently dead. Dark veins visible beneath pale skin occasionally formed Celtic symbols as they twisted just under the flesh. Her hair was black as a raven wing, eyes blacker still. She spoke first. "It is good to be united. I feel the power coursing through me."

Macha, more alive in appearance, flashed her fiery blue eyes. Her burgundy hair, held with a gold headband, glowed like burning coals. "We have never been more united in purpose. Let's move to the portal and summon the first. We make our presence known."

Nemain had ashen dry skin drawn tight over a skeletal face. She acknowledged the conversation with insane laughter: so loud and maniacal a laugh, the mountaintop quivered in evil ecstasy. She laughed again, even louder, then rose into the air and drifted toward Slievemore and a gateway to other worlds.

Her sisters followed in the night.

Ten minutes later, the crows landed one, two, three, on the portal tomb's capstone. They strutted atop the flat stone then stopped, forming the points of a triangle. As they morphed from bird form, they became smaller, light blue electrical fields dancing around each. A small bright white dome formed around each then dimmed and was gone. At the corners of the triangle, flattened against the tomb's capstone, sat three Capall cóiste Diabhal, Devil's coach horse beetles.

As if on cue, all three arched the rear portion of their bodies like a scorpion, flaring two white tips instead of a stinger. They lowered their backs to the stone and scurried over the tomb's front edge and vanished inside the blackness.

Several moments passed before a glass-shattering scream sounded from the tomb's opening. Again, the mountain's quartzite foundation shivered at the frequency and volume. The horrible sound came forth two more times, each louder and longer than the previous.

Then nothing.

The storm clouds slid between the moon and the sea, blanketing the island in darkness.

The three beetles emerged, hanging upside down on the underside of the capstone then scrabbling up the edge to the stone's top. There, they formed their triangle of the unholy trinity, then rushed toward each other. The beetle's mandibles touched each of the other's, locking in a bizarre kiss igniting the transformative light and they glowed and grew. When the white light faded, a single crow, the size of lamb, stood, head bent, watching the tomb's entrance from atop the capstone.

Scratching sounds mixed with the scraping of exoskeletons moving to freedom, anxious to leave their harsh world and feast on soft human flesh for the first time in two thousand years. Occasionally, from the ranks of the army moving forward, a short-lived flash of reddish-orange light illuminated the entrance to the tomb.

The huge crow cawed to announce victory, lifted its wings toward the wind and seemed to fly straight up into the night sky.

Several bolts of lightning strobed, revealing the monstrosities emerging from the tomb. The quickly flashing bright bolts revealed things, part animals, part insects. Things from the size of bees to the size of geese, now pouring from the underworld. As if part of a battle plan, the clacking, clicking, skittering things formed three columns and moved away. The first column moved toward Dugort, the second to Cashel and the third toward Keel.

The columns of hellish creatures grew longer and longer as they marched quickly to their targets. It was only when the head of the first column stopped outside the oil-fueled street lamps of Dugort that the creatures stopped emerging from the hole. More than a mile of monsters moved toward the head of the column, spreading right and left as they reached the village. In a very few minutes, the town was surrounded and cut off by creatures not seen on Earth since the Great Flood.

At midnight, they would attack and two thousand years of imprisonment would gain revenge.

The three sisters, now one, the dread Morrigan, circled over Dugort's rooftops, looking for signs of the halfling-changeling. Each pass over the town, the enormous bird dropped lower to improve its ability to sense the halfling. Each pass, the bird gave the belfry of Saint Thomas Chapel a wider berth at the voices singing a hymn behind the lamplit windows' colored glass. The colored glass displayed scenes troubling the Morrigan. She would not waste her strength getting to the pasty men, women, and children inside the false God's refuge. Not yet. Her strength would improve greatly tonight. Maybe tomorrow she would break the stained-glass images and remind those inside of the gods to be truly feared.

As midnight approached, the army surrounding Dugort began moving in from all sides. No humans were detected on the streets or backyards.

Thirsting for their prey's blood and fear, the creatures circled individual buildings. All the windows spilled light into the dark. They would find their revenge inside.

Silently, they approached the outer walls.

Some climbed up to the roofs, looking for cracks allowing entry. Others crawled under the buildings in search of weak places in the floors.

They all stayed away from the light coming from the windows. They heard no sounds of movement or excitement from the rooms inside.

They used their beaks, claws, mandibles, and teeth to quietly work their way through floorboard, siding, and shingles.

It would not take long.

"Branna," Michael said breaking the silence as they rode back to Dugort to meet with Father Bob. "Last night's haunts were the worst yet. People in the southeast of Achill saw the giant man who killed the O'Malleys. They claim he's at least nine feet tall and has a single eye, a clouded, blind, yellow eye in the center of his forehead. They think he is a god returned, one of the major deities named Balor."

"Hmm, interesting," Branna responded, feigning calm disinterest.

"People on the island's west coast saw crows. There were three. They traveled together," Michael expounded, hoping to elicit at least some excitement from the woman riding next to him. He moved his horse a little to the left, so his knee brushed Branna's.

Branna did not move away. She allowed their knees to touch as the horses swayed.

"What did the crows do that aroused and made people afraid?" Branna asked.

At least she had spoken to him. That was something, Michael thought.

"They would land in a yard and caw loudly until the people inside woke and looked out the window. Then the crows stood together and began glowing until they filled the area around the house with bright light. When the light dimmed, three creatures stood where the crows had been. One, a female warrior, singing an ancient battle song. Another one, dressed in queenly clothes, angrily sowed seeds in the yard. The third, a haggard, drawn skeletal woman with frightful hair and terrifying glowing eyes, wailed at and pointed a bony finger toward the people watching from behind the window. Her scream grew so the people had to cover their ears but even so, some of them fainted, and others had blood come from their ears or nose." Michael provided more detail than normal only because he saw Branna was listening.

"Did anyone die or suffer injury?" Branna wanted to know.

"Not as far as we know," Michael answered. "We haven't spoken with everyone on the island, so it is possible someone was injured or killed. So far, we think the hauntings were designed to make as many people as possible see them. The giant and crows moved from one house to the next, skipping houses in between their sightings."

"Hmmmmm," Branna said as she returned to silent thought.

They dropped off their horses at the livery stables. The stableman was absent.

The lights were on at the Slievemore Hotel, but no one was visible through the windows.

Branna and Michael walked past St. Thomas Chapel and marveled at the number of voices crammed inside the little building and the volume of sound created by their hymn.

They knocked on Father Bob's door. After a pause, they heard someone unlocking it from the inside. It was the first time either knew Bob to lock his door.

The priest ushered them into the familiar library.

Collin and Gladys sat in chairs on opposite sides of the fireplace. Four pieces of peat flamed in various stages of consumption, casting a warm light. Oil lamps lit the rest of the room, making it much brighter than past times Branna or Michael were there.

Father Bob ushered the new arrivals to their seats. Branna and Michael sat at the ends of the table, facing each other. Branna looked left toward the fireplace and acknowledged Collin and Gladys' greeting.

"Glad the two of you could make it before dark,"

Father Bob intoned seriously.

Michael realized the only thing missing from the room was the brandy bottle. He looked at Collin who seemed anxious.

"I told Branna of the events of last night," Michael said. "She has yet to say much about them."

"So, Branna," Father Bob said, "We are eager to learn about your journey."

"Yes," Michael joined in, "please tell us what happened in the sixteen hours you were at the caves."

"Collin and Gladys," Branna began, "You were right about so many things. At the same time, too much human story telling exaggerated and filled the basic tales with speculation designed to cause fear to make children obey their parents. Those children grew up with what they knew. Some true, mostly not."

Turning to the priest, Branna said, "Father, you were right about many of your beliefs as well, but in error about others. The Catholic Church manipulated local lore to blend into the church's doctrine, which itself began purely, but, over centuries, the church's hierarchy morphed their own religion to increase the church's power and wealth. As a result, many things the church taught you, no matter how well disguised, are either not true, or so twisted only a grain of truth remains."

Father Bob, forever questioning things taught him, interrupted Branna. "Exactly true. That's why the Cistercians took steps away from the direction the church headed and began living as monks lived centuries before."

"Well," Branna responded, "That was a step in the right direction."

Branna picked up where she was interrupted. "The sixteen hours I was missing from here," Branna said, "Was nearly three months to me with my mother, Oonaugh, a queen of the beings we call Sidhe."

Branna looked from face to face checking for signs of

doubt. Michael's face could not conceal his struggle to believe what Branna said. He wanted to, she could see that, but it was hard for him.

"The people we call Sidhe are as old as man. They are the children of Watchers, two hundred angels God sent to Earth to watch over humans."

Father Bob's eyes grew large. "Are they the fallen angels?"

"No," Branna said, "Not exactly. The fallen angels caused war in heaven and were cast down. The Watchers were angels who chose not to fight for God. They were sent here to protect humans but cursed by a two-edged sword; they live on earth, immortal, until judgment day. The other edge of the blade is on the last day, they will suffer the same fate as the fallen angels, never to see heaven again."

"This is not what it says..." Father Bob was interrupted by Branna.

"In the Bible," Branna answered. "Some of it is mentioned. Some are found in scriptures not canonized by the church, and in Hebrew scriptures. Some are not found in any human writings."

Branna scanned the faces again. Bringing up the Bible somehow poked Michael's disbelief. She knew he was such a sweet man, but a very conservative one, especially when it came to disturbing long-standing beliefs.

The priest asked, "Then are the fallen angels the demons invading Achill?"

"Michael," Branna singled him out, "I asked only you let me finish my story and trust I will never lie to you."

Michael nodded agreement, uncrossed his arms and opened himself to listen. He knew he could trust Branna to tell what she believed to be true. His job taught him witnesses to crimes often told different tales they thought were true.

"The answer, Father, is no, these demons are not the

Fallen. The Fallen are in hell with Satan. These demons are the descendants of the Nephilim," Branna paused and waited for a comment.

"Jesus, Mary, and Joseph! I never thought I'd live so long as to learn this truth," said Collin Gallagher. "Can we have a drink now? I'd like to celebrate."

"Not yet," said the priest, "We need clear minds to listen to all Branna has to say."

"It's hard to listen with a clear mind when a hammer is banging your head," Collin answered.

"Please, Collin," Father Bob implored, "just a bit longer."

Collin agreed but not happily.

When the attention returned again to Branna, Gladys pulled a small corked medicine bottle from her coat and passed it to Collin whose eyes lit with relief.

"We are told the Nephilim drowned in the Biblical flood so man could be pure again with the survival of Noah," the priest inflected it more question than a statement.

Branna replied, "Most were killed, but some went to a connected world. Just as the Sidhe left Earth for a different world. There is still much to tell," Branna said and waded into everything that happened during her three months among the Sidhe.

After twenty minutes of describing the Sidhe world and her training, an impatient Collin interrupted, "Why did your queen mother call you back? Why are you here, on Achill, now?" He glowered at Branna, seeing her as the reason he could not have a bigger bottle to stop the pounding in his head.

☐

Mary and Thomas at the Slievemore

Mary and Thomas Corrigan sat silently reading in their suite at the Slievemore Hotel. The few guests ensconced at the hotel stayed silently in their rooms. The other guests were either in a nearby church or with the group conspiring at the priest's rectory.

Mary said quietly, "That priest is a strange one. He actually worked for the Pope who sent him here on a mission."

"Well," said Thomas, "it might be time for him to start slinging buckets of holy water over the village."

Mary looked up from her Bible.

Thomas looked at her. "What is it?" he asked.

Mary shushed him and pointed to an outside bedroom wall. He faced the wall.

There was something. Thomas barely heard it. Thomas whispered for his wife to stay where she was as he tiptoed to the window. The noise became more defined the closer he came,

161

something like a squirrel or rat gnawing in a wall.

He pressed his back slowly against the wall by a mirror. He moved carefully so his head could look out the window.

The light in the room caused too much reflection. Thomas signaled his wife and whispered for her to turn out the electric lamps in the room.

She did.

There was fear in her eyes now as she heard similar noises from the other end of the same wall. Her husband stood with his back against the plaster, letting his eyes adjust to a darkened room.

Thomas eased around the window sill and looked outside.

He kept his fear and reaction in check as he waited for his eyes to adjust.

Then looking at buildings, he realized his eyes were adjusted.

The ground was a living carpet of writhing, clacking, clicking things. The mass covered every inch of the village streets and grounds except where trapezoidal patches of light formed below windows.

"Mary," Thomas said, his voice strangely quiet, "Gather up some lamps and candles, then meet me in the kitchen. I'll grab some things and be there in a minute."

"What is it? What do you see?" Mary said, approaching the window.

Thomas signaled her to stop. "Mary, please," Thomas whispered, "Just go. We have to get into the root cellar."

Thomas dropped and crawled from the window toward his bed. He noticed Mary had not moved. Even before they married, she'd been a stubborn girl. Marriage seemed to make her only more so.

"Mary, go now and hurry, you are putting our lives in danger," Thomas said, reaching under the bed for his double-barreled shotgun and a cloth bag containing shells.

"I don't know why we need so many lamps and candles," Mary said, standing on the third step from the cellar's floor.

"Okay, now light the candles and place them around the room," Thomas said ignoring her question.

With the shotgun and bag in his left hand, he descended into the flickering light of the stone-walled room. He paused long enough to pull closed the trap door in the kitchen floor. There was never a need for a lock, before now.

Thomas descended to the cold stone floor and sat on a narrow stair step. He lay the gun across his lap and counted the shells in the bag.

"What did you see, Thomas?" Mary asked, sitting on a stepstool in front of shelves filled with canned vegetables, jams, and pickles.

Thomas immediately wished he had put on a pair of socks before coming to the cold, small room. The continuous rain soaked the ground, and the stones in the floor and walls wept chilly moisture.

"Well, Thomas, what was out there?" Mary repeated, annoyed her husband ignored her.

"I don't know. But I can tell you this, whatever those things are, they've risen from hell. The things cover every inch of ground. There are layers of them, and they avoid light," Thomas answered, putting the extra shells in his coat pockets.

Mary no longer feigned bravery; she came to Thomas, who moved the shotgun out of the way so she could share the step upon which he sat. She snuggled close to her husband and asked, "What do they look like?"

"Oh, Mary." He put his arm around her. "It's all dark and shapes and shadows moving against each other. I couldn't see a single creature, just a jostling thickness of living things."

Mary said, "Should I light the lamps?"

"Not yet," he answered and squeezed her shoulder.

Their conversation paused.

They looked up towards the door overhead when they heard scratching and scrabbling on it.

The Corrigans looked at each other.

Thomas raised up to check the knot on the cord meant to keep the door closed.

"Holy Mary, mother of God," Mary began, gripping her rosary. As a child, all the people calling her name at mass seemed silly. But at the moment, it wasn't silly at all. It was all she had to keep insanity out of the root cellar.

☐

The Rectory

Branna leaned back and looked at the faces in the room.

Michael still struggled with the fanciful part of her story. Father Bob felt some of his beliefs validated by Branna's account of the Sidhe world. Her story provided missing pieces to the puzzle and answered many questions. Gladys stood, stretched and shared a knowing smile. Collin sat impatiently, waiting for her to answer his question.

Michael observed the other members of Branna's audience.

Michael saw Collin doubted nothing in Branna's narrative but preferred his more embellished version. Gladys seemed rejuvenated by the tale. Father Bob appeared troubled by the disagreement of things taught him his whole life and other supposed truths taught him through reading, observation, and reason. Branna had lost some of her energy. Her eyelids were heavy.

If any part of her story was true, she had a right to be exhausted and the troubles of the past few days were nothing compared to what was coming.

Michael stood to suggest everyone turn in for sleep and reconvene with fresh minds tomorrow after breakfast.

"I am here, called back," Branna continued, "because the Sidhe live time differently than humans or Nephilim." Branna looked directly at Collin, "They are able to view blurred moments of the future. As a result of one of those moments, my mother exchanged me, her infant, half-Sidhe, half-human, with the infant born to the Butlers. The Sidhe foresaw I should be raised in this place and time. The Sidhe needed a physical presence in our dimension to aid them in protecting us from what is to come."

"What is to come?" Father Bob asked.

"Dark times, very dark," Branna said, a sad frown on a face as she grew wearier by the moment.

"The one-eyed giant is, in fact, Balor. In other European mythologies he is called Arimaspi, Cyclops, Dajjal, and Hagen, just to name a few. They are brutal, mean-natured bullies in any language."

Continuing quickly, Branna said, "The three crows…"

"The Morrigan," Collin and Gladys interrupted simultaneously.

"Yes," replied Branna. "The three sisters, Badb Catha, the Battle Raven, Macha, Queen of the land and sea and Nemain, the spirit woman of fear and chaos. Together they form the Morrigan." Branna now looked at Father Bob. "Together they are one, an unholy trinity," she said. Branna went on, "She is, next to Saint Bridget, the most powerful of the Irish gods."

"The Morrigan is here now, back from the Nephilim's parallel world. They want to increase their power through fear, death, and suffering." Branna stopped and glanced at Michael, who unconsciously raised his hand to be called on in class.

"So, why begin here, on Achill?" Michael asked. "Why start on a sparsely populated island on the edge of the world?"

"The Morrigan was not just a god here. She exists in every Celtic country whose myths include her counterpart. Her worship and powers were not limited to Ireland."

"But," Michael asked again, "Why here?"

"The population on Achill has the highest percentage of people who still believe in the gold gods," Branna answered.

Father Bob injected, "Surely your mother does not expect you to stop the Morrigan alone?"

"There are changelings all over the world. Legions placed on Earth to deal with future crises as the times arise. There are many, like me, awakened, trained and called to prevent the plans the Morrigan has to bring misery," Branna offered, growing more tired by the moment.

"What plans?" Michael questioned.

Father Bob stood and stretched, his back to the room's window.

The hair on the back of Father Bob's neck stood up as a shiver ran across his shoulders.

Michael heard strange clicking, like a lobster claw clamping shut.

The clicking increased into a cacophony of clacking, scraping, thumping and scrabbling as the noises' creators rose along the room's outside walls.

Michael stepped to the window. The ground outside provided an unfocused scene of dark undulating, indistinct things covering the ground.

Michael startled when Father Bob, who now stood beside the inspector, said in a resolved, firm voice, "Branna, what do we do?"

Lynott's Pub

John Lynott never saw the pub so empty since he inherited it from his father, twenty years ago. Two Quinns, father, Pierce, and son, Donald, sat at the bar, drinking quietly and too quickly. Lynott kept glancing at the door hoping someone would open it and lift the mood.

"I'll bet you a half-crown you won't see another customer tonight," said the elder Quinn.

"A man can hope, can't he," replied Lynott, thankful at least someone was in the pub to help him pass the time.

"My wife tells me no one is leaving church tonight. She says that's where me and the boy would be if we had the sense of…" Quinn paused, trying to remember the word she used. His wife, Beth, was always reading something and knew some long words for an islander.

"Cabbage," Donald added, "if you had the sense of a cabbage."

"So, what about you then? You're on the stool next to me. Doesn't that make you cabbage brained as well?" teased Quinn. He thought he must be drunker than he cared to admit, thinking cabbage was a big word.

"Nah," Donald replied, teasing back, "She told me to

keep an eye on you so you wouldn't get lost on your way home. I'm only doing my duty as a good son."

Lynott chuckled then added, "I'll tell you true, if I knew a safer place tonight, I'd be there, pub license or not."

"You'd never leave us to draw our own beer," Quinn laughed.

"Truer words were never spoken," Lynott chortled.

Saving lamp oil, the pub was dimmer than most nights. Lynott saw no reason to light areas where no people sat.

What he just said about safer was true. Lynott and the pub weathered some devastating storms together. Storms where the Atlantic battered the shores with thirty-foot waves and winds a man could not stand in without holding a tree. The pub was of sound structure, stone walls, and flooring that could last another hundred years.

The only vulnerabilities were the front door and windows. The back door and windows were shuttered and the heavy wood locked from the inside.

Thinking about the unlocked front door and the paned glass windows, Lynott spoke, "Well, you are probably right about the place staying empty. I'm going to shutter the windows and lock the door. If anyone wants in, they'll have to knock hard."

Lynott cautiously peered into the dark outside then went about securing the windows.

When he reentered, he said, "I don't think I've seen Cashel ever so deserted. It's like all the people been taken somewhere else."

"So, what do you think is the root of the troubles?" Quinn asked.

Donald replied as if his father directed the question to him, "It's clear to me it started with the slaughter of Paddy Healy and that man Lewis up to the Dugort bog." Donald paused. "You know, John, I seen the bodies. I know you've heard descriptions, but I'm telling you nobody on this island ever saw anything like it before. I can't do it justice, an anyone who didn't see it can't either."

"Paddy didn't get to the pub often, but he was always welcome," Lynott said, trying to remember the last time he saw Paddy Healy.

"Another storm must be starting," Quinn said, looking at the ceiling.

John Lynott stopped polishing glasses that had not been washed in several days and listened. He heard the sound of rain, or something, on the roof.

"The roof," Lynott said softly.

"What about it?" Donald asked.

"It's thatch," Lynott said, looking up at the increasing noises above him.

"That sound is too sharp to be rain on straw," Quinn said.

"I hope you are wrong," Lynott said as the first sound of something scurrying across the plastered planks beneath the thatch.

All three kept their eyes on the ceiling as more things scuttled atop the ceiling above and a troublingly loud sound of buzzing began building.

☐

The Rectory

"The thing is," Branna said, now standing next to Michael, pressing toward the glass to glimpse some familiar shape, "Your and Collin's theory about seeing the Sidhe is true when it comes to the Sidhe, faeries and all beings from their world. If you don't believe, you can't see them. They are ethereal more than physical when they visit our world. The Nephilim manifest physically in our world but only by drawing vast amounts of power from the lines flowing through the quartzite."

"The Ley Lines," Father Bob said to Branna.

"Oh yes," Branna paused to think. "There may be a permanent solution for the local problems, but we don't have time for it now."

Michael watched Branna's calm beauty. Whatever happened to her in the land of the Sidhe certainly added to her courage. She seemed calm, almost relaxed, just as the first giant bugs came down the chimney and scampered across the tile roof.

Something thumped in the unlit parlor across the hall. Everyone thought the same thing and peered into the parlor.

171

Thump, scrabble.

Thump.

"There's at least three in there," Michael said. "There might be more. Some that didn't fall or are too small for us to hear." Michael removed his gun from its holster.

Father Bob placed an oil lamp on the floor near the door, signaled Collin to pass him the poker. Collin, eyes large and so quickly sobered, shook his head no. He was holding on to the poker.

"Then hand me the ash shovel." Father Bob held out his hand.

Armed with the small fireplace shovel, the priest slowly pushed the burning lamp across the hall toward the parlor.

The light began to illuminate the room.

Scurrying, scratching retreats sounded as bug feet backed over the polished wood floor toward darker recesses.

Only Branna had not found a weapon.

Everyone, including Branna, stared toward the oil lamp on the hallway floor.

"Get more light into the room," said Collin, voice laced with fear.

Gladys offered Father Bob a candle.

Hsssssssss!

A diminishing spray of milky white liquid fell short of hitting the lamp and spattered on the floor inches from the intended target.

They saw a diminishing spray of milky white liquid dropping short of the lamp and splattering the floor. A sinus burning, noxious odor rose at once. Acrid, caustic, its stink made them recoil.

"Sweet Jesus, save us," Collin blurted.

A few seconds later, a second stream from the opposite side of the parlor door hissed against the lantern's hot glass.

The glass cracked, then a section fell away.

The next spurt extinguished the lamp's wick.

Everyone's face dropped a little as they watched the last bit of smoke rise from the now useless lamp.

Branna thought she saw a flash reflect off a beetle's armor-like back as it moved behind a settee in the parlor, gaining ground toward the hall.

Oonaugh warned Branna she might feel weak when she returned to the human world, that it would take a few days for her to reacclimatize herself to the air and gravity.

Branna's forehead beaded with drops of sweat. Her face drained pale.

Everyone's eyes remained locked on the broken lamp and they held their noses, hoping the odor might dissipate soon. No one saw Branna collapse into Collin's chair by the fire.

Michael turned immediately and saw Branna passed out in the chair. He rushed to check her pulse.

"I'm alright," she said, weakly. "I know you are disappointed I am not more help, but I need more time to readjust."

She tried to stand.

Michael gently placed his hands on her shoulders. "You stay here." He decided not to add how sickly she appeared.

"Michael," Father Bob called over his shoulder, "There seems to be activity among our unwanted guests."

Michael looked in time to see a creature's head peeking around the side of the door frame.

Its head, whiskey bottle sized head, hovered two feet about the floor. Its antennae twitched like a dowser's stick then held steady toward the library. The horrid creature shifted its head, waved its antennae, and clacked its plate-like, serrated mandibles as it studied its adversaries.

Then, slowly, it lowered its head and moved into the room.

Two large, long, needle-sharp pinchers came first. Unlike a scorpion, dozens of legs on its centipede-like body propelled it forward like a crew of galley slaves manning oars. It was halfway across the hall, all four feet of its length visible. Like a scorpion, a nasty arched tail warned with a row of three-inch long stingers that glistened with drops of venom.

Father Bob threw the ash shovel at it. The blow struck it behind its head. It paused for a second, then continued but changed direction toward Father Bob.

Father Bob retreated until his back bumped into a narrow bookshelf below the window.

"Michael, I believe you are the one with the gun," he said.

The Slievemore Hotel

The giant insects, or whatever they were, clicked, clacked and scraped across the kitchen floor, spent five minutes wedging claws and legs down the cracks between the closed trap door and the frame around it. At times they actually raised it marginally, but the cord Thomas used to secure the door held.

Well, mostly held. After several attempts, the creatures pried it up a fraction of an inch, and the cord began to stretch.

One thing in the Corrigans' favor was every bug that joined the pile on the topside of the trap door made it that much more difficult to raise it up.

Thomas held the loop formed across the door's bottom, maintaining continuous downward pressure.

His hand felt as if it just dipped into hot grease. Blisters began forming before he could release his grip on the cord. He jerked his hand away from the cord and bumped

Mary on the steps as he lunged to pour water in a pan and soak his scream inducing wounded hand.

"Thomas, what happened?" Mary said, standing at the foot of the stairs.

Then Thomas saw his wife wearing fresh vomit on the front of her dress and her shoes.

At that second, the odor, like a descending cloud, reached him. The putrid vapor made him gag repeatedly.

Mary looked awful. Stomach emptied, she heaved every time she tried to stand straight.

Thomas smelled something else.

Looking at the trap door, the center of the cord on the door's bottom side was on fire. The burning cord began igniting the planks in the door. The burning kept the bugs off the door until it extinguished itself, leaving charred edges on the planks.

A scant second later, the sounds of creatures moving and lifting began in earnest. The door lifted an inch then dropped.

More insects' legs and claws squeezed through the spaces along the edges, widened in places by the fire.

Then the sounds of gnawing began.

Mary Corrigan continued saying Hail Marys as she moved to the corner of the room farthest from the foot of the stairs. Her terrified eyes spilled large tears to her cheeks.

Just as her mother commanded her as a child, she knelt in the corner facing the wall and continued praying as if the Rosary might project a shield of protection or transport her to a safer place.

Thomas found a large chopping knife, steeled himself, and ascended the stairs. Using the knife's edge, he pressed the sharp steel pinning the creature's appendages then pressed firmly. The insect-like parts were hard.

"Hail Mary full of Grace…" Mary's voice grew louder.

It felt like cutting through small sticks of hardwood.

176

Thomas rocked the blade against the door's frame. The owners of the trapped appendages struggled to pull their parts free. Some managed to escape, most just struggled against the honed blade holding them.

Thomas felt the wood sticks break beneath the knife's edge then fall to the floor.

"The Lord is with thee..." Mary's mantra became faster.

Thomas struggled.

Twice more the chopping knife performed its duty.

Each time more legs than were severed invaded the underside of the trap door.

"Blessed are thou among women..." Faster still.

The sound of gnawing.

A scorpion-like claw dug between the fire-blackened sides of two abutted boards in the door.

"And blessed is the fruit of thy womb Jesus..." Louder.

"Christ, Mary, please stop," Thomas said, too soft for her to hear.

Thomas set the knife's edge like a carpenter's plane, pressed hard and scraped the door's underside. He caught the claw against a plank's edge and leaned as much weight as he could into the assault.

"Holy Mary Mother of God..." Louder and faster.

The thing above freed its claw, but not before the knife cracked the hard exoskeleton.

Before Thomas selected another place to counterattack, a new claw larger than the first appeared two inches away between the same crevice.

The sounds coming from the floor above had expanded and changed. It was no longer possible to hear individual creatures. It had become a continuous clatter like hail pounding a roof.

"Pray for us sinners, now and in the hour of our death!" Mary nearly screamed the last line. She moved a bead on the rosary and started over. Now her repetitions were loud chants.

Thomas struggled.

He saw the demons would win. The boards in the trap door slowly shrank as splinters of wood and wet sawdust-like splinters sprinkled down.

Thomas looked behind and saw the kitchen floor directly over Mary showed early signs of attack, as Mary continuously repeated the magic words to ward off evil.

His mouth dry, arms exhausted, spirit and hope gone, Thomas looked and saw three more areas where the creatures progressed in the destruction of the kitchen floor.

He could not let Mary die by demons. He could not, would not, allow the gnawing, hard-bodied creatures to devour her an inch at a time.

Thomas came down the stairs, gathered up the lamps and emptied their oil reservoirs on the top stairs, then worked his way down, step-by-step.

A calm illogical reason told him dying in this manner would be far better than being nipped, pinched and eaten alive. In fact, dying in these circumstances would relieve having to endure one more minute of hellish waiting and calculating how long it would take before the monsters succeeded opening the floor and pouring into the cellar.

He struck a match and lit the stairs. The flames leaped from the lower step to the next.

Thomas moved to Mary, knelt, put his arm around her shoulder and began the Hail Mary mid-sentence with his wife.

The flames and smoke drove the creatures out of the kitchen.

When the fire consumed the oxygen in the root cellar, the denizens of another world slowly worked their way to the center of the kitchen.

The trap door, now charred thin boards, fell to their

assault. The creatures seemed gleeful as they dropped and climbed down to the basement floor.

Mary and Thomas, side-by-side, pressed together into the corner of the stone walls. The bugs covered them in an instant and began tearing out pieces of flesh. Thomas and Mary didn't move, didn't scream. They died of smoke inhalation long before the fire went out.

Hail Mary mother of God, they were in a safer place.

☐

The Rectory

Michael dubbed the thing a "scorpiopede,' for lack of a more fearsome name. He aimed his large caliber pistol, hammer cocked, at the four-foot length of unearthly beast.

"Please feel free to dispense of your target," the priest quipped as the scorpiopede stopped about two feet short of him.

It raised its head half its length and swayed like a cobra, antennae twitching as it tested for something.

"I think it may be blind," Collin said, brandishing his poker. "Gladys, wave your hand."

The creature did not react to the poker or Gladys' motions.

"Now throw something at it," Collin said, looking at Gladys.

The old gal grabbed the first thing she saw in the library, a book placed on the side table by the chair near the fireplace. She lifted it, aimed and threw it hard.

Better aimed than Father Bob's shovel and thrown so it

spun in flight, the book, a first edition of Grimms' Fairy Tales by the Brothers Grimm, struck the thing in the side of the head. The force of the blow knocked its head to the right and caused it to lower the upper portion of its body.

"Collin's right," Michael said, "it made no reaction until the book struck it." Only after recovering did it turn toward Gladys.

Michael took a step away from Gladys and warned, "I'm going to make a loud noise. Let's see if sound affects it." Michael howled like a wolf. The scorpiopede did not seem to notice.

The creature seemed confused. It kept changing its orientation. It would aim its antennae toward the priest, then back toward Gladys.

"So somehow you both remain threats," Michael said, as the monster's mucous-colored body segments shifted toward the priest and inched forward.

It assumed a different battle stance. Its front end crouched to the floor, pinchers thrusting blindly as it crept forward. The thing's tail cocked the back half of its body length.

"Sorry to be a bother, Michael, but would you mind shooting the damned thing?" the priest implored.

The scorpiopede's head was in Michael's sights.

"Cover your ears," Michael warned.

A long second crawled by as Michael gently squeezed the trigger.

The big-bore pistol roared in the confined space. It bucked in Michael's hand and, exactly as trained, the sub-inspector brought the weapon to bear on the same target readying the second shot.

Everyone felt the concussion.

Everyone except the creature. Its head simply exploded across the floor toward the hallway, radiating a spatter of yellowish-brown ooze. A horrific odor rose at once.

Branna, already feeling weak, gagged. Gladys pinched

her nose and held her breath.

The men grimaced and instinctively backed away.

The dead or dying scorpiopede's body writhed and twisted on itself, making its uncontrolled elongated body bump and roll. As it thrashed about, it oozed a stream of poison along the four stingers in its tail, which, one by one, came loose and fell to the floor.

The audience watched the monster's death throes, displaying looks ranging from primal fear to morbid disgust.

Just as it made itself into a tight ball, before anyone could speak, a second creature of the same type poked twitching antennae around the library door's frame.

Lynott's Pub

John Lynott went from behind the bar to close the door to the pub's attic. He had no intention of investigating the attic, only to close and lock the door to the stairs.

The door itself was something of a marvel. It was narrow because the entire door, top to bottom and side to side was made from a single piece of wood hewn from a huge tree felled two hundred years before. It was also nearly three inches thick, which made it impenetrable to anything less than an ax. The doorway it occupied was especially designed to fit it.

All John had to do was cross ten feet between the bar and the base of the stairs.

The Quinns stayed on their stools, craning to see over the bar as John began his journey.

He made it to less than three feet from the opened door when the Quinns saw a shadow the size of sparrow streak from the dark stairway and slam into Lynott's face.

John swiped the thing away from his face, exclaiming,

"Manky yoke!" He took the last step toward the door and gripped the handle. "Agh! Bugger me, that hurt." Lynott closed the attic door then turned back toward the bar.

The Quinns saw him as he stepped into the limited light.

"Jesus Christ Almighty, Lynott, what was that thing?" Pierce asked.

Lynott stopped and turned to look into the dusty mirror on the wall behind the bar. He moved two bottles of whiskey over to make room for his face.

The first thing John Lynott saw was a nose swelling at a rapid pace. The nostrils trailed mucous-mixed blood onto his lip.

It hurt like the devil before he touched it. When he did, the excruciating pain began where his finger touched the now-discolored nose and shot to all of his body's nerves. Though he had only gently touched it, he nearly collapsed from the pain.

After regaining his breath and recovering enough to move, he stared back into the grimy glass. This time, his purplish-red nose was the size of a plum. The nose stopped bleeding, but his sinus cavities made him moan with pain at the slightest movement of his head.

He reached for a bottle of Jameson whiskey. His coordination off, his hand failed to encircle the bottle, and he knocked it to the floor.

He bent to pick it up, but instead, fell forward, face down behind the bar. He moaned pitifully.

The Quinns, standing as they watched the pub's owner, scurried around the bar. Too tight for both to work behind the bar, they grabbed his feet and, gently as they could, dragged him out to the floor and turned him over.

"Turn up that lamp!" the elder Quinn ordered.

Donald reached for an oil lantern. He exposed more wick, and the light brightened immediately. He turned the lamp so its reflector maximized the light on Lynott.

"What in God's name?" Donald said, crossing himself.

Lynott lay on his back, eyes staring blankly at the ceiling. The nose and surrounding flesh were swollen till Lynott's face no longer looked human. The frontal sinus cavities displayed bulging blood vessels that pulsed with the rapid beat of the man's heart.

"What are we going to do, Da?" Donald asked, his eyes large with concern.

Pierce reached up, found Lynott's bar towel, then a pitcher half filled with water. He poured some water on Lynott's face. When the towel touched his nose, Lynott suffered a seizure, body quivering and eyes rolling up behind swollen lids.

"I don't know," he answered his son. "I think we better get John some help." Pierce paused then, looking up at the ceiling, said, "Get him some help away from here."

The results of the attack on Lynott distracted the Quinns from the ruckus taking place in the attic. Now, with their friend seriously injured or dying, the noises above recaptured their attention.

"I think we could carry him to the church," Donald said as the first chips of plaster fell from the ceiling.

Before Pierce answered, Donald watched as the shadowy thing that hit Lynott streaked over his shoulder and smashed his father's nose.

It happened so quickly the younger Quinn caught only the fleetest of glimpses. The thing, the size of a small bird with bat-like wings, pressed against his father's nose.

Pierce slapped both opened hands, catching and crushing the little monster. But before the two calloused hands slapped together, the creature inserted a long thin tail deep up Pierce's right nostril.

When Pierce pulled his hands apart, the dark, leathery thing's flattened body dangled over Quinn's mouth until the tail slipped from the nostril and fell to the floor.

"Jesus! Feels like a horse kicked me on the nose,"

185

Quinn complained. He tried to blow his nose. The only thing that came out was a scream.

"Da, we have to get to the church. Get you help," Quinn the younger's voice was desperate.

Pierce looked at his friend's face. Swollen in its entirety, the nostrils, mouth and eyes were visible as small slits in bloated flesh, reminding Pierce of a decomposing, gas-filled, pig.

The front of Pierce's head continued to rage with pain. His vision blurred. His ear tubes filled with pressure and liquid from sinuses. His eustachian tubes closed in both ears and that fast, he was deaf. "Go to the church, son," Pierce said, holding on to his son's hand and watching the first appendages of living creatures break through the plaster in several places. "Go now!"

Speaking those few words exploded the pain in his head, and he desperately fought to remain conscious.

"I'll not leave you, Da. I won't do it," Donald said. He took both his father's forearms and tried to lift him to his feet.

Pierce's last thought was, "You're a strong lad. I'm proud of you."

Pierce's body slumped and became dead weight, offering no aid to his son's efforts.

After a minute, Donald stopped trying to lift his father and began to drag him across the floor.

His eye caught something small and dark on Lynott's pasty-blue, bloated face. He returned his eye to something like caterpillars emerging from Lynott's nose.

"I'm sorry, Da. I don't know what else to do," Donald said and walked to the pub's front door with pieces of plaster raining down.

Donald unlocked and opened the door.

Looking out, he saw the ground and roads roiled with a covering of living shadows. He heard screams coming from the church. Horrible screams. He saw three structures in various stages of burning down.

Something hard touched his boot. Donald leaped as far as he could. His foot entered the moving carpet of demons. He almost lost his balance and fell into them. He made himself move forward one step at a time. Creatures clung to his boot and pants.

He could see the church.

Pulling his right leg out of the mass, he noticed his boot smoked.

Donald began to count the number of steps he made toward the church. He counted to six.

☐

Dawn

Completely hidden by clouds, the full moon's arc neared completion. Its reflected sunlight had not penetrated through the clouds this night. But the moon's other powers worked as always. It caused the seas to move. Its gravity was also felt in more subtle ways. It worked with the energies moving through quartzite, crystal-streaked stones and the Earth's tectonic plates. Many stones had been moved and erected in patterns by humans thousands of years ago. Many stones remained where glacial ice dropped them, or where, even before walls of ice moved, they were forged by unimaginable heat separated earth and stone then fused them together in alchemy only God could work.

The moon's gentler forces worked to manipulate the energy moving along the matrix of stones. Sometimes, coalescing with other natural occurrences, the energy waxed and waned. Tonight, though unseen, the moon's secret power caused the network of stones to become as powerful as they ever had been.

When the moon descended, its effects on the energy sank with it.

Branna's vigor began to return. Her face regained its normal healthy color, and her eyes ceased their dullness and sparkled, all of which reduced Michael's worry.

Though he had enough to worry about.

The area inside the library doorway contained bodies of six dead creatures. Michael shot and killed a second scorpiopede shortly after the first. Before the second one died, it lowered its spiked rear portion then flicked it forward like a catapult. Triggered during the death throe, unguided, the four stingers flew across the room. Striking no one, three bounced off the stone wall, and one stuck into a wooden baseboard.

For quite some time nothing happened. Even the noises in the parlor fell silent except for an occasional scrape of hard exoskeletons bumping against another.

"What are they doing, waiting for more blind reinforcements?" Michael asked rhetorically.

The minutes crawled by.

Armed with his iron poker, Collin crept toward the doorway.

"Careful, Collin," Gladys offered unnecessarily.

The largest of the library lamps went out.

Collin froze at the reduction of light.

Father Bob looked at Michael. "There's no more oil here. I'll have to go to the pantry for more."

"Everyone, lift a lamp, hold it waist high and move toward the door. Stop when I tell you," Michael said. "Bobby McGuire, the rest of the house is dark, you cannot vanish into it. I will not allow it." Michael said to the priest. "Stop, everyone," Michael said. "Stay where you are until something happens."

Michael took a place between Branna and Gladys.

Branna's hand slowly reached over, touched Michael's then their fingers intertwined.

"Something is changing," Branna said.

"Is it near sunrise?" she asked.

Four beetle-like things, each the size of a man's head, scurried into the hall, charging the library. The beasts' instincts at being in the light made their charge stall, restart, and stall again.

Michael aimed carefully at the thing nearest to Branna and fired. The bullet struck the thing's face and mandibles. Its legs twitched with no coordination, and it lay on the floor making itself spin in place.

Michael's second bullet missed the target entirely, penetrating and splintering the hardwood floor in front of its face. Unphased, it continued forward.

The third bullet found its mark and seemed to kill it instantly.

Aiming steadily, allowing the third beetle to close until it was almost straight below, Michael said, "Last bullet, get ready to kill the last one. Try not to get into each other's way."

The fourth shot sent the bullet near the diameter of a man's index finger almost straight down.

Before Michael could determine the monster's health, he heard Father Bob's voice.

"In the name of the Father!" the priest yelled.

The three foot tall brass cross came down on the fourth beetle, edge first, like a gleaming metal ax.

"And of the Son," the priest said with the second stroke. "And the Holy Ghost," he said with the final blow, rendering the animal into two separate, but equally destroyed pieces.

"Amen, to that," Collin said, crossing himself.

Everyone waited for the next onslaught.

The coming dawn lightened the outside.

"They are leaving," Father Bob said, pointing out the window.

Without yielding their positions, everyone craned to see outside.

Father Bob narrated, "There is still a tangle of demon

things all over the ground, but their movements are sluggish now. They appear to be moving toward Slievemore."

"The portal tomb," Branna said. "That's where they emerged. They are trying to return before the sun rises."

"Well," said Gladys, "I for one say let them go and good riddance."

Branna knew they would be back after sunset but said nothing as there was not anything she could do while the mass of creatures raced against time to return to their own world.

With each passing minute, the day became brighter. So long as clouds, mists, and fog kept the full strength of the sun's brightness from striking them directly, they functioned in a weakened and confused condition.

When the sun hung full above the horizon, the morning fog burned off and no clouds moved in the way, the undulating mass, like receding floodwaters, moved clumsily and slowly toward the tomb on Slievemore's side.

Now clearly visible, Father Bob studied them through the window. He maintained a running description. "There are dozens of species, all sizes. They aren't exactly insects, but if insects could limp, that's how they would move. Sluggishly, not in full control of their limbs."

The sun reached ten degrees above the horizon. The sea of demons began to emit tendrils of steam.

Then, jets of steam emerged from various joints in their armored bodies. Father Bob first heard the whistling. He could not tell if it was caused by the steam or the creatures immolating the sound of lobsters lowered into boiling water. In a matter of seconds, everyone heard it.

Some of the steaming creatures simply collapsed, cooked from the inside out. Others built up pressure and, even though probably cooked, exploded.

Another ten minutes passed, the sun shining as brightly as it had since Michael arrived, they heard the first whistling coming from the parlor. Another moment, a cacophony of whistles then explosions.

"It seems we rule the day," Father Bob said.

"By default," replied Michael.

☐

Na Clocha Ocras, the hungry stones

The crows soared toward a sacred spot atop Croaghaun. Flying line astern, they landed one, two, three, cawing and looking out to sea from the heights the cliffs.

They cawed at each other in a language no human ever mastered. They cawed and hopped, spread their wings so the wind lifted and made them hover, then cawed some more.

They looked healthier than yesterday; more sheen to their feathers, a brighter reflection in their eyes. They looked satisfied.

Hopping to form an equilateral triangle, they cocked and twisted their heads looking at one another until the blister of light formed above and around them. The brightness flared then faded, leaving a single large crow.

Bigger than a raven it was, but for centuries, over a thousand battlefields, men mistook it for a raven instead of crow. Battlefields were its garden; the fallen, its dung. The large crow, the three sisters united, became a single creature, the Great Queen, casting spells upon enemies while encouraging and strengthening her allies. Rarely she took the form of a warrior god and demolished enemy companies with each swipe of her sword.

The sisters' power came from fear, chaos, pain, suffering, and death. No greater source of food than a battlefield as their garden, filled with screams of every sort, of men maimed and dying. Those already dead remained of value. Their mangled corpses and pooling blood added more fear to those still living, feeding the Morrigan, the phantom queen, with every whimper, tear, and terror.

The crow spread black wings and allowed the ocean's wind to make it rise. It dove from the cliff, gathered speed and winged its way north to a peninsula a few miles north. To an ancient stone circle on another set of cliffs, another doorway to secret worlds.

The wind increased. Her wings beat faster. She played. Swooping, diving, turning, she frolicked. She landed in the circle of stones near Gleann an Ghad, named for the valley of the withes. In ancient times, the stone circle became known as na clocha ocras, the hungry stones.

The withes were small, tough and agile creatures that dwelled around the portal of stones. They hated trespassers and, once man arrived, the withes hated humans the most. They erected the circle, and their shamans, wise-women, and healers gathered all their tribes and, under a full moon, imbued the circle with power.

When any creature other than their own kind lingered near the circle it would become hungry. So hungry, if the trespassers had not their own provisions, that they would eat the grass and flowers then fall asleep. While asleep, nearly invisible wisps of vapor slowly rose from the ground around their bodies, forming tendrils attracted to the victim's breathing. They never woke. Instead, they became mist-like vapor and lowered into the ground. Cattle, sheep, pigs, and other useful creatures were revived in the world of the withes. Everything and everyone else was eaten by the withes.

It was here, in this thousands-of-years-old circle of poison, did the Morrigan land. She hopped to the stone closest to the sea and pecked on it. Then to a stone opposite the first and did the same. The vapor rose, the crow stood perfectly still and faded into the vapor and was then pulled down into the ground.

An hour later, the vapor rose, formed the shape of a crow and the Morrigan waited until the air around it cleared then lifted off, flying straight back to the sacred spot on the top of Croaghaun.

It landed and flashed brightly for a few seconds. When the light faded, the three sisters stood in their most human-like forms. Each held in her hand a light green egg, speckled with small, dark green patterns of three connected spirals.

The haggish one, locally known to humans as the Banshee, held the egg so her misaimed eye could see it, smiling broadly, exposing a few gaps in the top and bottom rows of saw-like teeth. "Tonight should do the trick," said she.

"I believe you are right, Sister Nemain. I tire of performing for so small an audience," replied Badb.

"Tomorrow our kingdom expands," smiled Macha.

"A toast, of a sort," said Badb, holding the egg near her mouth. "Le sláinte iomlán!"

"Slainte Agus cumhacht," replied the sisters as all consumed their eggs.

They flashed again and became three birds each standing on a triangle's point.

Without a single caw, they lifted and flew. One to Dugort, one to Cashel and the third, Badb Cath, to Mallaranny, a nearby mainland town, larger than any on Achill. From this night forward, The Seeing would expand fear and destruction among humans.

The five emerged from the rectory looking much worse than when they entered. Outside, in the light of day, the strange, frightening, and fierce creatures littered the ground in various stages of destruction. In the distance, toward Slievemore, they saw the carcasses increased geometrically the closer the fleeing mass neared the portal tomb. The power of the sun massacred them wholesale as it climbed the heavens. The creatures unable to remain below the other beasts made it the farthest. But as the cooked and exploded monsters increased exponentially and fell behind the desperate retreat, there were less and less to hide beneath. Very few regained the safety of the tomb's dark tunnels. Regardless of the destruction of one army, millions more waited at the doorway to this world, straining, praying to the Morrigan to unleash them.

Seeing no others about, hearing only the surf and hymns from the church, Michael stopped and spoke to the group. "I think we should go door to door and hunt for survivors."

"If we don't do some very heavy work before nightfall, we may relive last night," Branna offered, getting everyone's attention.

"Well, we will have to accomplish both," Father Bob answered. "Since Collin, Gladys and I live here, we will search the houses. We can tell those able to help Branna's heavy work to meet you. I am sure those who can will. What are you doing, and where should they meet you?"

"We are moving dirt, a lot of it. Anyone who can help should bring tools for that purpose. If they own a horse, bring it as well," Branna said.

"Are you planning to bury the portal?" the priest asked.

"No, we are going to redirect the energy to close the portals to this world," Branna said, eager to begin. "It's going to be a long day, so please hurry."

"Meet us on Bog Road below the tomb," Michael

added.

"Come along, Michael, let's get horses and reconnoiter," Branna said, tugging on his arm.

When they reached the livery, there were no horses to be found. No living horses, anyway.

The first door Gladys and Collin knocked upon produced no answer, nor did their calls to anyone inside. Still skittish, Gladys shook the ancient iron door lock. It opened. Inside, Widow Margaret McNulty sat in her rocker, what was left of her. On the floor between her legs was her dead husband's goose gun. Around her portrait of horror were three beetle beasts and one scorpiopede exhibiting the signs of shotgun pellets fired from close range. There were also many carcasses cooked by the sunlight. The top of Mrs. McNulty's skull was missing completely. The rest of her skeleton remained. Apparently, the bugs were gentle eaters when left to their own devices.

The priest found the church door locked. The sounds of someone trying to enter the door caused instant silence to wash like a wave from the back of the church to the altar.

"It's Father Bob, can someone open the door?" he called.

He heard shuffling, then a muffled voice from inside asked, "Are you alone? I mean are those things gone?"

"They're dead or gone," the priest replied, "now open the door."

One old fisherman opened the door while another stood back, double-bladed ax held ready to come down. The rest of the church's occupants stood back, forming a cautious semi-circle.

"It's safe," Father Bob offered in as hearty a voice as he could muster. "Come on out."

The men came out, one after the other, looking left and

right before stepping through the threshold. Most of the women and all of the children remained inside but came closer to the door.

"Jesus, Father," the man with the ax said excitedly, "What in God's name is happening? What were those things?"

Other people jumped in issuing a barrage of questions, "Will they be back? Did anyone get hurt? Where did they come from? Is this the doing of the Devil and all his demons?"

Father Bob found the last question the most interesting. He decided the best course was to get this force of potential laborers working at whatever Branna wanted to be done.

"I know you survived a terrifying night. So did everyone in Dugort." The priest didn't feel the need to tell them he had been knee deep in the things. "I will tell you what I know, which isn't much more than you."

Father Bob looked at the crowd, now gathered, silent waiting on his explanation.

"Our visitor, the Butler woman, is from Trinity University. She is an expert on the studies of the ancient ways." Father Bob stretched the truth. "She believes if we lay stone at the portal tomb, we can prevent these creatures from ever returning," Father Bob said.

The old man who opened the door asked, "Are you telling us these things came from underground? From below the tomb?"

"Yes." Father Bob wanted to keep things simple and avoid lengthy discussion. "She and the inspector are on their way now to determine exactly what needs to be done. We need you to go to your homes, gather tools to suit the purpose and meet them on Bog Road below the tomb. If you have horses, bring them as well."

"Father, was anyone hurt?" a fearful woman asked.

"I don't know. Gladys and Collin Gallagher, from

down Cashel way, are searching each building." The priest continued, "To be direct with you, there's no time to try and figure things out. The tomb must be sealed before dark, or we will suffer another night of the same. If you can help with the work, meet below the tomb. Bring horses if you have them. Now off with you."

Most of the residents between the rectory and the hotel were among the survivors at the church. They found no more bodies until they reached the Slievemore Hotel. In addition to the picked-clean skeletons of Thomas and Mary Corrigan, three guests had gathered in one of the upstairs rooms. They too would have gleamed had the sun shined on their bones.

Outside, a few shell-shocked survivors of the hellish night shambled along the main road.

A young couple expecting a child carried bundles over their shoulder as they sought to reach the mainland before nightfall. Last night they saw the creatures approaching. A column of creatures splintered from the main wave and pursued them to the beach and into the ocean. They stood thigh deep in cold waters, terrified the monsters would reach them, but either the salt in the sea, or the surf constantly washing them back to the sand kept them safe, though miserable until sunrise.

A woman with three children followed, all carrying quilts, custom packed to allow each child a portable bundle. They were headed to Achill Sound to flee the island. They survived by cramming inside a hole in their root cellar's wall and using the black, iron-rich stones which normally sealed it to block the entrance. The beasts found the root cellar quickly enough. They moved around all night but never made an attack on the people, huddled behind the wall of stones. Her husband Donald and father-in-law Pierce did not come home last night. She would stop by the pub in Cashel and give them what for.

The men's bodies were among the many skeletons found that day but never identified.

Gladys cried at the loss of Thomas and Mary Corrigan and the destruction of the hotel she'd worked in since childhood. Collin helped himself to an opened bottle of brandy and consoled the grieving old woman as best he could before they moved through the rest of the town. When they found someone alive, they told them of the work at the tomb. When they found the dead, they made a small pile of rocks outside their entrance.

Within an hour, some people, mostly men, recovered enough to walk to the portal tomb. They carried picks, shovels, hoes, ropes, and chains. Some, who lived far enough out of town and were not attacked, led horses, harnessed and yoked for pulling.

Collin and Gladys eventually made their way to the tomb, Gladys' eyes red from tears, Collin's from liquor.

Before leaving the livery stables on foot, Michael gathered a shovel and pitchfork, the only suitable tools he saw, hoisted them to his shoulder and walked to keep up with Branna's fast pace.

For once, Michael was not tongue-tied around Branna. He had nothing to say. He was exhausted, frightened and wanted to finish the construction, whatever it was, leave town with Branna and watch what happened from afar.

Branna bent down and crawled into the tomb enough to get her head in.

Michael did his best not to tell her to be careful. He did, however, keep a sharp eye on her.

She emerged saying, "I feel better about our plan."

"I might if I knew what the plan was," Michael answered.

"We have one more place before I know if this will

work. Then I will tell you the details. For now, let's move to the deserted village." Not intending rudeness, Branna turned in the direction of the village and, not taking the longer but easier road, marched along the slope.

Once in the center of the ruined village, Branna stood by the cistern, tasting and smelling the water it held. After a moment, she followed the stream up the shallow slope until she reached the source, a small stone ringed circle where the water rose to the surface.

"Just a few more minutes," Branna said, as she knelt to place her nose close to the water.

The constant movement of the water for a thousand years made particles rise and layer the stone circles inside with coarse black sand, which itself reddened from the discolored water.

Branna scooped a handful of the dark pebbles from the spring's head and let the water run from her hand. She pinched a small shard between her thumb and forefinger and put it between her front teeth, the way some tested the authenticity of gold.

"Very good," she said. "We will know in a moment."

"I'll have some for lunch, on your suggestion," Michael said.

Branna cast a chastising look then smiled at his poor attempt at humor. Branna rose, and studied the microtopography of the ground around the spring.

"Michael, would you be so kind as to bring the shovel to me?" she asked.

"I know I have not done much, if anything, to further your scheme, but I am sure my digging skills are more practiced, more efficient and enduring than yours. I will dig. Just tell me where," Michael replied as he approached her.

"Very well, I will allow your logic to prevail, just so long as you are not acting out of chivalry," Branna smiled. "Please dig here," she said, indicating a spot with her foot.

"Am I looking for buried treasure? At least share that with me," Michael said and pressed the cutting edge of the blade into the spot then stepped on the top with his weight, pressing it about eight inches into the soil. He immediately wished he had a peat shovel.

Branna watched him work. "You are mining for iron," she said.

"Iron? There's not been iron mined here. What makes you think I will find it?" Michael said, deepening the hole.

"You are right. Iron hasn't been brought from the ground in this area for thousands of years. What's here is not a high-quality ore. It's called Bog Iron, and there are likely buried veins of it all over Achill," Branna said, peering into the hole.

"So, now you are an expert in geology," Michael replied, joking but a little annoyed at her knowledge's breadth.

"Certainly not. It's just that I've done enough excavations to learn what minerals occupy the area where the digs are. It is just part of my job," she paused.

Michael's little mine was now two feet deep and three feet wide. Digging on a terraced area of Slievemore, the soil here was not as water-laden as elsewhere.

"What does it look like?" he asked.

"It is likely to be a layer of roughish small stones and coarse pebbles. They most likely will be a color between taupe to rusty red. There are other color combinations, depending on the type of ore, but I will recognize those as well," Branna said, watching the progress with more interest.

"How deep before we reach it?" Michael asked, his breathing a bit husky.

"The terrace and the spring's flow and color indicate it should be between four and ten feet," Branna said, not realizing the effort required to dig down ten feet.

Michael paused and leaned on the shovel's handle.

"What if we are not on the right spot?" he asked.

"Oh, my," Branna replied, for the first time realizing she might be wrong. "Oh my," she repeated.

Men began arriving with tools. Soon Branna had several men digging holes where she indicated. Oddly, the villagers trusted she knew what she was doing and that by digging, they would save themselves.

Branna told everyone to stop while she examined the soil a fisherman unearthed at three feet below the surface.

Michael, whose hole was now five feet and filling itself with seeping peat, was glad for the break.

Branna organized two teams of three men each to dig trenches above and below the exposed soil containing iron. Finding the streak on both sides of the original hole, she asked men to use ropes to form a straight line along the iron vein's axis. Once in position, she had men stake the path and instructed diggers to follow the line of stakes. If the vein did not continue along the staked line, the digger was to dig to either side to locate its new course.

More men arrived, a few with horses pulling peat sleds. Women and children came with water, bread, salted fish and tools for themselves.

Within two hours, the villagers created a trench two to three feet wide and ranging in depth from two to five feet. The vein of iron was certainly wider than the trench, but Branna felt this would allow the movement of more than enough iron ore.

The trench began a few feet south of where the spring emerged from the ground, followed the brook generally for about two hundred paces, then diverged from the staked line nearly perpendicular, due south direction.

She formed teams of men to load as much of the iron ore, mostly presented as various sized loose stones of fairly consistent color, onto the peat sleds and wheelbarrows, and transport it along the side of the hill to the portal tomb.

It was slow going. The horses pulling the peat sleds kept losing their loads as the stone slid off the sled. Then men pulling sleds or hauling bags soon learned to lighten the load as the slight incline made it backbreaking work.

Some boys were sent to the village to bring back planks, hammers, and nails. Upon their return, the sleds were quickly equipped with side panels to keep the ore from shaking off. This greatly improved the speed and efficiency of the horses.

In the meantime, Michael formed a separate team to create a similarly sized trench around the tomb. As they dug, the soil was thrown toward the tomb. At first, when moving the iron ore to the tomb was slow, Michael's team stayed ahead of the arrival of more ore. Once the sleds were fitted with side panels, Michael transferred some of the men pulling peat sleds or carrying rocks in bags to working on the trench around the portal tomb.

Michael had guessed Branna's plan based on their conversation last night. Branna said the quartzite in the mountain channeled energy through it. She must know iron might redirect it. Even so, something niggled at his mind, causing him to think about what else could be done should the iron circle defense fail.

An hour before sunset, the trench around the portal tomb held iron ore to a five-foot depth, and the tomb itself, including the entrance, was hidden under a ten-foot mound of dirt.

On the walk back to Dugort, the villagers were bone weary but in high spirits. They believed their work would prevent a repeat of the previous night.

Branna walked slowly by Michael's side. For the first time since going to the seal cave, she smiled easily and spoke cheerily. She confirmed Michael's guess about the iron redirecting the flow of energy and felt positive no unwanted guests would come from the portal tomb. She, however, reminded Michael she could not vouch for other megalithic structures hiding tunnels.

Father Bob spent the afternoon trying to understand how the church withstood invasion under the bugs' assault. He wanted to believe it was simply the power of God. After thinking and investigating details he'd never noticed before, he decided, indirectly, God was the reason the church was not breached.

The building's walls and basement floor were made from heavy, cut stones. The roof was one-inch slate shingles. All vents, grates and other openings were made of iron. The church was built to last for centuries.

The priest decided the house of God was the safest place in the village and set his own plan in motion. Within a few minutes, he had female disciples spreading his plan.

Father Bob waited where Bog Road entered Dugort.

As workers arrived, the priest explained women of the village had not been idle. They prepared food and placed water inside the church. Everyone would spend the night inside the 'mighty fortress,' as the Lutheran hymn said.

Even after Father Bob informed Branna and Michael of the deaths at the Slievemore Hotel, they insisted they go to clean up and change clothes before meeting everyone at the church.

Michael waited downstairs for Branna. His constant sense of observation indicated bottles missing from the bar's shelves. Collin's work no doubt.

Michael looked up as Branna descended the stairs. He did not know how anyone held so much power over him. He never experienced anything like it.

She was radiant, her hair pulled back in a pompadour, her skin perfect, smooth pale alabaster. She wore a white silk blouse under a buttoned vest and a floor length skirt. Her eyes and smile dazzled him. Michael felt like a schoolboy, unable to do anything other than stand dumb as this amazing creature approached him.

She rose on her toes, kissed his cheek and asked, "Is something wrong, Michael?"

It was obvious to Michael her feelings about him were not nearly as intense as his for her.

"Not really," Michael lied. He realized his feelings and thoughts about Branna were out of control. He was smitten by everything about her. It was a bundle of never-before-felt emotions. She distracted him so, he could hardly concentrate. If this was love, it was not what it was cracked up to be.

Michael escorted Branna to the church with little time to spare before twilight began graying the landscape.

Just before entering the house of worship, Michael studied the sky. No storm appeared to the horizon. Tomorrow, assuming he survived, he would use his motorcycle to see how other towns had faired.

The crowded church offered salvation of a different sort to the survivors of Dugort. People who had not seen each other or had suffered falling outs visited in frightened whispers yet hoped the iron circle provided protection.

The only windows in the structure, tall, narrow stained glass arched at the tops, were surrounded by lamps and candles, maximizing the light passing to the outside. The scents of food, the comradery, and the well-lit church created a sense everything would be alright for those in the church. Everyone except for Collin, who, though the church was crowded, slept on a front row pew.

Father Bob held up a hymnal and, in a voice without fear, said loud enough to hear, "Hymn number three fourteen, Guardian Angel from Heaven So Bright." He waited a few seconds as people picked up the songbook and found the hymn. Then in a booming voice with imperfect pitch, he sang out.

The Morrigan Strikes Again

Nemain flew toward the portal tomb. Halfway there she felt the disturbance in the flow of power. The closer she came, the interference grew enough to alter the course of the flow, forcing it to bend south, away from the tomb. She settled on a rock outside the trench circling the portal tomb.

"Damned the halfling bitch," she said with a long, angry caw. She laughed, a series of quick, short caws, "You feel safe now, do ye?"

She rose into the air toward the town of Dugort.

The crow landed on the beach north of Dugort. She allowed the breeze of the ocean to smooth her feathers. After a few minutes with no fanfare, her crow form grew as it changed into her most famous form, the one known as the Banshee.

Hovering a few feet above the sand, she gagged until the light green egg rose up her esophagus and into her mouth. She removed the egg and kept her hand near her mouth. She took a deep breath then closed her hand, crushing the egg.

A thick burnt umber cloud pulsated and roiled in her hand. Its heavy gas flowed from her hand down to the sand and slowly spread out. She pursed her lips and blew. The ever-increasing fog in her hand streamed east along the beach. Her powerful breath sent the thick storm-like cloud up the beach until, like a horizontal cyclone, it twisted and danced this way and that, anxious for release.

The Banshee lifted her hand, now empty of the brownish cloud, and waved it toward the little town of Dugort.

The three hundred yards of horizontal cyclone cloud hovering above the beach dropped to the sand and, like a slow, dense fog, crept up the escarpment.

It roiled in turmoil. Flashes of light the color of yellowed teeth flickered and ran like tiny lightning bolts to meet other flashes.

Once off the beach, the fog spread, slowly flowing in all directions. No lights shone in the town except in the church's windows. Lights or not, the burnt orange, foot deep cloud slowly crawled to cover all of Dugort.

Its movement surrounded St. Thomas Church. Each tendril reaching from the low ground covering cloud met solid stone. Seeking a way inside, no matter how small, the tendrils methodically searched for any crack or crevice.

They found openings in the church's front door. Though weather sealed with tight strips of felt, the porous material offered eventual entry.

□

Macha

The population of Keel had been virtually wiped out in the previous night's slaughter. Three people survived: an eight-year-old girl along with mother and father who found shelter by hiding under an upside down metal watering tub for stock. They were now with the survivors

208

of Cashel's dark night's attack. Packed in the church, singing hymns, drinking tea, armed with tools. They knew nothing of the iron trench. They expected the hard-backed bugs to come again. When they looked at one another, they saw the same fear in the eyes and frightened worry in the struggled smiles.

The town was black, except for the light filtering through the colored glass church windows, framed in iron.

Macha landed in the center of town. She changed into her most human looking form: a goddess queen of land and sea, a sovereign of all things living in her territory. Her dark red hair flowed over a ruby red cloak. Her pale green eyes shown with their own light, her right arm wrapped with a copper snake bracelet coiled around her wrists.

She brought up the egg from her stomach.

As she crushed its shell and the noxious brown cloud materialized in her hand, she heard music and song burst from the church.

"You now have something to sing about. Sing your dirges, lament your loss of hearth and home, pray your souls escape me," she said, as the heavy fog crawled in every direction, seeking to kill every living creature in the area.

☐

Badb

Badb traveled the farthest of the sisters. She landed on a mountain north of Mallaranny. Whatever rumors reached the people of this town, they had no idea of the wrath about to come down on them.

Badb remained a crow, took flight and circled the high slopes of Mount Nephin. It felt good to return to the place that was a doorway to her world of the last eight thousand years. She had no intention of returning, but it had offered a gate to the sanctuary from the Great Flood those millennia ago.

Before the deluge, her kind often gathered on its slopes and top to celebrate their special days. So long ago, yet it had not changed much. In those days, before the Great Flood, the humans called it Mount of the Nephilim.

Someday soon, relative to thousands of years, the Nephilim would rise and rule the world making human slaves to serve their every whim no matter how cruel or deadly.

She landed on the mountaintop. Looking toward Mallaranny, she saw many lit windows. Regardless of what the people thought they knew, tonight would bring terror never before known to them.

She changed from her crow form to another form, the one that lay buried in the peat at Dugort Bog, trapped by a Watcher's prayer until those fools uncovered her.

She became a nine-foot-tall version of Satan's wife. Her naked flesh dark burning red-colored scaled skin, covered with blisters in various stages of development. She stood on the rear legs of a goat with backward knees and four-toed hooves. Her fingernails were black, thick, slightly curved claws. Her black gums held double rows of pointed needle teeth.

Badb floated in the air then drifted a few feet off the ground toward the town below. She was in no hurry, she looked to enjoy her work.

As she neared the buildings, she heard screams coming from her right. "Good," Badb thought, "Balor has started." Balor's instructions were not to kill too many too quickly. He needed to take his time and breed horror with the remains.

☐

St. Thomas Church

The darkness brought fear to those in St. Thomas church. No one spoke, each locked in their own anticipation of their bones picked clean by the bugs. Twenty minutes went by. The door was not to be opened for any reason by order of Father Bob. The sub-inspector stationed himself at the door to make sure the door did not open.

One man cupped his hands around his eye and pressed against the clearest piece of the stained glass. He could see very little, but he announced no sign of creatures on the ground.

Gladys found a place too high for her to see out on the building's other side. She recruited a tall, willowy boy and soon he announced the same, nothing to be seen or heard.

Two women sat on a pew rearranged to both block the door and allow people to sit and place glasses between their ear and the door. Though the doors were thick, the glasses allowed a listener to pick up the signs of any gnawing, scratching, digging creatures.

The listening station had nothing to report: no sounds

211

of any kind.

Another hour went by. People began showing signs of relief. Hope began rising among those under siege by monsters.

Then, about two hours after dark, the first wisps of vapor filtered through the door's felt weather seal.

At first, it was invisible, odorless gas that squeezed its way through this wool strip on the doorframe's edges.

The church's occupants were almost joyous. They thanked Branna for knowing what to do, and each other for the hard work creating the trench.

Branna, though grateful, kept her exuberance in check. She was thankful the iron circle held the bugs at bay on their side of the gate between worlds, but it was not the nature of man's ancient enemy to give up so easily. She felt, more than knew, another shoe must drop.

Another thirty minutes and children near the door complained of itching and feeling hot. A quick examination revealed no fevers, only a mild rash.

Fifteen minutes later a child in front of the church, halfway between the door and the east wall said, "What's that?"

An older child next to him asked, "What's what?"

"Looks like smoke," answered the first boy.

The older boy studied where the boy pointed. After a second, he saw the lightest of shadows ripple through it.

"Well, it's something alright," the boy said.

The man who kept his eye to the window abandoned his station and stepped over. "What do you see?"

"Look there," both boys said and pointed.

The younger boy squatted and lowered his face to smell the vapor.

The man stared for two or three seconds. He was about to give up when the gas's movement made shadows ripple through it.

The younger boy began to cough. He went from a

tickle in his throat type cough, to a chest wracking, body-shaking cough in a few seconds.

The boy's face reddened. His mother stood him up and forced him to sip water between bouts of hacking.

The rumble of voices concerned about the boy attracted Michael. He observed the scene until he realized people were, in addition to the boy with the coughing fits, looking at something else on the floor.

"What are you looking at?" Michael said to the small group staring at the floor.

"Look there," the man from the window post said, pointing. "It was barely visible when the boys got my attention. Now it's like a thin, nearly colorless cloud. Watch the cloud make shadows as it moves through the light."

Michael watched. His eyes widened when he saw it.

"Father Bob," Michael called, "Branna, please come look at this."

"I see it too," said a woman on the opposite side of the church.

"It's here, and there!" shouted another woman, panic edging into her voice.

A girl standing by the door said, "I see it! I see it! It is turning brown here. Come look."

Some people started toward her, others moved away, toward the altar.

By the time Father Bob and Branna spent two minutes looking at the visibly thickening cloud, almost everyone on the front door side of the church complained of itching and feeling burning on their skin.

The boy who had squatted to smell the mystery gas vomited as blisters rose on his legs and face, the skin most exposed to the gas.

"The pox! The boy has the pox," a woman standing near the boy said, backing away and rubbing her hands subconsciously as if the act would clean the germs from her.

The boy's mother replied, "He does NOT! It's something in the fumes he's allergic to. I've seen the pox. I know its look and smell. This ain't it."

Father Bob made his way to the boy.

Collin woke with a start and sat up in the pew.

"What's that awful stink?" he asked in a hoarse voice.

Collin slept on the pew only a few inches above the top of the vapor cloud, which became more concentrated as time passed. An ammonia-like smell annoyed his nose and woke him. He stood and looked down. His dirty pants covered the tops of his Wellington Boots, so he did not feel any effects, but standing, the odor diminished.

"What's dat cloud thing on the floor? Where's the bugs? How long has it been dark?" he asked no one in particular of those closest to him.

Some people answered his different questions simultaneously, and Collin tried to hear them all.

"Well if there's no bugs, why don't we open the door and let the stink out of here?" he asked.

Gladys answered from the end of the pew, near a window. "Because the fog is coming in the door. If you want to know what's happening, stay awake more often."

The group between them chuckled.

"It's not the pox, not smallpox, anyway," Father Bob said after examining the boy. "Someone bring water and a cloth to wash his face and legs," then added, "and soap if we have it."

Collin stood next to Gladys, watching her stare out the windows.

"The cloud is much thicker out there," she said. "If we open the door we will be the worse for it."

"That smell reminds me of something," Collin said rhetorically.

Gladys continued looking out of the window as she

replied, "It makes me think of lye soap, but stronger. But, I've never known gas to come from lye."

"Well, I never knew of giant bugs, until last night," Collin added.

Gladys cracked a smile.

"I know where I smelled that before," Collin said, remembering. "It was up to the stone circle near Gleann an Ghad."

"I know that tale," Gladys said looking at Collin. "But there's been no stories about the withes for more than a hundred years, at least that I know of."

"Nor I," Collin said, staring down at the ever-so-slowly thickening cloud of ammonia-smelling vapor.

In the next few minutes, more people whose legs were protected by sturdy fabric began to itch and burn.

Collin watched as the epidemic of scratching spread throughout the church. "Folks. Folks, you must get your bodies out of the vapors." Some people listened. Two teenagers leaped up and stood on a pew.

"That's it. Get above it. Stand on the pews," Collin said. Seeing Michael and Branna stare at him. "Get up on the pews now. At least until the ones among you with clear minds figure out a way to get this stuff out of here."

Soon everyone stood or squatted on a pew. A third group began the early stage of itching and irritation. The infected group from before saw their first blisters and felt spots on their skin burn to form new ones.

The boy, though washed with water, which seemed to soothe his skin, burned with fever and coughed fluid from his lungs.

The priest gathered Michael and Branna and asked them to go to the altar, where they would be above the fumes.

"Any ideas?" Father Bob asked, looking at Branna.

She did not answer at first. Instead, she looked between Michael and Father Bob. Finally, she offered, "I have not come up with a solution. To be honest, I was not expecting anything like this. I was so focused on sealing off the bugs, I am taken completely off guard."

"What about you?" the priest said, looking hopefully at Michael.

"If there were a way to draw the fumes out of the church, we might send it out faster than it can enter, but I've no idea how to do such a thing in a building we picked as our fortress because it is so tightly closed," Michael said.

The boy's mother began to wail, lamenting her limp-bodied son.

"I must go comfort her. Keep thinking, there must be something we can do," Father Bob said, downing the two steps that raised the altar.

Before the priest reached the woman, the wailing ended. The mother held her little boy and kissed him while she cried.

"Oh Brian, my boy," she said holding him close to her. "I thought I lost you. It's a miracle, I tell you, a miracle from God."

The little boy, looking much more healthy, pulled back and said, "Mama, I'm hungry. I'm really hungry."

Someone handed the mother a lamb sandwich, and she held it for him to bite.

He took a small mouthful from the bread's crusty edge, barely chewed then swallowed it and reached for more.

"You'd think he was starving," a woman standing on the pew's seat next to the mother and child said.

The boy opened his mouth for another bite, but before his teeth reached the short distance to the sandwich, projectile vomit streamed three feet through the air and struck an old man watching from the pew in front of the boy's. The man stood as quickly as shakiness allowed, brushing the vile vomit from him.

"I'm really hungry, Mama," the boy said as he tried to

216

reach the sandwich and a slight cough produced spittle of blood and bile around his lips.

People moved away, looking for any place they could step to another bench without putting feet on the floor.

The mother pulled him to her and pressed the back of his head to her shoulder.

Father Bob stood on the pew behind, leaning forward.

Again, the boy yawned widely and long. "I'm hungry, ma."

His eyes half closed as his head hit her shoulder. His mouth opened wide as if to yawn and his teeth clamped down on the flesh above her collarbone.

The mother screamed and tried to escape, yet she did not let go or push her son away. She wanted his teeth out of her shoulder meat.

The boy shook his head violently, like a dog with a freshly caught prey.

He pulled away on his own. Looking at people around him, eyes glazed with death, he said with a mouth full of raw meat wet with blood, "I'm hungry. I'm sleepy. I'm hungry."

Branna and Michael watched one another as they thought of ways to help. Every few seconds one would start to offer an idea, then shake their head indicating whatever the idea, it would not work.

The group that became infected after the boy began to cough.

The third group showed blistering.

Father Bob's head snapped to look toward the front of the church. He nearly ran to the front door where the bug listeners kept their ears to the glass pressed against the wood. He looked up, then motioned Michael and Branna to join him.

"What is it," Michael asked. "A solution?"

While they made their way, the priest had the people on

the two back pews double up with others. With the two pews free of occupants, he began pulling to work one toward the front door.

Michael arrived, took the other end of the heavy wooden pew, and soon, they had it placed across the front door.

The priest motioned for Michael and Branna to climb onto the solid bench.

"Are you expecting a magical battering ram?" Michael questioned.

"Look up," the priest said.

Michael and Branna saw the opening to a small belfry rising eight feet higher than the peaked ceiling.

It dawned on Michael before Branna.

"It's closed. Otherwise, the bugs would have come through last night," Michael said.

"But it won't be hard to open, if we can reach it," the priest replied. "It was sealed before I arrived here," Father Bob said excitedly. "The bell cracked. The congregation continued to use it until it sounded like a call to hell rather than to church. They could not afford a new one, so they sold it for the bronze then sealed the belfry to keep the cold out."

"Do you know how it is sealed?" Michael asked.

"I looked at it when I went up to inspect the roof for damaged shingles. It's a cross-hatching of four iron bars and a layer of stucco walling above and another layer of plaster below."

"Sounds easy enough to tear out," Michael said, "if we have a man the thickness and length of an oar."

"The iron bars most likely kept the bugs from trying hard to get in," Branna observed.

Michael looked at the people in the church, searching for a person who might fit and still be able to work in the confined space.

"There are some recruits," he said, pointing to the two

teenagers who were first to step up on a pew, "but how do we get someone high enough and stable enough to hammer through?"

"They are not going anywhere for a while. We need to think how someone will be able to stand and work in the space on something stable enough to keep them steady," Michael said. Michael stooped to the floor, studying the pews from underneath.

Branna studied the items in the church, looking for anything to fit the requirements. "The men have tools. We can use those to take something apart to make it small enough to fit up the opening, we could…"

Michael interrupted, "Could remove the backs from the pews, turn the bench part upside down and use the leg panels as steps on a makeshift ladder," he said, looking at the other two.

"Brilliant!" Father Bob said, looking at the construction of the closest pew, making the people standing on it wonder if they were about to be evicted.

The priest used his belt to measure places on the pew.

"It's going to be harder than we thought," Father Bob said. "After removing the back, we will need to split the seat lengthwise along with the legs." Father Bob called the two boys chosen for the task. "Thomas, Stephen, over here, please!"

The boys looked at the priest as if they were caught masturbating in church. "Us?" Tom replied, looking as if he knew trouble was on its way.

"Yes, come here. But first, find Mike Brennan. Do you know him?" Father Bob shouted back.

By now, the people between the priest and the boys looked back and forth.

"Yes, Father, he's near the altar. I'll get him," said Stephen. "But what about the fog?"

"Keep your head high and move fast as you can," the priest replied.

By the time Mike Brennan arrived, the coughing among the people trapped in the church had worsened .

☐

Macha

Macha watched as a nearly invisible plague flowed toward the doors of The Church of Mary Immaculate. She waited for a few minutes hoping someone would stray through the town, but there was no death to be had except in the church.

Older than St. Thomas in Dugort, Mary Immaculate was solid as a fortress. The people inside sang, but with less hope than the night before.

Macha wished she had a few bugs just to tease them.

The shallow sea of plague surrounded the church, seeking any entry, no matter how small.

The entrance was old and well used with a double door. Behind the church, another door for the people who cleaned and a small office had a one-sixteenth-inch crack between the bottom of the door and the threshold. Someone made a temporary repair by tacking a sliver of wood to the transom to reduce the draft in winter.

The fog entered Mary Immaculate much faster than it had St. Thomas. The people noticed it almost immediately as it passed between the unsealed cracks of the church doors.

In the office, which the priest locked earlier to keep parishioners from snooping in his files, no one noticed it flowing beneath the door and filling the room three feet deep. As more gas entered the room, it no longer gained height but its potency doubled, then tripled as time passed.

The people trapped inside instinctively sought to avoid the drifting banks of gas. They climbed on pews, the altar, the organ, anything that would keep their feet out of the swirling cloud.

The top of the cloud leveled near the top of the pews' seats. After a few minutes, people began to show relief. But something changed within the cloud.

Its color became darker, almost a charcoal-colored taupe. It stopped rolling along the floor. Fear was born from seeing the top of the almost motionless cloud below their feet.

No one spoke. Everyone felt it.

A young woman, Margaret McGraw, coughed.

The first and only sound made in minutes.

The gas at the front edge of the cougher's feet issued forth a tendril. It licked the pew then turned toward her feet. Like a crippled, wispy blind snake, the tendril's tip felt around. It seemed difficult for the tendril to make any further progress. It kept reaching out and touching the area it had already searched.

Each repetition it touched near the woman's shoes. She held her hand over her mouth to keep from screaming. She tried to repress a cough. She failed. A triple cough issued forth.

The tendril withdrew from the bench to be replaced instantly with one closer to the woman's shoes. It moved faster, with more assurance. It touched the toe of her right shoe.

There was no room to move on the pew bench. The

other occupants of the oak pew refused to yield their spaces.

It had been donated in memory of Edith McGraw, who died twenty years ago. That had been her and her family's pew. Every Sunday, without fail, the three priests who served the church watched her children grow up, her husbands die, and her age until she died of a disease, The Cough, that had not occurred since Edith's childhood.

Out of respect, Margaret McGraw replaced her mother as the lone occupant of the pew every Sunday.

Edith would roll over in her grave if she knew people had their dirty shoes on her pew.

"Move over," Ms. McGraw ordered, "This is the McGraw family pew, and I'll not allow anyone to rob me of what is mine."

"You have your place. Don't be greedy," a woman holding a baby said.

Everyone watched the two women as the tendril, unfelt by Margaret, touched then reached and wrapped itself around Margaret's ankle. Margaret's ankle itched. Before she could reach to scratch it, the ankle burned.

As others noticed, they relinquished their claim to the space they fought for moments before.

Margaret's face formed sweat drops as a rapidly rising fever circulated through her body. A spasm wracked her chest. She coughed uncontrollably. Spittle flew all around her shaking head.

Someone on the pew behind Margaret coughed. It was the first, almost dainty, tickle of a throat cough Margaret issued only minutes before.

The tendril unwound and withdrew.

Someone on the pew behind screamed as it repeated its search and destroy mission.

Macha stood very close to the church doors. She listened intently. She knew the coughing death would spread quickly now and soon the church would be filled with corpses that could not be buried or even touched for days.

☐

St. Thomas Church

Mike, working with shovels, axes and picks brought to the church by people as weapons, finished the tasks. It had taken more than twice as long as it would have with his own tools. But it was done.

It took longer still because the pew's legs, built to withstand weight from above, would not hold at all against force applied from their sides. They would not hold as ladder steps. Mike used everything in the church to bind the legs to support cross beams formed from the unused portion of the bench: the bell rope, men's belts, boot laces, and braided rope the women made from fabric. It looked like the worse piece of carpentry Mike ever saw, but it would hold.

The makeshift ladder was placed on a normal, unmodified pew and lifted so its end reached into the belfry shaft.

It looked a little short. Michael gave Thomas a half-burned candle and waxed it to a lady's donated straw hat.

225

Thomas carried a chisel and hammer in his belt. They sent him up the not so well-made ladder. The second boy followed and stopped halfway so he could pass tools up to Thomas.

The hammering lasted a full five minutes. Several times, for lack of light, the hammer's blow missed the head of the chisel and struck Thomas' hand. Several profanities blurted out followed by, "Oh, sorry Father. Won't happen again." Until it happened again.

"I can see the cross bars!" the boy yelled down.

Michael, Branna and Father Bob cheered lowly.

"The stucco is more difficult," the boy said, his breath heavy.

"Have you a hole in the stucco?" Father Bob asked.

"A small one," came the response.

"How large a hole, Thomas?" Father Bob became more anxious as nearly one in three people were coughing or itching.

"I'm through two of the cross-bar sections," Thomas answered, still hammering.

"Keep at it until you clear one more section," the priest said. He turned to Michael and Branna, "Would you mind gathering as many pieces of the wood remaining from the destruction of the pew?"

They nodded, and the boot-clad priest walked through the cloud toward Mike Brennan, asked him to gather two men with axes and break the pew's back for firewood.

When Thomas completed stacking wooden strips from the broken pew through the hole in the once sealed belfry, he stuffed in some wadded paper torn from hymnals and backed down the thrown-together ladder.

The men pulled the ladder from the belfry chimney-like space.

Branna handed pieces of wood to Michael as he built what looked like a primitive pyramid shaped log cabin in the baptismal pedestal bowl brought from the altar area.

Father Bob lit the tied fabric around the long section of broken wood Mike Brennan stripped off the pew's back panel. He raised it to the hole inside the belfry and watched the fire placed on the crossbars at the belfry's top grow into a fire that would continue with no more help.

After he backed out with the strip of wood, he lit the papers inside the much larger pyramid shaped wood in the baptismal bowl.

As hoped, the smoke from the lower fire was slowly drawn up the belfry shaft. As the two fires gained strength and heat, the draft up the belfry became more obvious.

Branna said, "We better move away. This might actually work."

The three of them, so far protected by the knee-high Wellington boots they wore, could not afford to be in the area as the baptismal fire was fed more and more wood until it blazed.

The draught strengthened.

Michael felt the air passing him as it rose into the belfry.

"It's working!" Father Bob said excitedly.

Michael looked harder and saw the nearly invisible vapor sucked toward the belfry fire, then up into it and finally, with color changed, the draught pulled a steady stream of it out the top of the Belfry.

As the first of the gaseous cloud moved next to the baptismal fire, it flared on its way up and outside. These continual flarings made the fire hotter. The draught became stronger, pulling in more vapor. A self-feeding cycle was born. At one point the fire was so hot, the people feeding it wood from pews could not reach it because of the heat.

Father Bob began moving through the church, spreading the good news.

There was joy among the people as they listened to their priest and looked to see the vapor pulled slowly toward the door like an outgoing tide.

There was sorrow among the people. Many were in various stages of the plague brought by the fog. Many were dead, their loved ones too tired or frightened to lament loudly. Their grief came as soft sobs .

Before morning, the main area of the church appeared free of the plague-carrying fog. The thin streams of fog entering through the door's weather stripping was immediately pulled toward the fire, then out the top of the belfry.

As the sun rose in the sky, the window watchers announced the fog was burning off. When Michael and Branna looked out, they saw the fog was literally flaring in bursts of flames. Just as in the fire, as the tendrils rose and thinned, they flared and were gone. Within another hour, the fog was gone.

Father Bob opened the front door and stepped out.

Looking at the steps and ground around him, he was relieved to confirm no poison fog remained.

Then, looking up to see the town, the priest screamed and recoiled a step. "God have mercy upon us."

At Father Bob's voice, Michael, standing in the doorway, squeezed Branna's hand. They both recoiled and gasped but issued not a sound. Those who could see outside made every sound from whimpers to screams to curses.

Michael squeezed Branna's hand and looked at her. The silver that streaked her hair nearly shone with its own light. Her emerald eyes blazed like green fire. Her expression was fixed with determination. Yet terror caused her body to quake. A tear she could not hold back rolled down her cheek. Her mouth was tight in decision.

In the church's morning shadow, where the infectious fog lingered, stood the Morrigan, the Great Queen, in her unholy trinity.

On the left end of the trio, floating above the ground,

in her terrifying ghostly form, Nemain laughed loud enough everyone covered their ears. Then, in a shrill explosion, said, "Lúb do ghlúine!"

Collin, Gladys and two other old people who understood the old language went to their knees.

"Down," Collin said loudly, "She said, 'Bend your knee.'"

Everyone went down with the exceptions of Father Bob, Michael, and Branna.

Nemain's eyes, a putrid yellow color, glowed brightly as she focused on the priest. Her gossamer body shot forward so fast it appeared as if she vanished and reappeared in front of the priest at the same instant.

She towered over him, her horrid face looking down upon him. "Féach ar do banríon," she commanded.

Father Bob understood a little of the old Gaelic, enough to know she told him to look at her. He did not move.

"Féach ar do banríon!" she roared in a voice deep enough he could feel the vibrations of her voice move through his body.

Never so afraid in his life, he refused to bow to Lucifer or one of his demons. Even if it cost him his life.

But it did not cost him his life.

Thomas, the boy who lit the fire in the belfry, self-combusted. From head to foot, his body burst into a white-hot holocaust.

The priest heard the screams coming from the church. "What happened?" he asked without moving.

Michael replied, "The boy, Thomas, just burst into flames!"

Terrified, not for his own life now, he knew the corruption of life commanding him would kill them one at a time unless he did as the beast ordered. Father Bob said a silent prayer, forgive me Lord, then knelt.

The church's shadow shortened as the sun continued

to climb. As sunlight struck the fog around the Morrigan, the cloud-like gas sparked continuously until it burned itself away.

This time Nemain, a smug smile contorting her hideous face, drifted toward Michael and Branna. Her sick eyes drooled an infectious-looking viscous liquid. She stopped in front of Michael and diminished her size until her face was only a foot above him.

"Lúb do ghlúine." This time in a voice almost bored, no longer enjoying toying with these pitiful creatures.

Michael's reason for refusing to kneel was simple, at least to his thinking. Branna had not knelt. If he had to defend Branna, he could not do it from his knees. If Branna had a reason not to kneel, then his dropping to his knees would demonstrate a lack of faith in her reason. He would not kneel. Then again, he had not counted on his defiance causing innocent people to be killed.

"Branna," Michael asked softly, "What should I do?"

"Stand your ground," she replied in a steady voice.

Trusting Branna, Michael did not move.

The second boy recruited to help with the fires self-combusted, causing screams and lamentations from people in the church.

"For Christ sakes, kneel. Kneel!" someone inside yelled.

"Steady," Branna instructed.

Macha, dressed as a nine foot tall, dried-skin mummified queen, started to move forward.

The middle abomination stopped her. She stood in the form of the creature that murdered Healy and Lewis at the peat bog. Nine feet tall, naked and well-muscled, she could have stepped from a medieval painting of the Devil himself. Her dark-red body, spotted here and there with blackthorns like sharp, hard moles, she took a stride with legs shaped like the rear legs of a goat, but much bigger, much bigger. Her four-toed hoof landed. Then one more

230

step and a twenty-foot leap to land in front of Branna.

Her odor was of sulfur and burnt pork.

Michael did not know whether to let go or continue to hold her hand.

She bent down so her black horned, disproportioned head hovered inches above Branna's forehead. The devil raised her hand so a black clawed finger could point to Branna's face.

"Gan leanbh ag imirt níos mó," Badb said, revealing a black forked tongue heavy with mucous.

"I am not playing," Branna answered.

"Leath cine, níl tú láidir go leor ag leath," spoke Satan's half-human daughter.

Branna looked into Badb's huge snake-like eyes. "I am strong enough to send you back to hell. Michael, stand behind me please, in the doorway," Branna said. Then, looking past the horror in front of her, she saw the church's shadow had shortened until the two other aspects of the Morrigan had taken an involuntary step forward.

Badb knew when and why Macha and Nemain stepped forward. Seeing Branna look beyond her naturally intimidating face made her aware of the changeling's intentions.

"Ullmhaigh le bás, beith," whispered the spawn of evil as she pulled her hands back, preparing to strike.

"I am prepared to die, Badb, but it won't be today, and…" she said softly. She brought her hands to clasp at a slightly off angle.

The onyx ring on her right hand's index finger hovered slightly above the jasper ring on the left hand's forefinger. The quartz ring on her right hand's middle finger hovered a similar distance over the ring worn on the left's middle finger.

As Badb brought her hands together to meet and smash through Branna's head, the changeling allowed the rings to touch.

Nothing happened.

Until Badb's blow came within six inches of Branna's head. The hands slamming the intended target struck an immovable, invisible field with such force as to bounce away with the same energy applied to the blow, causing Badb to jerk backward.

"...I'm not the bitch. You are," Branna finished her comment.

Speaking in Gaelic, Badb said, anger lacing her voice, "That puny spell will not last long, Changeling."

"Long enough," Branna replied. "Father Bob," she called. "No one move. Pray for calm and peace. This will soon be over." Then glancing behind her, Branna instructed, "Michael, ask the people to face the altar and pray for strength and peace. Tell them no one else will die here. Then close the door."

Michael and the priest did as instructed.

Turning back to stare into the snake eyes before her, Branna smiled then said, "I believe the sun is warming you now. How long do you want to waste your energy waiting?"

Badb's eyes showed no fear; they never had, they never could. But at the same time, Branna saw her deep in thought.

The Morrigan knew what Branna knew: the longer they stood in the sun, their power drained unless a source replaced it. The people in the church was the major source this morning and now, they no longer offered their fear to the Morrigan.

"As you know, half-breed, this is not the end. You will all die soon enough," the monster said, as she looked at Branna's now fearless face.

When Branna did not reply even with a facial expression, Badb turned and walked back to join her sisters. They merged together in a show of light, and a huge crow flew toward the mountain caves, cawing loudly as it raced to darkness.

Father Bob came to the front door of the church. It troubled him Branna possessed the power to defend the people inside the church the entire time but allowed those two boys to die because he and Michael defied the Morrigan's order to kneel.

"Branna," Father Bob began, "Why did you not create the shield earlier? You could have saved those two boys."

"She saved everyone else," Michael said defensively, knowing Branna must have a reason for waiting before creating the barrier.

"It's okay, Michael," Branna said. Turning to Father Bob, she said, "I didn't have the power. I was pulling it into me as fast as I could. Remember, the power flows through the mountain's quartzite. Putting the iron trench around the tomb disturbed its natural flow. I'm a novice at this. I can't just summon it to fill me up in an instant. I began tapping into the flow the second we saw those three in the yard."

"I am not criticizing," the priest tempered his previous comment. "I know you saved us, and we all thank you for that."

Father Bob glanced at Michael. He knew how the inspector felt about Branna and did not want to trigger his defense of her. Looking back at Branna he said, "Perhaps, in these circumstances, you should do what you need to do to gather as much energy as you can then stay fully charged until you need it."

"I wish I could, Father Bob. But it doesn't work like that; the energy is not compatible with the human body's own natural energies. Storing it in the body for any length of time deteriorates bodily functions, sickening them, including the mind," Branna explained. "Again, I'm very new to this and don't yet know the maximum amount of the power I can acquire nor how long I can hold it without harming myself."

Father Bob thought about the yin and yang of Branna's situation. He concluded she had done exactly the right thing for the moment. "I am sorry," the priest said, "You may be new to it, but I do not have the slightest notion of what you can do or how it works. I'll be more patient in the future."

Branna said, "You must know, I never intended anyone to die. It hurts my heart to know those boys died because I could not gather energy any faster, but if I executed the spell any faster, it might have failed and the energy wasted."

They opened the door to the church and counted the dead and dying.

Their eyes were dark hollows, reddened and dry from endless tears. Out of nearly seventy people who entered the church before sundown yesterday, thirty-six were dead, another twenty-six would die. The eight survivors, in addition to Father Bob, Branna and Michael, had something in common: they all wore knee-high Wellington boots.

Some had burns and blisters. They would live but bear scars, physical and emotional, for the rest of their time.

☐

234

Horror at Cashel

"Be careful, Michael," Branna smiled as Michael cranked his motorcycle to life. She wanted to add, 'I love you,' but knew it was wrong to further entangle herself with the man she loved in such unsure circumstances. Either of them could be dead by nightfall.

Michael waved, blew her a kiss and returned her smile. The petrol-driven engine ran more loudly and the sub inspector was off to Cashel to count their dead, then to Keel.

"How long will he be gone?" Father Bob asked.

"Michael said he should be back within three hours at the most," she answered.

"We don't have the people or the energy to move, let alone bury, the bodies," Father Bob spoke sadly. "Everyone on the island will be dead after they come back tonight. What do you think about evacuating the island?" he asked.

"They won't be back," Branna replied. "There aren't enough people here now generate enough fear and death for them to feed. It would be a net energy loss."

She looked at Father Bob for reaction.

"Are you sure?" the priest double checked.

"The only thing they want here now is me," Branna

said, looking past Father Bob toward the sea.

"You are saying it is safe to stay, but convincing the survivors, scant number they are, may not be possible. Besides, they have lost so much, they might see no reason to stay." There were tears welling in the exhausted priest's eyes.

"I must ask a favor of you," Branna began. "I must return to the cave on Slievemore and go again to my mother for answers. Is there anyone that can take me?"

"I will grab some food, water and blankets and row you there. Once you go inside, I'll eat and try to sleep until you return. If I am not there when you come back to us, it means I have run out of food and will return shortly, or, less desirable, the Morrigan has eaten me and destroyed the boat," sighed the priest.

Branna said, "We have no time. I will gather the supplies you need and tell Gladys and Collin the plan so they can tell Michael when he finishes his inspection of the other towns," Branna said, taking the first step toward the church.

Father Bob went off to prepare a boat. As he readied the whaling boat to be pushed into the sea, he saw the three of them lugging bundled and filled blankets toward him.

Branna entered the boat silently. Gladys and Collin helped push the boat fully into the water and the priest climbed in and took the rowing seat.

Too weary to speak, Father Bob rowed and replayed the night's events. Branna sat still as a statue, deep in thought. The only sounds were wind, gulls and oar strokes splashing into water.

The spell of silence broke when the priest called to Branna, "Drop the anchor."

Atop the terrace on the mountain's side, they stood together, examining what they could not see in the cave's dark recesses.

Even though she knew what to expect, the harrowing experience to come remained most unpleasant. There was no choice, she must go.

She turned to Father Bob and gave him a gentle hug. "You are a good man, Father."

"And you a good woman, Branna Butler. I just hope you are as good a Sidhe as you are a human," the priest said. "I can make the food and water last for two days." Father Bob added, "If encounter any demons, please persuade them not to come out of this cave."

Branna laughed, faced the cavern's entrance then entered.

Father Bob stood at the entrance, watching Branna fade in the darkness as she moved deeper into what appeared a maw.

A waft of foul air pumped from the mouth of the cave, causing Father Bob to move away.

"You are one of the bravest people I have ever known, Branna Butler. May God be with you," he said, then began unpacking supplies for the vigil.

A despairing feeling descended on Michael Doyle as his Triumph motor bike stopped in the center of Cashel. There was no movement, no sound, not even birds. Usually a dog or cat might be visible moving through alleys, but today the town seemed empty of all life.

Dismounting, he braced himself and walked toward the church. The door was barred from the inside.

"A good sign," he lied to himself.

Michael knocked, then called inside, "This is Inspector Michael Doyle of the RIC. Please let me in."

No sounds.

Michael tried the door again, applying more force. The door did not relent. Michael walked around the church hoping he would not be forced to destroy a stained-glass window. He found the door to the church office behind the building. It was locked with an ancient iron bolt latch. It took him three times to kick in the door.

An odor most foul struck him as he crossed the threshold.

He held a handkerchief on his nose and called, "Is anyone here? This is Inspector Doyle of the RIC."

When the reply he no longer expected failed to sound, Michael moved through the office to the door to the main church. It was not locked.

Hand on the door handle, Michael steeled himself for what he knew waited behind it.

He opened the door.

Before him, like a painting of hell, was the grisliest sight he had ever seen, perhaps any man ever witnessed. It was unimaginable horror.

A room was filled with more than one hundred and fifty people slumped, lay, knelt, or leaned against whatever support was nearest them when they collapsed. Their bodies were blue from lack of oxygen. Some were covered with blisters, which had exploded, the crater left behind in the flesh caked with a thick layering of infected puss. Here and there, corpses had chunks of flesh torn from their bodies. The wounds reminded him of bite marks in raw meat.

Some died with eyes open, begging relief from pain, fear and loss. Some died covering their children in futile protection. Other bodies littered the altar, implying a grotesque Satan's Mass.

Too horrified to think, or move, Michael closed his eyes and turned his head toward heaven. The shaken inspector offered a prayer for the souls of the people of Cashel who fared far worse than those in Dugort.

Prayer, finished, offered him some comfort. He opened his eyes and staggered two steps toward the office door. A fresh terror filled the cathedral ceiling.

A dozen or so dog-sized, gargoyle-like beasts clung to

beams, ceiling or hovered. Their bodies faded from solid form to ghostly to invisible. A few stared at him with large, opaque eyes sunk deep into reptilian skulls. Most ignored him, seeing no threat. Many held chunks of raw flesh to their mouths, waiting to finish chewing the current morsel.

Man was not made to endure such sights.

Michael stepped backwards slowly and passed through the office door. He quietly closed it then walked outside.

He leaned forward and emptied his stomach of its contents. After the nausea allowed him to walk, he moved to a tree and sat in the shade, hoping for some sort of recovery.

The images of the church interior flashed one after the other in his mind. He could not think. His mission forgotten, he sat on the ground, elbows resting on pulled up knees, his head lowered heavy into his hands.

He stayed that way, not even aware of the passage of time, reliving the horror of all the events on Achill Island since his arrival. His mind developed its own agenda: stop projecting the terror, move away from it, bury it, bury it deep.

Michael was so glad Branna did not witness this. He was glad no one else came upon it. Those thoughts led to Branna. He wondered if she was safe. He fell into obsessing about her safety, envisioned all manner of the monsters manifested in the last two days. He decided to abandon the rest of his duty and return to the current ruins that was Dugort.

He walked slowly, trance-like, to his motor bike, drank some water and mounted, the entire time averting his eyes from the church.

He drove to the ironmonger shop where he purchased fuel before and filled the tank on his Triumph and the two jugs. He drank more water, filled his canteen and looked across the way at Lynott's Pub. He thought about going there for a shot or two of Irish whisky but remembered

239

what he saw there on his last visit.

Michael planned to return to Dugort and check on Branna but duty kicked in and he found himself heading east to cross Achill Sound and ride to Westport. His top commander, Commissioner Colonel Milling, needed to know with no uncertainty the events on Achill Island were not the result of the United Irishmen's League, unless they were in league with the devil.

☐

The Devastation of Mallaranny

Driving eastward, Michael saw several columns of smoke rising into the otherwise perfect sky. Reasoning the smoke most probably originated in Mallaranny, he headed toward the new menace.

As he approached the town, Michael saw small clusters of people ambling away from the town. He approached, drove past some and shut down the bike ahead of a group of three men. He removed his goggles and leather cap before approaching them.

They shuffled forward, heads down, victims of atrocities. Ashamed of fellow men and themselves. Michael tried to speak with them. They ignored him, as their feet mindlessly moved toward Westport.

"They won't talk to you," a voice said from behind the men.

Michael looked to see an old one-legged man using a crutch to move with the other refugees. He wore a tweed newsboy hat which, by its condition, may have been with him fifty years ago when he was a boy.

Michael moved to the man in the hat, who reminded him a bit of Collin.

"What happened?" Michael asked.

The man stopped just in front of Michael. He studied Michael then replied, "He wants to know what happened," he asked rhetorically. "The end of the bloody world, that's what happened."

Michael thought about moving on to find someone else to interview, knowing this man of the old Irish ways might tie him up an hour while he used many more times the words necessary to convey the answer.

Before Michael made up his mind, the old man asked, "Do you know what is said about the terrors on Achill Island?"

"Yes," Michael replied.

"Do you believe them?" the one-legged man asked.

"Yes," Michael responded.

"Then, since that motored bicycle tells me you are a man in a great hurry, I'll tell you straight out," the man under the weather-beaten cap said. "What happened is the old gods are here again. The Morrigan herself descended on Mallaranny with an army of little ghosts as thick as flies over a three-day-dead sheep. They swarmed around her, hundreds of them, doing her bidding."

The man paused to make sure his audience really listened.

Michael, thinking about the ghost-like creatures in the church asked, "How big were the ghosts?"

"How big were the ghosts, he wants to know?" the man beneath the tweed cap offered. "As if it made a difference. They were not actually ghosts, they were Caorthannach, man. Fire spitting air-demons. They hate us so much they stayed away for two thousand years. The Morrigan called them back and they came with a vengeance," the old man said.

Now knowing the cast of characters, Michael inquired,

"What did the Morrigan and the air-demons do?"

"Jesus, Mary and Joseph! I hate to tell it. It is sickening," the man said sincerely.

"Please tell me, I am a RIC inspector on my way to Mallaranny. I need to know," Michael revealed.

"Well, alright then." The man looked up at Michael as he pulled a small bottle of clear liquid out of a back pocket, took a swallow and said, "Alright then, if you have a need to know then tis my duty to tell it.

"In the beginning they went from house to house. Waking people into an awful fright. Then the Morrigan's booming voice boomed so everyone heard. She told everyone to assemble in the town center. The air-demons were everywhere. If people didn't do what they were told, they might bite out a piece of arm or leg. If they still didn't move toward the Morrigan, the little bastards set the house on fire. If the people ran outside and stayed or tried to go somewhere else, they set them on fire."

Michael shook his head at the scene the man painted.

"I took my crutch up right away because I knew who they were and I knew who it was that called us. By the time I reached the town center, most of the townsfolk were circled around the square. I saw the glow of fires outside of town and people continued to walk in.

"She announced who she was," he said, talking fast now.

"'I am the Morrigan, The Great Queen come to take back my home. Any who disobey will meet a pitiful death, no exceptions.' Then she looked around and said, 'You will perform a ritual to swear your fealty to me, your queen and god.'"

The old man paused and said, "Some in the crowd made the sign of the cross. Before they finished the movement, they burst into white-hot flame. In less than a minute, ashes was all that was left of them."

Michael saw a tear running down his cheek.

The man said, "So, we held her ritual, a sacrifice to her power. When a demon touched a man or woman's shoulder, they were to step forward and form a ring around the Morrigan, dressed for battle; she directed them to remove their clothes and prostrate themselves before her. Them that didn't suffered the same as the ones before. A white-hot fire that left a little bit of ashes on the ground. Others were called to replace them.

"When the dozen folks were on the ground, she removed her clothing. Now I know the Morrigan is a woman, but I swear, she had a man's part, it was proportionate to her being nine feet tall, if you can picture it. The people in the circle kept their eyes to the ground so they didn't see it.

"Anyway, she made them stand and bend over facing away from the circle. One by one, man or woman, she buggered them. They screamed for mercy. Begged her to stop, but it made no difference. She went from one to the next with that huge thing between her legs and made them suffer.

"The odd thing about it was, she didn't enjoy it. She seemed like she just wanted us to know she could do it.

"After she completed the circle she told them to stand and dress. Then she told them to leave Mallaranny and where to go. She told them they were to spread the word that the Morrigan had returned and would soon visit the town where they were sent to reclaim her land and the people's souls. Only praying to her could save their lives and their souls.

"She did three more circles of buggering and sent each circle's members to a different town. After they were gone, she told the remaining people to leave Mallaranny and become her apostles; to travel wide and far and tell what they saw that night.

"Then, just to show us, I guess, she made all the

244

buildings around the town center burst into flame with explosions of fire that blasted them apart.

"So here I am, a one-legged apostle heading to Westport to spread the gospel of the unholy trinity," he said, then took another swallow.

Other small groups had passed him and the man with the crutch as the old man relayed the story. Michael had seen enough on Achill not to doubt a word of the story. In fact, the story seemed like something the Morrigan would do to instill hate and fear.

"Has anyone disobeyed her?" Michael asked.

"Oh, after her majesty left, a few thought they would go somewhere else. There was no point in staying in Mallaranny. Those that started walking in a direction other than they were told screamed as an air-demon materialized and took a bite of them. If that didn't put them back on track, they just exploded into a standing pillar of fire. It didn't take long for us to figure out her air-demons were among us, watching."

"Thank you," was all he said and handed the man a half-crown coin. "For your new life," Michael offered and returned to his motorcycle.

Mallaranny town looked like a battlefield. It was empty of people and there were places that might have been the ashes of the spontaneous combustion victims.

Michael had no idea what he could do about any of this.

With shell-shocked people streaming into Westport, telling the same story, Colonel Milling could not possibly deny the supernatural nature of the troubles.

He started his bike and headed toward Dugort and Branna.

The scene in Dugort was worse than when Michael left, if that was possible. The survivors were pulling the bodies from St. Thomas Church into the yard and piling them around a wooden cross constructed and erected this morning.

The people intended to burn the bodies and then leave Dugort to the demons, another abandoned village.

Michael, furious again to discover Branna again went to the cave on Slievemore, took a boat and rowed himself.

Back to the Sidhe

Branna fell on the cave's slimy floor. This time the fall did not take so long. Her eyes opened to soft, diffused light. She lay on the canopied bed in her suite in her mother's castle. She heard the same deep bass drums tattooing a signal of purpose.

As she rose from the bed, she noticed the room had a window not present during her first visit. She walked to it and looked out. The spectacular view was utopian: low rolling fields of flowers and forest mixed with orchards, and enormous fountained gardens. Some distance beyond rose the most fantastical structure she ever saw.

It rose high into the sky, impossible to tell how high, dwarfing anything manmade. Though the sun was high in the sky and shining brightly, the building provided its own illumination, disallowing shadows around it.

She studied it intently, and realized it closely resembled a cathedral but at the same time more streamlined, more rounded, simpler in design. Mainly made of large polished quartz bricks, the tower was adorned with rings of silver, gold, emeralds, ruby and other gems.

Suddenly, Branna recognized its similarity of two structures on Earth. The lower portion an enormous cathedral, while the high tower seemed a much taller and much more elegant version of the Eiffel Tower in Paris.

Oonaugh's voice spoke softly to Branna's mind, "We are waiting in the temple."

"The building I see from my window?" Branna asked.

"Yes. We are waiting," Oonaugh repeated.

Branna looked again at the great distance to be traversed. "How will I get there?" she asked.

"Walk," Oonaugh replied.

"That will take a very long time," Branna answered as if talking to herself.

"It will take as long as you want it to take," Oonaugh quipped.

Branna wore her Sidhe fashioned silver overalls and sandals.

After walking through the first half-mile of gardens, Branna looked back to get a view of the castle from a different angle. There was nothing there.

As she hiked quickly through more gardens, orchards and fields, beautiful unknown plants, fluttering insects and small animals distracted her. When she reached the polished quartz temple, she saw the light refractions in it. It was like a giant crystal ball, allowing the observer to see within but not allowing the viewer to know what they saw.

Branna always preferred to recognize what she saw. She walked to within a foot of the wall and leaned to study the images more closely. She could see small flecks, tiny imperfections inside the bricks of quartz. One in particular drew closer examination.

The mind tries to make sense of light passing through the eye to the brain. In some cases, the brain might think it sees a misshapen face in a spot on a tile floor or finding the partial image of a lion hidden in the edge of a wheat field.

Branna, aware of this trick of light and dark spaces, tried to keep her brain from forming its own image of the spot at which she looked. She stared patiently at the unusual spot and thought about trying to find an entry into the temple. After all, they were waiting on her.

That was when the spot moved. She was sure of it. She still had no idea what she studied, but it had not been a trick of the eye, it had moved.

"Do you know what it is?" Oonaugh asked, startling Branna.

"You have to stop sneaking up on me," Branna said.

Oonaugh smiled, "It is not that I mean to, but rather you are always so intensely focused on what you are doing you don't see anything else. As you are learning, that is a two-edged sword. Now come with me."

A doorway had appeared where none existed a moment before, and Branna followed her mother into the enormous temple filled with thousands of Sidhe sitting on bleachers circling an arena. Branna had no idea how many Sidhes occupied the building. The bleachers rose one behind the other until the occupants in the top rows were so small as to be nearly invisible.

Then again, Branna thought, perhaps they were invisible.

The room provided not the slightest sound. All Branna heard was her own breathing.

The tens of thousands of Sidhe on the bleachers meditated. There was never a motion in the rows of occupants. Branna studied the closest Sidhe. They appeared in a deep trance. She tried but did not see one breathing.

Oonaugh took Branna's hand and led her into the circular arena. The floor was an enormous single slab, a single piece of quartz polished to look like clear glass. The flat, empty quartz floor appeared larger by the absence of any kind of furnishings or decorations. It amplified and made the sound of Branna's shoes echo as she walked.

But she only heard one pair of feet. Looking over, her

mother drifted an inch off the floor.

"Will I ever be able to do that?" Branna asked.

"Sssssssh," Oonaugh answered, her finger to her lips. "This is a sacred ritual."

The arena's center had been marked with an etched three-foot diameter circle.

Oonaugh nudged Branna to the center of the etched circle.

Every hair on Branna's body stood straight, repelled by her skin and her other hairs. Branna's nerves jittered and tingled. She felt electricity run up and down her spine. Branna felt like living things moved all about inside her. Goosebumps covered her body. This was not pleasant, she decided.

"You will be there only a moment, dear," her mother offered caringly. "Now look straight above you."

Branna looked up. Directly overhead was the apex of the incredibly tall tower she saw from the window in her room. The bottom was a hollowed opened circle. Larger than the arena, it nearly covered the entire building. Branna could not see to its top. She did see various colors of electrical flashes flickering inside the tower's crystal walls. When one sparked and flashed, it reached out and touched the end of another bolt's tip.

It was beautiful but frightening.

From somewhere came the sounds of the same orchestra as the night of the feast on her first visit. The symphony they played was different from the first night when Branna became part of the light, but no less mesmerizing.

Oonaugh said, "Do not move. I will be back in a moment."

The Sidhe queen walked across the arena and sat in a space on a front-row bench.

Beneath the music, a low hum began softly. Branna heard the hum below the music. The sounds were not unpleasant. Branna continued staring up into the hollow tower.

The music's volume decreased. As the hum's decibel level increased, so did the activity of the lightning bursts in the tower's walls as did the intensity of the feeling of something moving through Branna.

The hum provided a constantly increasing volume. Branna, arms dangling, staring up at the non-stop larger and longer bolts of electricity, felt her body go rigid. Her back arched, her arms, fingers, legs, and neck straightened and her joints locked.

She possessed no control of her body, none.

Now, the hum at full volume began to rise in tone. As the hum rose above the deep bass, so did Branna's body begin to rise from the floor. Still locked and looking up, Branna watched the top of the tower grow larger. That was the only indication she rose through the air.

The humming's pitch grew higher. Branna's ascent accelerated.

Her ears popped several times.

The wall around her was alive with energy.

Her mouth felt dry.

Her inner ears rang like church bells.

Every square inch of flesh tingled madly.

Her ascent stopped.

She hovered.

Suspended, her uplifted head positioned her to see the inside of the very top of the tower three feet above her.

The lightning ceased being individual bolts and flashes. Here, at the top of the tower, the walls were solid with energy, far too bright to look at. Branna closed her eyes.

Branna had no idea how long she hung, suspended at the top of that narrow cone. It seemed forever.

She ceased to hear the humming long before reaching the tower's apex.

She thought she heard it again and realized her descent

251

started without her knowledge.

The humming gradually returned to the bass, and she hovered above the gigantic slab quartz floor. Her body unlocked and then, weak-kneed, goosebumps vanished, hair subject to the laws of gravity, she stood on the floor.

Oonaugh suddenly appeared, an arm around her waist, helping her across the arena to a small room under the bleachers. They sat, both sipping the amazing elixir from Branna's last visit.

Oonaugh waited patiently for Branna to recover.

Branna's first words were not what Oonaugh expected. "It is a transmitter," Branna stated.

Oonaugh looked surprised.

"The Eiffel Tower," Branna repeated, "It's recently allowed the French Army to experiment sending wireless messages. Last year they transmitted a message received by the British Army at Dover. Its height made it perfect for this use."

"Very astute, Branna. The crystal tower is a transmitter but not of radio waves. It transmits waves of energy from this world to Earth," Oonaugh explained.

"Where is the tower that receives it?" Branna wanted to know.

"Why, wherever you are, my daughter," Oonaugh smiled. "It is tuned into your body's resonance. A combination of energy created by your heart and brain. Your personal radio frequency, you might say."

Branna already understood from previous lessons how to draw power from the quartzite mountain, but this must provide much more energy. "How can I receive it?" Branna questioned.

"Not so fast, daughter," Oonaugh replied. "Do not be so quick to receive the transmitted power. The more and longer you draw this power into you, the weaker your body becomes. Too much and your immortality becomes a burden."

"Immortality?" Branna's eyes widened.

"You are a changeling, half-human, half-Sidhe, as am I." Oonaugh watched her daughter. "We know the pure Sidhe, those of us with a full head of silver hair, are, by God's word, to live until judgement day. We do not know the length of halflings' lives. I am nearly three thousand years old."

While most people might dance with joy and excitement, Branna replied to her mother, "I must think about it." As if she could change the fact.

"You have all the time in the world," her mother answered. "Now it is time to begin training and understanding the reception of power."

The training began with the neophytes of the Crystal Tower. Branna learned the basics of gathering energy, amplifying it then sending it to halflings on Earth.

Next, she learned to focus the Crystal Tower on herself and cause the energy to flow into her. The energy moved at the speed of light, one danger was it began as a trickle and increased to a flooded river. If that much energy ever reached a receiver, it would destroy their mind and nervous system. They would continue to live until the last day but unaware of their environment, unable to think. Just empty eyes and ears trying to make sense of random noises.

Branna traded the rings on her fingers for a canteen filled with water from the sacred Spring of the Repentant. The intake of energy dehydrated the body quickly. A drop of the sacred water on her lips restored her body instantly.

Weeks, then months passed as Branna practiced calling the power to her along the Earth's energy lines. Letting it build to the necessary level then releasing it in many creative ways designed to stop or kill an enemy.

When Branna was ready, she asked her mother one last question before entering the cave of the Belly of the Beast. "Mother, if I am to live so long, what about men, a husband, children, a family?

Oonaugh frowned. "I tried to blend the two worlds in the early years. It ended sadly."

☐

Branna Returns... Again

The boat bumped against the boulder at the base of Slievemore. An exhausted Michael lowered a stone anchor at each end of the boat and gripped a shrub growing from the large stone. He worked his way to the top. As his head rose above the stone, he found his friend, Father Bob, sitting under a canvas tarp used to create a lean-to covering.

"Damn it, Robert," Michael said, before raising the rest of his body to the ledge.

"No foul language, Little Mike," the priest responded as he crawled and stepped out from beneath the canvas.

"I'm serious!" Michael fired back, anger streaking his voice. "Why the hell would you help Branna go back into that cave?"

"Michael, calm yourself," Father Bob offered soothingly. "If you haven't noticed, our defense against the things killing islanders by the dozens has not gone well. Branna knows she is our only hope. She was going back whether I brought her here or not. You know how stubborn she is," Father Bob said, hoping to calm Michael.

After thinking about the priest's words, Michael said,

"You are right about that. She is the most stubborn woman I have ever known." He paused then added, "But I love her and will not allow her to put her life in danger."

"Good luck, my friend," the priest replied. "I think you selected an unwinnable battle."

"How long has she been gone?" Michael asked, looking into the cave.

"Almost two days," Father Bob answered, realizing the forty-eight hours gone by since Branna entered the cave was nearly three times as long as she had been absent before.

"That is…" Michael began only to be interrupted by the priest.

"I know," Father Bob said, worry in his voice.

"I'm going in to find her," Michael said, leaning into the cave's entrance trying to see more.

A putrid, warmish air brushed past him from the cave. The smell made him grimace. "I have to," Michael said as much to himself as to Father Bob.

"Stop, Michael, think," the priest pleaded. "You have never declared love for a woman before, so I know you mean it. I know your nature is to protect those close to you. I can only imagine how far that extends to the first woman you have ever loved. That is noble and good and right." The priest paused to make sure Michael listened to his words. "Think Michael. How will she feel when she returns and learns the man she loves is missing, probably dead, in the very cave she emerged from?" The priest put his hand on his friend's shoulder.

Michael's eyes teared up, and he hugged his friend. "I feel so helpless. I failed at keeping the people on the island safe, I failed to keep Branna safe. I am useless."

"Nonsense," Father Bob whispered and released the hug. "When we were boys, you attempted things you couldn't possibly do because you saw them as helping someone. You grew into a man whose job is to protect whole populations. But this time you are not trying to subdue a horse thief or pub bully. This time you are facing demons, Michael. The denizens of the Dark Principalities. Unimaginable creatures whose only pleasure comes from torturously executing their master's commands. You cannot defeat them alone."

Michael thought about what he heard. He admitted the priest's words scared him, but he had been frightened many times. His job generated fear, he had learned to accept it and do his duty, regardless. Perhaps that wasn't enough in this case.

Then something came to him.

"Where is God?" Michael's anger and frustration returned. "Where is he in all of this? Why is he not sending angels to destroy the demons? Why is he not protecting us?"

Before the priest could offer a reply, Michael added, "And don't give me that 'works in mysterious ways' verse. It's the worst excuse the church has to offer and the one they use the most."

"I was not going to say that, Michael," Father Bob said softly, "My answer is, I do not know."

"When we studied in seminary together," Michael began, "Your faith made me question my own. Your faith never failed you. You accepted everything they taught. I saw my faith as merely a shadow of yours. My doubts and unanswered questions left me questioning the very existence of God, at least the God of the Catholic Church."

"I wish you had told me," Father Bob said.

"Why? So your 'gift of gab' could have swayed me to stay and become a priest for a

God and church in which I did not believe?" Michael paused and saw tears in his old friend's eyes.

There was a long silence. Neither man looked into the other's eyes.

257

Finally, the priest spoke. "Michael, I know how you live, you are a good man, a Christian man. You follow Christ's path better than the majority who are in their pews every Sunday thinking of money or plowing while the sermon slips past them. I want to ask you the only question that matters." Father Bob waited for Michael to issue some sign of permission.

Rather than tell the priest to go ahead, Michael answered the question he knew the priest wanted to ask, "I believe Jesus Christ is the son of God."

Father Bob grinned. "That's all you need, Michael. Anything more and you start to tread on governance rules established by churches to attract members to pay bills. But there is more, Michael. You and I have touched on it many times in conversations over the years," Father Bob continued.

"You do not have to believe in the church," the priest continued, knowing the Catholic Church would view his statements as heresy. "But every man must believe in something, something good. Without belief, we are lost. Without belief, we weaken ourselves, families and the world. The ancient Irish believed fervently in a mishmash of pagan gods, the Catholic Church's God and their own gods and goddesses who the church kidnapped, changed their clothes and reissued as saints. The power of that belief drove the demons away.

"Belief is power to the monsters attacking the island. People's belief in their existence makes the demons real. The energy they gain from terror, pain, and suffering, gives them power.

"The belief in the gods, Christian and Pagan, gradually eroded, removing the barrier between our and their worlds. Now they are back, and I for one do not have a notion how to restore balance."

Michael sat on the rocky terrace for a long moment. Looking out to sea, he said, "The Morrigan was in

Mallaranny last night."

"Was it the same as here?" the priest asked.

"Far worse. She brought an army of air-demons to enforce her rule. The town is gone, nothing but shattered and burned buildings. The Morrigan performed a ritual designed to emasculate and humiliate the people. Afterward, they were sent in all directions to spread the word that the Morrigan and all the old gods are back. Anything less than complete submission and loyalty will be met with a slow, painful death."

The priest's eyes grew large. "Sending forth apostles to spread the fear of her before her arrival. The more people they tell, the more fear fuels her power without her ever being among them.

"I doubt they will waste their energy on Achill again. Everyone here fears them or is beyond more suffering. They began here because this was the last spot on Earth where belief in the Morrigan lingered. From that spark, they will set Ireland afire," Father Bob said dejectedly.

"Will they stop with the British Isles?" Michael asked, afraid to think of a future.

Father Bob looked into a stiffening breeze of colder air. Winter was coming. He looked at his friend and said, "Unfortunately, Ireland was the final place the Morrigan manifested before being sent wherever it is dead goddesses go. She appeared throughout European myths in many forms and names, but always as three sisters. I fear Ireland and England are merely stepping stones for her path to rebirth."

"Lower a rope, please," Branna's voice came from the cave.

With rope harness across her back and under her arms, the two men pulled her upward. It was not she was down so far as much as the difficulty of climbing out.

Michael called as he pulled, "Are you hurt or ill?"

Branna lifted her face upward.

Michael had never seen a more beautiful or radiant woman. Butterflies fluttered in his stomach to the beat of his quickening heart. It bothered him she affected him so. At the same time, he did not know what he would do without her.

"I'm fine, Michael. How are you? Any more raids?"

Father Bob rowed the boat back to Dugort.

Michael relayed the events of last night to Branna who grew more serious as each portion unfolded. When Michael finished, she sat silently.

Listening to Michael's terrible news kept her conscious attention. Unconsciously, her appreciation of his looks, his actions, his goodness, made her want to lean over and kiss him. She almost did, then a wave pushed her back from him.

A swell in the ocean stopped my action, she thought. Something I wanted, I want, she corrected herself. A wave's swell may have helped or hurt. I do not yet know, she thought and turned her mind back to the new information regarding last night's attacks.

Dugort was a ghost town.

Even Gladys and Collin were nowhere found.

No horses were found alive. For that matter, no chicken, pig, sheep, goat, nor any living animal was so. They walked from Dugort to Cashel. Awkward as it was, Michael held his motorcycle up and pushed it along instead of riding. His idea was to hang what supplies, food, and water they had across it.

He chose this as opposed to riding the thirty miles from Dugort to Westport in two hours. Michael would walk the distance with Branna at his side.

They stopped to rest at Collin's house outside of Cashel, hoping to find him and Gladys there. The house was empty of any sign of life but otherwise, just as Branna left it after her first visit with Collin.

While Michael built a fire, Father Bob found some

salted fish and hard biscuits. He boiled the small fish and found nothing to soften the biscuits. It was poor fare, but no one complained.

Outside darkened. All agreed it was not safe to proceed in the dark so the group decided to stay until morning.

Branna sat in Collin's sagging comfy chair watching Michael stoke the fire and add more peat. Father Bob sat in a scuffed and cracked wooden chair that had at one time been part of a dining set.

Michael moved from the fire to the opposite side of the comfy chair, so Branna captured most of the heat from the fire. He sat on the small stool Collin used to rest his feet as he drank in the chair.

"I wonder where they are?" Michael asked rhetorically.

Father Bob replied, "Preparing to destroy another town, I suppose."

"I meant Collin and Gladys," Michael said, chuckled and added, "though I would not put the ability beyond them."

"I came to like them quite a lot," Branna said, still gazing into the small flames from the peat.

"So did I," the priest said. "They were trustworthy and dependable. Rare among people these days."

Michael interjected, "You told me they were. Hopefully, they are alive somewhere along the road with the other survivors, seeking refuge where none is to be had."

"Michael," Branna said softly. "They are alive. I feel it. We will find them soon."

As they thought about the two elders' fate, they heard something outside.

Michael was up like a spring released. Gun in hand, he moved toward the back door where the sound originated.

They heard scratching sounds, reminiscent of the night of the bugs in the rectory. Branna and Father Bob took a step away.

261

"I do not see anything out the window," Branna said, praying they would not have gone through all this to be devoured by horrid little creatures. Branna stood straight and spoke, "Do not open that door, Michael. Give me a moment, and I will prepare a Sidhe welcome for those monsters."

Her natural fear prevented her from instantly remembering her Sidhe training.

Branna held her index finger pointed upward then lowered it to point straight away from her. She stayed perfectly still then slowly turned clockwise. Her revolution slowed, then stopped.

Michael and Father Bob saw her finger twitch move slightly back toward the right.

Branna closed her eyes. Her face relaxed.

She began to hum, a deep sound for a woman, far too much bass for Branna's normally lyrical voice.

Her humming slowly climbed the register.

As it touched the high end of the scale, Branna slowly rose in the air and hovered a few inches above the floor.

The tip of Branna's finger glowed as if a very small firefly with a blue light landed on it. The color spread along the finger, the brightness intensified. Branna's hand became a bright blue fire.

Suddenly, Branna's floating body went rigid. Her hair crackled with tiny streaks of lightning as it stood straight out.

Her face illuminated a cyan blue; she opened her eyes. The pupils were rolled up, and the reflection of the blue fire danced in the whites of her eyes.

"Is she alright?" Michael whispered worriedly.

"I am not so worried about her as I am whatever is outside the door," the priest responded without taking his eyes off the spectacular light show. He imagined people who witnessed this in the past reported an angelic visitation.

The glowing hand subsided.

Branna slowly descended. When her feet felt the floor, her eyes were the only part of her showing a soft glow.

"I think we are ready to receive our guests," Branna said, standing calmly, watching the door. "Would you do the honors, Michael?"

Michael nodded and reached his left hand toward the broken door handle. He still held his pistol in his right. Whatever Branna had in store, he felt better holding the large caliber pistol as backup.

Branna spoke again. "And, Michael, be careful."

The entire time Branna stayed entranced, her electrified cyan hair spiked out, no sound had come from the door. Perhaps whatever had been there realized it was about to meet its maker and left.

Just before opening the door, Michael listened intently.

Michael threw the door open, stepped back and automatically aimed his pistol at the dark, thigh-high shape in the doorway.

The dog whimpered.

"It's Cromwell!" Branna laughed and started toward the door. "It's Collin's dog. Poor thing is probably starving. Let him in."

Michael lowered his gun and squatted. "Here, Cromwell, come here, boy." Michael held out his hand to befriend the matted, dirty canine.

The dog looked at him suspiciously. Clearly, he wanted his master.

Father Bob held out half a biscuit and clicked his tongue.

Cromwell's suspicious eyes moved to the priest, to the biscuit, back to the priest, then he slowly stepped inside, watching Michael with side glances.

Cromwell stopped, sat, ran his tongue around his chops, whined then stood and walked straight to Branna. He assumed the heel position and sat.

Branna laughed like a little girl. She knelt and roughed Cromwell's dirty head. He responded with a huge smile and licked her hands.

"Apparently you made a friend," Michael remarked, closing the door to retain the fire's heat.

"He did not seem to care about me when we met," Branna said. "I guess he had time to think." She laughed, continuing to rub Cromwell's head, neck and shoulders.

Father Bob walked toward her and held out the partial biscuit.

Cromwell looked at it, licked his chops again and looked at Branna.

"Go ahead, boy," Branna said, "Father Bob is offering you communion."

They all laughed as Cromwell, crunching like a machine, made short work of the hard bread.

After a few minutes of reliving the scare Cromwell provided, their lightened mood switched back to their situation; not just their situation, Ireland's situation.

Father Bob looked at Branna, "You told us of your training while you were with your mother. Did she speak of the Morrigan or any of the other gods of the Celtic pantheon?"

"The Sidhe already knew what the three of us learned about them. The good news is most of what we guess is correct. The bad news is the same," Branna said, sounding exhausted. "Oh my!" she exclaimed. "I didn't use the energy. I must discharge it before it makes me ill."

Michael rose, "What can we do to help?"

"You can watch. I've never done it before, so do not stand too close," Branna smiled.

They stepped into the cold.

Remembering her lessons, Branna began the hum in the high octave and gradually lowered it. Her body locked, bent backward, she rose above the wet ground. A light blue aura formed around her. Then a blinding blue lightning bolt shot from her body into the clouds. The loosed bolt of pure energy was followed immediately by a sound of thunder so intense it knocked the two men to the ground and made Cromwell run as if the devil was after him.

Branna, body trembling, lowered herself to the ground to regain balance. After the men were up, she said, "We should go inside and develop a strategy. It is a safe bet the Morrigan has one she's worked on for two thousand years."

Michael stoked and fueled the fireplace until it radiated a small space of steady heat. The three of them stood together huddled in tight rank. They faced the flames, warming themselves and hoping to at least partially dry their clothing.

Michael's hand gently touched Branna's shoulder. A soft squeeze invited her to snuggle against him. "You are freezing," he said.

Branna enjoyed his touch. There were so many things about him she liked. It was obvious he was head over heels in love with her. But he had fallen in love with the Branna before all of this. He knew that person. Now she was this other person, this halfling, empowered to destroy descendants of unrepentant angels. If it was too much for her, who lived it, to fully comprehend, how could she ask Michael to understand what she could not?

Oonaugh made clear the pitfalls of sharing human affairs. Her loves, one by one, would wither before her eyes, and a forever young Branna would grieve at their gravesides. If she chose to have children, they would be mixed. Oonaugh was half-angel, half-human, Branna was a quarter of the same mix, and her children would be an eighth. Oonaugh told her any dilution beyond one-quarter reduced the Nephilim blood to birthing a child with no chance of inheriting any of the Sidhe powers. They too would grow old and die before their mother.

265

Though her desire for Michael grew with each minute they spent together, she knew nothing good could come from it. Even so, she allowed Michael's arm to hold her against him.

Father Bob stepped away from the fire, leaving Michael and Branna to enjoy a moment alone. He felt sorry for Michael who could not see Branna did not share the same depth of feeling. There was nothing to be done. The disparity of emotions would make itself clear, eventually.

The priest, holding a candle, struggled to read book covers and papers strewn about tables, chairs and two small shelves. Opening and glancing at folded papers, he found a pre-construction map from 1883 showing the area which the Midland Great Western Railway would operate.

Father Bob returned to a place near the fire, knelt down and unfolded the map on the floor.

The adoring couple looked down.

"Excellent," Michael said, "We can use this in our strategy session."

Branna stepped away from Michael and, careful not to block any light from the fire, sat, legs crossed, on the floor.

Michael lowered himself to his knees and placed a candle on the far edge of the map.

"Let's approach this as if we were solving a crime, shall we," Michael offered. "Imagine we are plagued by livestock thieves. They have already struck these four areas," Michael said, pointing his finger at Keel, Dugort, Cashel, and Mallaranny. "They are very good thieves. With no livestock left in the area, they must look for new territory, new farms.

"The question is, pretending towns represent farms, where would they go next?" Michael asked, looking up at the other two.

"We are not dealing with chicken thieves, Michael," Branna said. "I know you are using farms and livestock to represent towns and people. I understand it, but the thieves, in this case, have been planning these attacks for two thousand years; they do not yet possess unlimited energy and must not waste what they have."

They sat looking at the map. When no revelations occurred, Father Bob stared off into a dark corner of the room.

Branna and Michael exchanged ideas both knew were flawed.

Father Bob stood, pacing the room, lost in thought. His most creative thinking emerged from moments like these, looking for solutions to someone's or his own problem. He noticed an old, worn stool on its side. He absently picked it up and placed its three legs on the floor. It wobbled, one of the legs shorter than the others.

Still lost in thought, hand on chin, the priest turned to face the fire. The fireplace itself was not exceptional. Mortared stones with an arched top. Something clicked into place. "It has to do with a triangle, with three. I'm not sure how exactly but I know I am right about the connection."

"I see the three sisters aspect," said Branna.

"There is the unholy trinity," Michael chimed.

Father Bob drew a pattern in dust and ash built up on the hearth. "What is that?" he asked.

The other two leaned closer. The priest's marks were three spirals. Each spiral's outside tail connected to the tail of another spiral. When all three tails connected in the center, an equilateral triangle was formed. The circular shapes of the three spirals formed their own triangular design.

"That is, among other things, the symbol of the Morrigan, the three sisters formed into one," Branna said instantly upon being able to make it out.

"Correct," Father Bob said. "Triangles are the strongest shape in construction. Even the arch," Father Bob placed his fingertip close to the keystone in the fireplace's arched stones. "Even the arch can be reduced to a triangle."

"I'm not sure I understand," Michael said, feeling slow.

"I see," Branna offered, "a three-legged stool cannot stand with a missing leg."

"I see now," Michael said, half-heartedly.

Father Bob spoke. "Is it possible they are most powerful when everything is associated with the number three?" Not waiting for an answer, he plunged ahead, "Until just now, I thought they attacked three towns at a time solely because there were only the three of them. Now, I am not so sure. What if their power is somehow boosted by threes or triangles?"

"The towns on Achill did not form a triangle," Michael said.

"True," Branna began slowly, then continued, "But they returned at Achill because it was the epicenter of what remained of the old belief system. The Morrigan's only choice was to begin there. Now they are loose, we might keep a triangle pattern in mind, but not limit ourselves to the idea. As Michael's point proves, it is not essential to their plans."

"Fair enough," Father Bob reacted. "What Michael learned from the man leaving Mallaranny suggests most of the town's people followed roads as they spread out.

"Those sent to northeast must travel more than thirty miles over bad roads and across bogs to reach Killala or Ballina, which both have less population than Achill. The other option, the people Michael met, took the coast road east for ten miles or so to Newport, then further south to Westport." The priest pointed out the mentioned towns on the map.

Michael spoke, "We do not know if the Morrigan is attacking other towns tonight, and if she is, where. Our first priority tomorrow is to gather intelligence and confirm our suspicions."

"I agree," Branna said, "That is why you should take

your motorbike to Westport. That is the fastest way. You can more likely gather news and see firsthand the effects the town is suffering."

"I do not think leaving you alone to walk the road is safe." Michael tried to squirm out of doing what he knew to be the right thing.

"We will be safe. We have Cromwell to protect us," Branna said.

Cromwell raised his head at his name, looked around then went back to sleep.

"She's right, Michael," the priest took Branna's side. "Your bike is an asset we need to employ."

"I know," Michael replied, wishing it were not the right thing to do.

"We will be lucky if we make it to Mallaranny based on your description," the priest said, still looking at the map.

"The Church of Saint Ignatius is a mile and a half west of Mallaranny. Branna and I will push to make it there. An old friend of mine, Father O'Connor, lives there. He's eighty-five years old but still healthy and clever. If anyone survived that night, it would be him. Branna and I will wait for you at his church."

"Yes, yes." Michael allowed his annoyance to be heard in his voice, "But what about a plan. Should we just wait until we have more information tomorrow?"

"Tomorrow will be a busy and strenuous day," Branna said. "We all need to get some rest. My feelings are the Morrigan used a lot of energy last night, and she will most likely spend tonight restoring power."

Not waiting for their agreement, Branna stretched out on the floor with her feet toward the fire, pulled her coat over her torso and said, "Goodnight." She rolled on her side and closed her eyes.

Michael placed as much peat on the fireplace grate as it could hold then followed suit by laying down on his side facing Branna's back.

Father Bob continued studying the map for a few minutes then slouched himself in Collin's comfy chair, positioned the footstool properly and fell asleep with his chin on his chest.

More hard biscuits and boiled salted fish for breakfast.

Alone with Branna outside by the motorcycle, Michael hesitantly and awkwardly tried to kiss Branna using their parting as an excuse.

"Sometimes you are such a boy," Branna said, before raising up and kissing him on the mouth. She held the kiss longer than she should have.

Waving goodbye to him as the bike moved away humming like a giant bee, she thought how difficult it would be to say goodbye to this man who loved her so greatly, especially since she now loved him but had to restrain showing her true feelings.

☐

To Westport

Westport was in a terrible state. Refugees from Achill and Mallaranny spread the nightmares of the last few days in the markets and pubs. The fear was palpable.

Michael made his way to the RIC barracks. Colonel Milling was absent. A message calling him to Dublin granted him excuse to depart the area, at least until things calmed.

Michael's direct supervisor, Captain Lowndes, was in Westport, but not in the barracks and no one knew when he might return.

"Tell me about the current situation," Michael asked a middle-aged desk sergeant working the desk in the barrack's lobby.

"The situation?" the man replied, arching one eyebrow. "With all due respect, Inspector, the situation is as you see."

"Please tell me how you see it, Sergeant," Michael asked again.

"Very well, Inspector. I am two years from pension. If

this rabble continues as they are I'll most likely be killed quelling a riot or calming a Donny-brook in a pub." The sergeant paused, looking at Michael, "I don't, I can't believe what the people from Mallaranny are saying but I have no clue as to what really happened. All I know as facts are: Mallaranny is in ruins, and its people are here, scared to the point of insanity. So, there you have it, my thoughts on our situation," he concluded, emphasizing the last word.

"Thank you," Michael said, thinking the information was useless for his purposes. He left the office and went to the pub closest to the station.

Called the Bishops Miter, both locals and refugees from Mallaranny filled its tables and bar. Their conversation blended into an unintelligible hubbub.

Michael squeezed inside and made his way to the near end of the bar.

The bartender's daughter, perhaps nine or ten years old, drew him a Guinness and collected his coin.

Michael had wedged himself next to the bar where its 'L' shape turned back toward the wall. On his left sat two men, one a dairy farmer from Mallaranny and the other an employee of the Midland Great Western Railroad Company. The latter continued to speak. Michael tried to listen.

"We added the last train cars to the Number Nine Engine this morning, and it left pulling more cars than any train from Westport before it," said the man on the stool against the wall.

"I saw it. People were stacked tight as peat on the flatcars. I just missed catchin' a ride meself," said the Mallaranny man. His eyes were both red and dry from crying too long a time. "I'm glad I missed it," he added.

"It's a terrible thing, the loss of your family and your home," the railroad worker said, then raised his glass saying, "You can stay with me and Mrs. O'Doul for a spell until things return to normal."

"Things will never be normal again," the bedraggled dairyman said, his hand did not lift a glass in a toast.

"Aww, now, don't say such a thing. The constables and Dublin will find out what really happened and I'm sure they will provide aid for the rebuilding of Mallaranny," O'Doul offered hope.

Michael waited, hoping for the conversation to turn to the events of the night before last. Then he realized he might learn nothing from the talk in the pubs or market other than the suffering experienced by the victims in Mallaranny. He finished his beer and was about to leave when the dairyman spoke.

"There is no hope," the man from Mallaranny said. "It's the old god, the Morrigan. She's back, not to drag us to hell, but to pull her hell over us, to enslave us. There's nothing we can do."

Michael moved toward the pub's door when a thought stopped him. In his conversations with Collin, Gladys, Father Bob and Branna, there was never talk of enslavement. The Morrigan didn't want slaves; she wanted fear, the pain of loss, suffering and sorrow from those witnessing it. What fear and sorrow came from enslaved men, with no hope? Eventually, only dread could come to her. If not to enslave men, what did she want? No answer came to mind.

But Michael understood something else. He needed to find Collin and Gladys. They were part of this, the same as he. God had brought them all together in this place to do something, somehow defeat the Morrigan and send her back to hell. He didn't know, but the same instincts that made him one of the best inspectors in Ireland told him he had to find the missing members of their team.

Michael arrived back at the RIC barracks just as the wizened desk sergeant held two drunk men by their collars and ushered them out the door. Their voices raised without care of consequences the way only drunken men do, they cursed the sergeant for not doing what they instructed to get the Mallaranny people out of Westport.

"Why, in all my years, keeping the peace in County Mayo I've seen nothing like this. When do our reinforcements arrive, Inspector?"

The sergeant looked at Michael expecting an answer.

"You will have to ask Milling or Lowndes or someone who is in charge," Michael answered.

"Far as I know, Inspector, you're in command." He looked at Michael. "No one of higher rank than yourself is about, and until you showed up, I might have been in charge, but I didn't want to admit it to myself." The veteran constable looked hopefully at Michael.

Michael looked back, thinking how quickly civilization disassembled itself when chaos and fear reigned.

After a moment, Michael said, "Sergeant, it looks as if you will remain the ranking constable here for a little longer."

The sergeant grimaced as a bedraggled woman entered the front door crying as she had lost her babies.

"Before you take care of her, Sergeant, tell me the best place to obtain horses," Michael wanted to know.

"Most are gone. Constables are riding ours. People here that had any sold them to Mallaranny folks who wanted to get farther away," the sergeant said, moving toward the distraught mother. Before he reached her, he turned and said, "There may be something that will do, in the stable, but you will have to figure it out." The sergeant put his arm around the mother and edged her to a seat.

Not knowing what to expect, Michael went to the stables behind the barracks. At first, all he saw were empty stalls. At the far end, the last stall door stood open. He walked there to close the door if nothing else.

Behind the opened door and backed into the stall, with its bonnet extending beyond the stall, sat an almost new

1903 Delahaye Type 16 motor car.

Michael was aware of this model vehicle but had no idea Westport's RIC Barracks warranted one. It could sit two comfortably in the front, or squeeze a third person in. Behind the front seat was a larger space suitable to enclose with a fabric top and comfortably accommodate four passengers on facing seats. This model was the first vehicle ever to possess a four-cylinder engine that allowed it, on smooth roads, to reach the incredible speed of forty-five miles per hour.

The Delahaye was a Godsend. All he had to do was figure out how to start it. He opened the top to the fuel tank and used the marked rod attached to the tank to measure the depth of the petrol. Three-quarters of a tank, the stick revealed, along with an approximate mileage number embossed into the rod. More than enough to travel to Dugort and back.

Michael knew a hand crank started the engine. He found it affixed beneath the front bumper. Next, he searched for printed instructions on how to start the motor. A cardboard card stuck out from a pocket attached under the dashboard. The necessary steps were numbered. He saw immediately it would be easier with two people.

Michael sat in the driver's seat. Following the steps, he switched on the magneto, pumped the gas pedal seven times and pulled the choke halfway out.

Checking the foot clutch, making sure the shift was set to neutral, then setting the handbrake, he put the card back where he found it, jumped out and walked to the vehicle's front.

He inserted the crank, placed his grip on the handle as illustrated on the card. Holding the handle as shown felt counter-intuitive, but he followed instructions to the letter.

Michael bent his legs slightly. As his legs rose, his arms lifted and rotated the handle in a clockwise direction.

It was much harder than Michael anticipated.

Turning the handle full circle made the four cylinders cycle once, opening and closing the magneto, which caused sparks to ignite the fuel in the engine and make the motor run on its own.

Easier said than done.

He tried again.

Then three more times.

He looked inside the vehicle to recheck the magneto and choke.

Michael went to the front, put his hand on the handle and heard a voice from the stable yard, "I can help you with that."

Looking up, Michael saw a tall, broad-shouldered boy of sixteen or seventeen. He dressed like a fisherman out of the Westport Quay.

The boy stood still, waiting for Michael to respond.

"Well, come on then," Michael waved the lad to himself.

"Sometimes these mechanical things don't tell you everything you need to know. My uncle has a combustion engine on his boat. It makes the job easier when it works," the boy said looking at the dashboard. "Sir, if you will get in the driver's seat, I'll tell you what to do," the young fisherman offered.

"Whatever you say, Captain," Michael replied.

"I ain't no captain, sir, not even a mate, just the lowliest last hand of the crew." The boy opened the bonnet and smelled the motor.

After he latched the bonnet, he stood ready at the crank.

"Switch off the magneto, push in the clutch and do not pump gas," he said as he turned the crank for the first time.

His crank, harder and faster than Michael's, elicited metallic grumblings from the engine.

He cranked the motor four more times in rapid

succession.

"When they've not been run for too long, you have to unfreeze the pistons before you try to start. Now open the choke halfway, turn the magneto on. When the motor catches, I'll signal to slowly close the choke. Once it is all the way in, pump a little petrol," the boy said, proud to be demonstrating his abilities.

Michael followed his instructions.

The third crank caused the engine to ignite and sputter.

"Choke half the distance to off," the boy yelled just before a cannon-like backfire.

The boy moved quickly to the driver's side. "If you don't mind, your honor, let me work it."

Michael moved over.

The boy worked the choke and petrol until the motor settled down and ran smoothly.

"I'll show you the gear pattern," the boy offered.

"I might have a better idea," Michael said. "Are you working?"

"No, sir. My uncle's wife is from Mallaranny. They are both on the road, talking to those who might've seen my aunt's sisters," the boy said, looking down.

"Wait here, please," Michael said, "I'll be back in five minutes with something for your troubles."

When Michael returned from the barracks, he held out his left hand holding a one-pound note. The other hand held out a sheet of paper with the word 'Voucher' printed across its top. "The note is yours."

Delighted, the boy took the money. "Thank you very much, sir. But I didn't do it to get money."

Michael smiled. "Some people will be very grateful for what you did. Believe me, you earned it." Michael paused then held out the sheet. "This is a voucher hiring you for one or more days. If you drive this vehicle for me, the RIC will pay you a pound a day."

"I never drove one of these before," the boy said,

hating to lose the money.

"Nor I," Michael said. "You know a great deal more about it and will learn as fast, or faster than I will. But before you say yes, we may run into some troubles. Some of the people on the road are not in good spirits, and we are going to Achill Island and Mallaranny."

"My name is Sean Bean , and I'll take the job." He held out his hand.

Taking the boy's hand, Michael replied, "I'm Inspector Doyle, but you may call me Michael."

Michael gave the lad a crumpled note. "I know everything here's been picked over, but we need some food and water for our journey. See what you can find, and I'll meet you here in an hour."

Sean opened the wadded banknote and beamed. "That's a ten-pound note. I've never had that much in my hand before. I'll be back with food, and your change, Michael."

As Sean moved on to the main street, Michael reentered the barracks to obtain more guns and ammunition. He wasn't sure what help the guns would provide but having them made him feel better.

☐

The Road to St. Ignatius

Father Bob and Branna spoke little during their trek to Mallaranny. They spoke not at all when they reached Cashel.

Cashel was exactly as Michael described it, a ghost town, empty of all life. They reached the street in front of the church.

Branna stopped, looked at the church then said, "Can you smell the death?"

The priest continued to stare at the front of the church. "My God, can you imagine the horror inside? The fear and agony of the dead and dying people? Branna, my heart has never pained me more." He paused, then looked at Branna. "I've smelled death many times, Branna, what you are smelling is not death, it is the scent of Satan escaping from a new doorway in Hell."

"Whatever it is," Branna said, "It smells awful. I suggest we move on."

There were few people on the road. None moved toward them. Most of the people they passed were people who lived away from the towns. They had witnessed none of the horrors but the stories they heard and all their friends abandoning their property convinced them to leave the Island.

Branna did not want to tell them she believed they would be safe at home now. She was afraid she might be wrong.

"What are we going to do, Branna?" Father Bob asked. "When you trained among the Sidhe," he paused, "That sounds so ridiculous, doesn't it?"

Before she could answer his rhetorical question, he went on, "Surely, in all this time, the Sidhe developed a plan to restrain these monsters. What is it? Why have they sat back and watched?"

Branna tried to find the best way to answer the priest's question. After a moment, she started, "Father Bob, I'll tell you what I know but I warn you, I don't think it will comfort you."

"It sounds like you better tell me everything. Otherwise, I will not worry enough," Father Bob said, only half joking.

Branna hesitated another moment, then said, "If you insist, but remember I warned you.

"Things are very different in the world of Sidhe than humans suppose. Some of the old folklore has truth in the stories. But what was true so long ago in many cases has changed." Branna paused to look at something on the road ahead then continued. "The Sidhe themselves lost the energy to manifest their physical bodies in our world. Their ability gradually faded as humans stopped believing in them. The same thing happened with the Nephilim. For a while, a thousand years or so, the Sidhe held the advantage. They continued to have a physical presence in our world because they draw energy not from belief in the faerie world alone, but also from human belief in God, the creator, the same God who sent their ancestors, the two hundred watchers to look after humans. When that didn't work out so well, Nephilim ran amuck. The Sidhe's ancestors repented and were given their world between Heaven and Earth. But the Sidhe repented and, though they will never enter Heaven again, they continue to help humans when and how they can. The loss of the ability to physically manifest as a physical being for more than a few seconds made it more and more difficult to overtly watch over humans. Their answer was to take a lesson from God, to move in mysterious ways, to accomplish their mission through guile and anticipating human and demon endeavors.

"But during the last four hundred years, belief in God has diminished in both the numbers of people and the fervor of their belief. Martin Luther started it. He was absolutely correct in publicizing the corruption within the Catholic Church." Branna looked at Father Bob who seemed nonplussed by the words.

"Do you want to disagree or question this?" Branna offered.

"Not yet," Father Bob replied, "I'll save my rebuttal until you are finished."

"Very well," Branna said and continued.

"It was not that Luther was wrong about the corruption, but the spreading of his complaints fueled smoldering coals in Europe. The vast majority of Catholics were relatively poor and felt the burden of paying the church for indulgences to extra 'donations' beyond tithes. They were resentful already of the unfairness of the church's representatives, priests, bishops, cardinals, all the way up to the Pope. Those smoldering coals, fanned by Luther's movement, burst into a devouring fire and weakened the Catholic Church far faster and with more damage than any could have believed.

"So, once the Church's hold as the only Christian church is broken, many churches, in many nations, opened their doors and ex-Catholics often flocked to them.

"So instead of a unified church, defining and enforcing what members were to believe, dozens, eventually hundreds of splinter groups preached their version of Christ. That loss of millions of people's unified, focused belief, prayers, hymns, weakened the power of the belief in God.

"As that faith dwindled, so did the power the Sidhe drew from God." Branna stopped and said, "That's what I learned."

Father Bob gazed into the distance.

Branna allowed him to think.

"Believe it or not," the priest said, "I've heard this theory before, not that it had anything to do with the Sidhe. In fact, it is an ongoing discussion at the Vatican, seeking ways to increase the Church's wealth and power with the remaining faithful."

Father Bob thought a second then went on, "If the Catholic Church recognized the damage done by the schism created by Protestant churches, then your account of the loss of overall faith is a plausible one."

The priest paused only a second before saying, "Interesting as that is, this is not the time or place to debate the damage Luther caused the church. We have more serious, more deadly matters with which to contend. Please go on about the Sidhe. At this point, they are no longer weakened by my lack of belief?"

Branna chuckled. "The Sidhe ability to be physically present on Earth requires tremendous energy for even a short visit. At a point of diminishing returns, they stopped coming. They only visited us when they were desperate to alter something in the present that would set the wheels in motion to help humans in the future. The Sidhe were forced to play the long game."

"Is that where changelings enter the picture?" Father Bob asked.

"Exactly," Branna responded.

"If changelings are Sidhe infants left in place of human babies, how is it your physical presence disputes what you have just told me?" Father Bob wanted to know.

"I am a different kind of changeling," Branna said, looking at the priest.

Suddenly, a motor car appeared from the far side of a hill. The man in the passenger seat stood, his upper torso above the windshield. He waved both arms in the air, then cupped his hands and called to them with words they had no chance of understanding.

Branna and Bob stopped and watched the vehicle draw closer.

"It's Michael! It's Michael!" Branna nearly cheered when she recognized him.

Father Bob saw the excitement in her and decided the rest of her story would wait. After a moment, he said, happily, "It's Michael alright, and he's found a fantastic way for us to move about. This is very helpful."

"He is always helpful," Branna said, her composure lost at seeing the man she should not love but did.

The motorcar slowed and stopped as Sean applied the handbrake. He stayed behind the wheel.

Michael leaped from the car and rapidly approached Branna. She walked toward him with a welcoming smile that quickened his heartbeat. They embraced in the hug of long-separated lovers, kept apart by war.

Cromwell followed Branna and nuzzled against Michael, wanting pets.

Branna could not help herself. She put her arms around his neck, raised on her toes and kissed Michael on the mouth. Not a passionate kiss, but long enough to tell

Michael her feelings for him were growing, which, of course, sent him into a euphoric state.

"Ahem," Father Bob said after waiting for an appropriate interval. "Where did you acquire this fine mode of transportation?"

Branna still snuggled into Michael's chest with her mouth by his neck, she said, "Oh, Michael, what are we going to do?"

Michael did not hesitate to respond, "What is best for us, darling." Michael spoke to Father Bob, "Courtesy of the RIC Westport barracks. The young man driving is Sean Bean. He knows combustion motors and is an excellent driver."

"Michael." The priest stood next to Michael so the teenager in the car could not hear. "Does he know what we might find? I don't think it a good idea to intentionally expose others to our perils, especially a child."

"He knows a little. It is hard for anyone in this part of the country not to know something," Michael said. "I plan to have him drive us until we find the Morrigan or their next target, then leave him to watch the automobile while we do whatever it is we decide to do."

"Very well," Father Bob answered. "We are very close to St. Ignatius Church. You must have passed it a mile or so back."

"Get in," Michael said, his hand indicating the priest to sit in the front passenger seat.

"Sean," Michael said, "This is Father Bob, an old and dear friend." Then he flashed a smile. "This is Branna Butler, she's a very special lady. You will find out more about her later. For now, please turn around and drive back to the church we just passed."

Branna and Michael shared one of the benches on the drive to the church. Michael wished the church was in Dublin and not just a few minutes away.

Cromwell, in the back of the car, stretched out on the

floor at Branna and Michael's feet, happy to rest.

The small stone church was nearly four hundred years old. Its slit windows filled with much newer stained glass reminded Michael of a tiny fortress. When built, it served parishioners from Achill Sound to Mallaranny. It was far enough away to escape the devastation of Mallaranny.

Inside sat Father Travis O'Connor, looking every bit of eighty years old. He sat in a front pew, sipping tea and looking at the crucifix above the altar.

Father Bob approached the old priest and sat beside him so the older man would not feel the need to stand.

Father Bob saw how exhausted Father O'Connor looked. His eyes glazed with cataracts, Bob realized he must be nearly blind. It had been far too long since they talked.

"It's Bob McGuire," the young priest said, "We've come to check on you."

O'Connor's expression did not change, the look of a shell-shocked soldier locked on his face.

When O'Connor did not respond, Father Bob repeated himself only louder.

O'Connor turned his head slightly, more toward the voice than what he saw.

"I've seen things, terrible things in my service to God. I've seen death and sorrow, suffering and pain, starvation and sickness, but never, never once in my eighty-five years has God forced me to endure such as the Godless ruin that is now Mallaranny." Tears ran from the old man's eyes.

Father Bob hugged him.

O'Connor, surprised at the touch, flinched, then, realizing it was a kindness, leaned into Father Bob and sobbed.

Michael and Branna sat in a pew a few rows behind the two holy men.

Sean Bean and Cromwell played outside.

Suddenly Cromwell entered and stopped halfway to the altar. The dog's ears stood, and he stared toward the back of the church.

Branna, sensing Cromwell more than seeing him, looked at the dog. "What is it, boy?"

Cromwell whimpered, gave Branna a side glance, then returned his focus to the door by the altar.

Father Bob looked at the dog, then the door where the animal stared.

Suddenly Cromwell, barking loudly, bolted toward the door, rose on his hind legs and scratched it frantically.

The door opened from the inside. Cromwell vanished inside continuing to whimper.

Father Bob was first to glance into the room. Michael and Branna were right behind.

Gladys sat in a rocking chair, looking toward the door. Collin lay on a cot, shivering under three blankets while Cromwell licked his sweating face.

"I think he is worn down. He has no strength to fight," Gladys said. "I've done what I can. Now I just wait and pray."

Branna stood over the old man on the cot. She watched his ragged breathing and fevered face. Branna said, "Gladys, would you mind going outside with Michael and Father Bob for a few minutes?"

As they left, Michael asked, "What are you going to do.?"

"Something I've never done before," Branna replied, feeling the old man's forehead.

"Something you learned from the Sidhe?" Michael questioned.

"Partly, but an idea mostly," Branna said, then added, "Please close the door."

Michael did so but stood just outside.

Michael saw cyan light outlining the cracks of the door. Then the light went out as if a switch were thrown.

He waited, wanting to call in but he knew it would disturb whatever Branna was doing.

He felt a chilly draft coming from the crack below the door.

He touched the brass door handle, but before he could tell Branna he was coming in, his hand shot back from the handle's stinging cold.

Within a few seconds, the draft in the doorway stopped, and Branna said, "You can stop lurking at the door and come in, Michael."

The handle was cold but no longer freezing.

Michael opened the door and entered. The space felt like a room in the middle of winter that had gone unheated all season.

As he reached the cot, he felt the chill replaced with warmer air.

Collin, still in sleep, no longer shivered, breathed easier and appeared clammy as if the fever had broken.

"What did you do?" Father Bob asked as he entered the room.

"I cooled him down," was all Branna said.

"He seems better," Gladys said feeling Collin's brow. "He can be a mean, grumpy sort, but he's only pretending." Her concern for Collin was plain as day.

Father O'Connor moaned from his pew by the altar. He sounded injured. Father Bob rushed to his side.

The old priest lay on his side on the pew. He held his chest with his left hand and continually crossed himself with his right hand.

"Travis, what can I do? What do you need?" The fear and sorrow in Father Bob's voice made his voice crack.

Travis O'Connor, a good and faithful priest and man, looked at Rob's eyes as if he saw clearly through those translucent, cataract-covered eyes. "What can you do? Pray, my son. Pray for an old man whose faith is breaking under this test. Pray for me to continue to believe in the

God I have served my whole life."

He blinked, tears rolled down his cheeks. "What do I need? I need for our God to show himself and strike down Satan's demon plague. I need for God to no longer remain absent. I need God to make people believe in him again."

Branna brought a communion cup filled with water. Father Bob raised the priest up enough he could sip it.

"Thank you," the priest said weakly. He looked at the shadowy figures that his eyes saw. "I cannot die until my faith is restored. I need restoration."

"I will tell you something, Father O'Connor," Branna said softly. "Soon, you will see the power of God on Earth Again. Forty-two of God's angels sent to watch over humans will send an army to chain and throw the usurpers back into their pit." Branna reached to touch his hand. "Take my hand, Father."

Travis O'Connor took her hand with a death grip.

"Oh, I see them," he said as a smile spread his face. "There are so many. Silver angels striking down demons with the fearful lightning of God's terrible swift sword. The people, oh dear God, the people come to witness the terrible battle. They fall to their knees, a sea of people praying on their knees and the demons vanish into a great hole that opened in the earth." The old man stopped, then continued, "Thank you. Thank you for showing me the future. I know God never deserted us. This horror around us is a test, and the angels will show us the way again.

"I am better, so much better. I need to sleep. Please let me sleep." O'Connor whispered as he drifted into a deep sleep.

"What did you do?" Father Bob asked.

"I didn't show him the future, if that is what you want to know," Branna replied. "I showed him a possible future, one that helped to restore his faith so if he passes, he will die in peace. Not feeling his life was wasted on a dying religion."

"Thank you," said the young priest.

Sean Bean entered the church and announced, "I'm hungry. I started a fire, and fresh fish is cooking for us."

Gladys, Branna, and Michael moved to exit.

Father Bob said, "I'll stay with Travis awhile, in case he wakes up."

The fish and soda bread filled them. By sundown, they were back in the church gathered around the iron stove.

Collin woke from his sleep and Gladys spooned fish broth past his cracked lips. An hour later, Father O'Connor woke and Gladys helped him with the broth.

Sean wanted to know if Michael wanted him to stay another day. Michael agreed.

Cromwell split his time between Collin, the main group, and Sean who stayed outside until dark.

"Branna, before the noisy motorcar interrupted our conversation, you were about to tell me what makes you a different type of changeling," Father Bob said, inviting her to finish her story.

☐

The Battle of Moytura, 5,000 B.C.

Three blackbirds, of raven sheen, sat upon the three tallest stones in a circle of stones. The birds, aggravated, turned their heads with sharp, twitchy motions, as all birds do when uncomfortable. They watched around them a great battle that roared three thousand years ago. A battle at which they were present.

The god-men, the Tuatha De Danann, who arrived in Ireland in ages past riding ships in the sky, waited, men and women in warrior garb, ranks straight, without waver. Their wizards gathered strength just inside the tree line behind the warriors. In numbers too few, they stood, their flanks anchored on two great lakes, as they waited for their enemy to attack.

The Morrigan circled in the sky above their formations. She waited for the orgasmic pleasure of terror, pain, and death that was soon to fill her with power.

Eochaid, king of the Fir Bolg, spoke to his warriors. He refused the offer of his enemy, King Nuada. The Fir Bolg did not come to share the land, they came to conquer it.

The Fir Bolg soldiers were large and fierce. Though their faces were handsome, in a bestial manner, their bones were large, allowing great muscles to bulge and gleam in the sunlight. They were tall with legs and arms disproportionately thicker and longer than humans. Coarse black, curled hairs populated their bodies.

Their lines were not perfect as the De Danann's. The front row's men wore huge broadswords beneath a sash worn across their middle and carried in their left hands a leather bag of stones, each as large as an apple. The long strap of a leather sling was attached to the right hand.

Behind the slingers were the Fir Bolgs selected for the length of their arms. Each carried three thick spears and wore the broadsword.

The final ranks were the largest of the Fir Bolg. They carried two-handed, double-edged swords with five-foot blades of unpolished iron.

All the Fir Bolg wore sleeveless, rough leather tunics over their bare, dark-complexioned torsos. The tunic was studded with closely-arranged iron rectangles sewn to the garment. The tunic's hood had the same iron rectangles.

A portion of the army, one-hundred men, wearing strapped leather bags between their upper arm and chest, with pipes jutting from the bag, assembled at intervals in front of the ranks. Their fingers covered holes on one of the pipes, and they took another into their mouth. They inflated their bags with breath and stood, allowing unintended hellish squeaks to escape.

Eochaid finished speaking, turned to face the enemy, and lifted his huge sword into the sky. The bagpipers began to play. It was an anthem, intended to inspire the Fir Bolg warriors. Eochaid lowered his sword and took a step forward.

The circling crow flew higher to lessen the horrible sound of the pipers. The Morrigan was angered by the annoying music. Shortly, she would show them the power of sound.

The Fir Bolgs walked quickly but did not charge.

As they reached archery range, they, without order, placed their hoods over their heads in such a manner the front hung out over their face, the heavy iron rectangles making the hood droop.

The first flight darkened the sky. The Tuatha De Danann's bows were made by elves. Nothing could compare to their range and accuracy. Before the first cloud of iron-tipped arrows reached their targets, a second cloud climbed upward.

The volley of arrows signaled the Fir Bolg to charge. Their long legs made quick strides. They rushed past the deploying slingers.

A volley of heavy stones arched into the air, then descended upon the enemy.

The army rushed past the spearmen as they stopped to hurl massive, iron-tipped spears over the heads of their kinsmen and into the ranks of defenders.

And finally, after volleys of large stones and spears, the huge, powerfully-built swordsmen crashed into what was left of the Tuatha De Danann's first ranks. Though suffering many casualties, the De Dananns did not retreat. The Fir Bolg respected them.

The long arms and five-foot swords cut swaths through the remaining enemy. The Tuatha De Danann's swords could not reach their enemy. Their light shafted spears were severed when thrust toward a Fir Bolg.

The Fir Bolg felt their surge through the defenders unstoppable. They were even more surprised that not a single enemy warrior had retreated.

Quickly eliminating the last soldiers in the last rank, the

Fir Bolg paused. The rest of the Dannan army had withdrawn.

Their ranks were still in the gap between the lakes, but now there were two hundred yards between the closest Fir Bolg and the enemy.

The successful attack was preplanned and practiced. Every Fir Bolg knew when and what to do. Now their organized ranks of slingers, spearmen and swordsmen were mingled. The pipes behind the disorganized mass of men that was their army continued to play the charge.

After a long minute, one Fir Bolg swordsman walked forward, towards the neat ranks of enemy soldiers. "Follow me!" the soldier called over his shoulder, and a second soldier obeyed. Then a third, a fourth. Then ten, twenty, one hundred, the entire mob of Fir Bolg soldiers moved toward the tight ranks of the Tuatha De Dananns.

Reorganizing while on the move is impossible. The mass was composed of intermingled groups, slingers, spearmen, swordsmen, even pipers, all mixed together.

King Eochaid, an arrow in his thigh and another in his sword arm, rallied himself but not his troops. He sent his officers forward to get the pipers to play the withdraw music.

Just as the mass was near the enemy's deadly bow range, a single piper, on his own, began playing the withdraw song. Another piper heard and joined in. The pipers spread the song throughout the mob, and the crowd of soldiers stopped and looked at one another. Soon the Fir Bolg began moving back toward their camp. They thought they had won and did not understand why the withdraw song sounded.

By night, Fir Bolg warriors sat in their camps, reunited with their comrades, at least most of them. The De Danann's downpour of arrows killed or wounded one in fifteen of the attacking waves. The soldiers thought themselves victorious and relived personal victories.

King Eochaid tried to recover from his wounds, more annoying than life threatening. He met with his leaders and went over the plan for tomorrow. Many of the soldiers would be busy until dawn making shields to defend against the arrows.

The sun rose behind the Tuatha De Danann camp. King Nuada stood fifty feet in front of the first rank of his defenders, soldiers who toiled through the night to complete many wooden palisades with long sharpened sapling trunks to slow the swordsmen's advance once they broke through. Yesterday's lesson was costly.

Once among his troops, the Fir Bolg swordsmen with their long arms and long swords prevented their targets offering an effective defense. The matrix of spiked palisades would not stop the enemy, but it would slow them down. Many of the poles affixed to driven stakes were parallel to the ground, others angled upward to prevent attackers from getting through by leaping over them.

Nuada looked out on the lake and was pleased. Today promised more sun and calm wind. He looked to make sure his flanks extended to the shores on both sides. He saw the large spiked logs, anchored end-to-end along the shores intended to impede any attempt to outflank his army through the water. He almost smiled as he surveyed the line of logs floating along both lakes' shores running between the two armies.

One last took toward the forming ranks of the Fir Bolg, and the king faded back through his troops.

He looked to the sky, hoping to see the large crow circling the battlefield. The Morrigan hated the Fir Bolg. His alliance with the demon goddess, undesirable as it might be, was based on that hate. King Nuada knew once the Fir Bolg were gone, she would turn on his race.

Yesterday, she did not intervene. Even as the Fir Bolg

swordsmen broke into the ranks with the murderous strokes of their huge swords, the Morrigan stayed over the carnage, relishing the meal of anguish served to her by the men on the ground.

The Morrigan did not contact Nuada since yesterday's battle ended. Nuada would not be surprised if she broke the alliance and came out only to feed amongst the freshly dead. No matter, his main motive for the alliance was to keep her from attacking both Fir Bolg and Tuatha De Danann.

The sound of the pipes playing screeching notes signaled the beginning of the day's carnage.

Frontlines of Fir Bolg slingers advanced. Twenty paces later, the spearmen followed. Then came the swordsmen, frighteningly big, packed shoulder to shoulder.

But something was different. The swordsmen each carried wooden shields, cut cross-sections of large threes. The shields were the size and shape of the section cut from the tree. Defenses against his bowmen, the shields might not render his arrows ineffective but would greatly reduce the damage and disruption they caused in the Fir Bolg ranks.

The Fir Bolg commanders had learned from yesterday, but, he hoped, his learning was the greater.

King Eochaid's wound prevented him leading today's attack. His replacement was much larger and fiercer in appearance than the king.

Silent, except for the discordant bagpipes, the Fir Bolg soldiers moved forward, unconcerned about a second battle with the Tuatha De Danann.

Nuada's archers, arrows nocked, their drawing hands holding two more arrows at the ready, waited for the command. When it came, a great thrumming sound resonated as the cloud of arrows arched upward to attain maximum range. Before the arrows reached their apex, the second arrow was nocked, drawn and released upon command. The first volley fell among the Fir Bolg a second before the third flight of arrows left their bows.

The wooden shields offered an additional layer of protection to the advancing enemy.

When in range, the remaining slingers loosed their apple-sized stones. They landed among archers within the matrix of palisades. They landed with great force, some breaking the wooden structures, others killing or wounding one to three men as they crashed down.

The arrows continued to rain down, but the shields reduced the number of combatants rendered ineffective.

Repeating yesterday's tactics, the spearmen came within range. Their heavy spears, easier to avoid than the slinger's stones, landed mostly among the palisades with much less damage done to the archer hiding and ducking behind timbers.

Nuada, anxious, watching his flanks, waited.

His archers fell quickly back through their own ranks of spear and sword.

Tuatha De Danann horns sounded as the charging Fir Bolg came within twenty paces of the first sharpened points of the palisades. Dannan men, hidden in holes spread along the length of the battle line, touched their burning torches to a shallow trench and ignited a portion of gelatinous material composed of resin, pitch, oils and animal fats.

A wall of flame, not so high as it was hot, sprang up, temporarily halting the advance.

More arrows swarmed into the paused men.

More swordsmen crowded into the Fir Bolg front, forcing some men into the fire. Pushed through to the other side of the blaze, they met with numerous arrows fired by kneeling archers hidden in the palisades.

The general leading the charge ordered men to hold his feet and legs and raise him to be seen and heard. He shouted in the unpleasant, guttural tongue of the Fir Bolg.

But before the troops could begin to rally, the Tuatha De Danann's trumpets sounded a second time.

Archers, hidden behind the logs floating from the lakes' shores, hundreds of them, rose and fired volley after volley into the flanks of the enemy.

The Fir Bolg's plated leather tunics were designed to deflect weapons from the front and rear. They offered little protection from the sides. Waves of them fell victim to the wicked arrowheads piercing the sides of their torsos and their legs.

Volley after volley reduced the enemy's numbers. Some gathered comrades and charged the water. The few that made it to the logs were killed before they could negotiate the spikes projecting from the floating tree trunks.

The pipes sounded the retreat.

Again, confused, but this time with a sense of defeat rather than victory, the Fir Bolg backed away from the opposing army.

Most of the Fir Bolg dead remained where they fell until an evening truce allowed their bodies to be recovered.

One casualty carried from the field was the general who rose above the heads of his men to rally them. His back bristled with arrows like a porcupine.

Though still much day remained, King Nuada did not feel another attack imminent and allowed his men to rest.

The third day, Fir Bolg hastily built siege machines that destroyed much of the palisades. When the swordsmen broke through this time, it was not as on the first day. They thought to repeat the slaughter, but their diminished number did not allow it. Still, they stubbornly pushed into the Tuatha De Danann's lines.

King Nuada led a counter-attack to drive the swordsmen back. It seemed to serve only to anger and inspire them. Not only did the counter-attack fail against their strength and reach, but King Nuada also left the field minus a hand.

Nuada held back his wizards until now. They stayed in the woods gathering energy from the power lines moving through the ground. The Tuatha De Danann king sent his youngest son to ask them to execute the spell.

For the next thirty minutes, the Fir Bolg siege machines moved closer and continued to destroy defenses. The swordsmen received a modest number of reinforcements, mostly spearmen, and pressed forward for the final breakthrough and the destruction of the enemy army.

Clouds began to form over each lake. They roiled together, growing thicker and darker. Black-purple clouds flashed ochre-yellow lightning within but never striking the water.

Either the Fir Bolg attackers, tasting their victory, did not see the clouds or did not care. Fighting in the rain was nothing new to them. They did not notice the clouds over Lough Mask move south, toward them. This movement, had they observed it, would not have concerned them. But they might have thought twice on continuing the killing had they seen the clouds over Lough Corrib blowing north, toward their position.

When the storm fronts met and merged directly over the strip of land between the lakes, they unleashed a downpour of fat, rust-colored, steaming drops. Warned in advance, the Tuatha De Danann drew back until they were out of the storm's line.

The Fir Bolgs, seeking to exploit their withdrawal, pressed forward. The grunting and whining began among them.

Where the rain found skin, a blister formed, then broke. The acid ate into their flesh. So deep it burned into their bodies, causing the hardened warriors to scream and cry. A few fled the battle and ran toward the cleaning water of the lakes.

When the acid rain plopped onto the iron rectangles sewn to their tunics, the metal began to rust until reddish channels scored the tunics along its drip line.

Within minutes, nothing living remained on the land between the lakes.

Again, the Morrigan had not entered the battle and Nuada, upon learning of the successful spell, felt sure she had abandoned their alliance and deserted him.

Just before dark, an envoy under a white flag approached the Tuatha De Danann defenses. A field officer went out to meet the enemy to parlay.

They stood talking, the Fir Bolg a head taller and half again as broad as the officer. The officer returned and sent a runner with a note to the king.

Within minutes, the runner returned with a different note and the officer marched off to again meet the waiting Fir Bolg. The Fir Bolg took the offered note and moved to rejoin his own army.

That night, the wounded King Eochaid and the wounded King Nuada each sought a champion for single combat that would decide the war.

The selected men would fight to the death at noon on the morrow.

King Nuada could not ask a man to face a Fir Bolg in single combat because he knew the person asked would accept only because the king requested. It was the way of the Tuatha De Danann; their king, Nuada or not, was the heart of their civilization, their civilization was the reason they survived so many millennia. If he asked for volunteers, the men would fight over who volunteered first. Good men were they all, brave men, men who suppressed fear to continue fighting alongside their brothers.

Whoever fought the Fir Bolg champion would have to be quick, for that was the only weakness Nuada saw in their physical aspects: lack of speed and dexterity. Their weapons, clothing, even siege machines were crudely made. It was more than lack of caring how the end piece looked, or how sharp an edge it held, or how the spear would not hold steady flight. It was a lack of dexterity, of coordination between the fingers and the eye. The Fir Bolg never needed it, so it never developed in them. Speed and finesse were how to defeat one in single combat. The champion must never allow a Fir Bolg's hand to close on him. Their physical strength was more than three times that of one of his own kind.

King Nuada decided on three men who possessed the best chance to win in single combat, but still, he could not ask, for they would all answer yes, whether they would have volunteered on their own or not.

He decided, that though he lost a hand to a blade only yesterday, he would offer himself. He would have a weapon made in the morning to compensate for his lost hand.

Before sunrise, the Fir Bolg pipes began playing dreary tunes that offended the mind by their awfulness. They sat at bonfires at the front of their line and burned great flames that carried sparks high into the sky. Somewhere, unseen behind their fires, they beat great drums.

Nuada called for the smith and handed him a drawing of what needed to be built.

Three hours later, with three hours left before the combat started, the smith returned with exactly what Nuada wanted.

The moment arrived. Nuada stood in the front rank of warriors at his end of the field. Many offered to fight instead of him, but he refused.

On the other end of the field, the Fir Bolg champion stepped out of the ranks and walked toward the center of the field. At first, in the distance, he looked like a larger than average Fir Bolg, but as he closed the distance, his true size became obvious. He was a monster of a man, perhaps eight feet tall, four feet across the shoulders. He wore his leather iron-studded tunic and carried the largest sword any had ever seen.

King Nuada swallowed hard and began his first step when a hand on his shoulder stopped him. He turned to say farewell to a comrade but instead saw a female warrior.

Raven black hair was made into a braided rope wrapped around her head and pinned with a miniature sword. She dressed in polished black leather, connected together with gold rings rather than stitches. She was tall, beautiful and poised.

"I am your champion," she said, looking into Nuada's eyes.

Nuada stared back into her eyes and saw who she was. In the depth of each eye, he saw the reflection of a crow.

She gently pushed King Nuada aside and strolled onto the field. As she walked, large black feathers seemed to appear and grow from her back until a pair of wings folded against her.

The pipes and drumming stopped. When they played again, the battle was to commence.

The Morrigan's current form created the image of a beautiful tall woman, taller than most men, with pale, perfect complexion, marine blue eyes. Her uncovered arms and legs spoke of unrevealed sinewy strength.

Her hands held weapons. A nine-inch, needle-sharp dagger was in each, each hilt gripped so the weapons pointed for thrusting.

The Fir Bolg realized she was a woman, looked over his shoulder and laughed.

The pipes sounded.

The giant champion did not alter his relaxed stance with his sword held by one hand laying across his shoulder. He stood as if he had not heard the pipes.

The tall woman of long limbs took a slow step toward him.

He pretended not to notice.

With the next step, she assumed a fighting stance,

301

positioning her two puny daggers.

The Fir Bolg monster finally responded. The sword came from his shoulder and powerfully swept low across his front. Had it found its mark, her legs would have been sliced clean just below the knees, and the fight would be over except for removing her pretty head.

Of course, the massive blow did nothing more than whine through empty air.

Which is where she was when it passed below her feet.

His left hand reached to grab her.

As gravity pulled her down and the powerful arm came toward her, she flicked the blade. When she landed in a squatting position, she rolled away from the angry beast. He stood looking at the deep cut on the inside of his forearm. Blood began flowing freely as he watched.

When he looked at her again, anger burned in his eyes. She looked back at him, raised one eyebrow and smiled.

He raised his sword high for a long-range downward blow; calculating she would step out of range, he brought it down with confidence the battle would be over.

The woman did not retreat. Instead, she dipped low and shot below his left arm, this time slicing the inside of the Fir Bolg's right thigh. After rolling away, she rose to face her adversary, to see him still turning to face her.

Now she toyed with him, darting in and out of his range. As he swiped his huge sword, sheets of blood flew from his wounded arm. With each move of his right leg, a thick stream of blood spurted from his wounded thigh.

Slow to begin with, he became even slower.

His coloring, at least the parts not smeared with blood, became ashen. First, she saw confusion in his angered, humiliated expression, which slowly turned to fear.

She moved around him with precision and speed never before seen by either side. There were many times his awkwardness presented killing strikes for her. Rather than take them, she preferred to watch the life flow from him.

As he became slightly unsteady, she said in perfect Fir Bolg, "You stupid bull, in a few minutes I am going to eat your testicles."

The last of his strength expended when he lunged forward, desperate to end this before he died. After a few seconds of futile chasing, he fell, face forward, his body exsanguinated.

The Morrigan turned him so his splayed legs faced the Fir Bolg. She lifted his blood-stained tunic, revealing his scrotum. With a performer's exaggerated moves, she slit the sack, sliced the balls loose, then one at a time popped them in her mouth and chewed loudly with an open mouth indicating it was delicious.

The Fir Bolg near enough to watch the battle went from ridiculous confidence to slight worry, then fear and finally horror as their champion fell to the ground. As she made such a show of dining on the fallen's testicles, they felt rage.

One left the safety of numbers and started toward the woman. Then others followed his lead.

Before the first man had gone thirty paces, the woman stood straight and drifted above the ground. An incredible light blue light flashed, temporarily blinding everyone who watched.

When the flash was gone and vision restored, three women stood where a moment before there had been one. The dagger-armed warrior stood now flanked by two others. On her right, a queenly looking woman, plump and pregnant. On her left, a hag, clothed in rags.

The three women drifted slowly toward the army.

King Eochaid, held erect by two men, watched the spectacle with growing concern. He realized they were not facing mortal creatures and screamed for the withdrawal. A few pipes began the first few notes, and the army became a route, an uncontrolled race to reach their ships on the beaches of Galway.

The three women increased their speed, floating into the woods.

The screams began.

The Tuatha De Danann scouts assigned to follow the retreating army heard never-ending screams all night. Just before sunrise, the last screams ended abruptly.

Moving toward Galway, the way was littered with unspeakable carnage. No Fir Bolg enjoyed a quick death. It appeared as if pain had been wrung from them drop by drop. Upon reaching Galway, all the Fir Bolg's ships sat at anchor. The few locals found attested to no Fir Bolg reaching the docks, nor even the town.

Sitting atop the three standing stones in the circle near the battlefield of three thousand years ago, the crows cawed, trilled and chattered in the pleasuring memory of the destruction they enjoyed on those four days.

In the not too distant future, they would recreate the feast of carnage but on a grander scale, a much grander scale.

In the meantime, they would enjoy spreading their horror to three more towns tonight. The number of apostles spreading their fear and horror grew exponentially. Even the towns so far untouched dreaded their coming. An underlying atmosphere of fear grew in the west of Ireland like a fog rising from the ground.

☐

Journey to Newgrange

Branna sat on a pew near the front of the church. Michael, Father Bob, and Gladys gathered around her.

"As I was saying, before we were so rudely rescued by the handsome scallywag in the obnoxious, noisy contraption," Branna paused and smiled at Michael who returned her smile with puppy eyes. "There are two types of changelings," Branna continued. "The most common is created when a Sidhe infant is altered to appear identical and swapped for a human infant then, when physically mature, they return to their worlds. The human changeling returns to its natural parents, the memory of being raised with the Sidhe eradicated and replaced with visions from the Sidhe's child from its human family.

"In most cases, this works, causing minimum disruption of the human family. In some cases, something breaks down in the human's mind and consequences,

305

sometimes severe, occur. Branna stopped to appraise her audience. "Yes, Father Bob, what is it?" she asked seeing the ever-inquisitive priest held a question in check.

"What is the purpose of this changeling type? What do the Sidhe gain?" he asked.

"The Sidhe child joins its own race, its knowledge of human nature instinctive instead of learned. The Sidhe child's physical body fades but he is able to manifest himself more physically and for longer in the human world, expediting what the Sidhe do in their manipulation of man's affairs. But, eventually, that changeling loses the manifestation ability and can no longer exist physically in the human world any longer than a natural Sidhe."

Branna paused, saw no one wanted to interrupt, and said, "I am, as is my mother, a halfling, changeling. My human mother, Lucy Margarette, unbeknownst to herself, became pregnant on the eve of my father Piers Edmond Butler's annual hunt in County Carlow. Father became temporarily lost in a thicket, then upon exiting, stumbled onto a huge Dolman atop a cairn. Thinking it was a never before recorded megalithic structure, he dismounted and examined it more closely.

"His account of the story is that while crawling under the capstone's low end, he rose too quickly and knocked himself unconscious. When he woke, three hours later and no longer able to hear the dogs baying, and not finding a dolman or cairn, he rode to the first house he saw and asked directions back to the manor in Carlow town.

"What happened under the dolman's capstone is, Piers, taken to my mother's world, woke under my mother's enchantment. They made passionate love for a full day, well beyond my father's usual stamina. My mother placed him in slumber and returned Piers to his world.

"The two babies were born within three days of each other, and my mother swapped me for the one born of Lucy Butler.

"You know the rest of the story; I only discovered this since arriving on Achill Island."

A short silence was broken by Father Bob. "So, what is the difference, and advantage to the Sidhe, of a halfling changeling?"

Branna looked at the priest. "The first advantage is obvious, as you can see; my physical body is always manifest in this world. There are no difficulties at all for me to live my entire life here."

Michael seemed relieved when she said she could stay here.

"I am," she said, "essentially an ambassador between Sidhe and Human. At the same time," Branna continued, "my Sidhe half allows me to learn and direct natural energy to produce certain effects."

"Hence the blue lightning outside Collin's house," the priest commented.

"Yes," Branna responded, "That was actually my first time trying it in this world. It was a little frightening."

"Branna," Michael's tone was cautious, "Does your plan to stop these things depend on you being close to them to use this energy?" Michael asked.

Branna beamed at Michael, "You sound as if you care."

"I care enough to do what can be done to protect you." Michael did not smile back but kept his eyes locked on hers and his expression serious.

"So, would you like to share your plan?" Father Bob asked.

"We are to travel to Newgrange," Branna said, adding, "Oonaugh will come to me there. That is all I know for now."

"Then it is off to Newgrange," Michael said, ringing his endorsement of Branna's instruction. "Sean," Michael asked, "are you up for a few days of facing the horrors of hell on the other side of Ireland?"

"Sir, I must try to find my family in Mallaranny before I

can commit to anything else," Sean said in a troubled voice.

"We will need more food, petrol and probably whiskey," Michael expounded.

"I'll stay and help Father O'Connor and Collin," Gladys said. "This is as far away from Achill I've ever been and don't intend to go farther from home. Morrigan or no Morrigan."

Father Bob left enough food to last the three of them four or five days. What was left would last those on the road to Newgrange only two days but the thinking was as they moved eastward, towns would be less disrupted, and they could purchase more.

Father Bob blessed and prayed for each who remained behind.

Sean drove the Delahaye motorcar along the road toward Mallaranny where the only human found was a salvager from Westport loading a wagon with pieces of lumber from partially destroyed buildings.

Everyone felt the shadow of evil about the town.

Michael said as they poked about the rubble, "It is as if great sin committed there drove God away."

"You know better, Mikey Doyle," Father Bob answered, referring to the inspector by his boyhood name. "God may abandon a place, but he is never driven from it. Like you, I feel the shadow of sin on this town, but God's sun will shine and drive it away."

"Well then," Michael answered, voice tense, as he looked at the rubble and thought of what the Morrigan did to the people in those ritual circles, "I ask you for the second time, where is God's light in all of this? I do not think he is here, nor do I think you can find him."

"Michael!" Branna spoke to Michael as his mother did when, as a boy, he violated a rule. "Do not give up, not now. You must believe. You already know belief is the ultimate power at our disposal."

"I believe in you," Michael said, unashamed. "I believe in our personal priest, but it is difficult for me to believe God allows this slaughter by foul creatures to destroy so many people."

"My faith in the God of the church is not strong," Branna answered, "but my faith in the creator of all things, 'seen and unseen,' grows with each atrocity. God is present, here and now, but not even my mother or her people, or the forty-two watchers can ever know why God does what he does."

Father Bob felt left out. After all, he was the holy man of the group. He thought he should add something to all this talk of God. "Seen and unseen has new meaning affixed to it. So many worlds, so many races. It is all part of His creation and plan. It hurts me, Michael, to hear you speak this way. I feel I have let you down."

"Oh, stop it, you overgrown altar boy. You have not let me or anyone else down. My faith is tested by this. When I do not see God's answer, I question my belief, that is just what happens."

Sean, who had walked up unnoticed, said, "Me Mum always said, 'If you believe in the Lord, everything will be alright in the end. If things are not alright, then it's not the end.'"

Michael laughed. "Well, if everything will be alright, we should get straight to the end." He laughed for the first time in days.

As they returned to the vehicle, Sean climbed into the driver's seat.

"Apparently you intend to stay with us," Michael said.

The boy looked at the inspector. "I can't really do anything to help find missing folk. If it's alright with you, sir, I will continue with you. The fishing has been off this year anyways."

They averaged between fifteen and twenty miles an hour, and it was dark by the time they entered

Roscommon. A single room was available at an inn, so they shared it for the night.

Shortly past midnight, people began arriving in the streets of Roscommon. Their crying and chatter woke Father Bob first, then Michael. They opened a window and listened.

It took little time for them to understand these people were fleeing the Morrigan's attack on Glenamaddy, about fifteen miles west of Roscommon. From the roof of the inn, looking in the direction of the latest attack, they saw the yellow glow of a perishing town.

Feeling he was empowered by knowing as much as possible, Michael went into the streets to learn what he could. The attack was similar to Mallaranny: air demons, humiliating ritual buggering, forced public worshipping of the Morrigan and turning from the false God. The trauma apparent in these victims surpassed anything Michael had seen in the survivors of Mallaranny.

Looking up at the inn, Michael saw the group's faces staring back from the window. He shook his head 'no' in a sad manner, indicating no good news.

The next morning, in the back of the car, Michael napped, or tried to, as the road allowed.

"Newgrange is one of the oldest, if not the oldest, ancient sites in Europe," Branna said as Sean turned left at a road with a sign directing them to the megalithic site.

"Are you a teacher, miss?" Sean asked, "I mean, how do you know so much of these things?"

"I'm a professor at Trinity University, I study very old things in our part of the world," Branna responded.

The answer seemed sufficient for Sean, who swerved to avoid a hole in the road.

Hearing no response from Sean, Branna continued speaking to Father Bob who turned to face the back from his seat. "There is no knowing who actually built it. Its size, a decorated inner chamber and an opening above the door that aligns with the sun on winter solstice make it remarkable among all other monuments so far discovered in the British Isles."

"I have heard," Father Bob spoke, "when viewed from above, the inner chamber is shaped like a cross, the same as many cathedrals."

"It is," replied Branna.

"It strikes me strange, the inner part, presumably the place of worship, sacrifice or whatever happened there, is shaped like a cross and built before Christ's life," Father Bob spoke, as the vehicle turned right and then stopped.

"We're here," said Sean, excitement in his voice. He leaped from the driver's seat and made his way toward the ancient site's entrance.

Cromwell jumped to relieve himself and terrorize local fauna.

"Hold up, Sean. This is Branna's expedition. Give her time to study and decide the best way to approach," Michael called.

Sean stopped and turned toward Michael. "Yes, sir. I'm just excited."

Branna, flanked by Michael and the priest, stood looking at the ancient spectacle. A mound, nearly forty feet high at its center was composed of two hundred thousand alternating layers of dirt and rock, mostly quartz. A fifteen foot high retaining wall, again built of quartz stones, circled the nearly one acre of ground the monument occupied. Megaliths, kerbstones, some four feet high and ten feet long, had been placed out from the wall and sat in a ring around the eerie place. It would have been beautiful, awe-inspiring, spiritually powerful except it was, for the most part, overgrown with weeds and natural shrubs concealing most of the art carvings in the kerbstones.

The large stone directly before the entrance contained a series of symbols from the megalithic period. The most prominent caught everyone's attention: tripled spirals formed a triangle. These spiral images did not flow elegantly together as did the symbol of the Morrigan but they were close enough in appearance to make everyone stop and think.

"Examinations of this area have revealed three mounds," Branna said. "Newgrange is by far the grandest. The three cairns, when seen from the air, form a triangle." Branna stopped and allowed her last statement to sink in.

The entrance to the mound, considered by archeologists to be a portal tomb, was a simple rectangle: a hearthstone at the bottom, two supporting stones on the sides and a lintel across the top. Above the lintel, a second rectangular opening allowed morning light to fill the inner chamber from the entrance to the altar. This 'lighting of the chamber' occurred during sunrise on the winter solstice.

Though overgrown and some of the quartz stone façade fallen to disrepair, everyone, including Sean, felt its power.

"I'm not sure about going inside, what with all the demons and the killings. It might be better for me to stay here and guard the automobile," Sean said, hoping for a quick agreement from someone.

Michael did not disappoint the boy. "Fine idea, Sean. Get a shotgun and light some lanterns for us to see what is inside."

Sean happily busied himself.

"If we go now, we will have the advantage of daylight for some part of the chamber," Michael said to Branna.

The priest looked at Branna. "What do you expect to find in there? Any monsters that bump or scrape in the night?"

"Not really, but Michael, I might be a good idea for you to arm yourself, just in case," she said, studying the entrance.

Sean arrived with three lit lanterns, a loaded shotgun

and a handful of shells.

"Better sooner than later," the priest said staring into the chamber's darkness.

"I'll lead," Michael said.

"Be careful," Branna offered unnecessarily.

Once inside, Michael had to stoop slightly to keep his head below the stone ceiling. "I will hold my lantern low to see where we walk. If you can, hold yours above my shoulders to light the rest of our walk."

As they moved slowly and carefully down the eighty-foot stone hallway, they saw many examples of megalithic artwork etched into stones. When they stopped at the end of the manmade tunnel, they looked at the two alcoves and altar.

Each heard only their own breathing.

Michael felt the strangeness of this place.

"Something is wrong," Branna said, moving to the center space between alcoves and altar. "The Earth energy is absent," she said, placing her lantern on the floor between feet and altar. "This is the most energetic place in Ireland, one of the most in the world," Branna said, her hands moving over megalithic art on the stones.

"The same type of energy at Dugort?" Michael asked.

"Yes," Branna answered absently, looking for a clue as to what had happened.

"Maybe iron has blocked the energy flow, the same way you had us fill the portal tomb's trench with iron," Michael offered.

Branna stopped, unable to feel any power inside the chamber. She turned to Michael. "I do not think so. Energy comes to Newgrange from several other sites. In fact, the energy in Dugort came from Slievemore and Croaghaun and are part of a network of energy moving here.

"This energy is from the Earth. The planet generates and emits it. The ancients, first aware of its existence, used it, then understanding the power's relationship with quartz and other crystals, built Neolithic stone structures to try and harness it," Branna said, turning toward the altar, fingers lightly touching the surfaces there.

"Eventually, when they knew enough, they created paths, or lines, to transfer the energy from one stone structure to the next. We call these lines, 'leys,' or 'ley lines,'" Branna said, glancing back at Father Bob.

Then she continued, "They built Newgrange as the central power station of Ireland, Britton, and parts of Europe. Stonehenge, Avebury, Glastonbury Tor, Carnac, all the major stone monuments were constructed after Newgrange; their purpose, to feed the Earth's power to Newgrange. No one knows how the builders used the energy."

"What is your theory?" Michael wanted to know.

"Since Achill Island, and my trip to the Sidhe world, I know one thing for sure. The power in the ancient sites opens and closes portals to other worlds. Hence the double entendre of calling this place, and many others, portal tombs. They were not only used by the dead on their passage to the next world but also, doorways to worlds we cannot see," Branna answered. "Ancient Gaelic lore is filled with tales of humans falling asleep at stone sites only to wake in faerie lands."

Father Bob, holding his lantern higher to closely examine the art on one of the stones, tossed out a fact. "In the Church, laymen are common worshippers. They are taught to 'walk the straight and narrow path.' Originally layman was spelled l-e-y-man, which gives new meaning to the phrase."

Michael quoted the Bible. "'Look not to the things that are seen but to the things that are unseen,' Second Corinthians. We have witnessed creatures from these worlds. We know they are real. Convincing others who have not experienced the Morrigan will prove challenging."

Branna looked at Michael. "If we can't find a way to stop her, we will not need to convince others of her existence, she will do that herself."

"Why are we here, Branna?" Father Bob asked, looking into Branna's eyes in the yellowish lantern light.

"Oonaugh said the Watchers told the Sidhe leaders the Morrigan would come here before leaving Ireland. At Newgrange, she can quickly amass the Earth energy she needs to continue to grow her power," Branna replied.

"As I said before, the Sidhe derive all their worldly power from the planet energies from our world and their own. The Morrigan needs a supply of Earth energies to maintain her corporeal presence in our world. Most of her demonic power, however, comes from feeding on fear, pain, death, and suffering of others. If she plans to leave Ireland, it will be essential to restore all of her Earth generated power."

"What if she does not come?" inquired the priest.

"The Watchers are the repentant angels, their ability to know the future is without equal, at least outside of heaven. The Morrigan will come," Branna responded.

Michael looked at the others. "The bigger question is, what do we do when they show up?"

The altar provided a low glow. As the altar's glow grew brighter, the alcove stones glowed. By the time the light around them glowed a white light, brilliant enough to wash colors out, it filled the entire passageway.

"The energy is back. It's not just back, it is pouring in as if it had been held back and now the dam is opened. The power is incredible," Branna said, touching the glowing stones, which made her fingers light with the same color.

Assuming the surging power was for her, she told the others to back away and positioned herself to receive the energy rushing as a flooded river.

The entire cave glowed softly as more and more energy filled the huge mound around and above the chamber. The quartz rocks surrounded the channel amplified and focused the incoming power.

The altar end of the chamber glowed brightly. Colors washed out in the white light.

Branna rose from the ground and hung, back arched, a few inches above the floor.

The Chamber's brightness increased until the entire cavity blinded Michael and Father Bob.

"Get out!" Branna spoke in a frightened voice.

Hearing the fear in her voice, Michael, unable to see anything in the blaze of whiteness, called to her, "Branna. I'm coming to get you."

Feeling along the wall that vibrated with energy, Michael took one step toward Branna suspended near the altar.

His hand snapped away from the wall as it shocked him. He tried to place it back on the wall but quickly jerked it away.

A series of electric bolts flashed from the surfaces of the chamber. The light diminished for a second and Michael saw a mesh of living energy formed around Branna. Then the light brightened, and all that could be seen was blank, infinite white.

"Get out of here now, Michael! This could kill you. Now go!" Branna's voice broke as she spoke.

At that moment, a gust of what felt like static electricity literally pushed the priest and Michael a foot toward the altar. Before they recovered, a second gust moved them back another foot.

"Michael, we have to go," Father Bob pleaded, no longer able to see even his hand in the brightest light ever seen on Earth.

Before Michael could answer, a gunshot from outside the mound sounded.

Sean Encounters The Morrigan

Sean thought how God smiled on him the day he helped the inspector with the automobile. He'd begun the greatest adventure of his life. The travels and talk of monsters and ancient gods repressed the thoughts of his parents for a time, but now the concern for his family was back.

He was worried they were hurt, away from their home, or worse, killed by those demonic creatures. He felt being here, at this moment, a curse and a blessing. The money he earned per day for driving and helping was more than he made for a week of fishing.

Cromwell bounded from the brush, a large fresh rabbit hanging from his mouth. The dog brought it to Sean, dropped it, backed up a step, smiled and wildly wagged his tail.

"Good boy, Cromwell, you are a good boy." Sean picked up the rabbit, found a piece of wood and staked the dead animal down. He took his knife from its sheath and began the task of cleaning and skinning the animal. He loved rabbit and looked forward to the surprised look on his companions' faces when they exited the chamber to the fine smell of fresh meat roasting on a spit.

Cromwell barked once then let loose a fit of barks and growls.

Sean looked at Cromwell to discover what the animal watched. The dog was looking toward him.

Suddenly a huge hand clasped his throat, lifted him into the air, took two steps and slammed him down on the Delahaye's bonnet. Sean felt his nose break, and some teeth rattled.

The beast released him.

Sean lay still, slightly moving his head to catch a glimpse of the thing that held him like a toy.

Sean saw the devil. At least he thought it was the devil at first then remembered the talk of the Morrigan in a red-skinned, hooved foot form.

The Morrigan stood before him, forked tongue flicking in and out between pointed teeth and a mouth which formed part of a disinterested expression.

The thing that was the Morrigan stared at him with its shining black eyes, opened its mouth and screamed like nothing ever heard by Sean. It hurt his ears, then his head, then his chest. Everything hurt.

Sean made himself roll to the other side of the bonnet, fell to the ground, placing both hands over his bleeding ears. The thing effortlessly leaped onto the bonnet, its hard black hooves bending the quarter-inch-thick steel downward.

The shotgun, shell chambered, leaned against the driver's door. The horrible shriek died out. Sean, every part of him hurting from the excruciating sound, obtained the gun, cocked the hammer and fired nearly point blank into the Morrigan's face.

The thing's features vanished as the large shotgun

318

pellets tore through the flesh, revealing emptiness between the front and back of the Morrigan's head.

The now headless monster regained its footing on the vehicle's bonnet. It stood, quivering for a moment as the red flesh cracked into papier-mâché-like fragments and fell to the vehicle.

Even as the empty dried skin fell, beneath it appeared a loathsome, bulbous skin of bluish dead flesh. Faster than the brain could understand the transition occurring, a fully grown, bloated animated giant corpse dropped from the vehicle with a solid thud with a disgusting rotting foot on either side of Sean's body.

Sean looked up into the creature's single, yellowed eye.

It reached an enormous pulpy hand towards Sean's face.

The shotgun fired again.

Sean saw the pellets enter and lodge into the monstrous palm above his face.

The hand twitched back before descending, more than covering Sean's entire face, cutting off the air, but careful not to assert so much pressure as to crush the skull.

Sean's hands struggled to remove the hand to unblock an airway. His own hands wrestled with the giant's fingers to pry them from their grip. He tried turning his head left or right, desperate for air.

He heard the huge corpse make a tiny sound. He heard it giggle, like a baby.

He felt rather than heard a series of running steps then nothing.

The creature released his face and stood.

Sean saw the creature had only one arm, a right one and it was busy vigorously shaking to unlock Cromwell's bite above the thing's wrist.

In a moment, Cromwell was shaken with enough force to pull a ham-size piece of dead flesh from the thing's arm. The dog, flung viciously against a kerbstone in front of the entrance to the chamber, cried and whimpered pitifully as his body slammed against the large megalith.

The single, murky yellow eye of a blind monster looked back at Sean as the boy struggled to remove himself from between the aberration's feet.

The giant placed the arch of his left foot on Sean's left thigh, pinning it firmly to the ground. He leaned over and, with his single hand, lifted a large rectangular cut stone, probably knocked over by drunken visitors. With not so much as a light grunt, he raised the stone over his head, looked at Sean's face for a second and smiled, showing teeth the size of rotten plums.

Sean lay, helplessly pinned, as the monster raised the stone a little higher and laughed a sound hollow of reason, a laugh with no cause.

A second shot came from outside the chamber.

Michael, reacting more than thinking, said, "Leave."

Father Bob, a few feet ahead of Michael, answered, "What do you think I am trying to do?"

Like blind men, they felt their way, placing one hand over the other on the chamber wall until the light softened and they were able to see a little more with each step.

They exited the chamber entrance and paused to allow their eyes to adjust to the twilight outside.

Michael and Father Bob's heads snapped toward the sound of laughter.

With no hesitation, Michael raised the shotgun taken from the Westport Barracks.

Sean would die when that stone came down.

Michael took a step toward the great, hideous thing he recognized as the creature that slaughtered the O'Malley lad and his mother in their home.

The naked giant's appearance looked like a five or six-week-old corpse pulled from a lake or river, bloated and rotting, wearing the color of death. The giant's smell suited his appearance.

"Over here, you murderous corpse!" Michael yelled, shouldering the new model Browning A-5, semi-automatic shotgun.

The creature offered no reaction.

Before the stone moved forward, Cromwell, severely injured but driven by instincts and love, was not out of the fight; the loyal dog ignored his pain, and leaped, mouth agape, onto the rear of the giant's thigh.

As the hideous, animated corpse turned to deal with the dog clamped to his leg, it was again thrown off balance.

Michael had closed the distance to less than twenty feet when he fired the first shot.

The twelve-gage shell exploded eight one-third inch diameter pellets down its smooth bore and struck the giant's lower back with enough force to knock him forward. At twenty feet, the eight projectiles all hit within a six-inch diameter pattern. Immediately, thick black liquid began flowing from the holes.

Michael fired the second shot, another load of buckshot into the same area.

The monster had not yet recovered his balance. Still turning to deal with the large dog death-grip and pushed forward when the lead pellets struck its back, he released the stone, which fell behind him.

Sean, filled with the coming of certain death, gathered his senses and rolled away from the towering hulk.

Cromwell also fell, pulling an oversized hunk of rotted meat from the creature's leg.

The second shot slammed its eight lead balls into the same area of the back. These pellets passed deeper through the area previously opened where two of them lodged in the lower spine.

The thing seemed to feel no pain but turned now to face Michael and the priest.

Father Bob carried a second Browning A-5. As he reached Michael's side, he fired four rounds. The intervals between shots were only the partial second it required to retarget.

His rounds fired much faster than Michael's, struck the foul-smelling beast near or in the rear of its left knee.

Its single eye lit with burning hatred.

Michael took careful aim, and eight pellets ripped through its eye, leaving a messy hollow splattered with black fluid and other goo. Michael's next shot passed through the hollow toward the thing's brain if it had one.

Michael, not oblivious to Father Bob's targeting, fired his final shot at the front of the left knee.

The massive creature's leg collapsed at the knee and broke apart as the terror crumpled to the ground.

It made no sound, nor did it move.

There was no sign of breathing.

Michael stood his ground and reloaded his weapon.

Father Bob kneeled and crossed himself in prayer.

"Bob, I think God is telling you to reload," Michael said, his hands pushing shells into the gun's tube as fast as he could.

"Yes, of course," the priest said, taking his friend's advice.

Beyond the fallen giant, Sean sat on the ground. Michael could not tell if he was wiping blood from his face, crying, or both.

Steam rose from the great corpse.

The odor forced the two men to step away.

The foul meat that lay where the monster stood glowed blue and short electrical streaks shot through it. The electric -aced blue formed a sphere. Shaped like an egg, narrow end upward, it grew to twelve feet tall and became increasingly bright as the electrical streaks increased in volume and size.

Suddenly, the blue orb evaporated.

In its place stood the three sisters, all staring at the two humans who dared to disrupt their evening plans.

Badb Catha wore the battle dress of five thousand years ago, Nemain, her famous banshee attire, and Macha, that of a queen witch, dressed in black. None wore a pleasant expression.

At first, the sisters stood where they appeared. Unmoving, their eyes never wavered from Michael and Father Bob.

Behind the sisters, Cromwell made his way to Sean, sat and tried to lick the blood and tears from the boy's face.

"You have done nothing, man of man's law and priest of God's law. You have temporarily disabled a projection of our power, a living image of our creation. You cannot harm us. We cannot die. What made you think you could defy us? Do you think the half-breed Watcher child could do anything but delay us? All men are fools. It has always been and will always be," spoke Badb in their minds.

"The girl? The halfling bitch, has already abandoned you. She knows neither she, nor any of her kind, can stand against us. They lost their power in this world thousands of years ago. They now huddle in fear inside a hidden world, no longer able to face us here," she continued.

Michael absently looked over his shoulder. No light came from the cave.

"She is no longer in the mound, man of man's law. No doubt she has fled to her mother's cowardly world where the Sidhe hide, helpless, waiting for their final day," Badb brayed. "Failed creatures God designed. Weak in their beliefs. They are such a waste of immortality." Badb spit a blackish slug of mucous to show her disgust.

"Michael," Father Bob whispered trying to avoid notice of the sisters. "Back toward the chamber. Slowly."

Macha floated above the ground, her black-witch queen

appearance a perfect image of evil, malevolent beauty. Her shadow moved ahead of her.

She stopped, her shadow continued. It remained connected at her feet but quickly lengthened until it shrouded Father Bob.

Father Bob looked up. Through the shadow covering him, he saw the sky in hell, bruised purple clouds, roiling against a sickly yellow sky. Bolts of magenta lightning firing up to the clouds, feeding the storm with energy. The fires of hell reflected dully from the bottoms of the clouds. A black, oily rain fell from the clouds.

Paralyzed by horror, Father Bob watched streams of foul liquid descend toward the shadow. A plump drop passed through the opening to hell created by the shadow. It struck his upturned face, and he dropped his head, turned and ran for the shelter of Newgrange's chamber.

"Run, Michael! The chamber! Run!" Father Bob moved toward the chamber entrance as fast as he could, wiping the devil's rain from his head which already started dissolving the flesh below it.

"Run, priest, worshipper of a vain God who deserted you when you questioned him," Macha called in his head.

Nemain, in her ear-shattering voice that made bodies' insides vibrate, filled the air with, "The god of vanity is your end. The end of man. Worship he who fled from your destruction."

The hand he used to wipe his head began to burn. Father Bob wiped it on his pants.

Inside the chamber entrance, the priest turned to confirm Michael's presence.

"Did any fall on you?" Father Bob asked.

"Any what?" Michael replied.

"Never mind," the priest said, "We should move to the altar."

The chamber no longer glowed. The lanterns they left behind were out. Though the outside provided twilight, a few steps past the chamber entrance, the depth of blackness was soul-quaking.

Hand over hand against the wall, they moved deeper, constantly casting backward glances to see what followed.

Michael counted the steps of their progress. "We are close," he said softly, finding himself growing dizzy in the utter blackness.

Father Bob's foot struck something.

"Stop," he whispered.

Michael heard something metallic move across the floor. More sounds of Father Bob's hands touching something.

"A lantern?" Michael asked.

A match snapped, and a flame touched the lantern's wick.

"Let there be light," said the priest.

The light allowed them to see the altar and alcoves. Branna was not there.

"She did not desert us," Michael stated.

"I know she did not, but where is she?" The priest lifted the light and examined the walls for cracks or openings.

The Banshee's voice hissed, echoing into the chamber, "We are coming for you."

"Oh, what pleasure we will take in sodomizing your virgin arses. We may bring Balfor back. Oh, how he loves to diddle with his enormous dead penis when we make it erect for him."

Both men cringed.

"Your fear and revulsion taste so delightful. May we have some more?" The hideous voice coaxed more emotions from them.

Several stones beneath the altar stone gave way as Branna pushed herself out from under the stone lintel.

Rather than stand, she held her finger to her lips and motioned them to follow her. She backed into the tunnel under the altar.

Michael immediately knelt and crawled in behind her.

The small tunnel's walls glowed enough light for Michael to follow Branna's rear ahead of him.

"What about concealing this passage?" Father Bob whispered as he followed Michael.

"Shhhh," Branna whispered.

"Shhhhh," Michael repeated.

"Shhhhh," Father Bob repeated to the person he pretended to be behind him.

After about fifty feet, the passage opened and appeared much like a mineshaft ascending, held solid by large quarried stones in a pier and beam fashion. Branna was able to stand. Michael and the priest had to stoop, but they were happy to no longer crawl.

The shaft made four switchbacks before it ended in a circular chamber, walls lined in interlocking polished quartz crystal pyramids. Inside each pyramid, hundreds of miniature spikes of electricity snapped on and off, creating a flickering light in the round chamber.

Branna looked at Michael. "This next part may be a little unnerving for you. Just trust me."

"I trust you with more than my life," Michael said, "What should I do?"

"Stand in the center of the room."

Rising to the Top of Newgrange

Michael followed her instructions. He looked up and saw a large, inverted pyramid with a four by four-foot base, pointing down. Constructed so the point was even with the rest of the ceiling. It was more than large enough to kill a person should it fall on them.

"Close your eyes," Branna said, adding, "Oh yes, don't move or you might be injured."

"Never crossed my mind," Michael replied sarcastically, eyes closed tightly, dizziness growing.

Branna hummed the unusual rhythm. Dampened by the room's crystal walls, Michael heard music; beautiful music played on various-sized flutes, lyres, harps, drums, timpans and other stringed instruments, as well as the unmistakable great pipes. The music somehow harmonized with Branna's humming, not the other way around.

Mesmerized by the music and distracted by growing vertigo, Michael did not feel himself rise from the ground.

Somehow the mixed experience made him smile.

Father Bob stood in silent disbelief as his childhood friend, smiling for only God knows why, lifted from the ground and passed upwards inside the crystal pyramid. He heard Branna's humming increase in intensity and then, quite abruptly, stop.

"It is your turn, Father Bob," Branna said, indicating he should stand under the pyramid's point.

Michael's vertigo no longer allowed him to stand without something to hold. He opened his eyes, recognized he stood atop the Newgrange mound and dropped. Someone caught him before he fell far, then stepped closer to support him.

"Come, sit here," Sean said and helped him sit on a patch of grass.

Michael wanted to talk, but with vomiting imminent, he instead mouthed, 'thank you,' and lay on his back, eyes closed, arms and legs spread-eagle hoping to regain his balance. As the world spun around, his fingers grabbed grass to steady himself. He slowly calmed then drifted to sleep.

A moment later, the sound of Father Bob retching nearby roused him, much of his balance returned.

He saw Sean helping Father Bob, Cromwell laying in a bloodied patch of grass and Branna sitting cross-legged on the ground, which, Michael guessed, was exactly atop the inverted pyramid's base.

Sitting up, Michael asked Branna, "Are they gone?"

Branna held up a hand asking for silence, as she finished whatever it was she was doing.

"Not yet," Branna said. "I hope we see them here, very soon."

"That is not my preference," Michael said. "I assume, as I have learned to do, that you have a plan. My question, since you no longer wish to share, is: is it a good one?"

"If it works, it is a brilliant idea. If it does not, well, I wish to apologize in advance for causing all of your deaths," Branna mused.

"Sometimes you are not as funny as you believe yourself to be," Michael stated, regaining his feet.

"I side with Michael in this case," the priest added.

"Is it brilliant?" Michael asked.

"The plan?" Branna responded. "I believe so. Mother and a world full of Sidhe thought of it."

Remembering what Branna first told him, then repeated in the Morrigan's recent words, Father Bob asked, "Is it true? The Sidhe can no longer exist in our world?"

Branna stood, looked to the sky and answered, "My people are unable to maintain a physical presence here for more than a second or two. It is too draining. As I said before, they taught themselves other ways to help humans. I am an example of one of those ways."

Three crows soared in from behind Branna. They circled her several times at blurring speed. Each revolution closed tighter until Branna appeared unable to move.

The birds began trailing electric-blue colored mist as they slowly widened the circle and slowed.

Thinking the vapor trails poison, Michael pivoted to dash inside the rings and pull Branna out with him. Before his body launched, the three crows flashed blinding light. The birds were replaced by the three sisters, surrounding Branna.

They stood three feet distance from Branna. Their eyes never left her for an instant. Appearing as they did earlier, the warrior-witch spoke. "We think it is time for you to go, dearie," she said, voice hissing and smacking.

The ground beneath Branna's feet vibrated. She widened her stance to stay balanced.

The vibrations' frequency made the earth on which Branna stood break apart. Tiny grains of soil rapidly bounced, dancing relentlessly to unheard rhythms.

The Morrigan cast a glance groundward asking, "What is this? A plan to shake us into pieces?"

Badb curled a nasty smile. Her clothing dissolved like wet paint and ran down her flesh. Her streaked, naked flesh sprouted large black feathers. Branna did not need to look to know the other two sisters sprouted their own oversized crow feathers.

At that moment, thinking what he could do to help, Michael realized his weapons were below, in the mound's crystal chamber.

Branna threw her head back and sounded a single, long and powerful note. All the mound's natural energy flooded upward from the mound.

The Morrigan felt it. She didn't understand why Branna would give Earth energy to her murderers, let alone so much. It made no sense.

Around the top of the mound's perimeter, a few feet inside the quartz retaining wall, beams of energy appeared and slowly, like a great water fountain gaining pressure, rose upward. Each stream of light flickered a spectrum of violet to midnight blue and grew wider as it rose higher into the sky.

Michael's vertigo and nausea attacked instantly and registered a much higher degree of sickness. Michael, unable to function, reached out his arms as he fell.

Father Bob landed next to Michael.

Their ears rang a consistent frequency, the music from before changed into various bell tones sounding at random times in addition to the ringing.

Sean fared no better. He lay on his side, pressed against the whining Cromwell.

None of them could even open their eyes to see what was next.

The Morrigan, filled with the Earth's energy as never before in its twelve thousand years, felt beyond powerful.

Her strength was limitless, her power unstoppable.

'But why,' she wondered? 'Why would this halfling make it so easy for her?"

The feeling of invincibility was fleeting.

The Morrigan felt a low-frequency vibration within her chest. The power continued pouring in, and it made her heart and other organs buzz inside her.

Surprised, she looked at Branna, genuine concern in her eyes for the first time in three millennia. "What do you think, little girl?" the Morrigan asked. "Do you think you can drown me in power?"

Branna made no reply. The note she sang changed to a higher one. She held it at an even, loud volume for an impossibly long time.

The widening beams around the mound's perimeter merged, creating a wall of living light that continued to reach higher as the full spectrum of midnight blue to violet danced in individual beams. As seconds passed, the dancing colors connected to their kin on either side until the encircling wall pulsed the spectrum around the mound.

The entire wall pulsed like a huge drum skin. A bass note sounded and The Morrigan felt the particles of her soul vibrate. The wall played a series of notes with increasing tempo until it became an oppressive deep buzzing.

The Morrigan felt the buzzing spread throughout her body. She began to burn inside, the heat gradually spreading outward.

Her transformation into a giant crow completed as the buzzing spread. She stood staring at Branna, a crow's head and chest with human arms and a naked lower half.

Looking beyond the halfling little bitch, she watched the movements within the wall of light, and she realized this was not the Sidhe's magic; these were forty-two angels, the repentant Watchers, fathers of the Sidhe.

That realization allowed an epiphany, and she instantly

understood the danger. The circle of energy, already closed around the circumference, rose and slowly folded inward. They constructed a cage. So long as the ley lines continued pouring energy into the mound, and, consequently, into her, she would be trapped for as long as it took them to figure out how to dispatch her ugly soul to hell.

The power inside the sisters could no longer be contained. It had to be released.

Each sister opened their crow beak and hurled a fiery cyclone toward Branna. The powerful spinning vortex quickly widened enough to encompass Branna. As the three attacks reached Branna, they triggered electric sparks revealing an invisible wall around the girl.

Branna quickly sank into the pyramid below the ground.

The sisters launched a different attack; stones rose from the ground and flung themselves at Branna. They laughed when Branna's entranced body reacted to dozens of stones pelting her before she completed her descent.

Badb tried to follow, but the energy in the pyramid struck at her as she came near.

She realized her spiteful attack on Branna was a waste of time, a diversion from the real threat, the cage closing as the forty-two continued their methodical construction.

The Morrigan's three incarnations released all the energy they possessed upward into the sky. Before the energy could again recharge to dangerous levels, each of them, standing on the points of their invisible triangle, lifted their wings. The crows took flight, beating wings to gain altitude as quickly as possible.

The crows flew nearly straight up, spiraling around each other as they ascended, like invisible cords braiding in the air. Each time the three crows spiraled around the others, three new crows popped into existence and joined the flight pattern, spawning three more crows along with the next three from the original. In seconds, the crows became a living column growing thicker and higher.

In seconds, thousands of real crows from outside the walls of light, called by the Morrigan, gathered and funneled into the growing mass of birds climbing upward. The air was black with crows.

The wall stopped sealing the top of the cage.

The wall of energy began sounding great, deep notes. The notes alternated with the cycling of the prismatic color transformation.

Like the walls of Jericho, the crows died. Birds fell by the thousands, then tens of thousands. Shattered creatures, small drops of blood seeped from them. They piled themselves in ever-deepening layers like a hailstorm of black feathered pieces.

The Morrigan struggled against the harmonic vibrations. Gaining the last feet of altitude challenged their will and muscles. Seeing how close to escape provided the final push needed and they climbed higher.

Suddenly, above them, similar to a camera's aperture, a swirling vortex opened, and before the three of them could even lose enough momentum to fall, they flew straight into Hell, a place of lakes of fire and mountains of flowing lava.

Behind them, the vortex snapped shut, trapping the would-be god in the world of their fathers.

☐

Life is Good Again

When the sun rose, a steady breeze ruffled feathers on the circle of piles of dead birds' broken wings.

People who lived close enough to witness the light in the night sky came in daylight to explore unusual event. The adults did not want to scale the retaining walls for fear of disease among so many dead birds. Some teenage boys, issuing escalating dares back and forth among themselves, made it to the mound blanketed with layers of dead birds. They called down, describing the scene.

The boys quickly lost interest in walking on the bodies of innocent dead birds and climbed down to share the scene with others interested to know.

A reporter and photographer arrived a day later to do a story for the Irish Times. By then, the birds provided a smell so foul no person could bring themselves to be with them.

People noticed house cats exploring the area. At first, they seemed determined to reach the fallen prey on top of the mound. Then, one by one, they went up for a second or two before they came leaping down the wall, eyes as large as half-crowns and ran for home as if the Devil himself chased them.

Curiosity wanes as it does and the smell kept people away for several days. By the time the odor allowed visitors again, the cameraman found nothing to photograph except heaps of bird bones.

Finally, the talk and speculation of what actually occurred died down and people went on with their usual lives, thankful that none of the rebels who burned towns in the southwest came closer.

After several weeks, it was generally believed the constabulary had dealt with the rebels, and there would be no more raids.

Life was good again.

Father O'Connor passed two days after their group left for Newgrange. His mood, much improved, stayed jovial until the hour he died.

No longer any people on the road, there was no point in holding service. Collin and Gladys dug a grave in the small cemetery behind St. Ignatius Church. The hole was probably too small and shallow compared to a proper grave, but digging was hard work, and Collin was still recovering. Gladys said a few words over the corpse of the priest she met two days before. Collin discovered to his horror, since his illness, he lost his taste for alcohol. He called his lack of wanting, and ability hold any strong drink down, the 'Curse of the Banshee.' Which he fully intended to incorporate in future tales.

Despite everything, Gladys and Collin were both drawn to return to Achill Island, even if no one else was there. It was their home. It was the geographic place where their hearts and minds settled into contentment.

They were surprised when they entered Collin's house.

The place was tidier than Collin ever saw it before. Gladys squinted about the room, ran her finger over a freshly dusted tabletop, then picked up and smelled a linen doily.

"Collin, the good people were here. The little ones, flitting about cleaning and repairing. My goodness, they must have felt they owed you a debt," Gladys said, delighted by the state of the house.

Collin fell into his freshly cleaned comfy chair. "Ow," he exclaimed. "I sat on something. Hope it's not one of the little maids you're talking about," he giggled, secretly glad the house was so clean. He decided that moment he might try to keep it better than he had.

Collin extracted a small burlap bag marked on the outside by a printed green shamrock.

"It's heavy," he said and reached inside. He stood, facing Gladys, saying, "Well, look what else the good neighbors gave us."

Collin turned the bag topside down.

Gladys squealed with a child's delight as a hundred gold coins fell onto the chair's cushion.

Collin opened the bag, added fifty coins then handed it to Gladys. "This is your share, you earned it as much or more than I did."

"Oh, go on with you. What am I going to do with that much money on a now deserted island?" Gladys asked.

Collin shook the bag indicating for her to take it and she did.

After a few days, they went to Dugort to scavenge flour, sugar, salt and other useful things. Though eerily quiet, the town, ocean, waves and sea air made them smile.

They moved into the Slievemore Hotel, made repairs then went to their work. Gladys planted a garden. Collin fixed up a boat for fishing.

At night, they sat by the fire in the hotel lobby. Gladys knitted and, eventually Collin took up reading.

Life was good again.

Father Bob crossed the Irish Sea, then the English Channel. He spent five days on a train to Rome. Once there, he visited with his papal friends asking for their help. He was sitting in a lavishly marbled and columned outer room. From stepping on the first boat of this journey to sitting on the cushioned chair waiting for the door to open, he practiced, revised and practiced again what he would say.

The door opened. A cardinal said, "His Holiness will see you now."

Life was good again.

Michael woke from a hard sleep. No dreams, no interruptions, just a dead sleep.

He opened his eyes to a room illuminated with soft white light that was somehow perfect. When his vision cleared, he saw the rounded wall was made of polished quartz bricks.

"They must defuse the light from outside," Michael mumbled to himself then added, "No need for windows."

But there was a window where Michael swore one did not exist a second earlier.

Michael got out of bed, noting it was the most comfortable bed he had ever been on and walked to the window.

On the way, he realized he wore a silvery fabric nightshirt.

Michael reached the window and looked out at a landscape more beautiful than he could have dreamed. Rolling green hills mixed with grass, orchards, and gardens and were decorated by natural rock outcroppings, springs, and waterfalls.

Michael looked downward.

He saw Sean and Cromwell frolicking in the freshly cut lush green grass. Sean laughed as Cromwell entertained him with his rolling, bounding, and barking that sounded exactly like a laugh.

He heard someone clearing their throat behind him. He recognized the voice at once and spun around.

A small table, set with a magnificent breakfast, had appeared in the room. Branna sat smiling broadly at Michael in one of the two chairs.

"Am I in Heaven?" Michael asked.

"You are closer than you were," Branna answered.

"Then I have wasted too much time already," Michael said, striding to the table. He reached down and tenderly raised Branna's chin and kissed her full on the lips. Nothing brotherly about this kiss. It conveyed a pent-up passion. The kiss lasted. Branna rose from the chair and circled her arms behind Michael. She pressed against him.

Branna felt her heart flutter. No matter what, she knew Michael was her man.

The kiss ended. The pair continued embracing.

"I want to spend the rest of my life with you," Michael said.

"I am in full agreement, Sub-inspector," Branna said, then added, "Can we start with breakfast?"

Life was good again — so very good.

The Morrigan

The three immortal crows issued panicked caws. Hell is hot, as it turns out. They flew in a V formation, climbing to rise about the furnace below which was the world.

Immortal though they were, the relentless flames superheated the air. Even immortal feathers singed and dried and made staying above the misery below difficult. They fought a losing battle to stay aloft.

To make matters worse, rumbling brown clouds containing blood red fires within moved toward them.

The Morrigan thought, "Father, General of warring angels, Creator of Chaos, hear my prayer. We are in your world. We have done nothing but evil. We have spared no one from torture. Help us to be good children of Satan. Save us from suffering in this world. We know you have no mercy, but we offer to redouble your works on humans. Amen."

The Morrigan suffered no false hopes. She knew he was a hard master. She began to fall downward, wings catching fire and crumpling to ash. The Morrigan could not even guess what living would be like in their new world of continuous torture.

Suddenly, she fell through a vortex and emerged into a clear blue sky where cotton ball clouds moved slowly south. She and her sisters inhaled the clean air at their altitude.

The disturbance on the surface ten thousand feet below caught her attention. Muted sounds of explosions rose from the earth. She descended and saw the earth below; for miles east and west had been scarred with ditches, networks of deep gullies parallel to each other.

She was low enough now to feel the air pressure as huge shells arched upward then fell on the enemies' trenches. The explosions ripped the earth asunder. Dirt geysers erupted into the air.

She felt power assailing her. It radiated from below.

In the trenches men, millions of them, killed and wounded their enemy. Sometimes, when waves of soldiers wearing metal hats rose from the trenches and charged across the barren middle ground already littered with death from previous attacks, the fear rose from them and filled the sisters' beaks with the taste of power.

They did nothing but remain high enough to avoid shells rising and falling. They circled the battlefield time and time again.

This was their heaven.

The End

About the Author
By Herbie Brennan

Steve Peek is the kind of author who, in the old days, was discovered. A publisher ttried one of his books, then another until one of them found itself in bookstore windows. Suddenly he would have been another Grisham, Clancy, Crichton, Patterson or even King, discovered by the New York Times Sunday edition. Unfortunately for readers, in today's world, that's not going to happen.

Peek's books are not formulaic novels with stereotypical characters struggling against standard villains. Each book is unique. Readers are surprised by his research and ability to blend facts with fiction. Every book twist and turns and never ends quite as expected.

I met Peek through writing in the 1970s. He published some of my books and games. More than that, he gave me concepts for my two most successful book series; Grail Quest and Faery Wars. After fifty years and one-hundred published titles, I know great writing when I read it. Peek has been a favorite author even before publishing his work. He has only improved since.

Peek studied in summer writers' workshops taught by greats including; Kurt Vonnegut, James Dickey, and his cousin, Pat Conroy. He began writing in earnest in 2012.

His fans look forward to his next book, whatever the genre.

Difficult to classify his books, they are always reviewed as unique and fresh storylines with believable characters. Often, he can't help sprinkling a touch of humor in an otherwise serious scene.

I promise if you read his work you will find: He is a master storyteller, his writing tight, and his books unique.

I hope you choose to discover Peek's talent.

Peek's books on Amazon include:

The Boy in the Well
Caligula: Murderer Immortal
W-G-O-D: In your Dreams, All night, Every Night
The Island Builders
Your Money or Your Mustard
Longclaws
Alien Agenda
Coyote Dreaming
Otherworld
The Game Inventors Handbook
Million Dollar Monster (Short Story)
The Sword of the Stone (Short Story)
Global Warning (Short Story)
New Roads (Short Story)
The Sword of the Flame (Short Story)
One Day Sale (Short Story)
Aboard the Starship Warden (Short Story)
Hell on Earth (Short Story)

He appreciates the magic of life and the interconnection of all things.

He would like to hear from you via steve peek author on Facebook or jstephenpeek@gmail.com

LONG CLAWS
The Following is an Excerpt from Long Claws
Background of Sample

Remote Alabama. Cut off by rain flooded rivers: a veteran with a secret, a runaway teenage boy, and a Cherokee medicine woman face terrifying creatures – the Long Claws, a clan of cunning beings equipped to track and kill with speed and strength like nothing seen before.

Chapter Four

The World that Rains Fire

There was nothing for them between the jetties but death. Even if they could reach the beach below before other larger predators swarmed to the frenzy, they were creatures of the land. The sea offered only death.

Leader had lived too long to allow his clan to walk into disaster. He ordered the clan to move.

Old for his kind, he had survived sixteen years due to intelligence. Many creatures were more powerful than his kind and could devour a longclaw in a second—if they could catch one.

Catching one was the trick. Leader's race survived a brutal environment by guile and cunning. With instincts, senses, and abilities precision-honed by disinterested evolution, longclaws were perfect for their niche. Yet even perfection afforded only a tenuous hold for any creature.

Leader was responsible for the clan's lives, and owned their instant, unquestioning obedience. He became the clan's leader when a great crawler ate his father. Death by any other means than predator was nonexistent.

Before his father's body was completely in the creature's mouth, Leader took command. The clan instantly accepted him: no communication necessary, no time wasted in transition. His mother—the dead leader's

343

mate, still able to bear young—paired with the Watcher, the member responsible for guarding the rear while the rest focused on hunting or escape. His mate became the new Speaker. His oldest son replaced him as Scout. This all happened within seconds of his father's death as they fled across a parched, flat valley floor between towering cliffs.

The old leader's death left the clan with eight members. Six to twelve was good for a clan, but his did not have enough females. More than twelve longclaws attracted too many predators. When a clan grew to twelve members, the leader divided it, creating two clans, each going separate directions. In his lifetime, his clan had split three times, forming new clans with the dead leaders' sons as clan heads.

The clan hunted. Scout captured a slow-moving, plated creature with venom-injecting fangs and claws. He sliced off the shellback's head with a killing claw and placed it on flat, open ground in a rock-strewn gorge. The clan could not eat shellbacks' poisoned meat, but they could eat many animals that fed on shellbacks. They waited anxiously behind rocks, downwind, sniffing for prey and predators.

Watcher dutifully did not sense the area immediately around the dead shellback, but focused on the sky and rocky cliff faces.

Only a few moments passed before Watcher mind-spoke to Leader. "Cave flyers, above, across."

Leader did not answer, nor did Watcher expect one, as he scanned and sniffed to detect attacks.

Sharp-bills had scented the bait and sniffed eagerly, ready to dart out and pick the shellback's exposed feet and neck with razor-edged beaks.

The clan waited.

Watcher mind-spoke again. "Cave flyers come."

Leader cast his eyes upward, seeing a pack of cave flyers gliding toward them. Their wings—taut, tough hide-sheets attached along their sides, arms, and legs—allowed the cliff-cave dwellers to glide, but not gain much altitude. Leader could not tell if they were after the clan, the bait, or the sharp-bills hidden in the rocks.

He waited, observing everything.

The sharp-bills swarmed from hiding, ferociously tearing meat from the dead animal. The cave flyers stayed on course, quickening their descent. They would be among the sharp-bills in seconds. Leader waited.

As the cave flyers swooped past the frantically feeding sharp-bills, each attempted to snatch with one clawed foot while the other sank and re-sank wickedly curved, two-inch, needle-sharp talons into flesh. Some were successful. Others missed or were themselves injured by the sharp-bills' edged beaks as they scrambled for safety.

The successful cave flyers landed, lustily devouring meals in gulping bites. Their narrow throats swelled with passing food. The less-successful flyers chased sharp-bills on foot.

Leader mind-spoke. "Kill."

Scout, the two hunters, and Leader sprang from the rocks, darting into the midst of the feeding cave flyers. The three females formed a rough perimeter around the killing party while Watcher stood away, alert for more predators.

A cave flyer, intent on feeding, saw its attacker too late. It leapt, positioning its talons between itself and its assailant, but Leader was too quick. Leader's left killing claw thrust into the animal's vulnerable belly. Burying its full nine inches before jerking it across, he sliced through the creature's vital organs. At the same time, he thrust his right killing claw into the flyer's face. It hit hard bone, glanced off it, and skidded down, parting flesh like a zipper opening. The dying creature retreated, desperately trying to free itself from the fire in its innards. Leader moved with it, keeping his left claw deep inside. His right claw flashed, cutting cleanly across the victim's neck. Its head fell back like an opened trunk lid. Leader rode the prey to the ground, heart still pumping, talons reflexively clawing the air. Leader extended and opened his snout, placed it on the exposed throat, and sucked the warm, spurting blood.

In less than a minute, sated, he offered the quivering prey to his mate.

The other hunters also fared well, though his oldest son, Scout, received a nasty wound on the thigh. They formed a perimeter while the females and Watcher drank.

The cave flyers retreated a short distance. Snarling, snapping jaws filled with jagged teeth, leaping, and showing talons, they scampered to safety up the cliff facing.

Another minute and Leader mind-spoke, "Flee."

The clan ran. Scout took his position at the column's head, followed by the hunters, then Leader slightly ahead of the females, with Watcher bringing up the rear.

They ran upright on powerful, horse-like legs, each stride covering four feet. Their goat-like hooves, impervious to rough terrain, carried them sure-footedly away, easily outdistancing another group of attacking cave flyers.

The clan did not run blindly. To do so would invite disaster. They were always hunted and always hunting. Complete alertness kept them alive. If for a moment they stopped concentrating on survival, their demise would be swift and merciless. Everything was a predator, no rival species given an instant's advantage.

The clan of longclaws stopped at a narrow stream that smelled strongly of sulfur. They took long, quick drinks and continued their flight, sensing for trouble with every stride.

They ran along a plateau's edge. To their right, a terrifying landscape dropped away. Spread between the clan and the horizon, spaced unevenly and intermingled with mesas and jutting, barren rock hills, six volcanoes spewed dirty smoke into the sky, their red glow like demon beacons marking a dead sea.

Always running between or near fields of boulders, they trotted to a temporary lair. Twice Scout signaled trouble, and the clan hid among large, craggy, yellow-crusted rocks, waiting until it was safe to continue.

Reaching a steep hillside and quickly climbing its slanted, loose, shale base, they used powerful hands and arms to pull themselves up the cliff. Precarious, inch-wide ledges provided footing until they gained entrance to a small cave halfway up.

When they started their journey, after the kill, the sun had been three quarters away across its arc. Still above the horizon, its light diffused through dirty clouds, the sun was a pale orb creating a daylong dusk. As they reached the cave, thick storm clouds reduced the sun to a faint, purplish glow, dimmer than the most distant volcano. Their inner eyelids reflexively opened, allowing owl-like, nocturnal eyes perfect night vision.

A crawler—a spider-like creature a foot across—occupied the cave, patiently digging its trap. Scout speared it with a killing claw before climbing through. The clan followed.

The setting sun left the night lit only by lava flows and sporadic, molten eruptions in the distance. An unseen moon journeyed across the sky behind lightning-laced clouds. Just enough light entered the cave to keep it from total blackness. The clan members were creatures of the dark. The brightest days wore a twilight quality. Evolution provided large, nocturnal eyes, with large, slit pupils like a cat covering most of the exposed surface.

Watcher squatted at the cave's entrance, sniffing and watching for any hint of attackers. The rest of the clan formed a circle.

347

"Mind-speak to others," Leader ordered.

Crouched in a circle, they linked minds and let Speaker's thoughts become their own. Soon they were engaged in the sunset mind-speak with other clans.

Less than twenty miles away, the Clan of Red Mountain told of a skirmish with howlers. Both species lost heavily, but the carnage ended with the appearance of a great flyer. The most feared predator, great flyers were enormous creatures so powerful only another of its kind could kill it. Usually they sought larger food than longclaws or howlers, but for the two species to draw attention to themselves in open combat was rare.

The Clan of Deep River joined the linking of thoughts with a strong message. A mass pursued them toward the great plateau. They ran at an angle, hoping to move beyond the mass's left flank before reaching the precipice.

Leader knew their plight. He spoke to his own clan and they broke the mind link. They scampered out of the cave to avoid sharing the fate that might befall the Clan of Deep River.

Feeling the flow of the energy lines crisscrossing the planet, Leader moved south, hoping to move below the westward-moving mass.

The mass consisted of billions of insect-like creatures. A foot in length, each wielded oversized, powerful mandibles, two sharp, crab-like claws, and a barbed, poisonous, whip-like tail. Every few years, colonies hatched billions of eggs, then emerged from underground hives. They joined forces, creating a carpet of death miles across. No living thing stood against them. Relentlessly scrambling over, around, up, or down obstacles in a solid sheet of murderous clacking, they trapped creatures that killed thousands of them before succumbing to smothering torture as the mass covered and devoured it.

Leader set a fast pace. After several miles, the escarpment sloped downward, eventually melding with a vast plain. Leader located a narrow crevice in the escarpment's face and moved his clan to shelter for a brief rest.

Scout began to limp. The ugly wound inflicted by the cave flyer's claws had festered. His normally light-gray skin had turned blackish purple around the ragged gash. Scout caught Leader examining his leg. Their eyes met. Scout blinked his big eyes, but neither spoke. They knew if the wound worsened, Scout would leave the clan to avoid attracting predators with the scent of infection. Gnat-sized insects already buzzed around the seeping gash.

After resting, they trotted eastward, following a line of power to a tangled forest of wicked thorn trees. They caught a saw-jaw, a four-foot reptile with thousand-toothed jaws. After draining its blood, they used its body to lure a family of tusks out from the thicket. The clan killed two animals, each twice the size of a longclaw. The others snorted angrily from the cover of impenetrable thorns as the clan sucked blood from the beasts' throats.

They followed the same energy path eastward, skirting the forest. A few hundred yards from their last kill, Watcher mind-spoke of a group of smallish flyers passing over from the north. They seemed to be zeroing in on the two corpses left beside the thorn tangles.

Flyers came in all shapes and sizes, from no larger than a longclaw's hand to those like the one attracted to the battle between the longclaws and pack of howlers. So large its beating wings drove the clouds, its claws able to encompass and lift creatures twenty times larger than a longclaw. The great flyers flew alone, high above the clouds, feeding on smaller flyers. Smaller varieties flocked together: the smaller the flyer, the larger the flock. Some were flying reptiles, others nightmare gargoyles: they all dropped soundlessly through the clouds hoping to catch unwary prey. Some hovered above cave entrances to snatch the heads of cave flyers or other animals foolish enough to come out. Feared and respected, their ability to fly was a huge advantage, especially on days when clouds were low and they skimmed only yards above the surface, looking for food.

Leader increased the pace as the clan turned north.

They traveled a dozen miles before seeing bodies of the mass littered as far as they could see. Gassy tendrils steamed from each corpse as digestive acids ate through decaying stomachs. These mindless creatures starved to death on their march. Eventually millions died because they were so far to the rear no food lasted long enough for them to reach. When the mass dwindled, the survivors burrowed, forming colonies until the next time. It would be days before this mass burrowed.

With no food left in the mass's wake, Leader ordered the clan to backtrack, then headed for a favorite hunting area. They fed three times before stopping in a high cave to mind-speak with other clans at sunset.

Scout's leg was bad. A thick, milky pus oozed from the torn flesh when squeezed. Leader mind-spoke, "Squeeze poison out, sun rise, leg good, clan go toward Path of Two Hands."

Scout's eyes darted from Leader's. If his leg was not better by sunrise, Leader had told him the clan's destination so he could follow, but he could no longer threaten them with his presence.

They headed to a place where six lines of power crossed, a dangerous place for creatures that used the energy paths for reckoning. The conjunction of the lines of power often caused dizziness and disorientation, often attracting sick or wounded creatures, making them easy prey. It was called Path of Two Hands because longclaws' hands each had three fingers; therefore, both hands equaled the number of bisecting lines of power. A longclaw's hand had an opposing thumb, an index finger, and a finger nearly as long where a human's little finger would be. Between, where the ring and middle finger would occupy a human hand, was a large knuckle. A killing claw, with a dozen or so growth rings at its base, grew from the knuckle. The lethal appendage was eight to nine inches of bone-hard, ivory-like substance that gently curved into a wicked point. Though rounded for strength at the top, the underside tapered wedge-like to a fine, serrated cutting edge, which, like flint, self-sharpened as old growth fell away and was replaced by a new edge.

Speaker could not function for the Sunset Mind-Speak with Others. Her pregnancy was full term and she would deliver very soon. Watcher's mate easily filled her role. The clan gathered and listened.

The Clan of Brown Rain had been decimated, five of eight killed in attacks by two separate howler packs. Three survivors lived only because the howlers turned to fight predators drawn to the fray.

This news caused concern. Howlers were an intelligent species. Though inferior to longclaws in brainpower, their natural packing instincts made them fearsome enemies. Unlike many creatures that lived and hunted together, the howlers devised strategies and cooperated, making them extremely dangerous.

Howlers knew there was prey less dangerous than longclaws, and it was rare for the rival species to meet in combat. At least it had been. In two days, there had been three attacks. The howlers' activity always reached maniacal levels when the sallow full moon sailed on visibility's edge behind constant clouds. It was during these times, if at all, a pack—running flat out, howling into the night—sometimes stumbled into a fight with longclaws. Lately, something had caused howlers to aggressively attack at every encounter.

The clan stayed in the cave half an hour before moving twenty miles to another shelter. There, Leader's mate gave birth to twins: a male and female. Since she could carry only one and still function, Scout's mate, herself pregnant, became the female infant's nursemaid and protector.

Before sunrise, the clan set out for the Path of Two Hands. Leader's hunter-son replaced his brother as Scout. The wounded son could no longer stay with the clan. He waited until they were a mile ahead before following.

The energy forming the lines of power naturally fluctuated, but the longclaws had noticed a gradual increase over the last few days. Nearing the six intersecting lines, the energy's intensity was disarming. The clan stopped to realign itself several times. Leader began to think the power was so strong even wounded animals would stay away. They were on a rise overlooking a rolling, ash-covered plain. The lines of power crossing the plain actually became visible as they neared the focus. The clan cautiously observed the pulsing glow, waiting for Leader's instructions.

One instant the flat, dried earth was empty, then it filled with flashes of lightning and peals of thunder like never before. When the longclaws' eyes adjusted, they stared in disbelief. An alien thing sat on the ground dripping water from its sides. A huge thing—multicolored but mostly brown—it tilted to one side and did not move.

The clan shrank back as one. Leader was unsure, the event so outside experience that he froze. The smell of prey was about the thing. Not a smell he recognized, but unmistakably the odor of food.

Then he saw them, moving slowly over the brown thing. Some jumped from the listing side, while others climbed down ropes at the thing's ends. Their scent overpowered. Perhaps there was danger, but there was also food.

"Kill," Leader mind-spoke, and the clan flashed forward. Crossing the plain, they were among the prey without warning.

It was slaughter. Not much smaller than a longclaw,

the two-legged, soft-skinned animals seemed slow and puny. Frightened, fleeing their assailants, some jumped from the brown thing and ran; others vanished into the brown thing's belly. Longclaws easily caught the ones they chased, decapitating most with a single swipe, gorging on the spurting blood. It was a feast. Normal feeding order broke as female longclaws, two with infants wrapped tightly around their necks, joined in.

The old scout caught up to the group and killed three escaping in his direction.

The butchery was massive. In a feeding frenzy, unable to control primal urges, longclaws went through the brown thing, sniffing the easily killed creatures from hiding. Blood was everywhere. The scent would be strong to other predators. The longclaws could drink no more. A few animals still lived, crying strange sounds from behind a smooth wall at the end of a narrow tunnel. Scout scraped a killing claw across it, gouging its surface. Again, and the gouge deepened. He thrust his claw into the wall. It penetrated, then stuck momentarily as he yanked it back. The scent came through the hole.

Again he thrust, this time prying the splintering surface, ripping it as he pulled free.

As the hole grew larger, the terrified creatures beyond the wall jumped through an opening and ran for their lives.

Many helpless creatures postponed death simply because longclaws were busy killing and feeding.

Watcher mind-spoke urgently, "Many flyers come. A great crawler also. Maybe howlers."

Leader, covered in blood like the other longclaws, pulled his dripping claw from the dead animal's back and lifted his nose. Many predators approached, drawn by the carnage.

Leader mind-spoke, "Flee."

They ran at top speed, kicking up a dust cloud. They blurred past two weak animals from the brown thing. In seconds, they were far enough away to chance a backward glance.

Various-sized flyers swarmed, finishing the remaining animals. A great crawler towered into the sky, its ten legs skittering toward the smell of food.

The old scout—Leader's oldest son, unable to move at full speed on his bad leg—fought two flyers with a third coming in. Despite his strength and quickness, it was only a matter of time before needle-sharp claws and fangs ripped the flesh from his bones.

Leader increased the pace. They would have to travel far from this place to be safe. Other animals, scenting increasing death, converged.

The thing had been a mystery, a gift from the Power. In seasons past without number, the Power had been more generous with its gifts.

Hunger sated, the clan ran on. Leader considered the thing and longclaw legends. He remembered stories of the howlers' gift and power lines. He thought many things while his senses constantly searched for danger. He would have much to say at the sunset mind-speak to other clans.

Reaching a shallow stream, they washed the blood from their bodies in sulfurous waters.□

The Following is an Excerpt From

THE ISLAND BUILDERS

Background

This mind-bending novel manages to convince the end of the world is not just nigh but may turn out not to be such a bad thing. Steve Peek's, The Island Builders tells the story of new islands suddenly risen from the sea. Their sudden appearance leads to the disappearance of tens of millions of people and collapse of civilization.

Against this terrifying background, the story follows a rogue physicist, an unstable President, a beautiful TV reporter, and three of the weirdest aliens ever to appear in literature, as they attempt to survive a world gone mad.

A novel that haunts your imagination.

DAY 1: Columbus Day

The perky, strawberry-blonde looked directly into camera three, crossed her famous legs, and said from the left end of the studio sofa, "Hi, I'm Kelley Regent."

"And I'm Charley Fuller," the tiny, old man on the other end of the sofa said for what seemed like the millionth time in an overly-long career driven by fear of anonymity.

Then, a heartbeat later, they said in unison, "And this is American Sunrise."

Filmed live at 6:00 a.m. EST, the daily gifts for the audience members, if not the show's popularity, always filled the four-hundred-seat studio. The early-rising audience applauded and cheered as instructed by the flashing LED lights in the sign above the set.

Charlie began, "Say, Kelley, did you see those photos coming into the website?" Before she could answer, had she chosen to, he continued, "No one seems to know what kind of hoax this is, but there couldn't be a better one for Columbus Day."

A smiling Kelley, who was closer to sixty than fifty, but tried her best to look thirty, said, "Let's take a look at some of the photos and see if the audience has a clue."

The giant monitor in the studio began showing photographs of islands taken with sunrise backgrounds.

Kelley furrowed her brow as much as last week's Botox injection allowed and said, "Why are we showing these to you? What's special about them?" She paused for two seconds, a very long time in TV Land. "They are not particularly beautiful. They are not great quality. And, most importantly, they are not real." She paused again for effect, then continued. "Go through the images again, and watch where they were taken."

The first slide filled TV screens along the eastern seaboard. Its caption read, "Coast of India, 8:15 a.m. local time." The photo itself was unremarkable. Taken from a rocky beach facing eastward, it showed a landmass just inside the horizon. The distance and poor quality of the photograph showed something that filled the camera frame from north to south. It looked like land, but the quality of the photo suggested it could be a large, dense fog bank.

The next photo came from South Africa, again facing eastward. The landmass – fog, or whatever it was – seemed about the same proportions and distance from shore as the first slide, but the quality was better. In this one, the "mountains" seemed higher and more distinct. It had a slightly greenish hue, suggesting it was not fog.

The third image came from the coast of Maine, the camera operated by a professional nature photographer with a telephoto lens. Instead of capturing the endangered crested loon, she had snapped a photo that was a bit fuzzy but, if studied, revealed granite-like cliffs in what first appeared to be fog.

"What the heck are we looking at?" the little man with too much makeup exclaimed to the audience. "Kelley, any idea what these photos are of?"

"Not sure, Charley, but at the moment, the bet is this is some kind of Columbus Day hoax. These same and other photos like them are pouring into newsrooms around the world. Either they show landmasses that do not exist off every coast in the world, or similar fog banks at the same time of day, or they are faked."

"It's Columbus Day, and we are receiving photos of

'New Lands, New Worlds.' Is it possible that a group of people orchestrated a huge hoax using the Internet? One man thinks so. He is Doctor Aaron Rothschild, an expert in the psychological and social aspects of the Internet on human society. We've all heard of or experienced flash-mobs. Doctor Rothschild thinks we might be seeing the first Internet flash-hoax. He will join us when we return, so stay tuned to learn more about these weird photographs, right after these words from our sponsors." Kelley finished, stood up, covered her mike, pulled down her short skirt, which had hiked up too far, and said softly, "Jesus, Charley, what the hell are these things?"

"Damned if I know, Kelley, damned if I know."☐

DAY 1: Little Creek, Virginia

Lieutenant J.G. Johnson-Picket, JP to his friends, stood in the cockpit of Coast Guard rapid response boat NLCV3. The forty-five-foot, self-righting vessel sped toward the mysterious fogbank at thirty-eight knots. The spray continually soaked the deck as the hull hammered the swells. Four wiper-blades worked to clear the windshield.

JP gripped a rough-water rail with one hand, held binoculars in the other, and listened intently to the message coming from the Coast Guard helicopter.

"Little Creek Victor 3, this is NCLC6, out of Little Creek, Virginia. Do you copy?"

The rapid response boat was five miles from the fogbank. The helicopter had passed overhead a couple of minutes ago and was by now no more than two miles from the objective.

As Johnson-Pickett's boat approached the objective, his high-powered binoculars showed that he was in fact looking at a landmass, with beaches, trees, mountains, a river, and natural rock formations. The radar and infrared onboard the vessel indicated otherwise. The scopes were empty, not a blipping thing except for the helicopter.

"This is Little Creek Victor 3, we copy, go ahead." JP released the talk button.

"Roger, Little Creek, we are approximately one mile off the objective's coast and holding." The voice in the helicopter paused, then, mustering as much cool and calm it could, said, "This is a landmass, not fog. Repeat, this IS a landmass. Do you copy?"

JP had earned a reputation in high school, college, and the Coast Guard Academy for unflappability. At this moment, inside, he was fully flapping. This made absolutely no sense. It simply could not be real. It had to be some sort of optical illusion. He'd once read that, on occasion, someone many miles from a structure might see it as a mirage. Something about how light and thermals played bumper shots when conditions were right. He felt sure that what he was seeing was one of those. He hoped it was, anyway. The sheer size of the thing belied hope for a simple explanation otherwise.

Technically, though the chopper pilot marginally outranked him, the boat's officer on this mission was in command. The boat was responsible for the safety of the chopper.

Lt. Johnson-Pickett pressed talk. "We copy. Visual from here shows land, but radar and infrared are clear. Hold your position until we arrive. ETA in five minutes. Over."

"Roger, Little Creek. We have negative readings on ES as well. Diagnostics show no malfunction. In fact, we've had you on radar since we started. Over." The voice on the chopper sounded nervous.

Eight minutes later, less than a mile from the objective's clearly visible beach, Lieutenant J.G. Johnson-Pickett and four other crew members scanned the heavily wooded mountainside for signs of life. Through their binoculars, they could even make out the types of some of the trees. Johnson-Pickett thought it could have been the Shenandoah Mountains if it weren't for where it was.

The helicopter had been slowly moving toward the land and now hovered about five hundred feet above the treetops halfway up the mountain, which Johnson-Pickett estimated to be about 3,500 feet high.

"Hold position, NCLC6. We are awaiting instructions from base." Johnson-Pickett kept staring at the impossible, familiar landscape.

He knew this same scenario was playing out up and down the eastern seaboard. The information transmitted by his boat and the helicopter was received by the local Coast Guard base in Little Creek, Virginia, and by God knew who else. His last instructions were to hold position until otherwise instructed.

When the instructions came, they were simply, "NLCV3. Proceed with caution."

JP ordered the boat to a quarter of a mile from shore and the helicopter rose to four thousand feet, then drifted toward the mountain ridge at about thirty knots.

"Little Creek, we are proceeding toward the ridgeline. Everything is the same as before, a lot of nice forest below us. No sign of life. We are approaching the crest and should see the other side of the moun— What the devil? Jason, what just happened?"

Day 1: Farallon Islands
The Miss Conception was two hours south of Bodega Bay, on her way to a favorite whale-watching spot west of the Farallon Islands Marine Life Preserve. The eastern sky had begun its first vague glow a half-hour ago and Robert Campbell, owner, skipper and crew, was in the cabin drinking ridiculously strong coffee. This time of day was about as happy as he ever felt. It was still dark; hardly anyone else was out. It was that brief period right before light chased away the shadows that hid the mess that was

his life.

The Miss Conception was a twenty-six-year-old forty-foot fishing boat. People often laughed and told Campbell it reminded them of The Orca, Captain Quint's boat in the movie "Jaws."

Robert Campbell opened another can of tuna, bent back the lid, and set it on the deck beside his captain's chair. Even in the dim red light, the lack of cleanliness was made more apparent by the half-dozen empty cans of salmon and tuna around the chair.

Admiral Nelson, Robert's one-eyed cat, quit mewing at the bottom of the chair and hunched greedily over the banquet.

"That's a good cat, eat it up, but remember: you've had yours, so don't start your begging when it's my time for lunch," he said, pouring another cup of coffee from the large thermos and looking at the tabby, which made a point of completely ignoring him while it ate.

Robert sipped the coffee beneath diminishing starlight, surveying the dark body of water. An hour earlier, the moon, bright enough to read by, had slipped beneath the horizon. Now there was only the last of the starry night, Admiral Nelson's excited chewing, the smooth, muted sound of Miss Conception's well-maintained engines, the smell of coffee, and the hope and anticipation.

It began on water, Robert thought, sipping the black coffee; it's only fitting it end on it as well.

Robert Campbell's life was the U.S. Navy, or at least it had been until he retired with thirty years a decade ago. Most of that life was spent at sea as a Chief Warrant Officer in charge of bomb loader crews on Nimitz Class aircraft carriers.

In May 1985, while cruising off Guam, Chief Robert Campbell saw something. Standing on the portside of the U.S.S. Harry S. Truman, smoking a cigarette and watching dolphins race alongside the massive ship, he saw a sea serpent.

He stared in disbelief. Swimming in the opposite direction, just below the surface, the fifty-foot, eel-like creature rippled past. A long dorsal fin broke the ocean several times, making the dolphins veer. Robert's eyes locked on the head. Too far below the surface to present clear details, it was long and triangular, knife-length teeth protruding from a down-turned mouth. Behind and above the mouth, an unblinking eye the size of a bus tire stared back at him.

Robert called to an approaching seaman, but when he looked back, the sea was empty.

From that moment, he became fascinated with the mysteries of the deep. He read everything he could find, even books and articles debunking the persistent sightings. Those unemotional volumes of reason and evidence had no impact on his belief. After all, he had seen one with his own eyes; he knew they were real.

Though retired, Robert never lost his love for the sea. He bought the Miss Conception with his life savings. His retirement pay was not enough to keep her moored and maintained, so during different seasons – fishing, crabbing, and whale-watching – he chartered the boat to the Bodega Bay Marine Excursion Company and took out men and their girlfriends, then three or four years later, their families, and still later, the men with their kids on every other weekend or summer vacation. He hated having passengers onboard. It was his home, for Christ's sake. He shouldn't have to scrub it down so some snotty little kid or phony girlfriend could splash their seasick ballast all over the deck.

But this was the only way he could combine his love of water and his fascination with strange creatures of the sea. Eventually, his wife, Anna, whom he dearly loved, could stand the poor sailor's life no more and ran off with a plumber to fix her broken heart.

The stars were all but gone in the brightening light. About five miles to starboard, he saw a long fog bank stretching north to south. He had checked the weather; fog was supposed to be light today. But then again, this was the San Francisco area. Weather could vary every half-mile by every half-hour.

As the light increased, he noticed a greenish cast to the fog. He took his binoculars from a hook and focused them on the apparition forming in the ocean.

It looked like land. His binoculars were not the best for someone at sea, but they were powerful enough that he thought he made out a beach and trees.

Probably a mirage or smeared lenses, he thought, staring harder into the glasses.

What the hell. He was on the ocean to explore, he thought, as he clicked off the autopilot and headed Miss Conception toward the fog bank.

The ocean surface was a series of slow, low swells, and the boat rode easily as it cut through the water.

Robert kept the binoculars with him and took another look every few minutes. The closer he came, the more distinct the features of an enormously long island were revealed. About fifty yards behind the breakers, Robert turned south, put the boat in neutral, and dropped the stern anchor. He studied the surf rushing onto a beautiful beach. He left the cabin and stared at the land without the hindrance of weathered glass. He stayed just like that for minutes, trying to decide what to do.

The landmass stretched from horizon to horizon. It was simply impossible. The impossibility of its existence was sinking in when he noticed a huge container ship coming from the south.

For some reason, the thought of someone else "discovering" his new land kicked him into action. He opened a storage cabinet on the aft deck's side and removed an inflatable raft. Robert tethered the line to a cleat, pulled the self-inflate handle, and tossed the raft over the side. It popped open with compressed air as it hit the water. He gathered up the short oars, pulled the raft to the stern and retied it to the ladder going into the water.

Without another thought for safety, he stepped into the raft. He affixed the oars to the nylon boat and pushed off, but not before Admiral Nelson made a courageous leap into the raft.

Together, they moved toward the shore.

The breakers were small, between two and three feet, and breaking about twenty feet off the beach. Getting back out to the Miss Conception would not be too difficult.

Robert, facing away from the beach, rowed smoothly, feeling more exhilarated than he had in years.

Looking over his shoulder, he set the raft up to catch a wave and rode it to shore. Just as the bottom of the raft scraped coarse sand, he was surrounded by a blinding light. He slammed his eyes closed and could not move for several seconds. When the light subsided, he felt the raft bobbing in the swells.

Robert opened his eyes and looked around. He was very confused. He had gone into the island bow first. Now he was facing the island with the raft's bow faced away, as if he had gone through the island.

He looked away from the island, expecting to see his boat and the California coastline. Instead he saw nothing but the vast Pacific.

Somehow, he had passed right through an island that was not supposed to exist. Robert looked back toward the shore and saw Admiral Nelson bouncing and bounding across the beach, chasing something into the forest.

He stopped thinking. This was too much for his mind. He turned the raft's bow toward the shore and rowed as fast as he could, hoping to save his cat.

Instead, he experienced a freakishly bright white light,

and found himself rowing toward the Miss Conception – without the company of Admiral Nelson.

He heard the rotors of a helicopter and looked up to see a Coast Guard chopper coming toward him. The speakers blared for him to get back to his boat and move away from the island. Robert had no issue with complying.

By the time he climbed back aboard his boat, Robert saw Coast Guard boats and helicopters of all sizes up and down the waters just off the island. Back toward the east, an increasing number of civilian vessels out to see what was happening were being held back by helicopters and boats of various agencies.

Robert returned to his captain's chair to set a course for Bodega Bay. He stepped on an empty tuna can, looked down, and started to cry.

The following is a excerpt from

CALIGULA: Killer with a Thousand Faces

1854, Saint Joseph, Louisiana

He knew who he was. One instant, a barefoot twelve-year-old following a rutted dirt road to the Mississippi River, the next, someone completely different. Looking down, beyond mismatched knee patches on faded overalls, dust covered his bare black feet. He stopped swishing a cane pole through tall weeds browned by a hot summer and carried the pole more spear-like.

He planned to meet Pete and Woodrow at the abandoned river barge landing, catch some catfish, swim, then sneak by the back of the Saint Jo Mercantile where black male slaves sometimes played dice for Liberty Head pennies. As he formed those thoughts, a slight pressure built at the base of his skull. It expanded up the back of his head, moved forward, then exploded in a flash of cognitive light, and he knew who he was. The leisurely plans changed. Just like that.

Awareness of his true self always came as mental lightning, always at puberty. He knew two lives, his real one, the person he once was, and the young boy's life in which he was bottled until this moment. He could recall every detail of his own life up until the moment of his first death. The other knew everything about his new life—which wasn't hopeful. The fifth child of a Louisiana slave, his father kept him chopping sugar cane, which allowed no time for education. He could not remember anything about the other lives between his original life and this poor peasant's. They were leaves on a tree, forgotten and replaced hundreds of times.

Maybe it was possible to change this boy's destiny. He might make it work, to turn this poor slave's life into something enjoyable. He felt he accomplished it before, but it required strength and cunning. But why waste time?

Reaching the disused river barge dock, he decided. At least he would have some fun first. He walked out on the rotting planks and sat dangling his feet in the muddy water, waiting.

"Woodrow, can I go swimmin' witcha? I won't tell on you if you let me."

It was a little girl's voice, Woodrow's sister. The more the merrier, he thought.

He stood facing the shore watching them top the bank. Woodrow carried two fishing poles in one hand and a rusty trowel in the other.

"Pete ain't comin'. His ma caught him skippin' Sunday school," Woodrow said. "I had to bring Ruthie or I couldn't come neither," he added apologetically.

The plantation masters who owned them were Christians and gave everyone the day off on Sunday provided they attend church. Of course, the slaves had to build their own church building but when it was finished, the plantation owners provided a piano.

Looking at the two of them against a cloudless blue sky, he saw coal black, close-cropped hair over large, excited dark eyes. The anticipation of fun and adventure in the boy's reminded of his youth, and his trusting sister.

"That's all right, she can dig worms while we fish," he grinned, coming toward them.

"Unh-unh," Ruthie said, screwing up her face, "I ain't diggin' no worms."

"All right then, you go in the field and bring back some grasshoppers and crickets. They make good bait. Me and Woodrow will get the worms."

"What can I put them in?" she asked with childish curiosity.

Both boys looked up and down the shore. Before the new dock opened in St Joseph, this had been a well-traveled place. Discarded items littered the area.

"There's a bottle. Use it." Woodrow pointed toward a brown glass vessel half buried in mud.

The little girl ran over and pried it up.

"It's broke," she said, holding the bottle up. "See."

The neck of the bottle was gone, creating a jagged hole.

"Just be careful, that's all. Them bugs ain't able to get out," her brother responded.

She nodded and moved up the bank holding the bottle away from her. When she disappeared into the field, Woodrow said, "Let's see. Seems there was good worms by them trees." He pointed downstream.

"I'll dig if you untwist the poles," he said to Woodrow. "Hand me the trowel."

Woodrow passed it to him. Its rusty narrow blade had been bent and straightened. The wooden handle was split, held together by bailing wire. He hefted it, looking at the point.

Woodrow squatted and, holding the hook carefully, started untangling the line on a pole.

"Hey, Woodrow, ever see one of them birds before?"

Woodrow looked at the sky beyond his friend to see. He turned toward Woodrow. The hand clenched the trowel in an iron grip. Shooting forward with sickening accuracy, the rusty point entered Woodrow's left eye, sunk an inch, struck skull and stopped. The blow knocked the boy over.

Sprawled on his back, reaching for his wounded eye, Woodrow screamed as blood welled and gushed on the dock. Straddling Woodrow, he kicked the other boy's crotch several times. He kneeled, lifted the dripping trowel high and plunged it into Woodrow's throat below the Adam's apple.

Woodrow gagged, clutched at his neck and tried to roll away. Crimson fountained across the attacker's chest.

He brought the trowel down three more times, mangling Woodrow's neck when the high-pitched scream started.

Ruthie stood, horror-frozen, holding the broken bottle. She screamed and screamed a little girl's life or death siren.

The boy, sticky with blood, left the quivering corpse and lunged toward the girl. One stride, two strides, three strides, he slipped going up the bank. Amazingly the girl had not moved. She stood screaming.

As he lost his footing, their eyes met. Something registered, and she turned to run, but too late. He had her black pigtail hair before she had gone ten feet. Kicking, screaming, sobbing, he dragged her toward the river. At the levy's crest, he turned her around, yanked down on her hair exposing her throat and thrust the wicked tool up into the flesh beneath her lower jaw. He jerked it free and stabbed her below the sternum. When the silent body sagged, he released the tightly braided hair, and she crumpled down the slope.

He examined the debris along the shore. He found a stone anchor with five feet of frayed dry rotted rope braided to an iron ring.

Struggling, he brought the twenty-pound anchor to the dock. Calmly, he untangled the fishing line from the three poles and removed Woodrow's belt. He brought Ruthie's body and laid it on the dock next to her brother's. The oozing viscous blood felt oddly wonderful and reminded him of better times. Moving purposefully, the thin smile never leaving his face, he tied the bodies together at the ankles then to his ankle. Using the belt, he fixed the knotted fishing line and his ankle to the anchor. He checked it to make sure the knots were tight.

Confident everything would hold long enough, he pushed the bodies into the water. The current immediately pulled them, and he struggled to maintain balance. Finally, bent over, tethered by the belt and rope, he lifted the anchor chest high and heaved it into the river. He followed as it sank, dragging the bodies beneath the muddy waters.

His eyes were opened wide, staring at the cloudy brown water. The anchor hit bottom, Woodrow's bloodless face bobbed accusingly close to his own then swirled down. The sight of Woodrow made his smile bigger, letting out some of the air that stuffed his cheeks.

Yes, maybe he could have made something from this peasant's life. But black slaves were considered less than human, much like in his original life. No, it was better this way. They might find the bodies—an insoluble mystery, three murdered children. Who would be blamed? Oh, so sad.

He saw the sun above the murky water. For an instant, he thought about trying to unfasten the anchor, but only an instant. Old instincts die hard. He opened his mouth and watched the bubbles rise.

I told you, long ago: I have existed from the morning of the world, and I shall exist until the last star falls from the night. Although I have taken this form, I am all men as I am no man and therefore I am a God.

Caligula laughed.